NOW YOU SEE ME

NOW YOU SEE ME

S. J. Bolton

First published 2011
by Bantam Press
This Large Print edition published 2012
by AudioGO Ltd
by arrangement with
Transworld Publishers Ltd

Hardcover ISBN: 978 1 445 84242 4
Softcover ISBN: 978 1 445 84243 1

British Library Cataloguing in Publication Data available

Printed and bound in Great Britain by
MPG Books Group Limited

For Andrew, who reads my books first; and for Hal, who can't wait to get started.

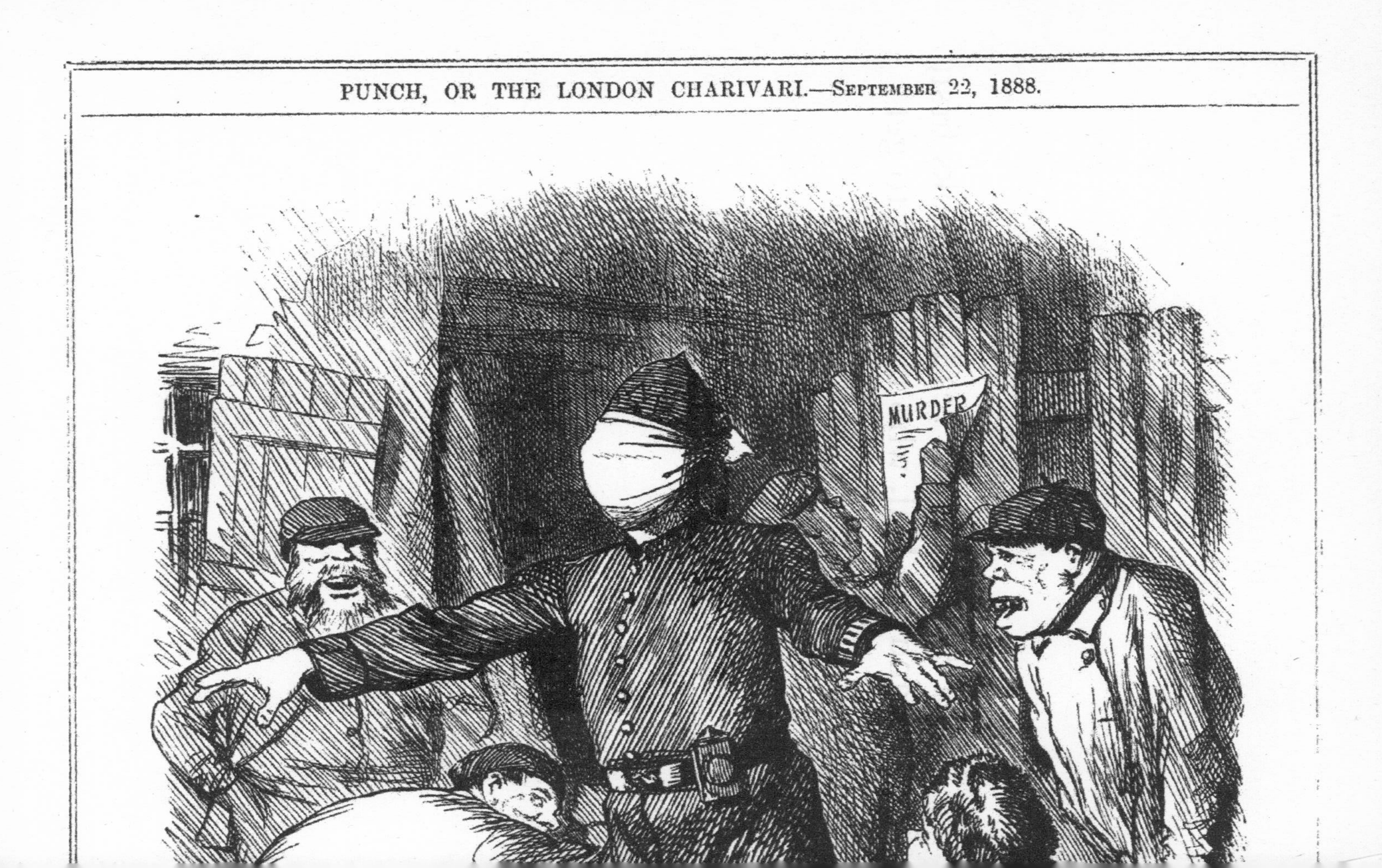
MURDER

BLIND-MAN'S BUFF.

(*As played by the Police.*)

"TURN ROUND THREE TIMES,
AND CATCH WHOM YOU MAY!"

Prologue

Eleven years ago

Leaves, mud and grass deaden sound. Even screams. The girl knows this. Any sound she might make can't possibly travel the quarter-mile to the car headlights and streetlamps, to the illuminated windows of tall buildings that she can see beyond the wall. The nearby city isn't going to help her and screaming will just burn up energy she can't spare.

She's alone. A moment ago she wasn't.

'Cathy,' she says. 'Cathy, this isn't funny.'

Difficult to imagine anything less funny. So why is someone giggling? Then another sound. A grinding, scraping noise.

She could run. The bridge isn't far. She might make it.

If she runs, she leaves Cathy behind.

A breeze stirs the leaves of the tree she's standing beside and she finds she can't stop shaking. She dressed, a few hours ago, for a hot pub and a heated bus-ride home, not this open space at midnight. Knowing that any second now she may have to run, she lifts first one foot and then the other and takes off her shoes.

'I've had enough now,' she says, in a voice that doesn't sound like her own. She steps forward, away from the tree, a little closer to the great slab of rock lying ahead of her on the grass. 'Cathy,' she says, 'where are you?'

Only the scraping answers back.

The stones look taller at night. Not just bigger, but blacker and older. Yet the circle they make seems to have shrunk. She has a sense of those just out of her line of sight slipping closer, playing grandmother's footsteps; that if she spins round now, there they'll be, close enough to touch.

Unthinkable not to turn with an idea like that in her head; not to whimper when a dark shape plainly is moving closer. One of the tall stones has split in two like a splinter of rock breaking away from a cliff. The splinter stands free and steps forward.

She runs then, but not for long. Another black shape is blocking her path, cutting off her route to the bridge. She turns. Another. And another. Dark figures make their way towards her. Impossible to run. Useless to scream. All she can do is turn on the spot, like a rat caught in a trap. They take hold of her and drag her towards the great, flat rock and one thing, at least, becomes clear.

The sound she can hear is that of a blade being sharpened against stone.

▪ ▪ ▪ ▪

Part One: Polly

▪ ▪ ▪ ▪

'The brutality of the murder is beyond conception and beyond description.'

Star, 31 August 1888

1

Friday 31 August

A dead woman was leaning against my car.

Somehow managing to stand upright, arms outstretched, fingers grasping the rim of the passenger door, a dead woman was spewing blood over the car's paintwork, each spatter overlaying the last as the pattern began to resemble a spider's web.

A second later she turned and her eyes met mine. Dead eyes. A savage wound across her throat gaped open; her abdomen was a mass of scarlet. She reached out; I couldn't move. She was clutching me, strong for a dead woman.

I know, I know, she was on her feet, still moving, but it was impossible to look into those eyes and think of her as anything other than dead. Technically, the body might be clinging on, the weakening heart still beating, she had a little control over her muscles. Technicalities, all of them. Those eyes knew the game was up.

Suddenly I was hot. Before the sun went down, it had been a warm evening, the sort when London's buildings and pavements cling to the heat of the day, hitting you with a wave of hot air when you venture outside. This was something new, though, this pumping, sticky warmth. This heat had nothing to do with the weather.

I hadn't seen the knife. But I could feel the handle of it now, pressing against me. She was holding me so tightly, was pushing the blade further into her own body.

No, don't do that.

I tried to hold her away, just enough to take the pressure off the knife. She coughed, except the cough came from the wound on her throat, not her mouth. Something splashed over my face and then the world turned around us.

We'd fallen. She sank to the ground and I went with her, hitting the tarmac hard and jarring my shoulder. Now she was lying flat on the pavement, staring up at the sky, and I was kneeling over her. Her chest was still moving — just.

There's still time, I told myself, knowing there wasn't. I needed help. None to be had. The small car park was deserted. Tall buildings of six- and eight-storey blocks of flats surrounded us and, for a second, I caught a movement on one of the balconies. Then nothing. The twilight was deepening by the second.

She'd been attacked moments ago. Whoever had done it would be close.

I was reaching for my radio, patting pockets, not finding it, and all the while watching the woman's eyes. My bag had fallen a few feet away. I fumbled inside and found my mobile, summoning police and ambulance to the car park outside Victoria House on the Brendon Estate in Kennington. When I ended the call, I realized she'd taken hold of my hand.

A dead woman was holding my hand, and it was almost beyond me to look into those eyes and see them trying to focus on mine. I had to talk to her, keep her conscious. I couldn't listen to the voice in my head telling me it was over.

'It's OK,' I was saying. 'It's OK.'

The situation was clearly a very long way from OK.

'Help's coming,' I said, knowing she was beyond help. 'Everything's going to be fine.'

We lie to dying people, I realized that evening, just as the first sirens sounded in the distance.

'Can you hear them? People are coming.

Just hold on.' Both her hand and mine were sticky with blood. The metal strap of her watch pressed into me. 'Come on, stay with me.' Sirens getting louder. 'Can you hear them? They're almost here.'

Footsteps running. I looked up to see flashing blue lights reflected in several windows. A patrol car had pulled up next to my Golf and a uniformed constable was jogging towards us, speaking into his radio. He reached us and crouched down.

'Hold on now,' I said. 'People are here, we'll take care of you.'

The constable had a hand on my shoulder. 'Take it easy,' he was saying, just as I'd done seconds earlier, only he was saying it to me. 'There's an ambulance on its way. Just take it easy.'

The officer was in his mid forties, heavy set, with thinning grey hair. I thought perhaps I'd seen him before.

'Can you tell me where you're hurt?' he asked.

I turned back to the dead woman. Really dead now.

'Love, can you talk to me? Can you tell me your name? Tell me where you're injured?'

No doubt about it. Pale-blue eyes fixed. Body motionless. I wondered if she'd heard anything I'd said to her. She had the most beautiful hair, I noticed then, the palest shade of ash blonde. It spread out around her head like a fan. Her earrings were reflecting light from the streetlamps and there was something about the way they sparkled through strands of her hair that struck me as familiar. I released her hand and began pushing myself up from the pavement. Gently, someone kept me where I was.

'I don't think you should move, love. Wait till the ambulance gets here.'

I hadn't the heart to argue, so I just kept staring at the dead woman. Blood had spattered across the lower part of her face. Her throat and chest were awash with it. It was pooling beneath her on the pavement, finding tiny nicks in the paving stones to travel along. In the middle of her chest, I could just make out the fabric of her shirt. Lower down her body, it was impossible. The wound on her throat wasn't the worst of her injuries, not by any means. I remembered hearing once that the average female body contained around five litres of blood. I'd just never considered quite what it would look like when it was all spilling out.

2

'I'm ok, I'm not hurt. It's not my blood.'

I wanted to stand up; they wouldn't let me move.

Three paramedics were huddled around the blonde woman. They seemed to be holding pressure pads against the wound on her abdomen. I heard mention of a tracheotomy. Then something about a peripheral pulse.

Shall we call it? I think so, she's gone.

They were turning to me now. I got to my feet. The woman's blood was sticky against my skin, already drying in the warm air. I felt myself sway and saw movement. The blocks of flats surrounding the square had long balconies running the length of every floor. A few minutes ago they'd been deserted. Now they were packed with people. From the back pocket of my jeans I pulled out my warrant card and held it up to the nearest officer.

'DC Lacey Flint,' I said.

He read it and looked into my eyes for confirmation. 'Thought you looked familiar,' he said. 'Based at Southwark, are you?'

I nodded.

'CID,' he said to the hovering paramedics who, having realized there was nothing they could do for the blonde woman, had turned their attention on me. One of them moved forward. I stepped back.

'You shouldn't touch me,' I said. 'I'm not hurt.' I looked down at my bloodstained clothes, feeling dozens of eyes staring at me. 'I'm evidence.'

I wasn't allowed to slink off quietly to the anonymity of the nearest police station. DC Stenning, the first detective on the scene, had received a call from the DI in charge. She was on her way and didn't want me going anywhere until she'd had chance to speak to me.

Pete Stenning had been a colleague of mine at Southwark before he'd joined the area's Major Investigation Team, or MIT, based at Lewisham. He wasn't much older than me, maybe around thirty, and was one of those lucky types blessed with almost universal popularity. Men liked him because he worked hard, but not so hard anyone around felt threatened, he liked down-to-earth, working-class sports like football but could hold down a conversation about golf or cricket, he didn't talk over-much but whatever he said was sensible. Women liked him because he was tall and slim, with curly dark hair and a cheeky grin.

He nodded in my direction, but was too busy trying to keep the public back to come over. By this time, screens has been erected around the blonde woman's body. Deprived of the more exciting sight, everyone wanted to look at me. News had spread. People had sent text messages to friends, who'd hot-footed it over to join in the fun. I sat in the back of a patrol car, avoiding prying eyes and trying to do my job.

The first sixty minutes after a major incident are the most important, when evidence is fresh and the trail to the perpetrator still hot. There are strict protocols we have to follow. I didn't work on a murder team, my day-to-day job involved tracing owners of stolen property and was far less exciting, but I knew I had to remember as much as possible. I was good at detail, a fact I wasn't always grateful for when the dull jobs invariably came my way, but I should be glad of it now.

'Got you a cup of tea, love.' The PC who'd

appointed himself my minder was back. 'You might want to drink it quick,' he added, handing it over. 'The DI's arrived.'

I followed his glance and saw that a silver Mercedes sports car had pulled up not far from my own car. Two people got out. The man was tall and even at a distance I could see he was no stranger to the gym. He was wearing jeans and a grey polo shirt. Tanned arms. Sunglasses.

The woman I recognized immediately from photographs. Slim as a model, with shiny, dark hair cut into a chin-length bob, she was wearing the sort of jeans women pay over a hundred pounds for. She was the newest senior recruit to the twenty-seven major investigation teams based around London and her arrival had been covered officially, in internal circulars, and unofficially on the various police blog sites. She was young for the role of DI, not much more than mid thirties, but she'd just worked a high-profile case in Scotland. She was also rumoured to know more about HOLMES 2, the major incident computer system, than practically any other serving UK police officer. Of course, it didn't hurt, one or two of the less supportive blogs had remarked, that she was female and not entirely white.

I watched her and the man pull on pale-blue Tyvek suits and shoe covers. She tucked her hair into the hood. Then they went behind the screens, the man standing aside at the last moment to allow her to go first.

By this time, white-suited figures were making their way around the site like phantoms. The scene-of-crime officers had arrived. They would establish an inner cordon around the body and an outer one around the crime scene. From now on, everyone entering the cordons would be signed in and out, the exact time of their arrival and departure being recorded. I'd learned all this at the crime academy, only a few months ago, but it was the first time I'd seen it in practice.

A gazebo-like structure was being erected over the spot where the corpse still lay. Screens has already been put up to create walls and within seconds the investigators had a large, enclosed area in which to work. Police tape was set up around my car. Lights were being unloaded from the van just as the DI and her companion emerged. They spoke together for a few seconds then the man turned and walked off, striding over the striped tape that marked the edge of the cordon. The DI came my way.

'I'll leave you to it,' said my minder. I handed him my cup and he moved away. The new DI was standing in front of me. Even in the Tyvek suit she looked elegant. Her skin was a rich, dark cream and her eyes green. I remembered reading that her mother had been Indian.

'DC Flint?' she asked, in a soft Scottish accent. I nodded.

'We haven't met,' she went on. 'I'm Dana Tulloch.'

3

'Ok,' said DI Tulloch. 'Go slowly and keep talking.'

I set off, my feet rustling on the pavement. Tulloch had taken one look at me and insisted that a Tyvek suit and slippers be brought. I'd be getting cold, she said, in spite of the warm evening, and I'd attract much less attention if the bloodstains were covered up. I was also wearing a pair of latex gloves to preserve any evidence on my hands.

'I'd been on the third floor,' I said. 'Flat 37. I came down that flight of stairs and turned right.'

'What were you doing there?'

'Talking to a witness.' I stopped and corrected myself. 'A potential witness,' I went on. 'I've been coming over on Friday evenings for a few weeks now. It's the one time I can be pretty certain not to see her mother. I'm trying to persuade her to testify in a case and her mother isn't keen.'

'Did you succeed?' asked Tulloch.

I shook my head. 'No,' I admitted.

We reached the end of the walkway and could see the square again. Uniform were trying to persuade people to go home and not having much luck.

'Guess there isn't much on TV tonight,' muttered Tulloch. 'Which case?'

'Gang rape,' I replied, knowing I could probably expect trouble. I didn't work on crime involving sexual assault and earlier that evening I'd been moonlighting. A few years ago the Met set up a number of bespoke teams known as the Sapphire Units to deal with all such offences. It was the sort of work I'd joined the police service to do and I was waiting for a vacancy to come up. In the meantime, I kept up to speed on what was going on. I couldn't help myself.

'Was the passage empty when you came out of the stairwell?' Tulloch asked.

'I think so,' I said, although the truth was I wasn't sure. I'd been annoyed at the response I'd got from Rona, my potential witness; I'd been thinking about my next move, if I even had one. I hadn't been paying much attention to what was going on around me.

'When you came out into the square, what

did you see? How many people?'

Slowly, we retraced the last time I'd walked this way, with Tulloch firing questions at me every few seconds. Annoyed with myself for not being more alert earlier, I tried my best. I didn't think there'd been anyone around. There'd been music, some sort of loud rap that I hadn't recognized. A helicopter had passed overhead, lower than normal, because I'd glanced up at it. I was certain I'd never seen the blonde woman before tonight. There had been something, for a second, as I'd looked at her, something niggling, but no, it had gone.

'I was looking back at this point,' I said, as I turned on the spot. 'There was a loud noise behind me.'

I met Tulloch's eye and knew what she was thinking. I'd looked back and had probably missed seeing the attack by seconds. Split seconds.

'When did you see her?' she asked me.

'I was a bit closer,' I replied. 'I was fumbling in my bag as I was walking — I thought I might have left my car keys behind — then I looked up and saw her.'

We were right back in the thick of it. A white-suited figure was taking photographs of the blood spatter on my car.

'Go on,' she told me.

'I didn't see the blood at first,' I said. 'I thought she'd stopped to ask directions, that maybe she thought there was someone in the car.'

'Tell me what she looked like. Describe her to me.'

'Tall,' I began, not sure where this was going. She'd just seen the woman in question for herself.

She sighed. 'You're a detective, Flint. How tall?'

'Five ten,' I guessed. 'Taller than both of us. And slim.'

Her eyebrows went up.

'Size twelve,' I said quickly. 'From the back I thought she was young, probably because she was slim and well dressed, but when I saw her face, she seemed older than I expected.'

'Go on.'

'She looked good,' I went on, warming to my theme. If Tulloch wanted endless detail I could oblige. 'She was well dressed. Her clothes looked expensive. Simple, but well made. Her hair had been professionally done. That colour doesn't come out of a bottle you buy at Boots and there was no sign of roots. Her skin was good and so were her teeth, but she had lines around her eyes and her jawline wasn't that tight.'

'So you'd put her age at . . .'

'I'd say well-preserved mid forties.'

'Yes, so would I.' There was movement all around us, but Tulloch's eyes weren't leaving my face. There could have been just the two of us in the car park.

'Did she have ID?' I asked. 'Do we know who she is?'

'Nothing in her bag,' said a man's voice. I turned. Tulloch's companion of earlier had joined us. He'd pushed his sunglasses on to the top of his head. There was scarring around his right eye that looked recent. 'No ID, no car keys, some cash and bits of make-up,' he went on. 'Mystery how she got here. We're some distance from the Tube and she doesn't strike me as a bus type.'

Tulloch was looking at the large blocks of flats that surrounded the square.

'Course, her car keys could have been stolen along with the car. A woman like that probably drives a nice motor,' he said. He had a faint south London accent.

'She had diamond studs in her ears,' I said. 'This wasn't a robbery.'

He looked at me. His eyes were blue, almost turquoise. The one with the scarring around it was bloodshot. 'Could have been fake,' he suggested.

'If I was slitting someone's throat and cutting open their stomach to rob them, I'd take any visible jewellery on the off-chance, wouldn't you?' I said. 'And she had a nice-looking wristwatch too. I could feel it scratching against my hand as she died.'

He didn't like that, I could tell. He raised his hand to rub his sore eye and frowned at me.

'Flint, this is DI Joesbury,' said Tulloch. 'Nothing to do with the investigation. He only came out with me tonight because he's bored. This is DC Flint. Lacey, I think, is that right?'

'Which reminds me,' said Joesbury, who'd barely acknowledged the introduction. 'Lewisham want to know when you're bringing her in.'

Tulloch was still looking at the buildings around us. 'I don't get it, Mark,' she said. 'We're surrounded by flats and it isn't that late, dozens of people could have witnessed what happened. Why would you murder someone here?'

From somewhere nearby I could hear a dog barking.

'Well, she wasn't here by chance,' replied Joesbury. 'That woman belongs in Knightsbridge, not Kennington. Thanks to DC Flint's knowledge of jewellery, we know that robbery seems unlikely, although we do need to find her car.'

'Kids round here wouldn't kill for a car,' I said as they both turned to me. 'Oh, they'd steal it, no question, but they'd just snatch the keys, give her a shove. They wouldn't need to —'

'Slash her throat so deeply they cut right through her windpipe?' finished Joesbury. 'Cut her abdomen from the breastbone down to the pubic bone. No, you're right, DC Flint, that does seem like overkill.'

OK, I was definitely not getting good vibes from this bloke. I took a step back, then another. For some reason, probably shock, I'd talked much more than I would normally. Maybe I just needed to quieten down for a while. Keep a low profile.

'How?' said Tulloch.

'Sorry?' said Joesbury, who'd been watching me back away.

'She was still on her feet when DC Flint saw her,' said Tulloch. 'Still alive, although horribly injured. That means she was attacked seconds before. Probably even while Flint was wandering around fumbling in her bag for her keys. How did he do it? How did he inflict those injuries then disappear completely?'

Wandering and fumbling? Tulloch had made the attack sound like it was my fault.

I almost opened my mouth again and remembered just in time. Low profile.

'There are no CCTV cameras in the square,' said Joesbury. 'But the high street is just yards away. Stenning has gone to round up any footage. If our villain left the estate, he'll have been picked up on one of them.'

Maybe it had been my fault. If I'd had my wits about me, I might have seen the attacker before he struck. I could have yelled for help, summoned local uniform on my radio. I could have stopped the attack. Shit, that sort of guilt trip was all I needed.

'Whoever did it would be covered in blood,' said Joesbury, still looking at me. 'They'll have left a trail.' He glanced behind. 'Sounds like the dogs are here.'

We looked towards the car park. Two dogs had arrived. German Shepherds, each with its own handler.

'Not necessarily,' I said, before I could stop myself. They both turned back to me. 'If her throat was cut from behind, whoever did it might have escaped being splashed. All her blood spattered forward. On to my car.'

'And then on to you,' said Joesbury, his eyes dropping away from my face to the bloodstains that were just about visible through the Tyvek. 'Are we done here,

Tully?' he went on. 'You really need to get DC Flint back to the station.'

Tulloch looked uncertain for a moment. 'I just need to make sure Neil —'

'Anderson knows exactly what he's doing,' said Joesbury. 'He's got six officers taking witness statements, the traffic has been redirected and they'll start the door-to-door as soon as the dogs are done.'

'Can you take her back?' asked Tulloch. 'I want to have a good look round when things quieten down.'

Joesbury looked as though he were about to argue, then smiled at her. He had very good teeth. 'Do I get to drive the Tully-mobile?' he asked.

Shaking her head, Tulloch pulled down the zip of her pale-blue suit and dug into her pocket. Glaring, she handed over her car keys. 'Prang it and I prang you,' she warned.

'Come on, Flint, before she changes her mind.' Joesbury had put a hand on my elbow and was steering me towards the DI's silver Mercedes.

'And make sure she keeps that suit on,' called Tulloch, as Joesbury held the passenger door open and I climbed inside. The interior looked showroom new. I sank back against the leather seat and closed my eyes.

4

It was gone nine o'clock by this time, but the streets were still busy and we didn't make great progress. I was still smarting from Tulloch's comments about wandering and fumbling, so I kept my eyes closed and asked myself what I could have done differently. Joesbury said nothing.

After ten, maybe fifteen minutes of silence, he switched on the car stereo and the eerie notes of Clannad filled the car.

'Oh, you are kidding me,' he muttered under his breath. 'Is there anything in the glove compartment?'

I opened my eyes and, still wearing latex gloves, pulled out the only CD in the small compartment. 'Medieval plainsong,' I said, reading the cover.

Joesbury shook his head. 'If you get chance to speak to her about her taste in music, go for it,' he said. 'She had me listening to Westlife the other night.'

He lapsed into silence again as we reached the Old Kent Road. Occasionally, as the streetlights caught the car windscreen at the right angle, I could see his reflection. Nothing out of the ordinary. Late thirties, I guessed, brown hair cut short. He hadn't shaved for a couple of days. His face and bare forearms were suntanned. His teeth, I'd already noticed, were even and very white.

Another ten minutes passed without either of us speaking. I had a sense, though, partly from the way his head kept tilting, that he was watching me in the car windscreen too.

Wandering and fumbling.

'If I'd got to her sooner, would she have lived?' I asked, as we turned off Lewisham High Street and into the car park behind the station.

'Guess we'll never know,' replied Joesbury. There were no spaces left so he parked directly behind a green Audi, completely blocking it in.

'She was still alive seconds before the ambulance arrived,' I said. 'I should have put something against the wound, shouldn't I? Tried to stop the bleeding.'

If I was hoping for any sort of comfort from this guy, I was wasting my breath. 'I'm a police officer, not a paramedic,' he replied, switching off the engine. 'Looks like you're expected.'

The station's duty sergeant, a scene-of-crime officer and a police doctor were waiting for us. Together we walked through the barred rear door of Lewisham police station and my arrival was officially recorded. I'd worked for the Metropolitan Police for nearly four years, but had a feeling I was about to see it from a very different perspective.

Some time later, I sat staring at dirty cream walls and grey floor tiles. My left shoulder was sore from where I'd fallen on it earlier and I could feel a headache threatening. Over the past hour, I'd been asked to undress completely before being examined by a police doctor. After a shower, I'd been examined again, and photographed. My fingernails had been clipped, my saliva swabbed and my hair combed thoroughly and painfully. Then I'd been given a pair of orange overalls normally issued to prisoners in custody.

I hadn't eaten that evening and, whether it was due to low blood sugar, shock or just a cold room, I was finding it hard to stop shivering. I kept seeing pale-blue eyes, staring at me.

I could have saved her. If I hadn't been in my own little world, we might not be kicking off a murder investigation right now. And everyone knew that. It would be my legacy, for as long as I stayed in the service: the DC who'd let a woman be stabbed to death right in front of her.

The door opened and DI Joesbury came in. In the small room he seemed taller than he had on the street or even in DI Tulloch's car. DC Gayle Mizon, the detective who'd assisted the police doctor in examining me, was with him. The two of them had been laughing at something in the corridor outside and he was still smiling as he held the door open for her. He had a great smile. Then he turned to me and the smile faded.

'Still bored?' I asked, before I could stop myself.

I might not have spoken. I got no reaction whatsoever.

Mizon was an attractive blonde woman of around thirty-three or -four. She'd brought me coffee. I put my hand on the mug for warmth but didn't dare pick it up. I was shaking too much. Joesbury continued to study me, my hair still wet from the shower, my face dry and pink because it hadn't been moisturized, and my prisoner-in-custody uniform. He didn't look impressed.

‘Right,’ he said. ‘Let’s take a statement.’

By the time he called a halt, I’d barely the energy left to sit upright in my chair. If I’d wanted to be tactful about DI Joesbury’s interviewing technique, I’d have said he was thorough. If honesty had been the order of the day, I’d have called him a sadistic shit.

Before we started, they explained that Gayle Mizon would be taking the statement, Joesbury only sitting in on an advisory capacity. They’d even given me chance to request he leave the room. I’d shrugged and muttered something about it being fine. Big mistake, because the moment the interview kicked off, he took charge.

What followed didn’t feel like any witness statement I’d ever been a party to before. More like I was about to be charged. He made me go over every detail several times, until even Mizon was looking uncomfortable. And he kept going back to the same point. How could I not have seen something? How could I have missed the attack and yet been close enough for her to die in my arms? Every second I was waiting for him to say that the blonde woman would still be alive if I hadn’t messed up.

Finally, he terminated the interview and switched off the recording equipment. The clock on the wall said ten past eleven.

'Is there someone you'd like us to call?' asked Mizon, as Joesbury took the disc out of the recording machine and labelled it.

I shook my head.

'Will there be someone at home when you get there?' she asked me. 'Flatmate? Boyfriend? You've had a nasty shock. You probably shouldn't be on your own.'

'I live on my own,' I said. 'But I'm fine,' I added, when she looked concerned. 'Is it OK if I go now?'

'Family?' Mizon wasn't giving up easily.

'They don't live in London,' I said, which was true, if a bit disingenuous. They don't live anywhere. I have no family. 'Look, I'm tired, I haven't eaten, I just want to get home and —'

Joesbury looked up, frowning. 'Did nobody offer you food?' he asked, and really, you had to admire the way he made it sound like it was my own fault.

'Really not a problem. Can I go now?' I stood up. 'Sir,' I added, for good measure.

Joesbury turned to Mizon. 'Gayle, if we'd brought the killer in red-handed, knife dangling from his teeth, we'd have fed him. One of our own, we leave to starve.'

'I thought someone else was . . .' Mizon began.

'It's really not . . .' I tried.

'Sorry,' she said to me. I shrugged, managed a smile.

Joesbury stood up and crossed the room. 'Come on,' he said, holding the door open.

'Where are we going now?' I hadn't the energy to even try being polite any more. Not that previous efforts had been all that successful.

'I'm getting you fed, then I'm getting you home,' he replied. He nodded at the disc on the table. 'Can you get that processed?' he said to a rather surprised-looking Mizon. Then he walked me out of the station.

Tulloch's silver Mercedes had already been moved and Joesbury opened up the green Audi we'd blocked in previously. He turned on the engine, put the car into gear and began flicking through a stack of CDs.

'Got any Westlife?' I asked, as he reversed the car out of the parking space and turned it round. When he didn't reply, I made a mental note that a sense of humour wasn't high on this guy's list of attributes. And that I could probably cross out fair-minded and compassionate as well. In fact, so far, the only box I could tick was a healthy respect for a woman's need to eat. He pushed a CD into the stereo. Back on Lewisham High Street, he turned the volume right up and rhythmic, percussion-based club music filled the car. Message received and understood, DI Joesbury, I wasn't meant to talk.

5

The garden is long and narrow. And very dark. Whilst high walls on three sides keep out most of the streetlight, the dense foliage of over-mature shrubs seems to soak up any light that does seep through. The garden is overlooked by several windows, but the intruder moving slowly down the slim gravel path is dressed entirely in black and is unlikely to be seen.

The garden is scented. The intruder stops for a moment and takes a deep breath, before stretching out a hand to a tiny, star-shaped flower. Jasmine.

At the bottom of the garden is a small, neat wooden shed, partially hidden by vegetation. Ivy creeps up its walls and overhanging tree branches rest on its roof. The door is locked, but the intruder thinks for a moment before reaching up to run a hand along the rim of the low, flat roof. After a few seconds the hand finds what it is looking for. A key.

The door opens easily. The intruder starts back with a muttered curse.

For a moment, a human form appears to be hanging in the shed. It swings gently, turning on the spot. Human in form, but not human. This has a soft, cylindrical torso, it wears clothes but is limbless. Its head — male — once stared out from a shop window.

The intruder touches it lightly. It spins on the chain that suspends it from the shed roof and the head lolls like that of a drunk. Or a crazy man.

'What a good idea,' says the intruder. 'Oh Lacey, what a brilliantly good idea.'

6

'Are you veggie, lactose intolerant, allergic to sesame seeds . . . ?' Joesbury was asking me, practically the first words to come out of his mouth since we'd left the station. We were in a small Chinese restaurant, not far from where I live, that I didn't think I'd ever noticed before. The owner, a slim Chinese man in his fifties called Trev, had greeted Joesbury like an old friend.

'If it stays still long enough I'll eat it,' I replied.

Joesbury's eyes opened a little wider. He and Trev shared a look, had a short, muttered conversation and then the Chinese man disappeared. Joesbury took the seat opposite mine and I waited with something like interest. He was going to have to talk to me now.

He picked up a fork and ran the prongs down a paper napkin, before leaning back to admire the four perfectly straight lines he'd made. He glanced up, caught my eye and looked down again. The fork made its way down the napkin once more. It was becoming blindingly obvious that DI Joesbury and I weren't of the same mind on the talking issue.

'If you're not part of the MIT, what do you do?' I asked. 'Traffic?'

If you want to insult a fellow cop, you ask him if he works on traffic. Quite why I was insulting a senior officer I'd only just met was, of course, a good question.

'I work for SO10,' he replied.

I thought about it for a second. SO stood for Special Operations. The divisions were numbered according to the particular function they served. SO1 protected public figures, SO14, the royal family. 'SO10 do undercover work, don't they?' I asked.

He inclined his head. 'Covert operations is the term they prefer these days,' he said.

'Then you're based at Scotland Yard?' I asked, slightly encouraged at getting a whole sentence out of him.

Another brief nod. 'Technically,' he said.

Now what did that mean? Either you're based somewhere or you're not.

'So how come you ended up at the scene tonight?'

He sighed, as though wondering why I was

bothering him with this tiresome conversation business. 'I'm convalescing,' he said. 'Dislocated my shoulder and nearly lost an eye in a fight. Officially, I'm on light duties only until November, but as both you and DI Tulloch have been at pains to point out, I'm bored.'

Trev arrived back with drinks. He put a bottle of South American beer down in front of each of us. I hadn't been asked what I wanted.

'The look on your face says you're not a beer drinker,' said Joesbury, reaching across and pouring the contents of my bottle into a glass. 'And the look on mine should tell you, I know that — you're far too skinny to be a beer drinker — but it's good for shock.'

I picked up my glass. I'm not a beer drinker, but alcohol of any description was starting to feel like a very good idea. Joesbury watched me drink nearly a third of its contents before coming up for air.

'What brought you into the police?' he asked me.

'An early fascination with serial killers,' I replied. It was the truth, although I didn't usually advertise the fact in quite so blunt a fashion. I'd been intrigued by violent crime and its perpetrators for as long as I could remember and it was this that had led me, through a long and circuitous path, into the police service.

Joesbury raised one eyebrow at me.

'Sadistic, psychopathic predators specifically,' I went on. 'You know, the type who kill to satisfy some deviant sexual longing. Sutcliffe, West, Brady. When I was a kid I couldn't get enough of them.'

The eyebrow stayed up as I realized my glass was now more than half empty and that I really needed to slow down a bit.

'You know, if you're bored, you should think about golf,' I said. 'A lot of middle-aged men find it fills the hours quite nicely.'

Joesbury's lips tightened, but he wasn't about to dignify such a cheap jibe with a response. And I really had to get a grip. Winding up a senior officer, however unpleasant, just wasn't me. I was low-profile girl.

'Sir, I apologize,' I said. 'I've had one hell of an evening and —' Movement at my side. The food had arrived.

'Don't call him Sir,' said Trev, putting a plate of noodles with prawns and vegetables in front of me and something with beef and black beans in Joesbury's place. 'Young female officers calling him Sir turns him on something rotten.'

'I'll remember that,' I muttered, thinking

it probably shouldn't be too hard. Joesbury was definitely not my type. I didn't actually have a type. But if I had, he wouldn't be it.

'Now this is for Dana,' Trev went on, putting a covered plastic dish on the table. 'Give her my love, tell her to come and see me soon, and if she ever gets tired —'

'Trev,' drawled Joesbury. 'How many times . . . ?'

'A man can dream,' said Trev, as he made his way back to the kitchen. When I looked up, Joesbury was intent on his food.

'How did he know I'm police?' I asked, picking up my fork and pushing a prawn around in a circle.

'You're wearing an orange Andy Pandy suit with PROPERTY OF THE METROPOLITAN POLICE on the collar,' said Joesbury, without looking up.

'I could be a villain,' I said, putting the prawn in my mouth. It sat there, large and uncomfortably dry, on my tongue.

'Yeah,' said Joesbury, putting his fork down and lifting his eyes. 'The thought had crossed my mind.'

7

I live just off the Wandsworth Road, less than five minutes' walk from Trev's Chinese restaurant, in part of an old Victorian house. The letting agent who rented it to me called it the garden flat. In truth, it was the basement, accessible via a dozen stone steps that led down from the pavement, just to the right of the house's front door. Out of habit, I checked the small area of shadow in the under-well of the steps. If I was unlucky (and careless) one night, someone could be waiting. It had never happened yet and I rather hoped tonight wouldn't be the first time; I was hardly in the mood. The stairwell was empty and the padlock on the door of the shed where I keep my bike hadn't been disturbed. I slipped my key into the lock and went inside.

I walked through my living room, past the tiny galley kitchen and into my bedroom. I'd changed the sheets that morning, as I always do on Friday. They were crisp white cotton, one of the very few luxuries I allow myself. Normally, getting into bed on a Friday night is one of the highlights of my week.

But I had just the worst feeling that if I lay down on them, when I got up again, they'd be stained the dark red of another woman's blood. Stupid, I'd showered until my skin felt raw, but . . .

I carried on walking, through a sort of lean-to conservatory and into the garden. It's long and very narrow, like lots of gardens behind London's terraced streets, attracting practically no direct sunlight. Luckily, though, whoever designed it knew what they were doing. All the plants thrive in the shade and it's full of small trees and dense shrubs. High brick walls on either side give me privacy. There's a side door that leads to an alley. I keep it locked.

I closed my eyes, and saw pale-blue ones staring into mine. Oh no.

DI Joesbury, objectionable git that he was, had actually taken my mind off the events of earlier. Being with him, trying to find something to talk about, trying even harder not to say anything inappropriate, had given me something to focus on. Now, on my own, it was all coming back.

London is never quiet, and even at this hour I could hear the constant hum of traffic, the sound of people walking past in the street and high-pitched yelling from very nearby.

There is a park not a hundred metres from my flat. When the sun goes down the teenagers of south London claim it for their own, swinging around the play equipment like monkeys, screeching and howling at each other. They were on form tonight. From what I could hear there was some sort of chase going on. Girls were squealing. Music playing. They were letting off some steam.

Which, exhausted or not, was exactly what I needed to do. And I had a playground of my own I could go to.

8

Camden town has long been one of the trendiest places in north London and especially so since the development of the Camden Stables Market. Once an extensive network of tunnels, arches, viaducts and passageways, the area was sold off to developers some years ago and transformed into a vast complex of shops, bars, market stalls and cafés. It's popular in the daytime as a place to browse, eat and just hang out. At night, people flock here. At least once a week, usually on a Friday, I'm one of them.

My car had been taken away by the scene-of-crime officers so I'd had to travel by bus. As I approached the Horse Hospital, once stabling for sick or tired horses that worked on the railways, I took off my jacket and tucked it into the small rucksack I was carrying over one shoulder.

Horses, or rather their replicas, are the predominant feature of the Stables Market.

Back in the days of the railway's construction, hundreds of them were kept to transport goods and equipment to, from and around the site. Nothing so unusual in that, but in Camden the working horses led a largely subterranean life, moving from one area to another through tunnels, built specifically to allow them a safe and convenient passage around. At one time they were even stabled underground.

These days, the living, working beasts are long gone, but equine images are everywhere you turn. There are wall hangings, massive free-standing statues, motifs built into railings, on lamp posts, even on bins. I like horses, but even I'm inclined to feel the developers have overdone it a bit.

The heat hit me like a wall when I stepped through the main door of the Horse Hospital. Violet lights twinkled on either side as I made my way through the central passageway, past the original layout of loose boxes and stable furniture. Even at this hour the place was full and the air was thick with the smell of alcohol and humanity.

A party was going on in one of the boxes and for a second I considered gate-crashing. Then I noticed red helium balloons around the iron grilles. They swayed, gleaming, in the hot air. Like blood droplets. I carried on, pushed my way to the bar and bought a Bombay Sapphire on ice. I can't bear the taste so I drink it very slowly, but if I need a quick shot, it does the job. The clock behind the bar told me it was five to one in the morning. The place closed at two.

A few more paces and I was surrounded by the soft tangerine light of the photographic gallery. Around me golden faces glistened with heat. A band had been playing earlier and up on the stage someone was packing away sound equipment.

'Hey baby!' Four boys, barely old enough to drink, were blocking my way. The one who'd spoken staggered closer, put a hand out towards me.

'Want to step outside?' he offered.

The hand had made contact with my hip. He was having trouble focusing and I didn't think it was just the booze.

'Well, it's a sweet thought,' I said, 'but I haven't had the all-clear from the clinic yet. I'll get back to you.'

I smiled quickly at a tall, dark-haired boy who seemed more sober than the rest. He grinned back and I stepped past them. Before I'd gone more than a few feet I felt a hand on my arm. The dark-haired boy had followed me.

'Don't rush off,' he said.

I looked at him and thought about it. Younger than I preferred, but otherwise definitely possible. Tall, just starting to fill out. He had a strong jawline and his face an almost regal look about it. His hair was curly, a few inches long, and he had pale skin. The sort that was very soft.

'What's your name?' I said.

'Ben,' he replied. 'Yours?'

Three pairs of eyes were watching us, willing him on. Scratch a gang of mates and you get a gang. I didn't like gangs.

'Catch you another time,' I said. 'Come without your friends.'

I turned away, moved back through the Horse Hospital's loose boxes and stepped outside. A wide, curved walkway known as the horse creep takes you down, past another giant equine statue, to the market below. The night was cooling down. Most of the outdoor stalls had closed up for the night, but those serving food were still doing business. Everywhere I looked, people were huddled in groups, leaning against walls and railings, keeping warm under outdoor heaters, eating, drinking.

At the centre of the piazza, wide steps lead down to more market stalls. The top was as good a vantage point as any. About halfway down, a fair-haired man was watching me.

As I stared back he didn't look away. When I smiled, he smiled too.

He seemed to be alone, leaning against one of the metal horse statues. Around thirty, I guessed, maybe a bit older, still in a business suit. He'd removed his tie and unbuttoned the top of his shirt. If he'd come straight from work he'd been here a long time, but, even at this distance, I didn't think he was drunk.

As I set off down the stairs he realized I was heading his way. He'd straightened up and was running a finger around his collar. His eyes hadn't left mine and I didn't think he was going to be one of my more difficult conquests. Then something made me look up and I stopped dead.

Mark Joesbury was directly opposite me, on the balcony that ran round the steps. He was leaning forward against the railing, his eyes going from me to the man I was heading towards. As he realized I'd seen him, his eyes narrowed.

I carried on walking, blanking the fair-haired man. At the bottom of the steps, I went left and shoved my way through the crowds, pushing a leather-clad girl out of the way, squeezing through bodies. I just had to hope Joesbury didn't know Camden as well as I did.

The crowd was thinning out but getting less respectable as I walked quickly past the toilets. This was where drug deals went down. I pushed through the swing door and started to run up concrete steps. I had to go up several flights to get back to street level.

If Joesbury didn't know about this way out, I could skirt my way around the market stalls, cut through Camden Lock Place and get across the roving bridge. On the other side, I could jog a few hundred yards and get a night bus home. I had flat shoes in my bag.

As I made my way towards the lock, I was shivering again and honestly couldn't have said this time whether it was cold, delayed shock or just plain fury. By the time I'd reached the canal, I'd decided.

What the hell was Joesbury doing here? I come to Camden for a reason, damn it. It's the other side of frigging London from where I live and work and the chances of coming across anyone I know are tiny. It could not be coincidence that he was here. He'd dropped me off, hung around outside my flat and followed me here. Why?

It was after two by the time I got home. I walked straight through the flat. There is a tiny shed at the bottom of the garden. I've put foam matting on the floor and hung a large punchbag from the middle of the shed roof. I've humanized it, giving it a head that once belonged to a shop dummy, dressing it in clothes, so that it resembles a human figure. I rarely bother with gloves.

I hit it as hard as I could; so hard my bruised shoulder yelled at me. Ignoring the pain, I hit it again, then again, until I was so weary I lost my balance and fell over. I gave the bag one last kick and wondered whether, just once, I'd get away with screaming my head off. Instead, I closed my eyes.

I can never remember my dreams. Come morning I have no idea what's passed through my head in the dark hours and yet I always know if my dreams have been bad. They must have been very bad that night, because I woke, hardly an hour after falling asleep, to find myself drenched in sweat and hardly able to breathe. I scrabbled backwards until I hit the shed door and found myself, wide awake, in the garden.

Awake or not, it seemed the dream was hovering around. I could see pale-blue eyes, the dead woman's eyes, staring into mine with something like rage. No, that wasn't right, the eyes had been terrified. Except now the terror was mine. And the eyes were getting closer all the time . . .

The chill night air was taking away some of the heat. I was OK, it was just delayed shock. Just a dream, my first for a very long time. I stumbled halfway across the garden and stopped.

Music was coming from close by, possibly the park. But it wasn't the sort of pounding, pulsing sound I was used to hearing here at night. This was a melody, soft and light, drifting across the rooftops. Julie Andrews from *The Sound of Music,* the song she sings to comfort the children scared of the storm. *Raindrops and roses,* it begins. 'My Favourite Things'.

As a child, I'd been enchanted by *The Sound of Music.* I'd loved this particular song and played the game myself, making lists of my favourite things. When life got completely shit (regular occurrence when I was a kid) I'd played the game and made myself feel a little bit better. But it had all been so long ago.

I took a step closer to the house.

The music was still playing, softly, sweetly, and beneath it, on the other side of the garden wall, I could hear scuffling. Quickly, I checked the side door that led to the alley. The bolt was shut. Something moved again, something brushing against the wall. I wouldn't normally describe myself as a timid person but I felt a sudden need to get indoors.

I hurried across the garden and in through the conservatory, checking the locks more carefully than I normally do. Probably just one of those weird coincidences, and yet, as I pulled a spare blanket from the cupboard and curled up on the sofa, I couldn't help wondering why it should be tonight, of all nights, that someone should decide to play 'My Favourite Things'.

I woke to the sound of my phone ringing. It was the duty sergeant at Southwark. I'd left instructions that if a certain person called for me, I was to be found. That person was now waiting at the station. So, day off or not, I was going into work.

9

Saturday 1 September

'They was three of them. At first they was three of them. Then more arrive.'

I sat very still on the wooden bench, not wanting to do anything that might distract her. I really wanted to make notes, but she'd refused to let me. She hadn't allowed me to turn on the tiny recorder I'd brought with me either. She wasn't making a statement, she'd said repeatedly, until she was certain I understood. She wasn't even prepared to stay in the station. So we'd gone out, had walked down towards the river, to the place where Shakespeare's Globe had been re-created on the South Bank.

Rona Dawson was fifteen years old, plump, with gleaming skin and braided hair. Eyes like dark chocolate. She was a good-looking black girl like dozens of others from south London. And like dozens of others, she'd been raped by her boyfriend and several of his mates.

Rape crime, particularly rape by gangs of young men and boys, has become a huge problem in south London. Not too long ago, Scotland Yard statistics showed a trebling in the incidence of gang attacks across the city over the past four years. More than a third of the reported victims were under sixteen.

When it comes to rape, of course, reported incidents are the tip of the iceberg.

'When you arrived at the flat, there was just the three of them?' I asked, when she didn't go on. 'One of them was Miles?'

She nodded.

'And Miles had phoned to ask you to come round?'

She nodded again. 'He say come round and watch a DVD. I thought it would be just the two of us.'

'Miles is your friend, boyfriend . . .?'

She shrugged. 'I suppose,' she said. 'He's just someone I know.'

A little way to our left the Millennium Bridge was already busy, two steady streams of foot traffic flowing gently along it. Visitors from the north bank crossing to view the Globe or visit the Tate Modern; others walking in the opposite direction, heading for St Paul's Cathedral or the shops and galleries further north. On the first day of September, London was still in peak tourist season.

'Had you had sex with him before?' I asked her. 'Before that day?'

She nodded, without taking her eyes off the river.

'What happened when you arrived?'

'I seen these other two. I didn't know them but I seen them around. We started to watch a film but it didn't feel right.'

A passenger boat was heading our way, its bow sending waves across the water. 'In what way didn't it feel right?' I asked her.

'They was looking at each other, not at the film,' she said. 'They wasn't watching the film. I didn't like it and I said I had to go. That I was meeting Bethany.'

'Did you get up to go?'

She nodded. 'Miles wouldn't let me,' she said. 'He said to come into the bedroom. I didn't want to, I said I had to go, but he pushed me in and shut the door. I said I had a stomachache, but he pushed me down on the bed. I thought if I let him get it over with I could go.'

She looked up at me again, eyes hard, daring me to blame her, to say it was her fault, she'd let him, she hadn't even put up a fight.

'I understand,' I said. 'So you had sex?'

She nodded. 'He was doing it and I heard the door open. I saw the other two standing in the doorway.'

'What did you do?'

'I yelled at them to get out. I told Miles to make them get out, but he just put his hand over my mouth and told me to keep quiet. Then he got up and I tried to get up too, but he pushed me back down again and then the other two were on me.'

Rona's hand was beside me on the bench. I gave it a quick pat, but stopped when she looked surprised. The passenger boat arrived and docked at a small river pier. We watched the crew hook ropes over giant cleats and the passengers begin to disembark.

'Did they threaten you?' I asked, when most of the passengers were on dry land.

She gave a little shrug. 'They just kept saying to keep quiet and they'd let me go,' she said. 'To keep quiet and I wouldn't get hurt.'

The boat was loading up new passengers now. Nothing Rona had told me so far was surprising. I'd heard variations of it several times already from other girls. I'd read countless reports. It was all horribly familiar.

'What happened next, Rona?'

'One of them was kneeling on my shoulders. He pulled my bra up round my neck and put his hands on my . . .' She stopped. She was looking down at her body.

'He put his hands on your breasts?' I asked.

She nodded. 'He was holding me, saying they was the biggest he'd ever seen, he kept repeating it, all the time his mate was doing it to me. It was humiliating, you know what I'm saying?'

'I know. Did you ask them to stop?'

She looked down at her hands.

'I understand that you were scared, Rona,' I said. 'I'm sorry I have to ask you all these questions. I know how hard it must be to answer them. Are you able to go on?'

She nodded. 'When the one who was doing it to me had finished, they swapped. Then, same thing again.'

'Where was Miles while this was happening?'

'Sitting in a chair, watching.'

'Did they let you go, when the third one had raped you?'

She looked at me and shook her head. 'No,' she said. 'They didn't let me go. Two more of them arrived.'

10

The underground space is vast and dark and smells of decay, like the cathedral of a city whose inhabitants are long since dead. The day outside was bright and clear, close to noon. Down here, the darkness is all consuming and time has become meaningless. The black-clad figure moves slowly and the huge structure amplifies sound like the inside of a great shell. The echo of each footstep seems to dance away into the distance, as though endlessly repeating itself somewhere out of earshot. The chamber feels like a crypt.

'Perfect,' says a voice.

The water, twenty feet below the searching eyes, looks black as moleskin in the light of the torch. It's shining, giving off the peculiar odour of petrol and salt water that always seems to hover around a river when the tide is heading out. Except this water never moves. This water is still as death.

A sudden sound above. Airborne creatures live in here, whether birds or bats or something new entirely, it's impossible to tell. A stone or piece of brickwork falls into the water. The sound, like glass breaking, cuts through the silence so sharply the air seems to shimmer around it for a moment. Then all is still again.

As the figure in black moves on, the smell seems to evolve. Humanity, street drugs and paraffin: echoes, all of them. It's been years since anyone has been down here. Years, probably, since anyone has even remembered it was once a home.

And yet there are traces, as the footsteps move on, of the people this vaulted space once knew. A lantern with a candle stub inside it, a small, upturned calor-gas stove. The people made dens for themselves with boxes, old curtains, even what looks like a hospital screen. They divided up the huge space to give themselves territory, erected walls for privacy, and most of their structures still exist. Along this long, suspended gallery are a dozen or more hiding places.

A discarded sheet of polythene moves in a sudden breeze and it sounds like the rattle of old bones. The polythene marks the way. The figure reaches out and pushes it to one side. Then steps through.

A smaller space. Still cold, damp and dark, but more containable. There is a mattress on the floor, even an old fold-up chair.

'Perfect,' whispers the voice again. Then, softer still, 'Lacey, I'm home.'

11

I talked to Rona for more than an hour. When we were tired of watching the river, we got up and wandered down Bankside. At the bridge we turned back again and joined the crowds admiring the black and white, surprisingly tiny, circular theatre. Everything she told me was off the record. She wasn't prepared to press charges, just wanted someone to talk to. She told me how two more boys had arrived, the older one she thought was seventeen, the younger, her age — fifteen. The five boys had stripped her naked and then the two new arrivals had taken turns to rape her. Then they'd forced her to kneel at the foot of the bed and perform fellatio on each of them. It was an act, she told me, known as a lineup. When that was over, the oldest of the boys had turned her face-down on the bed and raped her anally. Only when they saw how much she was bleeding did they let her go.

Just before she half crawled out of the front door, Miles had given her the money for her bus fare home.

We both knew this case was never coming to court. Rona knew other girls who'd suffered in the same way, she knew the form. If she brought charges against the boys, they'd either deny anything had happened or they'd claim she consented. The fact that she already had a sexual relationship with one of the boys and had gone willingly to his flat would be held against her. The boys had used condoms, again implying some level of consent. Even if they were charged, they were young and could well be released on bail and be back in the neighbourhood. They would have friends, who would be only too happy to intimidate potential witnesses. If Rona went public, she wouldn't be safe.

When she'd finished, it would have been difficult to say which of the two of us was the more exhausted.

'What can I do for you, Rona?' I asked. 'I understand that you don't feel able to press charges right now, but is there anything I can do? Do you need medical attention? I can probably arrange for you to see a counsellor if you like.'

She shook her head. 'Can you sort out

protection?' she asked.

'Protection?' I repeated. 'For you?'

'No,' she said. 'There's been talk, at school. Girls say they got their eye on Tia now.'

'Tia?' I was lost.

'My sister. People are saying Miles and the others are coming after Tia next.' She stopped, and for the first time I thought perhaps she might be close to tears. 'Miss Flint, you have to do something,' she said. 'She only twelve.'

12

I said goodbye to Rona and walked back to the station, knowing I was probably as powerless to protect Tia as Rona was.

The official line from Scotland Yard is that all reported rapes and sexual crimes are taken seriously. Spokesmen point to millions of taxpayers' money invested in the Sapphire Units. The truth is they are failing and all over London young women and girls are being let down. Because those in a position to address the problem simply dare not confront its true nature.

What the official reports and even most newspaper coverage will not say is that gang rape is endemic among young black communities. It's not the sort of thing people want to hear, but the number of reported cases goes way beyond what demographics can explain.

The girls themselves believe nothing can be done. They hate the fear they live in daily, but know they are powerless to protect themselves against these boys. And they certainly know that no one, not the police, nor their communities, not even their parents, will act or speak to help them.

And what was I going to do about it? I honestly didn't know. Yet.

Detectives operate a skeleton staff at weekends and I was expecting to find my room at Southwark police station empty. To my surprise, DC Pete Stenning was there, leaning against my desk, cheeky grin turned up to maximum. Stenning and I worked in the same team for just over a year before he'd finished his training and successfully applied to join the MIT at Lewisham. He wasn't a friend — I don't make friends at work — but we were on friendly enough terms. Normally, I wouldn't be sorry to see him, but I had a feeling this wasn't a social visit.

'I was just about to put out a call for you,' he said, as I walked over. 'You're wanted at Lewisham.'

'Have they identified the victim yet?' I asked, as Stenning drove us away from the station.

He glanced over. 'I had very clear instructions not to talk to you about the case,' he told me. 'DI Joesbury was at pains to remind me that you're a witness, not an investigating officer.'

It made sense and there was no reason for me to be pissed off. Except I really hadn't liked DI Joesbury.

'He's still around then?' I asked, wondering if the real problem had been that DI Joesbury hadn't seemed to like me.

Stenning must have picked up something in my tone. I saw him smiling to himself. 'You remember that drug ring we busted a couple of weeks ago?' he said.

I did. Sixteen million pounds' worth of heroin taken off the streets and nearly a dozen people arrested and charged. Three of them major players.

'He was a big part of it for six months,' said Stenning. 'Spent nearly a year before that just working his way into the organization. Almost got himself killed when the arrest went down.'

Well, thank heaven we were spared that loss, I thought. 'So, the victim, who is she?'

Stenning was still smiling. 'Rearrange this sentence,' he said. 'Sealed. Lips. My. Are.'

'Don't make me read it in the papers,' I pleaded.

'My instructions are to drop you off and

then get back to the estate,' he said. 'We have to knock on every door, see if anyone saw or heard anything. It's going to take days.'

Stenning was making an effort to look bored, but not really managing it. He was fired up, eager to drop me off and get out. Even in inner London, the opportunity to work on a murder investigation didn't come along every day.

'Have they had the post-mortem?' I asked, because it was worth one last try.

Stenning could turn his grin on and off like a light. 'You don't give up, do you?'

'This will all be public information in a matter of hours.'

'OK, OK. They had the PM first thing this morning,' he said. 'The DI was there. The full report won't be in for a while, but time of death fits with everything you told us and the cause was extensive blood loss. Still no clue as to who she was. No one's been reported missing. They're going to put her picture on the news tonight, see if anyone comes forward. Happy now?'

'They're putting a photograph of a corpse on national television?' I asked in disbelief, imagining a horror-struck family seeing their mother with her throat cut.

'Not a photograph, bozo, a drawing.

There's an artist over at the mortuary now working on it,' replied Stenning.

He turned into Lewisham's station car park. 'She was wearing thousands of pounds' worth of jewellery and had cash in her bag, so it wasn't about robbery. It all hinges on who she was, according to the DI. We find that out, and what she was doing on the Brendon Estate, and it should become obvious why she was killed. Everyone seems to think it'll be wrapped up pretty quickly. Oh, and there's something odd about the murder weapon, but Tulloch was keeping that pretty close to her chest.'

The room where Dana Tulloch's murder-investigation team was based was already crowded. I stopped at the open door, not quite having the nerve to go in. Tulloch had arranged for a street map of the area to be projected on to a white screen at the far end of the room. She was standing in front of it and a dozen people were grouped around her, some sitting, others leaning against desks. Then I realized that someone at the back of the room had turned to face me. Suntanned skin, turquoise eyes, one of them bloodshot. And my day was complete.

13

A couple of minutes later, Tulloch brought the meeting to a close. People began drifting out, one or two nodding to me. Gayle Mizon paused in the act of biting on an apple to give me a smile.

'Lacey, how are you?' Tulloch beckoned me inside. She indicated a seat and then sat down herself. She looked tired. There were shadows under her eyes and her make-up had all but disappeared. Joesbury perched himself on the desk behind her with a proprietorial air.

'I'm fine, thank you,' I said, thinking that if I concentrated on Tulloch, I wouldn't be tempted to raise my eyes a few inches and look at the man directly behind.

'Sleep well?' asked Joesbury. We both ignored him.

'Lacey, I've put in a request to have you transferred to one of the other stations until this investigation is over,' said Tulloch. 'One north of the river. I know it —'

'What?' I said, before correcting myself. 'I'm sorry, ma'am, but surely that's not —'

'Call me Dana,' she interrupted, 'and I'm afraid it is necessary. You're an important witness and if the wrong person saw you last night, I want you well out of the way.'

'I can't leave Southwark,' I said. 'That witness I was telling you about, she came in this morning. I'm just getting closer to her. I may be able to persuade her to press charges.'

There was the tiniest glint in her eyes. 'We'll make sure someone takes over . . .' she began.

'But she trusts me,' I said, making an effort not to talk too quickly. 'Or at least, she's starting to. She's seriously scared. If I leave now she'll think I've run out on her.'

Tulloch sighed. 'I understand how you feel, but last night's murder has to take priority.'

I should just agree. It made no real difference to me what station I worked from. Besides, I was low-profile girl, I didn't rock boats. 'She was raped by five boys,' I said. 'She thinks they're going after her twelve-year-old sister next. Her mother is out of her head on drugs most of the time and these girls have no one to look out for them.'

Those green eyes suddenly looked a whole lot colder. 'The decision's made, Flint,' she said. 'Deal with it.' She stood up and turned away from me. I watched her walk halfway across the room.

'Hold up a sec, Tully. Why doesn't she come here?'

Tulloch stopped and turned round. 'What?' she said.

'Bring her here,' said Joesbury, talking over my head. 'She'll be close enough to Southwark to stay with her current cases.'

Tulloch looked at him like he was simple. 'I can't have her near the investigation,' she said. 'Her credibility in court will be completely undermined if it comes out that —'

'If a detective on your team had arrived before your victim died, you'd have exactly the same issues with him,' said Joesbury. 'Keep her at arm's length, if you have to,' he went on. 'But you're going to want her on hand. She needs to go through the CCTV footage, for one thing.'

Tulloch frowned at him. A muscle beneath her left eye was flickering. 'That will take hours, at most,' she said.

'If you go ahead with the reconstruction, she'll be involved in that.'

'Yes, but —'

'You need to make sure she gets trauma

counselling, unless you want the Met to face a personal-injury claim. Much easier to see that happens if she's here.'

Tulloch stared at him for a moment, then said, 'Mark, can I talk to you for a second?'

He stood and started to follow her out of the room, before stopping and looking down at me. He took his time, taking in my lace-up brogues, pale chinos that I always wore a little too big, and the loose white shirt. My hair, as usual, was tied back at the nape of my neck and plaited. I wore my dark-rimmed glasses. No make-up or jewellery. Exactly how I always look at work.

'You certainly scrub up well,' he said at last.

'Mark!' Tulloch was at the end of her patience with both of us. Without another word, he joined her and they left the room.

I gave them a two-minute head start and then followed. I was feeling the need for caffeine. I walked the length of the corridor towards the drinks machine at the far end. I stopped just before I reached it.

The deep voice with its distinctive south London accent had already become unpleasantly familiar. Joesbury was feet away, just out of sight around the corner. 'All I'm saying is, keep an eye on her,' he said. 'You can do that a lot better if she's close. And let me make a few discreet inquiries.'

'And this has nothing to do with the fact that she's gor—'

Joesbury didn't let Tulloch finish. 'Let's just say my spider sense is tingling,' he said, in a voice I could barely hear above the gurgling of the drinks machine. 'Indulge me on this, sweetheart, OK?'

Back in the incident room, I sat alone, waiting. If I transferred to Lewisham I could stay in contact with Rona and her friends on the estate, and I'd get to see how the murder investigation panned out. The woman had died holding my hand. I couldn't help but be curious. On the other hand, I didn't really want to be surrounded by people who knew how badly I'd screwed up last night. And I still wasn't sure what to make of Joesbury and his antics.

I moved to a desk and, using a remote access password, opened up the Met's website and keyed in SO10.

Which was no longer SO10, I learned, but had been renamed the Specialist Crime Directorate, or SCD10 for short. Informally and colloquially, though, SO10 had stuck. I read that it had been formed in the 1960s to collect information on organized crime and prominent criminals. Due to advances in technology, the website claimed, the command had become a recognized world leader in covert policing methods.

So, I'd attracted the attention of a senior officer from a division with a worldwide reputation for specialist investigative techniques. Well, wasn't that a result?

After an hour, one of Tulloch's team, a good-looking black bloke in his late twenties who introduced himself as Tom Barrett, asked me to come and look at the CCTV footage from the murder site. Barrett and I crossed the small inner courtyard to another wing of the station and a tiny windowless room with a TV screen. For the next three hours I watched seemingly endless recordings of people and traffic around the estate where the murder had taken place. I saw myself, driving my black Golf along the Camberwell New Road and turning off towards the car park.

'What's that?' I asked a few minutes later. Thirty minutes or so after I drove my car into the car park, another vehicle — one decidedly out of place on an inner London council estate — went the same way.

'We've already spotted that,' replied Barrett, glancing down at some scribbled notes.

'It's a Lexus LS 460, Tuscan Olive in colour, retails at upwards of sixty grand. We can only make out the last couple of letters on the registration so it'll take time to track it down, but it's definitely of interest.'

'It's the sort of car she would have driven,' I said.

Barrett agreed with me and we got back to work. By three o'clock I was ready to slit my own wrists. There had been nothing, absolutely nothing out of the ordinary and I wasn't sure quite what we'd expected. A wild-eyed madman, perhaps dripping with blood, staggering down Camberwell New Road?

At ten past four we watched the last recording and I had a sense of freedom looming. I'd go home, draw the blinds, put on a film and curl up on the sofa. If I was lucky, I wouldn't wake till morning.

It wasn't to be. We hadn't even switched the machine off when the door opened to reveal Tulloch, a blue cotton trench coat loose around her shoulders. This time, she was alone. She nodded at Barrett and then turned to me. 'Looks like I'm stuck with you, Flint,' she said. 'You're based here until further notice and you'll bring your ongoing projects from Southwark with you.

Come on, I'll give you a lift home. We can talk on the way.'

14

'We've found the victim's car,' Tulloch told me as we pulled out of the car park.

'The Lexus?' I asked.

She nodded. 'We'll keep it under surveillance for a couple of days,' she said.

It was standard procedure. Plain-clothes officers would watch the car, see if anyone approached it. Anyone who showed a particular interest could well have some bearing on why the woman had been in that part of London. On the other hand . . .

'Sixty grand's worth of luxury vehicle on that estate won't go unnoticed for very long,' I said.

'Probably not,' agreed Tulloch. 'We found the keys as well. Behind a wall not far from where you found her.'

'So how . . . ?' I began.

'We think whoever killed her took the keys, meaning to drive away in her car,' said Tulloch. 'The dogs tracked someone to the alley you emerged from, but then he backtracked.'

'He heard me coming,' I said.

'Makes sense,' said Tulloch. 'You'd cut off his escape route so he had to change his plans. He ditched the keys, ran further down the block, round the rear of the buildings and made for the A3. The dogs lost him at Kennington Tube.'

'You must know who she is by now,' I said. 'The car would have been registered.'

She nodded. 'We have a pretty good idea.'

I waited. 'Are you allowed to tell me?' I asked, after a moment.

Tulloch sighed. 'It'll probably be on the news tonight,' she said. 'The car was registered to a Mr David Jones. Lives in Chiswick, married to Geraldine. We've got officers round there already, but only the au pair's at home. I'm on my way over now.'

Geraldine Jones. The name meant absolutely nothing. 'Can I come?' I found myself asking.

'Absolutely not,' she replied, glancing sideways at me. 'You should try and get some rest. You look like you need it.'

I couldn't argue with her on that one. We were silent for a while. There was something I wanted to say to her, I just didn't know how to start. So she drove and I looked at my fingernails. When I glanced up again, we were on the Wandsworth Road, not far from my flat.

'I heard there was something unusual about the murder weapon,' I said, knowing I was chancing my luck.

'That will definitely not be on the news tonight,' she replied, with a tiny half-smile as she turned into my road and pulled up against the kerb. I put my hand on the door handle and opened the door. Now or never.

'I'm sorry I screwed up,' I said. 'I know if I'd had my wits about me, she probably wouldn't have died.'

Tulloch took both hands off the wheel and twisted round in her seat to face me properly. 'What are you talking about?' she said.

'If I'd seen the attack, I could have stopped it,' I said. 'Even if it was too late for that, I could have identified who did it.'

She nodded her head slowly. 'Yes, that's possible,' she said. 'Or I might have two dead women on my hands right now and Southwark would have lost an officer.'

She turned the ignition key and the engine died. 'In any case,' she went on, 'the dogs tracked the killer to the alleyway you came out of, remember? He heard you coming and backtracked. He'd killed her and left her to die before you got anywhere near.'

She was right. I hadn't thought of that. Oh thank God.

'Lacey, you're not responsible for what happened to Geraldine Jones,' Tulloch went on. 'If that's what's been going through your head, forget it. And get some rest.'

It hadn't been my fault. Geraldine Jones hadn't died because of me. I got out of the car and thanked Tulloch for the lift. She told me to turn up at Lewisham first thing on Monday morning and drove away the minute I closed the car door. I watched the silver Mercedes turn on to the main road and felt strangely left out.

Nothing I could do. I was a witness, not an investigating officer, and finally I was home. Tulloch was right, I should rest.

But all around me life was going on and the evening was filled with that golden light September is so often blessed with. It really wasn't an evening for staying at home alone. Even if you were me. I went inside and jumped in the shower. Thirty minutes later I was on my way out, determined to make up for lost time.

Or maybe not. The top step leading down to my basement didn't normally have a scruffy-looking girl in a pink jacket standing on it, as though she couldn't quite make up her mind whether to approach my door or not. She started when I appeared, then moved back and waited for me to join her at pavement level.

'Lacey,' she said, to my surprise, because I knew I'd never seen her before. 'Can I have a word? About the murder last night? There's something you really need to know.'

15

'Do I know you?' I asked.

The girl was in her early twenties and, whilst I don't like myself for saying this, not the sort of person it's easy to look at. Her dyed black hair was slicked back with some greasy-looking substance and she'd tried, and failed, to cover a crop of spots around her chin with too much make-up. I counted six studs in her left ear. She didn't have a right ear. The burns scars around her lower jaw and the right side of her neck were dreadful.

'I'm Emma Boston,' she said, in a voice that might have belonged to an elderly smoker. 'I'm working on last night's murder. I've got information for you. Can we go inside?'

'What do you mean, you're working on the case?' I asked, trying to remember if I'd seen her at Lewisham or even Southwark.

Boston was wearing large sunglasses, the

sort that make it impossible to see the eyes behind them. I wondered if her eyes had suffered fire damage too. 'You were the one who found her,' she was saying. 'I heard she was still alive. Is that true?'

This woman wasn't a police officer. 'I'm going to ask you one more time, then I'm going to ask you to get off my step. What exactly are you doing here?'

Boston was about to respond when she broke into a fit of coughing. 'Did she say anything before she died?' she managed, when she got her breath back. 'Do you know who she is yet?'

Light dawned. 'Are you a reporter?' I asked.

Her lips hardened. She was used to people not responding well to her. 'Look, we both have jobs to do,' she said. 'I just think we can help each other.' She looked round the street. 'Is there somewhere we can talk?' she went on. 'I really do have some information.'

'Detective Inspector Tulloch is heading up the investigation,' I said. 'She's based at Lewisham police station.'

'OK,' she said. 'But I've had a letter that could be from the killer, and seeing as how it mentions you by name, I thought you'd be interested. My mistake.'

She pushed past me and walked up the

street towards Wandsworth Road. I watched her go, fairly sure she was lying, but . . .

I caught up with her ten metres from the corner. 'I'm sorry,' I said. 'It's been a long day.'

The lips relaxed and she glanced towards the pub on the corner. 'Want to buy me a drink?' she asked.

It was Saturday night and the pub was busy, but we went out into the beer garden and found an empty stretch of wall to lean against. Boston pulled a pack of cigarettes out of her pocket and lit one. I sipped my Diet Coke and waited. She coughed again and caught me looking at the packet.

'I shouldn't smoke,' she said, 'but my lungs are fucked up anyway, so I figure, what's the difference?'

'I'm sorry,' I said. Everything was relative. My life wasn't much to write home about, but it would be a whole lot worse if I looked like she did.

'Anything you tell me can be off the record,' she said, when she'd drawn deeply on her cigarette. 'I wouldn't quote you or anything.'

'I understand,' I said, knowing officers lost their jobs and their reputations for talking off the record to the press. Emma Boston hadn't taken out a notepad and I wondered if she was recording the conversation. She'd placed a scuffed canvas bag very close to me. 'But it sounds like you know more than I do right now,' I went on. 'I'm not part of the investigation.'

'But you found her?'

I nodded.

'Did she say anything?'

'You said you had a letter?' I asked. I couldn't afford to tell Boston more than I should because I felt sorry for her. 'A letter that mentioned me,' I went on. 'If that was a trick to get me here, I'm going home now.'

She reached into her bag and took out a thin, clear plastic folder with paper inside.

'No one's touched it but me,' she said. 'I didn't realize what it was till I pulled it from the envelope, but then I put it in a folder straight away. That was the right thing to do, wasn't it?' She seemed to want my approval now.

'Was it posted?' I asked.

She shook her head. 'No. It was pushed through the door of my house sometime last night. I found it this morning.'

'Can I see it?'

She handed it over. Inside the plastic was a sheet of fawn-coloured paper, the standard size for personal stationery. It had been folded down the middle lengthways and then twice horizontally. The fold marks were quite distinct. The handwriting was neat and legible. In red ink. There was something disturbingly familiar about it. I read it quickly. Before I was halfway through, I could feel a tingling in my cheeks.

> Dear Miss Bosston
> I keep on hearing Saucy Jacky is back. How I have laughed. Is it true? If it is, I hope the police are clever and on the right track.
> Ask DC Flint for me — did the lady squeal? No time to clip her ears but plenty more time for funny little games.
> Yours truly
> A f(r)iend
> Hope you like the proper red stuff.

I handed it back. 'It's gibberish,' I said. 'Some nutter's idea of a joke.'

Boston inclined her head, as though behind the dark sunglasses she was looking at me more closely. 'Are you sure?' she asked. 'You've gone very pale.'

I made a mental note that Boston probably shouldn't be underestimated.

'Actually, a joke is what I thought at first,' she went on. 'But then I found out you were with her when she died and it made me think twice. Not many people would know that.'

I was more bothered than I wanted to admit that my name was being bandied about by people I didn't know. But not nearly as bothered as I was that I knew I'd seen that letter, or something very like it, before. 'Well, if you found it out, it can't have been that hard,' I said, playing for time.

'We listen in to police radio transmissions,' she said, as if daring me to object. 'My boyfriend made a recording of last night's activity. Most people don't have the equipment to do that. But what really rung a bell with me was that reference to Saucy Jacky.'

I took it back and read the first couple of lines again. *Dear Miss Bosston, I keep on hearing Saucy Jacky is back. How I have laughed.*

'Who's Saucy Jacky?' I asked, as two things happened at once. My mobile beeped, letting me know I had a text message, and I remembered who Saucy Jacky was.

'Try Googling it,' Boston was saying. 'You'll find thousands of references. Saucy Jacky is one of the nicknames given to —'

'Jack the Ripper,' I finished for her. 'He called himself Saucy Jacky, didn't he? In letters he sent to the police.'

'And to the press,' said Boston, as I realized I was staring at her rather too hard. I pulled my phone out of my bag. The text was from Pete Stenning, letting me know that he and some of the others were heading to the Nag's Head in Peckham if I wanted to join them. Seeing me twice in twenty-four hours must have made him think of old times. Maybe he'd forgotten I'd never once accepted an invitation to go drinking with him.

'I know very little about Jack the Ripper,' I said, not sure why I was lying. 'Didn't he kill prostitutes?'

'Yes, he did,' Boston replied. 'A lot of them. Generally speaking, he cut their throats and then mutilated their abdomens. Just like what happened to that woman on Friday night. His first victim, a woman called Polly Nichols, was on 31 August 1888, but there were others after that. I think you might have a copycat on your hands.'

'Can I keep this?' I asked, indicating the letter.

'What can you tell me in return?' she replied.

I shook my head.

'No, then,' she said.

I held the letter out for her to take, and

realized my hand was shaking. 'I'll look into what you've told me,' I said. 'I'll do it tonight. And if I think it stacks up, I'll arrange for you to meet with DI Tulloch. It'll be up to her what she tells you, but if you hold off publishing anything until you've seen her, she'll be much more likely to cooperate.'

Boston was carefully putting the plastic folder back into the envelope. 'I need to meet her tomorrow,' she said, 'or I'm running with this.'

'Do you have access to scanning equipment?' I asked. When she nodded, I scribbled down my email address at work and gave it to her. I had to hope it would automatically be re-routed to Lewisham. 'Scan it and send it to me,' I said. 'And don't let anyone else touch the original. Now, how can I get in touch with you tomorrow?'

Boston wrote down her address and phone numbers for me. I took a last sip of Coke and left the pub. I went home, and some dozen years back in time.

16

My bedroom as a teenager was nothing like the plain, half-empty room I sleep in now. My old room was piled high with books: crammed into shelves, balanced on chests, falling off the wardrobe, even stuffed under the bed. I'd owned so many books at one time, lots of them crime novels, most of them accounts of true crime. If I'd ever appeared on *Mastermind,* violent crime could have been my specialist subject.

I'd been home only a few minutes, but my flat seemed to have grown warmer, and too small. As if the walls had moved a few inches closer together. I needed air. Outside, I walked to the jasmine that pours over the wall from the neighbouring garden. I breathed in deeply, sucking in the soft, sweet scent as though it might clear my head a little, bring me back out of the past.

It wasn't working. I'd gone back twelve, maybe fourteen years, to a history class at school. I'd been bored, doodling in my exercise book, whispering to the girl next to me. I remember the teacher fixing me with a weak-eyed stare. She'd been a little afraid of me, that teacher, but every now and again she'd get the urge to face her demons. 'So do you have a favourite character from history?' she'd asked me.

I'd been listening with half an ear, I've always been able to do that, and I'd heard my classmates name Oliver Cromwell, Leonardo da Vinci, Elizabeth the First, Einstein.

'Jack the Ripper,' I'd replied without missing a beat and the class had fallen about laughing. The teacher had blinked twice and, with more courage than normal, had made me explain why. So I did. I told her and the class about the arrogance and the misery of Victorian London and about a killer who'd changed the way we think about human evil. I told them about the fear that spread through the East End like a Victorian pea souper and the glee with which people watched the helplessness of the police.

And I told them my own particular theory about Jack. How, if I were right, over a century later, the killer (or the killer's ghost) was probably still laughing at us.

I'd wiped it all out of my mind until now.

I'd honestly forgotten that, once, I'd named my favourite character from history as Jack the Ripper. And now a letter, signed with one of his pseudonyms, had linked me with Friday night's murder.

17

I walked into the Nag's Head to find Stenning and a few others from the MIT crowded around a fruit machine. I recognized Tom Barrett, the DC who'd sat and watched footage with me for several hours earlier that day. Stenning spotted me and came over, nearly sending a table filled with drinks flying.

'Shit, Flint,' he said, when he was close enough. 'What did you do to yourself?'

Men! I'd loosened my hair, put on a bit of make-up and changed into jeans and a top that fitted me properly. I'd done very little, in fact, but I learned when I was a teenager how tiny the difference can be between a woman nobody notices, and one whom everybody does. Most of the time, especially at work, I prefer to be invisible. Plain clothes worn a size too big, no make-up, heavy glasses that I don't actually need and hair swept tightly back. I don't speak without something to say and, until I became an unwilling player in a murder investigation, I'd have bet most people at Southwark nick wouldn't have had a clue who I was. When I go out in the evening, I look very different.

I wouldn't normally have made any sort of effort to meet work colleagues. Hell, I wouldn't normally meet work colleagues socially, but I'd changed earlier in readiness for a night out and after Emma's visit and the whole Jack the Ripper stuff I'd been too keyed up to stay indoors any longer.

'Did you just get back from Chiswick?' I asked, when we were settled at the bar. 'Was she definitely Geraldine Jones?'

'Officially, we still haven't confirmed identity,' he replied.

'Unofficially?'

'Unofficially, there were photographs in the house,' he said. 'It's her. And the au pair says she hasn't seen Mrs Jones since Friday morning. She thought perhaps she'd changed her mind and gone away with Mr Jones and his eldest son. They're on a golf weekend near Bath. Or at least they were. They should be back by now. DI Tulloch stayed behind to talk to him when he arrived.'

'And take him to identify the body?'

Stenning nodded.

'Any idea what she was doing in that part of London?' I asked, as the pub door opened and a familiar tall figure came in. Shit.

'We did a basic search of the house,' Stenning was saying. 'The au pair couldn't tell us much, she seemed pretty freaked out having so many police in the house. But nothing out of the ordinary that we could see. No plastic bags of cocaine in the cistern. On the surface, it seems to be a perfectly ordinary, upper-middle-class London family. He's something senior in insurance, she worked part-time at a gallery. Two sons, one a junior doctor, the other at university.'

'What about the youngest son?' I said. 'If the oldest is with his dad, where's he?'

'He's travelling,' said Stenning. 'Due back in a couple of days, just in time to go back to uni.'

Joesbury was on his way over. Shit and corruption.

'Evening, Flint,' he said, as he reached the bar and walked further than he needed to in order to stand at my side. 'What'll you both have?'

Two hours later, I still hadn't mentioned my visit from Emma Boston. On the one hand, I knew I really had to. On the other, the most senior officer present was Joesbury and I was very reluctant to get into wild and wonderful theories abut nineteenth-century serial killers in front of him until I was a bit more sure of my facts. If he didn't dismiss the idea out of hand, he'd want details I didn't have after all this time. I think I was just plucking up the courage to say something when he took a phone call from Tulloch and left. Shortly afterwards, the group broke up.

And it really hadn't helped that everyone else seemed to consider him the best thing since Mr Warburton had invented the slicing machine. For most of the evening, he'd been entertaining the group with stories of his undercover work.

'So there I am,' he'd been saying at one point, 'in this police minibus, under arrest with a whole load of Tottenham fans, and I spotted a megaphone on the floor. So I picked it up and started giving it the verbal out the window and what do you think they all said to me: "Shut up, you'll get us in trouble." '

The group had fallen about laughing. I'd forced a polite smile when I realized Joesbury was looking my way and felt yet another stab of guilt. This was a murder investigation. I had information that might be important.

After Stenning, who'd insisted on driving me home, roared away, I hurried down the steps. Quick check of the under-stairs space and then inside. The neatly made bed I could see through the open door had never looked more inviting, but it would have to wait. Instead I pulled the blind down, opened my laptop, typed *Jack the Ripper murders* into the search engine . . .

. . . and became that teenage girl again, head stuffed with information about Jack the Ripper and the Whitechapel murders of the late nineteenth century.

In 1888, the year after Queen Victoria celebrated her Golden Jubilee, a serial killer who became known as Jack the Ripper stalked the streets of Whitechapel and Spitalfields, preying upon those least able to protect themselves. Jack's victims were 'unfortunates', if you were Victorian and polite. If you were less so — if you were Jack himself, for example — they were whores. Middle-aged, alcoholic, homeless prostitutes who sold their bodies to strangers several times nightly for the price of a glass of gin.

There were eleven Whitechapel murders

in all, starting in April 1888 and concluding in February 1891. The last few months of 1888, when the majority had taken place, had become known as the Autumn of Terror. At one time, I could have quoted victims' names, dates of death, details of injuries inflicted and locations of bodies. At ten minutes past one in the morning, I closed my eyes and found I still could.

Jack had been a killer ahead of his time, I realized that night, looking at the case again with grown-up, professional eyes. In the nineteenth century, someone who struck at random and without motive was something quite new. The police at the time had been close to helpless.

One reaction I'd had as a teenager remained the same. The most puzzling and the most frightening aspect of the murders had been Jack's ability to arrive from nowhere and disappear without trace. Many of the murders took place within yards of crowded lodging houses or major thoroughfares, but he moved silently and invisibly.

Then, as suddenly as they'd begun, the murders ceased. Jack vanished, leaving behind one of the most enduring murder mysteries the world has ever known.

I sat back a while, thinking, trying to make a connection between what had taken place in Victorian London and the murder I'd come close to witnessing twenty-four hours ago.

To my considerable relief, I couldn't do it. Married to a wealthy man, with a family, a nice home, a job, Geraldine Jones was the direct opposite of the women Jack had preyed upon. The original victims had been chosen at random, in the wrong place at the wrong time. Geraldine must have been in that part of London for a reason. And Kennington was a long way from Whitechapel.

Admittedly, Jones's injuries were very similar to those inflicted on more than one Ripper victim, but 31 August didn't even mark the anniversary of the first Whitechapel killing. The death of Polly Nichols that day had been the third murder. The first, that of Emma Smith, had been early in April 1888 and the second, Martha Tabram, on 7 August.

Something was still bothering me though. Something I couldn't quite put my finger on. Determined to leave no stone unturned, I checked whether there'd been other murders in London earlier in the year, specifically the first two weeks of April and August. I couldn't access the Met's computers from home but I searched the various news sites that cover events in and around the capital.

Nothing. There'd been a shooting on 5 August but the man in question, a nineteen-year-old of Grenadian origin, was recovering in hospital. Nothing in early April. There was no connection. So why couldn't I just go to bed?

Even the similar mode of death meant nothing. The original Ripper hadn't stuck to one modus operandi, his methods had evolved, even changed completely. There was no copycat. The letter sent to Emma Boston was a daft prank, possibly even the work of Emma herself to get an inside track on the investigation. I'd had it.

I printed off a couple of pages of summary information that I could use to brief the team the next day, closed the laptop and double-checked the front door. It occurred to me, for the first time, that I probably needed a stronger lock on it. Not something I'd ever worried about before. I picked up the printed sheets, meaning to put them in my bag ready for the morning. I was halfway across the bedroom when I caught site of the sub-heading halfway down the first page. A single word that stopped me in my tracks. Canonical.

Eleven Whitechapel murders. Few people, if any, believed them all to have been the work of Jack the Ripper. Experts argued endlessly about who had and who hadn't been a true Ripper victim. Emma Smith, almost certainly not. Martha Tabram, the jury was still out on. Personally, I was inclined to think probably not. Her injuries, multiple stab wounds from some sort of bayonet, were very different to the murders that followed. Polly Nichols, on the other hand, number three, nobody doubted. Killed on the last day of August 1888, she'd been the first victim that just about everyone agreed was a true Ripper killing. She had been the first of the canonical five.

The bedside clock told me it was three o'clock in the morning. I've said already that London is never quiet. It was then. I couldn't hear a thing. Not the traffic outside, not people in the flats upstairs, not even the sound of my own breathing.

The 31 August, the night Geraldine Jones had been killed, marked the anniversary of the first, undisputed Ripper murder. I checked the notes. Her injuries were practically identical to those inflicted on Polly Nichols and whoever killed Geraldine had disappeared without a trace.

I was going to have to wake up Tulloch and Joesbury, probably with the same phone call. Wasn't that going to make me popular?

18

Sunday 2 September

'Why didn't you mention this earlier?' asked Joesbury. It was an hour later, just coming up for four in the morning, and he was standing behind Tulloch's desk, leaning over her shoulder, both of them staring down at the letter that Emma, true to her word, had scanned and emailed to me at work.

'I wanted to be sure,' I replied, knowing how feeble an excuse it sounded. 'I needed time to do some reading.' Feeble as hell, but still a whole lot better than 'I didn't want to make an idiot of myself in front of you.'

Tulloch looked like she was struggling not to yawn. 'Did you see the original?' she said.

I nodded.

'The handwriting is red?' she asked. 'Please tell me it's somewhere safe.'

'Emma wouldn't give it to me,' I answered.

'But she seems to be looking after it. She has it in clear plastic. Saved the envelope as well. And I'm pretty certain the writing is in red ink.'

'That smudge on the bottom corner doesn't look like ink,' said Joesbury. 'Why the hell didn't you tell us about this in the pub?'

'Mark, back off,' sighed Tulloch. 'You know as well as I do the switchboard's been jammed with crank calls since Friday night.' She looked at me again. 'I know nothing about Jack the Ripper,' she said. 'What did you say the five murders were called? The ones that are supposed to be the work of the Ripper?'

'Canonical,' I said.

'What does that mean? It sounds religious.'

'Conforming to the established order,' replied Joesbury. 'Reducing things to their simplest form.'

Tulloch looked blank. 'I still don't . . .'

'Nobody really knows why they're called that,' I said. 'It's just tradition among people who describe themselves as Ripperologists. Five of the murders, between August and December, are called the canonical five.'

Joesbury raised an eyebrow. His right eye was still bloodshot. 'How do you know so much about Jack the Ripper?' he asked.

I didn't tell him Jack was my favourite character from history. Somehow, I doubted that would go down too well. 'I told you I'm interested in criminals,' I said. 'I always have been. Isn't that why lots of people join the police?'

'And the first of the canonical five was called Polly?' Tulloch asked. 'Are you sure about that?'

I nodded. 'Strictly speaking, her name was Mary Ann,' I said. 'But everybody knew her as Polly.'

Tulloch shot a glance at Joesbury. He stared back at her for a second and then shrugged.

'Why is that . . . ?' I began.

Tulloch waved me to be silent as she picked up the phone and dialled an internal extension. 'Find the record of all calls coming into the switchboard since Friday,' she ordered. 'Have somebody do a count-up of how many mention Jack the Ripper. Yes, you heard me, Jack the Ripper. I need it now.'

She put the phone down and looked at me again. She opened her mouth, but Joesbury got in first.

'Didn't the original Ripper send letters?' he asked. 'Taunted the police with them, from what I can remember.'

'Lots of letters were sent at the time,' I said. 'Not just to the police, but to newspapers as well. Even private citizens. They're generally believed to be fakes. Not actually from the killer.'

'I saw a film once. Didn't one have a body part in it?' asked Joesbury. He was leaning back against the window ledge now. 'Mind you,' he went on, 'the Ripper turned out to be Queen Victoria's grandson.'

'Someone did send a human kidney to the head of one of the vigilante groups,' I said. 'In a letter described as coming *"From Hell"*. And one of the victims was missing a kidney. But at the time, there was no way to establish whether it was really hers or just another prank.'

'Geraldine Jones wasn't missing any body parts,' said Tulloch.

'Whoever killed Geraldine Jones didn't have time to take souvenirs,' replied Joesbury. 'DC Flint saw to that. I think we need to see these letters. Come on, Flint, you seem to be our resident Ripperologist, find us a website.'

It wasn't easy with Tulloch and Joesbury breathing down my neck, but after a few false starts, I found the site I was looking for. It dealt specifically with the hundreds of Ripper letters.

Text at the top explained what I'd already told Tulloch and Joesbury, that most of the 'Ripper' letters were considered fakes, either the work of journalists trying to stir up a story or of fools intent on wasting police time. Just three, according to the site, may have been genuine.

The first of these, the infamous *Dear Boss* letter, had been sent to the Central News Agency on 27 September 1888 and had been the first to use the term 'Jack the Ripper'; the second was a postcard, in similar handwriting to the *Dear Boss* letter and referring to details of the crimes that, supposedly, only the killer would be in a position to know; the third had been the *From Hell* letter that accompanied the human kidney.

The phone rang just as I was pulling one of them up on the screen. As Tulloch answered it, her face seemed to tighten. She muttered her thanks and put the phone down.

'Six callers mentioned the date as that of one of the Ripper murders,' she said.

'You need to see this, Tully,' said Joesbury, who'd been staring at the screen. He lifted my hand from the mouse and enlarged the image. Written in rather elegant copperplate hand, it was the letter of the 27 September

1888, the one sent to *The Boss* of the Central News Agency. We read it together, Joesbury speaking the words in a just audible voice. Before we were halfway through, I was feeling sick.

Dear Boss

I keep on hearing the police have caught me but they won't fix me just yet. I have laughed when they look so clever and talk about being on the right track. That joke about leather apron give me such fits. I am down on whores and I won't quit ripping them till I do get buckled. Grand work the last job was. I gave the lady no time to squeal. How can they catch me now. I love my work and want to start again. You will soon hear of me with my funny little games. I saved some of the proper red stuff in a ginger beer bottle over the last job to write with but it went thick like glue and I can't use it. Red ink is fit enough I hope. Ha ha. The next job I do I shall clip the lady's ears off and send to the police officers just for jolly wouldn't you. Keep this letter back till I do a bit more work then give it out straight. My knife's so nice and sharp. I want to get to work right away if I get a chance. Good luck.

Yours truly
Jack the Ripper
Don't mind me giving the trade name.

Mark Joesbury picked up a pink highlighter pen from Tulloch's desk and started highlighting words and phrases on the letter Emma Boston had emailed to me earlier that morning. *I keep on hearing . . . How I have laughed . . . clever . . . on the right track . . . lady . . . squeal . . . clip . . . ears off . . . funny little games . . . proper red stuff.*

In the short note pushed through Emma's front door in the early hours of Saturday morning, twenty-two words had been directly lifted from the original letter. When he'd finished going through it, Joesbury drew a big circle round the misspelling of Emma Boston's name. *Dear Miss Bosston.*

'Christ,' muttered Tulloch.

'Bastard's sent us a *Dear Boss* letter,' said Joesbury, in case one of us hadn't got it. From the look on Tulloch's face, and the ache at the back of my jaw that usually means I'm about to vomit, it seemed fair to say we both had.

Tulloch looked at me. 'Do you have her address?' she said.

I nodded, fished around in my bag for the note I'd made and handed it over. Tulloch headed for the door.

'Dana, you don't have to go yourself,' Joesbury began.

Tulloch turned, glanced at me and then spoke to Joesbury. 'Do not let her out of your sight,' she told him, before disappearing.

19

For a few seconds neither of us spoke. Joesbury was right behind me, close enough for me to hear his breathing. To get out of the room I'd have to leap over the desk and run for it, or turn and face him. I think I was half bracing myself for the jump when he spoke.

'If you were on my team, you'd be on suspension by now.'

Maybe if I didn't move, didn't speak, he might get bored and leave himself.

'You had that note at eight o'clock last night,' he said. 'You were in the company of half the officers on the case for three hours after that. It's nearly four a.m. now and we've lost eight hours. You know how critical that is.'

He wasn't being fair. High-profile murder cases always attract crank calls and anonymous notes, weird conspiracy theories and attention-seekers. To follow up on all of them would require resources no investigation team could dream of. We make judgement calls. Sometimes they're right and sometimes not. I'd half suspected Emma of writing the letter herself to get my attention and trick me into revealing some juicy detail.

Which might still be the case. Emma could have copied the original *Dear Boss* letter. I found myself really hoping she had. In the meantime, I had to get out of the room with some shred of dignity. I turned.

Joesbury's tan seemed to be fading. Maybe he was just tired. The scarring around his eye looked more livid, if anything. He was wearing a loose blue cotton shirt and he'd rolled up the cuffs. The hairs on his wrist were a soft golden brown.

'What's the Polly connection?' I asked, without thinking. 'The name Polly meant something to you and DI Tulloch. What?'

He shook his head. He still hadn't shaved. Like most British men, his beard stubble was a mixture of brown, blond and red. There were even tiny grey hairs.

'You can't have it both ways,' I said. 'You can't insist I have nothing to do with the investigation, then give me a right royal bollocking because I don't respond to something immediately. If I'd known about the

Polly thing, whatever it is, I would have said something earlier. Although, admittedly, I'd have missed the very great pleasure of dragging you and DI Tulloch out of bed.'

A flash of something that could have been anger, but actually looked more like surprise, crossed his face.

'Shut the door,' he said.

Suddenly nervous, I did what he said and stayed right up against it.

'The knife that killed Geraldine Jones was a bog-standard kitchen knife, the sort you can buy in cooking shops and department stores just about everywhere,' he said. 'The team are trying to trace it back to where it was bought, but as several hundred seem to be made and sold every week, they're not too hopeful.'

I nodded, with no clue where this was going.

'The knife was unusual in one respect,' he went on. 'Five letters had been etched into the blade, along the cutting edge, just a centimetre below the handle. Five letters making up a name.'

'Polly,' I said.

He inclined his head. 'And if you repeat it to anyone I will throttle you myself.'

An hour later I'd bitten my tongue so many

times I could taste blood. Joesbury had decided, in Tulloch's absence, that we had to know as much as possible about the original Ripper murders and that I would be in charge of research.

We were in the incident room and he'd cleared one of the walls for Ripper information. I'd been told to have a file ready on each of the victims, paying particular attention to post-mortem reports of their injuries.

To his credit, I suppose, he was helping. He'd found a massive street map of Whitechapel and had fixed eleven small flags to indicate the locations of the original murders. The canonical five were red, the others yellow. He'd printed out internet photographs of the victims, all of them taken after death. These too had been put on the wall and I found myself looking, for the first time in years, at Polly Nichols. She'd been forty-five, small, dumpy, scruffily dressed and in poor health. It was hard to imagine two women more different than she and Geraldine Jones.

When I'd questioned the point of the map, given that Geraldine Jones hadn't been killed anywhere near Whitechapel, Joesbury said he wanted me to give a presentation on the Ripper murders to the whole team as soon as they got in.

As the night drifted away and the sun dragged itself up, people began to arrive. News of a breakthrough spread quickly and the incident room filled up. Joesbury's mortuary photographs proved something of a hit. I was halfway through a compilation of the various eye-witness reports (surprisingly few, given how heavily populated nineteenth-century Whitechapel had been) when Tulloch and Detective Sergeant Neil Anderson came in.

'That is one ugly-looking woman,' muttered Anderson, before crossing to the coffee machine. 'If I'd had breakfast I'd have brought it up.'

DS Anderson was no oil painting himself, with thinning red hair and a receding chin line. And a personalized programme at the local gym wouldn't have hurt. I looked down quickly when he caught me watching at him.

'The letter sent to the freelance journalist Emma Boston has gone over to Forensics,' Tulloch said, speaking to the team at large. 'They've promised to give it top priority. Neil and I have had a good chat with Miss Boston, but she hasn't been able to tell us anything new. The letter arrived some time early yesterday morning. She and her boyfriend went through recordings of our conversations on Friday night and realized DC Flint was directly involved in the murder. She ferreted out her home address and approached her last night.'

'Is she still here?' I asked.

Tulloch nodded. 'I don't want her going home until we've had chance to properly turn over her flat. She's not happy, but I can live with that.'

An avuncular-looking sergeant I remembered from the pub the previous night, who seemed to be called George, had been looking at Joesbury's artwork on the walls. 'Are we taking this Ripper business seriously then?' he asked. 'I mean, it's just the date, that's all.'

'Let me be very clear,' said Tulloch, in a voice you could probably strip paint with. 'I don't want anyone even thinking the name Jack the Ripper outside this room until we have the forensic report on the letter. In the meantime, we need to know as much as we can about what we're dealing with.'

'Well, that's good,' said Joesbury. 'Because DC Flint's been working on a presentation since the small hours. Take it away, Flint.'

I turned to him in dismay. 'It's nowhere near ready.'

'We'll take a work in progress,' he said.

I realized how tempting it could be, in

certain circumstances, to stick a knife in someone's gut.

'Tell us what you can, Lacey,' said Tulloch. 'Just take your time.'

Everyone was looking at me. There was no getting out of it. And this might be my best chance to win back some credibility, with Tulloch at least. So I took a deep breath, went over to the flip chart, and told my new colleagues the story of the most notorious killer who ever lived.

20

'Jack the Ripper was a real man,' I began. 'But he's become a myth. And that makes summarizing the case hard because the first thing you have to do is separate the known facts from the legend.'

Tulloch pulled a chair out from under a desk, Joesbury crossed the room and stood behind her. I was suddenly conscious that I was still in the 'look at me' clothes I'd worn to go to the pub the night before. And that the entire MIT was now doing exactly that. So much for low-profile girl.

'It's been over a hundred years since the murders took place,' I went on, 'and thousands of people all over the world have been drawn into the puzzle. Going right back to the time of the murders, facts got misreported, quite often by the press, sometimes by the police, but then those mistakes were repeated until they became accepted as facts.'

Chairs were being scraped across the tiled floor as people settled themselves down. Over twenty officers, all senior to me, listening to what I had to say.

'Over the years, books were written based on errors, and then more books, based on the flawed books,' I said. 'Senior police officers who'd been involved with the case got to the end of their careers and wrote memoirs. To make them sell, they'd include their own pet theories about who Jack might have been. But quite often, these theories bear no relation to what the officers who worked on the cases actually thought.'

Tulloch wrote something down on a notepad.

'Misunderstandings have been perpetuated time and time again,' I said. 'There are thousands of websites dedicated to the murders, dozens of books, films, documentaries. Tourists go on guided walks around Whitechapel, looking at the sites of the murders and hearing someone describe what happened.'

'I've been on one of those,' said Tom Barrett from the back of the room. 'I had a girlfriend loved that sort of thing. I couldn't wait to get to the pub.'

I smiled at him, grateful for the interruption. It gave me a chance to get my breath.

Since I'd started speaking everyone in the room had been listening hard. Even here, I realized, amongst people for whom murder and violence were regular occurrences, Jack could still weave his spell.

'So, if you're going to make any sort of accurate analysis of what went on,' I said, 'you have to ignore all these secondary sources and go right back to the original documentation. The reports of the constables and the police surgeons who were there at the time, the inquest reports, witness statements, photographs. There isn't much to go on, but unless you focus on the primary-source information alone, you're going to go wrong. Does that make any sort of sense?'

'Perfect sense,' said Tulloch and I saw a couple of other people nodding their heads.

Slightly encouraged, I went on. 'There were nine murders in Whitechapel in 1888 and early 1889,' I said, turning to Joesbury's wall map. 'A couple more a few months later. The victims were all prostitutes, most were middle-aged and in very unfortunate circumstances. They weren't good-looking, they weren't even healthy. They were the most vulnerable of all because they were the ones no one really cared about.'

Only DS Anderson wasn't looking at me,

he was leaning back in his chair and gazing at the wall. He was listening, though, I could tell by his stillness.

'Mainly because of the injuries inflicted on the victims,' I went on, 'people generally agree that just five of the murders were definitely the work of one man. The first of these took place on 31 August 1888.' I stopped. The air conditioning in the room was quite harsh and my throat was starting to feel uncomfortable.

'Go on, Lacey,' said Tulloch, with something like impatience in her voice. Joesbury moved out of my line of sight.

'Mary Ann Nichols, known as Polly Nichols, was found at 3.40 a.m. in a dark alleyway called Bucks Row,' I said. 'She was probably still alive when she was found, but she'd died by the time a surgeon arrived. She was taken to the mortuary, where a post-mortem was carried out. There were two deep incisions on her throat. Both carotid arteries and tissue down to the vertebrae had been cut. The cuts were made with what the police doctor called a strong-bladed knife, moderately sharp and used with great violence. There were also several incisions on her abdomen, made by a knife stabbing violently downwards.'

I stopped and swallowed hard.

'The doctor thought that the attacker must have had some anatomical knowledge because he attacked all the major organs,' I said. 'This, incidentally, is the almost throwaway remark that led to the theory that Jack was a surgeon. The doctor concluded that the murder could have been committed in just four or five minutes.'

Around me several eyebrows raised. Then Joesbury appeared in front of me with a glass of water in his hand. Without making eye contact, he held it out and I took it.

'One of the phrases you'll hear often about the Ripper,' I said, after a couple of gulps, 'is "without a trace". Because that's how he worked. The police at the time searched the area around Bucks Row thoroughly and found nothing. There were people sleeping yards from where Polly was killed and they didn't hear a sound. When she was found, she was still alive, even with those terrible injuries, so the killer could only just have left. Nobody saw anything.'

'Sounds a hell of a lot like what happened on Friday night,' said Stenning from his desk by the window.

For a moment no one spoke.

'On the other hand, Kennington is a long way from Whitechapel, Geraldine Jones was not a prostitute and she wasn't killed in the small hours,' said Mark Joesbury. 'Let's not get carried away just yet. When did he strike again, Flint?'

'Hold on a second,' said Tulloch. 'Can I just —'

There was knock on the door. Everyone's head turned. I didn't know the man who was standing on the other side, but Tulloch got up and nodded at him.

'We'll take a break,' she said. 'Thanks, Lacey.'

Back at the temporary desk I'd been assigned, I tried to find out a bit more about Emma Boston. None of the online directories of journalists listed her. She wasn't a member of the National Union of Journalists, nor could I find her byline in the archives of any of the national or bigger regional papers. I did, though, find several references to her on the unofficial and anonymous police blogging community.

Emma Boston had upset more than one of my colleagues in her short career as a journalist in the capital. According to Dave of Dagenham, a much-followed police blog, she was a loose-tongued bitch, as physically repulsive as she was morally repellent, who lied for a living and would sell her granny's puppy if it earned her a few quid. Another blogger suggested she had a drugs habit and recommended regular raids of the slum she called home.

The clock crept towards noon and Stenning popped his head round the door to say that the team were off to the nearby pub for a late breakfast/early lunch. I shook my head when he asked me to join them, mainly because I'd caught sight of Joesbury leaving the building with the others. There was just something about that man that unsettled me.

Instead I bought sandwiches, crisps and bottled water from the canteen before making my way down to the interview suite.

'Hi,' I said, as I pushed open the door.

'How long are you going to keep me here?' Time in police custody had done nothing to improve Emma Boston's appearance. She seemed to have lost even more colour from her skin and her spots stood out red and livid. She still wore her sunglasses, even though the room had no daylight.

'It's necessary,' I said, sitting down and offering her first choice of the sandwiches. 'We need to find out who wrote that letter. If he left any trace at your flat, we need it.'

'He pushed it through the letterbox,' she answered. 'Any trace he left would be on the front door. You're trying to prove I wrote it myself.'

No point arguing. 'Well, we need to rule that out,' I said. 'Did anyone offer you lunch?'

'I didn't write it.'

'I know,' I said, realizing that I really didn't think Emma was a liar. 'But if it's genuine, you have to be very careful. Whoever killed Geraldine Jones picked you out. He knows where you live.'

We both thought about that for a second.

'Have a sandwich,' I said.

'Actually, somebody did . . .' Boston shrugged and pulled a wrapped tuna sandwich towards her, looked at it and screwed up her nose.

'The canteen's not at its best at the weekend,' I said, just as the door opened behind me. I turned my head to see Joesbury in the doorway, a large Prêt A Manger bag under one arm. He gave me a sharp look that lasted a nanosecond and then turned to Emma. Who'd taken off her sunglasses to look directly at him. She had the most beautiful hazel-brown eyes.

'Don't tell me she's feeding you canteen food,' Joesbury said to her. 'You can have her up before the Police Complaints Commission for that. Remind me later, I'll get you a form.' He emptied the bag on to the table. 'Chicken, avocado and pesto dressing,' he said. 'Got you the last one.' He picked up the still-wrapped tuna sandwich, glanced down at me again and then shrugged at Emma as if to say, *What can you do?*

'Have a nice lunch, ladies,' he told us, on his way out.

The door closed and we heard his footsteps travelling a few paces down the corridor. He stopped to talk to someone, probably the duty sergeant, who burst out laughing.

'He's nice,' said Emma, unscrewing the top off a bottle of freshly squeezed orange juice. 'Not like all the other troglodytes in here. No offence.'

I'd been staring at the door. I turned back to Emma again. 'Oh, none taken,' I said.

'He came in earlier to talk about getting a camera put over my front door,' she went on. 'In case whoever delivered the letter comes back.'

I was about to unwrap the tuna sandwich when we heard sharp heels clicking in the corridor outside, then Gayle Mizon exchanging a few low-pitched sentences with Joesbury. The door opened and she looked in at us. 'Boss wants you upstairs,' she said to me.

'She's called everyone back from the pub,' Mizon told me as we walked back towards the stairs. 'The smudge mark on Emma Boston's letter is human blood.'

I opened the door at the end of the corridor and looked at her. She nodded at me. 'It's Geraldine's,' she said.

21

I got to my usual Camden haunt at ten thirty. The place was just starting to fill up and the music was loud enough to drown out any possible conversation. I took my drink out to the piazza and wandered over to one of the horse statues, already regretting the impulse that had brought me here.

I'd spent the afternoon trying (and largely failing) to find something to do. Even at a distance from the team I could sense that the mood around the station had shifted. The possibility of Geraldine Jones's murder being just the start changed everything. As I heard Joesbury pointing out, the goalposts had been stretched the width of the entire bloody football field.

At the end of the day I'd nipped into the ladies'. It was empty. A minute later, the door opened and someone entered the next cubicle. I'd just pressed the flush button when I heard the sound of my next-door neighbour vomiting. I washed my hands and waited for her to stop.

'You OK?' I asked, when I figured she had. 'Can I get you anything?'

I waited a few more seconds, but there was no response. I turned to leave, but behind the door, where it had missed the hook and fallen to the floor, was a blue trench coat. Tulloch's. Guess I wasn't the only one feeling edgy.

So I'd come out on a whim, knowing that an evening in my flat with nothing but my own thoughts could drive me half daft. And there'd been that tune I simply couldn't get out of my head. 'My Favourite Things'. It made no sense. I hadn't thought about that old game in years, but it was like the dam I'd built in my head was rupturing, letting through old memories like trickles of water.

I wasn't even sure any more what had been on the list. Flowers maybe, and perhaps books. Ponies, definitely ponies. I'd loved equine creatures of all shapes and sizes, even donkeys — which was probably why I liked the Camden Stables Market so much — but cute, plump, cheeky ponies had been my favourite.

If I left now, I could still get the Tube home.

'Where did you disappear to Friday night?'

I turned round and looked up. The fair-haired man I remembered from my last visit was casually dressed for Sunday evening in jeans and a white, short-sleeved button-down. A college sweatshirt was around his shoulders. The casual style suited him more than the business suit he'd been wearing early Saturday morning. I glanced down. His shoes looked expensive.

'You ran like the Furies were after you,' he continued when I didn't reply. He was better looking than I remembered and a bit older. No wedding ring on his left hand. He was over thirty-five, he'd probably have his own place.

'I'd left the gas on,' I said.

He smiled. 'Was there an explosion?'

I smiled too. 'Not yet.'

I left his house just after two, pleading an early start at work. He got up with me, offering to get me a cab. I told him I'd called someone already while he'd been dozing. He seemed almost reluctant to let me walk out of the door.

Uncomplicated, unconditional sex with a beautiful stranger. Wasn't that most men's fantasy? It was what I offered and I was never surprised by how easy it was to get a man I'd barely met to invite me to his home. What did surprise me was the number who wanted to see me again. I usually left my number, with a couple of the digits in the wrong order. Maybe on the other side of London a happily married mother of four was getting all my booty calls.

When the front door closed and his footsteps faded away down the hall, I stood for a few seconds on the top step, breathing in the cool night air, waiting for my ride home.

My early encounters with men and sex were abusive. Nothing so very unusual in that, but I realized some years ago that women with my history have a choice. All too often they become wary, fearful of intimacy of any sort, and then clingy and dependent if a decent man does come along. Some avoid men altogether, taking matters into their own hands, if you get my drift. Then there are those who take control.

The minicab pulled up after two minutes. The same driver has been taking me home in the small hours for a couple of years now. He greets me like an old friend.

Oh, I know what I do comes with a built-in risk, I'm not stupid, but I've become a pretty good judge of man-flesh over the years. On the rare occasions I get it wrong, I can look after myself. Keeping yourself fit, being able to handle difficult physical situations, is part and parcel of being a young police officer. If all else fails, which it hasn't yet, I plan to show the bugger my warrant card and threaten him with a night at the local nick.

All things considered, I'm not remotely scared of a bit of male aggression. I have more than enough of my own to counter it.

Back at my flat, I climbed out of the cab, paid the driver and wished him goodnight. Finally, I was feeling genuinely tired. Like I might actually sleep at last. I made my way down the steps.

I was still wearing high-heeled shoes, so when the hand grabbed the back of my hair I was thrown completely off balance. There was nothing to brace myself against, no way to fight back, as I was pulled down the last two steps and into the shadow beneath. A weight I hadn't a hope of resisting pushed me forward until my face was up against the wood of my front door. I felt something cold and hard press against my neck and knew there was a knife at my throat.

'This is how easy it is,' said a voice in my ear. 'This is the last thing Geraldine felt.'

22

Without warning, the weight pushing against me moved away. I almost fell but managed to grab hold of the door-frame. Taking a deep breath, I turned round slowly.

Mark Joesbury was shaking his head at me, like I was something forced into his way but far beneath his notice. In his right hand he held his car keys. It had been a key, not a knife, at my throat.

'Are you out of your fucking mind?' he said, in a voice that would have carried easily up to the street.

'How dare you touch me?' I spat back at him. 'I'll have you up on a charge for this —'

'Oh, you're really going to tell Tulloch you were out shagging your way around north London when she specifically told you to come home, lock your doors and go to bed?'

Any second now, he'd wake the people in the upstairs flats.

'Why the hell are you following me, you sad, pathetic —'

'There is a man out there who gets off on slicing women open.' Joesbury took a step closer, lowered his voice just a fraction. 'You narrowly missed a close encounter with him on Friday and, just in case this hasn't sunk in yet, he knows your name and probably where you live.'

'That does not give you the right —'

'Shut up,' he went on. 'Most women in your position would be scared shitless. How come you're not?'

'I haven't the faintest idea . . .' Any second now I'd wake the people upstairs.

Joesbury was so close I could feel his breath on my face. 'This is your last chance to tell me voluntarily, Flint,' he said. He wasn't shouting any more, just quietly furious. 'If you know anything about Friday night's stabbing that you haven't already owned up to, I strongly advise you to cough up now.'

Raindrops and roses. Pale-blue eyes, staring into mine.

'Because if you don't and I find out,' he continued, 'I will wipe the frigging floor with you.'

Deep breath. Get hold of the last of my nerve. 'Go fuck yourself,' I managed.

For a second, just from the look in his eyes, I thought he was going to hit me. Then he got a hold of himself, taking a deep breath himself and letting it out slowly. He shook his head again, and I didn't think I'd ever seen anyone look at me with quite such contempt.

'Given the choice, I'd wipe my hands of you, Flint,' he said. 'I think you're trouble. But Dana, for some reason, has taken a bit of a shine to you and she cannot deal with any more stress right now. So for her sake, I'm giving you a warning. Keep your nose clean or I'll break it.'

At that moment, he looked perfectly capable of doing so. 'You are way out of line,' I told him.

He stepped closer still, clearly one of those men who use their size to intimidate. 'You are a member of the Metropolitan police service,' he said. 'I suggest you try and remember that. And I really hope you're not up to anything you shouldn't be in Camden. But if you are, I'll find out. Watch your back.'

He'd turned away and was heading for the steps when I came to my senses. I could not let this man launch a serious investigation into me. He was halfway up before I found my voice.

'DI Joesbury.'

I watched him register the change in my voice, saw his shoulders moving as he took in another deep breath.

'I go to Camden for sex,' I said, quietly, but knowing he was listening hard. I let my jacket slip off my shoulders and saw him turn as it fell to the ground. The dress I was wearing was sleeveless, held up by thin straps.

'I don't have a regular boyfriend and I don't want one,' I went on. Joesbury didn't move. I saw the light from the streetlamp was turning his skin a soft gold. 'But there are times when what I can do on my own just isn't enough. Can you understand that?'

His right hand clenched around his car keys and he took a step forward. He was coming back down the steps. What the hell had I done? I hadn't planned for this, would never be ready for this, and how could I not have realized before — Mark Joesbury scared me.

I'd stepped backwards, could feel the stone wall cold against my skin. Joesbury saw the panic in my face and stopped moving. His eyes narrowed and we stared at each other for a second longer. Then he turned, climbed the rest of the steps and disappeared.

I stayed where I was for a long time, long after I heard his car drive away. I didn't even bother picking up my jacket. When I could no longer be sure whether I was trembling with fury, fear, or just plain cold, I made my way inside.

23

27 October, eleven years earlier

The girl slips barefoot across the carpeted landing. She stops at the bathroom door, leaning close.

'Cathy,' she says, in a voice that even she can barely hear. 'Are you in there?'

Silence behind the door. She sees her warm breath condense against the cold paintwork and taps gently with one finger. 'Cathy, are you OK?'

She hears the sound of a tap running, then the towel-ring banging against tiles.

'Cathy,' she tries again. 'There's nobody else upstairs. Let me in.'

Cathy isn't answering. The girl tries the door handle. It moves, the door doesn't. Locked.

She waits for another second or so, then steps away, heading back towards the bedroom. The light is still on. She sees the bloodstained clothes on the carpet and turns back again.

'Cathy,' rapping louder this time. The TV is on downstairs, she won't be heard. 'Cathy, are you bleeding again?' No answer. 'Cathy, this is serious. They said this might happen. If you've got an infection we need to get you seen. Please Cathy, just let me in.'

She waits. And waits.

■ ■ ■ ■

Part Two: Annie

■ ■ ■ ■

'London lies today under the spell of a great terror.'

Star, 8 September 1888

24

Friday 7 September

'Detective Inspector Tulloch, how certain can you be that the killer won't strike again tonight?'

'I can't be certain of anything,' Tulloch replied, in the measured tones we'd all come to be wary of. 'But, for the third time in ten minutes, there is no reason at this stage to believe we are likely to see another incident like the one on the 31 August.'

We were at New Scotland Yard for the latest press conference. Tulloch was at the front with Southwark's borough commander, Chief Superintendent Raymond Puller, and her immediate boss on the Murder Investigation Team, Detective Superintendent David Weaver. They'd had to admit that the team were following up no solid leads in the Geraldine Jones killing. Hours of tramping around the Brendon Estate and endless conversations with

Geraldine's family and friends had turned up nothing we could work on. Pete Stenning had even taken the Jones's au pair out for a drink, hoping to catch her off guard. Everything had been meticulously inputted on HOLMES. Nothing.

'DI Tulloch, how ready are you to head up an investigation of this magnitude?' called a voice from the floor. 'Given the events of last year . . .'

The two men on the platform exchanged glances and the chief superintendent stood up. 'Thank you, ladies and gentlemen,' he said. 'As the investigation into the death of Mrs Geraldine Jones continues, we will release information as it becomes appropriate.'

Tulloch and Weaver both got to their feet and followed the chief out. Those of us at the back filed out before the reporters could collar us.

Since Emma Boston had run with her Ripper copycat story just three days ago, the investigation had been bombarded by media interest. And the public had caught Ripper fever with a vengeance. Attendance at the nightly Jack the Ripper tours around Whitechapel had increased fourfold. Tulloch had even been invited to appear on *Good Morning Britain* to discuss the nation's newfound interest in Ripperology. She'd declined.

I had one reason to be grateful to Emma. I was referred to, in the papers, as 'an unnamed young detective'.

By the time we got back to Lewisham, daylight was fading. Stenning, Anderson and I had all gone to the press conference in one car. As we approached the rear door of the station, I caught sight of a green Audi with Mark Joesbury at the wheel pulling into the car park. He hadn't been at the press conference. In fact, he and I hadn't spoken, had barely seen each other, since our encounter outside my flat four days ago.

The two men went ahead as Tulloch's silver Mercedes pulled up behind Joesbury's car. She climbed out and, without speaking, walked over to him. When she got close enough, he pulled her towards him and she dropped her head on to his shoulder.

Feeling like a peeping Tom, I spun round, dived along the corridor and headed for the stairs. At the top, I walked straight into a young Polish girl who works in the cafeteria. She'd been carrying a tray overfilled with dirty crockery.

'Watch where you're going,' I snapped, above the sound of shattering cups and saucers.

The girl's eyes opened wide with shock and she dropped to her knees.

'Oh God, I'm sorry.' I knelt down beside her, feeling like a real heel. 'It was my fault,' I said. 'I was going too fast, look, let me . . .'

By the time we'd cleaned up the mess, the rest of the team were settled in the incident room.

'Good of you to join us, Flint,' said Tulloch. She seemed to have shrunk. The press conference had taken a lot out of her. As had the frustration of the past few days.

'OK,' she went on, as I perched on a desk at the back. 'Can someone confirm what extra uniform presence we've got out tonight?'

'Just about every constable available has been drafted in,' replied Anderson. 'The section heads will be along shortly for a briefing. We're going to concentrate activity on and around the Brendon Estate. All the CCTV cameras are in working order and we've got extra staff monitoring them.'

'What about in Whitechapel?' asked Tulloch.

'They've increased their numbers as much as they can,' the sergeant replied. 'They're going to have a bigger headache than us, though. They've already got bozos hanging round the sites of the original murders.'

'He won't strike in Whitechapel,' said Stenning. 'Not knowing half the local population's out looking for him.'

'We don't know he's going to strike at all,' sighed Tulloch.

There was movement behind me as the section heads of the various uniformed divisions arrived for their briefing. Tulloch thanked them all for coming and, a second later, I was called to the front. Still not allowed officially to join the investigative team, I'd spent the past few days doing little other than brush up on everything I'd once known about the Whitechapel murders. An urgent online order had delivered just about every book on the murders currently in print. By this stage, I could have given a Ripper tour myself, and the team had been drawn together now to hear what I had to say about the second canonical Ripper murder.

'Annie Chapman was in her mid forties, short, overweight and missing several of her teeth,' I said, spotting Mark Joesbury at the back, his eyes on his shoes. Around the room, all other eyes were travelling from me to the blown-up photograph of Annie Chapman in the mortuary. It showed a plump, plain face surrounded by dark, curly hair.

I didn't need to look at my notes. I told

them the story of the last night of Annie Chapman's life, of the killer who'd struck without making a sound or leaving a trace. Twice while I was speaking, Joesbury glanced up, caught my eye for a split second and looked back down. When I mentioned that she was last seen alive at five thirty a.m., I saw several people looking at the clock. Five thirty a.m. was less than ten hours away.

'Any truth the Ripper was a member of the royal family?' someone called from the back. Tulloch and I shared a look. She nodded at me to answer.

'You're talking about Prince Albert Victor,' I said. 'He was a grandson of Queen Victoria and in direct line to the throne. There are two theories relating to Prince Albert. The first is that he was suffering insanity brought on by syphilis and that he went on a murderous rampage of the East End. It doesn't really stack up because, as a member of the royal family, his whereabouts at the time are a matter of public record. It's pretty much impossible that he carried out the murders himself.'

'What's the other theory?' prompted Tulloch, and I got the feeling she wanted me to speed up.

'The second involved a Masonic

conspiracy,' I said. 'According to this one, Prince Albert entered into a secret marriage with a young Catholic woman and had a baby daughter. The woman was locked up in an asylum but the child's nursemaid, Mary Kelly, escaped with the child to the East End and told what she knew to a group of prostitutes, who then hatched a plot to blackmail the government. The prime minister at the time was a Freemason. He brought in a few of his Mason buddies and the story goes that they lured the women into the royal carriage, where they were murdered in accordance with Masonic rituals.'

'Is it possible?' asked one of the uniformed sergeants.

'Unlikely,' I said. 'For one thing, the women were killed where they were found. The amount of blood at the scenes and the lack of any in the surrounding area make that pretty clear. And the attacks just don't seem like calculated executions, they were done in a frenzy, by someone barely able to control his rage.'

'OK, OK.' Tulloch was on her feet now, looking at her watch. 'Thanks, Lacey, but we can talk about Ripper suspects all night and I'm not sure it'll take us anywhere. Let's get out there, shall we?'

Quickly, the station cleared. As groups made their way out of the building I could almost see the tension hovering above them. Waiting for something bad to happen; it was always so much worse than actually dealing with it.

'Anything in particular you're looking for?' one of the CCTV operators asked me.

I'd gone back to my old station at Southwark, covertly following the rest of the MIT, and had made for the room where all the CCTV cameras across the borough are monitored. Thirty television screens are permanently broadcasting live footage. The operators can zoom in on any particular image in seconds and the detail is impressive. Look at people sitting outside a pub and you can see the ice gleaming in their drinks.

'DI Tulloch just wants me to watch for a while,' I lied. 'See if it jogs my memory about last week. Can you see any of our people?'

They began switching screens and we spotted several members of the MIT, parked in cars on street corners, wandering past pubs and shops. Mark Joesbury's car was parked about two hundred yards from the murder site. The driver door opened and he got out. Then DS Anderson appeared from the passenger side. As I watched the two men disappear into the estate, I wondered, for the hundredth time, about Joesbury's threat to have me investigated. And whether he'd actually followed it up.

A figure in a blue coat caught my eye on a screen higher up. Dana Tulloch was crossing the square outside Southwark Cathedral.

If Joesbury had done the most cursory of searches, he'd have found out that I joined the police aged twenty-six, a little over three years ago after a spell in the RAF reserves, that I got good marks on all my training courses, had studied for a law degree in my spare time and was accepted on to the detective programme the first time I applied.

If he'd accessed my personal records — unlikely, but if he had — he'd know that I'd studied law at Lancaster University, but had dropped out before completing my second year. He'd know that when I was fifteen I was cautioned on the street for having a half-smoked joint in my pocket, and that a year later, I was admitted to hospital having taken too much GHB in a nightclub. On my release the next day, I'd been given another police caution.

I watched Tulloch pull open the main

doors of Southwark Cathedral and step inside. I stood up, thanked the two operators and left the room.

If Joesbury had really gone to town, he might have learned that I was born in Shropshire, that I never knew my father, and that my brother and I were raised by grandparents, and occasionally in care, after my teenage, drug-addict mother found the responsibilities of parenthood too great to deal with. He might know that after my grandparents died and my own drug problem escalated, I'd spent several years just drifting, living off the grid. He might even know that my brother lived in Canada and that he and I hadn't spoken in years.

That had to be it. I hoped.

25

The cathedral was getting ready to close for the night. An elderly verger held up both hands at me, fingers splayed, and smiled before nodding towards the door. I had ten minutes.

Tulloch was staring ahead as I approached, her eyes on the central stained-glass window above the altar. She must have heard me getting closer but she was as still as the stone images around us. I almost turned to go, then changed my mind and spoke quietly to her. 'Ma'am,' I said.

She started, as if I'd woken her from a nap. 'What are you doing here?' she said.

Good question. 'Sorry,' I began. 'I saw you coming in and . . .' I stopped. I really wasn't sure why I'd followed her.

'And you wondered why I was in here instead of pounding the streets?' she said, turning away from me again. 'It would make quite a headline, wouldn't it? MURDER

TEAM CHIEF PRAYS FOR GUIDANCE WHILE KILLER ATTACKS AGAIN.'

I couldn't reply to that. In terms of what I'd been thinking, she was pretty close.

'You missed Evensong,' she said, after a second.

'I'm not much of a churchgoer,' I replied.

'I never used to be,' she said, her eyes still fixed ahead. 'But now I think I'd give anything to know that someone up there's in charge. That there's a plan.'

I'd never thought of it that way. Nor was I about to start.

Tulloch half rose and moved along a chair, giving me little choice but to sit down beside her. I sat. And waited.

'I know it was you in the ladies' room the other day,' she said softly.

'Sorry,' I said again. 'I didn't mean to pry.'

No reply. I tapped my foot against the crimson hassock in front of me, making it swing on its hook. 'I just assumed you'd eaten something that didn't quite . . .' I stopped. I'd assumed nothing of the kind and this wasn't a woman you could bullshit.

'That would be just about everything I put in my mouth, Lacey,' she said. 'I can't eat.'

I sneaked a sideways glance. I'd never be allowed through the door at Weightwatchers but I was chunky compared to Tulloch.

'I had an eating disorder when I was a teenager,' she went on. 'I thought I was over it. Apparently I'm not. If I eat, I throw up. I'm surviving on skimmed milk, orange juice and vitamins right now.'

I gave the hassock another kick. I was beginning to wish I'd never gone into the CCTV room. Tulloch looked down at the swinging hassock, then back up again to the window.

'You want to know what I'm doing here?' she asked. 'I'm composing my request-for-redeployment letter.'

Requesting redeployment meant resigning from the inquiry. It would be the end of her career as a detective.

'It's going quite well,' she went on, in a conversational tone, as though the two of us were discussing television we'd watched the previous night. 'It's modest but dignified. Apologetic, of course. No way around that, really.'

There was nothing I could say.

'All my friends,' Tulloch carried on, 'which isn't a huge number, but all of them begged me not to take this promotion.'

I should have gone straight home. This was way beyond me. And I was getting a nervous twitch in my leg. The hassock was going to go flying, any second now.

'They said I wasn't ready. That I needed more time.' She glanced my way. 'But how often do opportunities like this come along, Lacey?' she said. 'I could have waited five years for another chance.' She turned back to the altar again and gave a little sigh. 'And London was so far away.'

'From Scotland?' I risked.

Her head gave a little sideways dart, towards me and then back again. 'What do you know about Scotland?' she asked.

'Nothing,' I said truthfully. 'Well, practically nothing. Just that it was a big case.'

For a moment Tulloch was silent. Then she said, 'It was a bad case. Unimaginable. Some scars run so deep.'

When I looked at her again, her eyes were closed. She was tugging at the sleeves of her coat, pulling them further down over her hands. Then she seemed to sense me looking at her, because she opened her eyes and faced me.

'I thought, what's the worst that can happen in south London?' she went on. 'The odd knife attack? A domestic taken a bit far? I could have dealt with that. I just wasn't prepared for this.'

'*This* hasn't happened yet,' I said, more firmly than I felt. 'There is no *this*. We have one murder, that's all.'

This time she didn't look away. Unusually, on a woman of her colour, she had a light scattering of freckles across her nose and cheeks. Behind her, I could see the verger making his way down the side aisle, past the massive pale stone arches that lined the nave. Tulloch didn't take her eyes off me.

'The police in the original investigation were crucified,' she said. 'At the time, and ever since. Charles Warren resigned over his failure to find Jack. Well, I'm going to get in first. I can't have five women's deaths on my conscience, Lacey, I just can't.'

One had to see her point. The few hours when I'd thought I could have kept Geraldine Jones alive had been pretty uncomfortable ones. I also knew that if there were more killings, and no one was caught, Tulloch would take the blame.

'Can I ask you something?' I said, thinking that if a senior officer could be this confiding with me, I could probably get away with an opinion or two of my own.

She gave a little shrug with her chin. I took it as a yes.

'How many mistakes have you made so far?' I asked.

A crease line appeared between perfectly

shaped eyebrows. 'I'm not sure . . .'

'If you had to start the whole investigation again, what would you do differently?'

She was shaking her head. She wasn't having it.

'If someone more experienced had been in charge, who didn't have any of your personal issues,' I went on, 'what would they have done that you didn't?'

She sighed and turned back to the front. I looked the same way, at the double row of statues above the altar, and at the three arched stained-glass windows above them.

'You've done OK,' I said. 'Nobody's so much as hinting otherwise. And we don't know anything else is going to happen. I'd give it another twenty-four hours if I were you.'

Tulloch leaned forward until her elbows were on her knees and her chin in her hands. 'Why do you think I've been telling you all this?' she said.

Bloody good question. 'I'm handy,' I offered.

'I've been making it inevitable,' she replied. 'The simple act of telling you about my resignation has made it a fait accompli. I can't lead a murder team if even one of them knows I feel like this.'

'Well, it's lucky I'm not on the team then,

isn't it?' I sat back in my chair, knowing I sounded a tiny bit smug. 'You've been very clear on that.'

She made a sound that could have been a soft laugh. It could also have been a small sob. 'You remind me of someone,' she said.

'Is that good or bad?'

Close by, the verger was hovering. He caught my eye and stepped closer. He raised his left wrist and pointed at his watch.

'So sorry,' he said. 'Time's up.'

Dana stood. I did the same and we walked to the rear of the cathedral, our footsteps unnaturally loud in the now empty building.

'Mainly good,' she said. 'She was a good friend of mine. But she was a meddler. Couldn't seem to grasp that when you stick your head above the parapet, someone will take a shot at it. I rather suspect you have the same problem.'

She was right, I had to get over this parapet business.

'By the way,' said Tulloch, as we stepped out into the night, 'what have you done to Mark?'

I couldn't look at her. 'Do you mean DI Joesbury?' I asked after a second.

She gave a soft laugh. 'Yes, that's the one. Did you two have words?'

'Well, I . . . I'm not sure the two of us really hit it off,' I managed. 'Sorry.'

She didn't reply, but when I glanced across again she was smiling.

'Have you known him long?' I asked, a second before I realized I didn't want to know anything about Tulloch's relationship with Joesbury.

'We went through training together,' she said. 'I wanted to change the world, Mark wanted all the free time off the service gave him to play rugby.' She smiled again. 'After a year or so they clamped down on that and he didn't have a plan B.'

We stopped to wait for the lights at the pedestrian crossing. I wasn't about to feel sorry for Joesbury. I figured he'd found his niche as an undercover thug.

'We were very close for a long time,' Dana was saying. 'I'm even godmother to his son. Then I had a long-term relationship breakup just as he was going through his divorce. We helped each other through it.'

The lights changed and we crossed.

'I've barely seen him the last two years,' she went on. 'He's been off the radar with this drug gang and I was up in Scotland. I suppose I'm just making up for lost time. He's practically the closest I have to family now.'

We'd reached the station.

'This business about him hanging around the investigation because he's bored,' I said. 'That's not actually true, is it?'

Tulloch gave me the small, slightly smug smile of a woman who knows she's loved. 'Of course not,' she said. 'He's watching my back.'

She wished me goodnight and a safe journey as she went inside. As I climbed into my car I was thinking that, whilst Tulloch might not have much in the way of family and friends, she was a whole lot better off than me.

26

Amanda Weston can't stop shivering. Except, shivering is something you do when you are cold. She has a feeling she might be cold — she's naked, after all — but this spasmodic shaking has nothing to do with temperature. This isn't cold. This is terror.

High above her head, suspended from the ceiling, hang large, coloured shapes. She sees red, blue and yellow paint peeling away and thinks she should know what they are but her petrified brain can't seem to process normal information any more. Just the minutiae of what's happening to her body. The rough wooden bench she's lying on feels like a thousand tiny creatures are biting into her. An itch below her right eye has become so intense it makes her want to weep and she's sure something is crawling up her left leg. Nothing she can do.

Not that it stops her trying. Hands, then arms, head and legs. Tugging and twisting and pulling until exhaustion gets the better of her again. One last effort, whole body, one massive buck, do it now. Useless. She can't move.

A noise behind her head. Someone coming back.

A hand touching her face. Then a sudden burning as the tape across her mouth is ripped away and the cold air stings raw skin.

'How're you doing?' whispers the voice in her ear.

Amanda tries to think of something to say. Something that will strike a chord, make a difference. Something other than the old clichés. *Why are you doing this? Please don't hurt me. Let me go now, I won't say a word, I promise.*

'This is a mistake,' she chooses. 'I'm not the person you think I am. I've done nothing.' Amanda thinks it isn't possible to be any more afraid. Then she realizes it is.

'Tell me something about yourself, Amanda,' whispers the voice. 'Tell me about your children.'

Her children? Her stomach turns cold. Impossible. Abigail is at school. Someone would have called her if she'd gone missing? When did she last talk to Daniel? Amanda strains her eyes, looking left and right, as though she might see them, strapped down like she is, one on either side. No one there. She and the voice in her ear are alone.

'What are their names?' asks the voice. 'I'll know if you're lying. You'll know too. What's your daughter called?'

'Ab— Abigail,' Amanda manages.

'Sweet. And your son? Tell me all about your son.'

'Daniel,' she says.

'You must be very proud of them. Mothers will do anything, won't they, for their children? Are you a good mother, Amanda?'

'I try. I don't understand. Why are . . .'

Suddenly, Amanda isn't cold any more. She's hot. Sauna hot. She watches a figure in white move away from her towards a bench at the far wall. She sees a hand reach out, a finger tap gently on a small, portable CD player.

'Let's have some music, shall we?' says the voice. 'This is one of my favourites.'

The tune rings out, light, jolly, familiar, as the white figure comes back towards her. It's a tune from childhood. The lyrics start just as something that feels like ice is traced slowly across Amanda's stomach. The trail it leaves behind begins to prickle and then sting. She can almost hear her hot blood sizzling as it meets the cold air.

27

Saturday 8 September

The next day, the mood at the station was tired but upbeat. Five thirty a.m. on 8 September had come and gone and no real disturbances had been reported. I'd arrived late, but even so I was one of the first. The rest of the team drifted in, yawning and bleary-eyed, towards midday. I saw nothing of Tulloch, but if she'd resigned from the investigation, it wasn't yet public knowledge.

During the afternoon, Emma Boston sent me several texts, wanting to know whether there was any news. I replied each time in the negative, but politely. Since Emma had come up with an original angle on a recent murder, her stock with the national press had shot up, and she still had the ability to plaster my name, and possibly my photograph, all over the papers.

The day shift came to an end and still no one wanted to go home. We could relax at midnight, when 8 September was over, and not before. I wandered through to the incident room and no one told me to leave. People started sending out for food. At nine twenty I was about to make yet another trip to the coffee machine when the call came through from the control room.

Anderson took it, rising to his feet and motioning the room to quieten down. Someone leaned across and switched off the TV just as he replaced the receiver.

'Pete — get the boss,' he said. 'We've had a call from a bloke on the industrial estate by Mandela Way. Half hysterical, by all accounts. Screaming down the phone about a mutilated body.'

I watched the last of the cars leave the yard just as another text came in from Emma.

Can u meet me Forest Hill Swm Pls? Urgt info on G Jones case.

She wanted me to meet her at a swimming pool? I checked my watch. At half past nine? I didn't need to look up Forest Hill. I knew exactly where it was, on the Dartmouth Road between Dulwich and Catford. When I was younger, swimming had been one of the few things I was really good at and Forest Hill, one of the old-fashioned Victorian pools, had reminded me of pools I'd visited as a child. I'd used it until it closed down. I couldn't imagine what Emma was doing there, or what it could possibly have to do with Geraldine Jones.

There was no answer from Emma's mobile number, even though she'd just sent me a text. I sat for a second, thinking. Did I really want to start driving around London this late? Then another text flashed up on my phone. Emma again. As I read it, something cold crept down between my shoulder blades.

Don't phone. Just come. Please.

This needed some very careful handling. Everyone on the team had just been called out to what could be the next murder site and I was being summoned in the opposite direction by someone with a known connection to the killer.

I picked up the desk phone and told the control room where I was going and who I was planning to meet. They agreed to pass the information on to a member of my team just as soon as they could. As I left the building, Mark Joesbury was coming down the stairs. He stopped when he saw me. I was sure he was about to speak when the door behind him opened and Anderson appeared. I turned and hurried out of the station.

Driving down the Bromley Road, I told myself I was taking no risks. I was just going to be close by. In case. When I was about ten minutes away I had a radio call from Tulloch wanting to know where I was. I filled her in quickly.

'Lacey, I'm sending a team after you,' she said. 'Do not get out of your car until they're with you. Do you understand?'

'Well, yes, but —'

'Don't argue with me, Flint. The callout to Mandela Way was a hoax. There's no body here. And I do not like the fact that you are on your own on the other side of London.'

She and I both.

'OK, understood,' I said. 'I'll get to the pool and wait for you.'

'Mark and Neil will probably be with you first. They never actually left the station.'

I parked a little way down the street from the pool and looked up and down the road. Traffic was still constant. The street was well lit. Nothing out of the ordinary. But no sign of Emma.

I pulled my mobile out of my bag. No new texts, which didn't feel right. If she was here, she'd be looking out for my car, she'd have seen me arrive. If she hadn't approached it was because something was wrong.

On the other hand, I'd made faster time than I'd expected. She was probably still on her way. Then the phone beeped. Just two words this time.

Help me

28

I was out of the car. Still no one in sight.

'Emma!' I'd intended to shout, but not much sound came out. I leaned back in through the driver door, hating the moment my back was to the street, and pulled out the hand-held radio. Shoving it into my pocket and holding my mobile tightly, I stepped away from the car.

Help would be here any second and I certainly wasn't going far. I just needed to look. I half ran down the street until the massive and elaborate red-brick building soared above me. Plenty of shadows. I reached the steps that led to the front door.

'Emma,' I tried again. I climbed the steps, looking round continually, telling myself my car was close. I could be safely locked inside it in minutes.

Geraldine Jones's killer hadn't needed minutes.

At the top of the steps I found the front

door locked. Where the hell was everyone? Conscious that minutes had past since Emma's last message, I ran back down to the street.

The Ripper hadn't needed minutes.

At the side of the building, I remembered an old metal fire escape led up to the first floor. It was still there. What I didn't remember from my last visit was the pair of sunglasses, their frames wrapped around the metal rail. They looked a lot like Emma's.

'DC Flint to Control.'

A moment's pause while I listened to static. And something loud and steady that I thought might be my own heartbeat. Then, 'Go ahead, DC Flint.'

'DC Flint requesting immediate back-up,' I said. 'Serious injuries, maybe fatalities, suspected.'

I backed away from the metal steps and looked up. At the top a window had been broken and the door wasn't quite closed. Someone was inside.

Tulloch didn't want another woman's death on her conscience. Shit, neither did I. And I was a whole lot closer to the action.

On the first two steps up my legs were shaking, the way legs do when you've spent too much time on the treadmill. By the fifth step they were on autopilot, taking me steadily upwards, and the stairs creaked with every step.

I reached the top and risked taking my eyes off the building for a second to scan the street. I was going to kill Anderson. I would knock Joesbury to the ground and stamp on his head. Where the hell were they?

Knowing I was taking a risk, but unable to do nothing, I took my mobile from my pocket and speed-dialled Emma's number. Then I pressed my face close to the broken window and listened. On the street, cars went by. Somewhere in the sky there was a helicopter. Hardly a second of silence. Then one came and I could hear the ringing. Faint but clear. Emma's phone was somewhere inside this building.

Then the ringing was completely drowned out by a loud and terrified scream. When it stopped I was on the other side of the door.

There is something so unnerving, even at the best of times, about buildings out of context. A school at night will be spooky. A department store, once the customers have gone home, even more so. This place, that I remembered so well from years ago, seemed unable to leave its past behind. As I peered forward into the darkness I could almost hear the squeals and splashes of children playing, and those strange rhythmic echoes that you only hear in buildings with large spaces and water.

I swear I could still smell the chlorine.

A few feet away a streetlamp was shining in through a window. In its soft, orange glow lay a shoe. On tiptoe, I walked up to it and bent down. There was no dust on it. This shoe hadn't been here long. It was Emma's. I knew it.

Breadcrumbs, yelled the voice of common sense. This is a trail of breadcrumbs. He's leading you in.

Common sense won. I was out of there. I took a step back towards the door just as I heard the fire escape creak. Outside, someone had stepped on it.

Not a trail then, a trap.

29

Horribly close to panic, my eyes were darting round like those of a terrified mouse. I was in a large space that had once been an office. Desks and chairs were still scattered around. In the centre of the room, dividing one half from the other, stood a row of lockers. I moved quickly across and stepped into the shadows behind them. From somewhere in the building I could still hear Emma's mobile ringing, but if I tried to stop it now, the beeping sound my own phone would make would give me away. Sometime in the last few seconds I'd stopped breathing. Softly, I made myself exhale.

Whoever was coming up the stairs was making more noise than I had. A heavier person. I heard the gentle swish of two pieces of wood sliding together as the door was pushed open. A footstep inside. Then another.

Silence. He was listening, waiting for his

eyes to adjust to the darkness. Any second now he'd see Emma's shoe, spot the trail in the dust I'd made when I'd moved it. He'd know I was here. The footsteps started again, more softly this time. He knew where I was.

A black shape appeared from behind the row of lockers. In the darkness it looked massive. Then it stepped into a pool of light and I thought I might die of relief.

'I'm here,' I whispered.

Joesbury shot round as I hurried over to him, surprisingly pleased to see someone I thoroughly disliked. Even feet away he was still little more than shadow, but his eyes were shining at me. Not in a friendly way.

'There's someone here,' I told him, 'I heard a scream. He's inside somewhere. We have to —'

Joesbury held a finger to his lips and then raised his radio. 'She's here,' he said into it. 'Yeah, toss you for who throttles her when we get out. Can you hear a phone?'

I couldn't catch Anderson's reply, but a second later Joesbury was moving towards the furthest door of the room and beckoning me to follow. At the door he stopped and listened, then pulled it open and stepped through.

I did the same. We were in the gallery that

runs almost the full circumference of the larger of the two pools. In the old days, when swimming had been strictly segregated, it had been known as the men's plunge. Up in the gallery there was still bench seating from when schools had competed here and proud parents had needed somewhere to sit. Joesbury made his way slowly down the wide, shallow steps of the gallery, peering along each row of benches. He was carrying a torch, but he hadn't turned it on. The ringing sound of Emma's phone had become louder.

Looking back to check I was still with him, Joesbury made his way to the side of the gallery where we could get down to ground level. We passed dead rodents and take-away wrappers. I stepped over broken glass and what looked horribly like human excrement. When we emerged at the bottom of the stairs, DS Anderson appeared through an archway at the far end of the hall. From memory I thought it led to the smaller of the two pool halls, the one reserved for women back in Victorian times. Anderson saw us and shook his head. He'd found nothing. Joesbury had moved to the pool, his feet just touching the edge of the carved stone that rimmed it.

Without water the cavity looked vast. It

was nearly thirty yards long and fifteen wide. In the old days, the pool had had a five-yard-high diving board and the deep end had been very deep. Since then, the cavity had been used for dumping. Cafeteria chairs, lifebuoys, lifeguards' seats, even part of the old diving board had been thrown in.

Joesbury was looking at a huge canvas sheet that bulged upwards from the floor of the pool. The ringing sound was coming from beneath it. Realizing my phone was still making the call, I reached into my pocket and switched it off.

'That was me,' I explained in a quiet voice, when both men looked surprised. 'It's Emma Boston's phone. I was calling it. I followed the sound inside.'

Joesbury switched on his torch and shone it down. Even with light it was impossible to say what lay beneath the canvas.

He turned to Anderson. 'Any possibility of back-up?' he asked.

Anderson spoke into his radio for a few seconds. Then he looked up. 'About five minutes away,' he said. 'The boss has called out the Ninjas too. They'll be here in ten.'

Ninjas is Met slang for CO19, the armed police division. Tulloch must be seriously concerned to have requested their presence.

'Tell them to contain the building,' Joesbury instructed, speaking in a low voice as Anderson had done. 'Four entrances, including the fire escape. And make 'em come in carefully. I think it's safe to say this is a crime scene.'

As Anderson stepped away to pass the instructions on, Joesbury turned back to me. 'Call her again,' he said. My hands were shaking but I did as I was told.

From beneath the canvas Emma's mobile resumed its shrill ringing tone and Joesbury muttered the sort of word you wouldn't use in front of your granny. Putting his torch on the floor, he crouched low and jumped down.

'Switch it off, Flint, it's doing my head in,' he called back as he stepped closer to the canvas. Once again, I did what I was told. It had been doing my head in too. Soft footsteps on the tiles told me Anderson had moved closer.

'Hold on, Boss,' he said, before jumping down beside Joesbury. I stepped closer to the edge. Both men kept their torches on the anonymous shape in front of them. Neither seemed able to go any closer.

'For God's sake, she could still be alive,' I said, jumping down to join them and striding towards the canvas. Joesbury's hand shot up and caught me square in the chest. I stopped moving as he bent down, took hold of two corners of the canvas and pulled it back.

A moan escaped Anderson a second before we realized what we were looking at. The human form before us lay on its back, its sightless eyes staring at the ceiling. Its left arm lay across its chest and both legs had been drawn up and splayed apart. Fair hair spread out around its head. A human form, but not human.

It was an old-fashioned rescue-training dummy, the sort I'd used myself when I'd trained for my life-saving award years ago. The fair hair was a cheap wig. Other people coming across this might have laughed, if only to release tension. We didn't. We all knew enough about Ripper case lore by this stage to know that the dummy had been left in the exact position Annie Chapman's body had been found in. Emma Boston's mobile phone lay by the mannequin's feet, just as Chapman's personal effects had been left by the original Ripper. Above the dummy's right shoulder was a clear plastic bag. Joesbury was staring at the bag. I don't think he was even blinking. I glanced towards Anderson. Same. Then Joesbury cleared his throat.

'OK, Flint, you're our expert on all things Ripper-related,' he said. 'Our man took trophies, didn't he? Body parts cut out of his victims that he sent to the police to taunt them?'

It was hardly the time to get into the various theories about what had happened to the Ripper victims' entrails, so I just nodded as Joesbury took a step closer to the plastic bag. He shone his torch and then crouched down to get a better look.

'Weren't you telling me one of the victims was missing her kidneys?' he said.

'That isn't a kidney,' said Anderson, who'd also stepped closer. 'Kidneys aren't that shape.'

In the bag was a piece of muscular tissue, roughly triangular, about eight centimetres long and around five centimetres at its widest point. It was surrounded by traces of clotted blood. I didn't need to get any closer to know what it was.

'Annie Chapman still had both kidneys,' I said. 'She was missing her uterus.'

30

Half an hour later, Tulloch pulled up outside the row of run-down terraced houses in Shepherd's Bush where Emma lived. Other than a terse 'What part of "Stay in the car" was difficult to understand, Flint?' she'd barely said a word to me since she'd arrived at the pool. It was pretty clear I was with her now so she could keep an eye on me, not because of anything useful I might have to contribute.

The flickering blue lights of two patrol cars had been waiting for us, their occupants watching the front and rear of the house until we could get here. As the car engine died, I saw Joesbury making his way towards us from where he'd parked down the street. Tulloch turned to me and opened her mouth.

'I had a text message saying "Help me" and I heard screams,' I said. 'What would you have done?'

'I'd have done what I was bloody well told,' she replied, her eyes darting from me to Joesbury.

Well, I could hardly call a DI a liar to her face. 'We're the police,' I said. 'We're supposed to help people.'

Tulloch's eyes narrowed. She reached for the door handle. 'Do I need to say the words?' she asked me.

'Consider me glued to the seat.'

As she got out of the car and went to join Joesbury, I pressed the button that would open the passenger window. She hadn't said I couldn't listen. She and Joesbury walked up the short path to the door.

In the tiny front garden dustbins overflowed with rubbish. An animal, probably a fox, had broken into one of the bin liners. The whole area stank of rotting food.

Joesbury banged hard on the door, making it shake in its frame. Then he bent down and pushed open the letterbox.

'Police!' he called. 'Open this door.'

Joesbury banged again, then stepped back and looked up at the house. 'Don't have a good feeling about that,' he said, indicating the camera he'd arranged to be positioned above Emma's front door. Sometime since it had been installed, someone had hurled a brick at it.

'Someone's coming,' said Tulloch as we heard noises inside the house, the rustle of paper, a clanging and a soft cursing sound. Then the door opened inwards. Tulloch stepped forward and held up her warrant card as a thin, unhealthy-looking boy of about twenty stuttered that he didn't know where Emma Boston was, he had nothing to do with Emma Boston, his own flat was below hers, he hadn't been in earlier that day when it had happened and it had all been some serious shit, man.

'Shut up and step aside,' said Tulloch. 'Mark, see he doesn't go anywhere.'

After a brief argument with Joesbury about who was going to go in first, Tulloch led the way along the corridor and up the stairs. The boy followed, then Joesbury, then one of the uniformed constables. The other stayed at the front door.

We waited. I saw a light go on in a first-floor window. The uniformed constable had a short conversation with someone on his radio. I was itching to get out of the car. Knew Tulloch would tear me apart if I did.

Emma Boston had been obnoxious and opinionated and in a position to make life pretty uncomfortable for me. But I'd actually quite liked her. I really didn't want to think about what Tulloch and Joesbury might have found in the room upstairs.

Noises on the stairs. I saw Joesbury's jeans-clad legs, then both he and Tulloch came into view. In the dim hall lights I scanned both faces. They looked tense, puzzled, not shocked.

'Is she there?' I asked, realizing I'd got out of the car.

'Place has been broken into,' said Joesbury. 'Trashed about a bit. No sign of Emma.'

'About ten o'clock this morning, according to her downstairs neighbour,' said Tulloch. 'He heard crashing about but didn't bother investigating. He didn't see anything. Says he didn't hear anyone calling for help either.'

'She doesn't live alone,' I said. 'Any sign of her boyfriend?'

Tulloch shook her head, just as the uniformed officer who'd accompanied them inside appeared, with one hand on the boy's shoulder. Out of the corner of my eye, I saw movement and turned.

'Oh thank God,' I said, stepping forward.

Not three metres away, in the light of a streetlamp, stood Emma Boston, her burned scar livid against her pale face, looking pissed off but very much alive.

31

'You've had how many text messages from Emma Boston today?' Tulloch asked me.

'Six,' I repeated. 'The first late this morning and then at two-hourly intervals. With a break for lunch.'

Emma, in another interview room at the station, had already confirmed that her flat had been broken into early that day and her phone taken. The text messages I'd been getting all day could not have been from her and, so far, I was managing not to think about the full implications of that.

Emma had also identified the sunglasses and the shoe I'd found at Forest Hill as hers. When asked why she hadn't reported the break-in she'd given us a withering look. Clearly yet another Londoner who didn't have much confidence in the Met's ability to investigate burglaries.

'Did you reply to any of her texts?' asked Joesbury. I explained about my brief, polite responses.

'The sixth being the one you got shortly before half past nine this evening?' asked Tulloch. 'The one that came in just after we all left?'

'That's right,' I said. 'That was the one asking me to meet Emma at Forest Hill.'

'If Boston's telling the truth, someone broke into her flat and stole her phone just to get access to you,' said Joesbury. I ignored him. I really could have done without him in the room. I needed my wits about me and, somehow, they never seemed to be when he was around.

'I tried to phone her after the one asking me to go to Forest Hill,' I told Tulloch. 'She didn't answer, just sent another message, asking me to come. I called it into control and then I went.'

Tulloch nodded. 'And then shortly after you got there, you received the last one? The one saying *Help me*?'

'Whoever sent that had seen you arrive,' said Joesbury. 'Did you notice anyone in the street? See anything unusual?'

'Nothing,' I said to Tulloch. 'It all looked completely normal. Until I saw the sunglasses on the fire escape. And the broken window at the top.'

'When I saw you, you said you'd heard

someone screaming,' said Joesbury. 'When was this?'

I took a breath and gave myself a second. 'It was when I was at the top of the fire escape,' I said to the tabletop. 'I heard what I thought was screaming, coming from inside.'

'Inarticulate screaming or words?' asked Joesbury.

I shook my head. 'Just screaming, I think. I don't remember any words.'

'Man or woman?' he asked.

Oh, could the guy not go get a cup of coffee? Another deep breath. 'I'm not sure, it only lasted a second. Female, I think.'

'How old? Child, adult, elderly?'

If I did much more deep breathing I'd be hyperventilating. 'I don't know,' I said. 'It might not even have come from the building. It could have been kids nearby. I was scared and I wasn't thinking straight.'

'When I found you, you weren't scared, you were petrified,' said Joesbury. 'Why would you be that frightened if you'd just heard kids?'

I turned round so quickly I almost toppled the chair. 'Well, shit, let me think,' I said, speaking directly to Joesbury for the first time since we'd entered the room. 'Eight days ago a woman was stabbed to death.

She died in my arms. Maybe I'm still a bit twitchy.'

Joesbury was just thrilled to have broken my cool. 'Past catching up on you, Flint?' he said, leaning back in his chair as I glowered at him. 'Any of your old friends been in touch?' He turned to Tulloch. 'Did you know your new pet was cautioned for possession when she was a teenager?'

'Yes, I did actually,' said Tulloch, as I looked at her in surprise and Joesbury frowned. 'And don't tell me you haven't come across that before.'

Tulloch's support gave me that extra bit of courage I needed. To go too far. 'Why are you even here, Joesbury?' I said. 'You're not part of this investigation.'

His eyes narrowed. 'Well, you're certainly not,' he replied. 'And yet you keep finding yourself in the thick of it. I have to wonder why that is. And another thing I'm wondering, Flint, is where you were before ten thirty this morning, which is the time I've been told you arrived for work.'

'Mark —'

'At home,' I said, interrupting Tulloch. 'I needed to see my landlord about something. I had permission from the sergeant to come in late.'

'So your landlord can confirm this?' Joesbury wanted to know.

'He phoned to rearrange,' I said. 'What is this about?'

'OK, you two . . .'

I turned to Tulloch. 'I want him out of here,' I said, as her eyebrows shot into her hair. 'I want him out of here or I want a solicitor.'

Joesbury was smiling at me now. And it wasn't his usual grin, this one was mean. 'Something to hide, Flint?' he smirked.

'Fuck you.'

'Mark —'

'OK, OK. I'll catch you ladies later.' He pushed himself up from his chair and sauntered out. The door closed and I dropped my head on to my hands. Tulloch didn't speak. After a second I heard her stand up and cross the room. A moment later a box of tissues had been pushed in front of me. I hadn't even realized I was crying.

'Bull in a china shop doesn't really cover it,' she said. 'But he has a point. Someone does seem fixated on you. We have to ask why.'

I took off my glasses and wiped my eyes. What the hell had got into me? I never cried. Tulloch got up again and brought me a glass of water from a tray on the side table.

As she held the glass out, the sleeve of her shirt fell back and I caught a glimpse of a scar on her right wrist. It was about two inches long, running across the inside of her wrist, pale and ugly against her café-au-lait skin.

What had she said in the cathedral last night? Scars run deep? I hadn't taken her literally. As I took the glass, she pulled her hand away and tugged the shirt cuff back into place. I drank most of the water, blew my nose and then polished and replaced my specs.

'It's what the Ripper did,' I said, when I trusted myself to speak. 'He picked people out — people in the police, the press, even the local vigilante committees. He picked them out and he sent them messages. He played with them. Our guy's just following the historical pattern.'

There was a knock on the door.

' 'Scuse me, Boss.' It was DS Anderson. 'SOCs are closing up Forest Hill. They'll go back first thing, but nothing else to report for now. Entry through the fire escape, as we thought. No sign of how he got out. Boston's mobile and the other personal effects have gone to Forensics. There are traces of fingerprints, but it will take a while to sort them all out.'

'What about the body part?' asked Tulloch, looking exhausted, and I realized the last thing she needed was Joesbury and me going at each other like a cock-fight.

'Gone to the mortuary at St Thomas's,' Anderson replied, his eyes flicking from me to Tulloch. 'They'll have someone look at it first thing in the morning. Let us know when we can go over.'

'Thanks,' said Tulloch.

'Could easily be a prank, you know, Boss,' said Anderson. 'Lots of medical students in this city. Could just be someone winding us up, sending us on a wild goose chase over to Mandela Way, then leaving behind a little present from anatomy class for Flint and me to find.'

'Let's hope so,' she agreed. 'How's the missing-persons search?'

'We're running the check for women aged sixteen to sixty reported missing in London over the last week,' said Anderson. 'Nothing so far.'

'Thanks, Neil. I'll be down in a second.'

Anderson gave me one last puzzled glance and left the room.

'Something you need to know, Lacey,' said Tulloch, as I looked up. She'd taken Joesbury's chair. 'Mark persuaded the police doctor to sign him off fit for active duty and

I've had him seconded on to the team for the next few weeks.'

Oh great.

'Our killer overstepped the line tonight,' she went on. 'Cutting out women's organs and leaving them lying around the place is a step too far in my book. I intend to catch him now.'

I waited. I could tell from the look on her face that she had more to say.

'But I'm not one of these macho types who think they can do it by themselves,' she said. 'I need Mark. I think perhaps I might need you too. And it would really help if the two of you —'

'I know.' I didn't give her chance to finish. I was feeling pretty ashamed of myself by this time. 'Of course. I'm sorry.'

'What will happen to Emma and her boyfriend?' I asked, as Tulloch and I made our way downstairs.

'I'll give them the option of staying here for the night,' said Tulloch. 'If they've got somewhere else to go they can leave, but the flat is out of bounds until our people have finished with it.'

'Emma's going to run the story first thing in the morning,' I said.

'At the moment, she doesn't have a story,'

replied Tulloch. 'She doesn't know where we found her phone or what else was there. I've told her there'll be an announcement in the next couple of days and that I'll give her fifteen minutes alone with me afterwards. As long as she continues to keep you out of the papers.'

'Thanks,' I said. We'd arrived at the incident room. Way after midnight, it was still full. Joesbury was in there, talking quietly to DS Anderson. As we walked in everyone looked up.

Tulloch raised her voice. 'OK, we're assuming there is another victim out there until we get confirmation the body part is either from an animal or a fake,' she said to the room at large. 'Now, here is the problem. When Flint arrived at Forest Hill earlier this evening she heard a woman's scream. She's pretty certain it came from inside the building, so we might be forgiven for assuming it was the voice of our victim.'

'Seems fair enough,' agreed Anderson.

'So what happened to her?' asked Tulloch. 'I mean the 95 per cent of her that isn't currently in the mortuary at St Thomas's?'

'It can't have been the victim,' I said. 'There just wasn't time. It could only have been five, maybe ten minutes from when I heard the screaming to when we found the phone and the dummy in the pool. It just wouldn't be possible to kill someone, cut out major organs, pop one of them in a plastic bag and then leave the building with a body over your shoulder. Sorry to be glib, it just wouldn't.'

'You wouldn't think so, would you?' agreed Tulloch, before turning to Anderson. 'SOCs found nothing else down there?'

He shook his head. 'Nothing so far.'

'I was wrong then,' I said. 'It must have come from outside the pool.'

'We've got uniform still searching the surrounding area,' said Anderson. 'The body could have been dumped nearby.'

'There still wouldn't be time,' I said. 'Wherever the voice came from, there still wouldn't be time for him to do — what he did — and leave. The screaming can't have been connected to what we found.'

'Blood-curdling screams within a fifty-yard radius of a body part is stretching coincidence for me,' said Joesbury. 'Could you have heard a recording?'

I nodded. I hadn't thought of that.

'You think the killer recorded the victim's screams and then played them back when he knew Lacey would hear them?' asked Anderson.

'Someone wanted her in that building,'

said Joesbury. 'He practically pinned up arrow signs.'

Tulloch gave me one last dirty look. I still wasn't forgiven for going into the pool alone. 'OK everyone, if you're not doing something essential and urgent, I want you home,' she called out. 'There'll be a team briefing in the morning, depending upon what time we're needed at the mortuary.'

Around us, people started to leave. Tulloch turned to me.

'Your car is still at Forest Hill, isn't it?'

'That's right,' I said, wondering if perhaps Stenning would offer to drive me over. I really didn't fancy getting a cab.

'I'm going to have it brought back in,' said Tulloch. 'Just in case whoever lured you into the pool building decided to touch it when you were inside.'

Great. I was losing my car for the second time in just over a week.

Tulloch raised her voice again. 'I need someone to take DC Flint home and check her flat out,' she said.

'I'll do it,' said Joesbury, getting up off the desk he'd been leaning against. 'I have to drive past her place anyway,' he added. 'And besides, I think Flint and I need to bury the hatchet.'

'I could get a cab . . .' I tried.

'No,' said Tulloch, glancing my way. 'You're staying with someone I trust and Mark lives just across the river from you.' She leaned over the desk to reach the phone and caught the look on my face. 'Oh, for heaven's sake, Flint,' she snapped. 'He doesn't bite.'

Knowing that to argue any further would make me look childish and make a nonsense of what I'd just promised Tulloch, I picked up my bag and headed for the door. As I passed Tulloch, I saw her giving Joesbury one of her eyebrows-to-the-ceiling looks. That was him told, too.

32

Best intentions or not, there wasn't much burying of hatchets in evidence on the drive home. Joesbury turned on the car stereo as we pulled out of Lewisham car park and cranked up the volume. I sat in the passenger seat, hugging my bag to my chest, listening to a hypnotic blend of house and jazz club music. After a while the bright orange and white lights of south London started to hurt my eyes and I closed them. I was a lot more tired than I'd realized.

The city had quietened down by this time and it didn't take us long. Joesbury slowed the car as we turned into my road and I opened my eyes.

'Thank you,' I said, as he pulled up to the kerb. I made myself blink, wishing my head didn't feel so fuzzy. The hot, noisy car had acted like a drug. I needed cold air and silence. As I pushed open the door I noticed he'd turned off the engine. Without looking back, I got out and stood up. I heard a door slamming and realized Joesbury, too, was out of the car.

'You're not coming in,' I said, turning to face him.

He didn't flinch. 'Wrong,' he said over the roof of the car. 'I'm not leaving you until I know there are no bogeymen under the bed and that all your entries and exits are secure. Tully would never let me hear the end of it. Would you like me to go in first?'

I turned and walked slowly down the steps. I took my time finding keys, although I knew exactly where in my bag they'd be. All the while I could feel him, inches away, hear him breathing softly.

Fuck it, nobody came into my flat. Nobody.

'Would you mind checking the space under the basement steps?' I asked him as I put the key in the lock. 'I've had some real low-lifes hide under there and spring out at me.'

'You're wasting your breath, DC Flint,' he said. 'It's impossible to insult me.'

I turned on the spot, looked him up and down. 'Maybe I just haven't seen enough of you yet,' I replied.

For a second I thought he might laugh. Then both corners of his mouth stretched into a slow smile. He didn't take his eyes off me. 'Well,' he said, 'that sounds like a bridge we should cross when we come to it.'

I turned back to the door, unlocked it, found the light switch and stepped inside. What the hell was I thinking? That was twice now I'd given this man the come-on. Even if he hadn't been one of the most obnoxious men I'd met in a long time, there was almost certainly something close and romantic between him and Tulloch. I dropped my bag on a chair and walked over to the fireplace, automatically taking off my glasses and leaving them on the mantelpiece. Just get it over with. Let him do what he had to do and leave.

When I turned back he was standing just inside the doorway, taking in the largest room of my flat, not even trying to hide his surprise at the clean white space, the minimum of furniture and, apart from plants, the complete lack of personal possessions. When I said nothing, he got to work.

First, by checking the front door. It was a Yale lock, ridiculously inadequate by London standards, but it's not like I have anything to steal. Then he crossed the living room and the small galley kitchen and disappeared. I heard him open the door to the bathroom and pull back the shower curtain. What he was hoping to find in the bathroom cabinet I don't know, but I heard that open and close too. The sound of wardrobe doors told me he was in the bedroom. Then I heard the creak of the conservatory door. He'd gone outside.

Curious, I followed. I heard the sound of something heavy landing on soft ground, as though he'd jumped from a height. He re-appeared just as I arrived at the rear door.

'Shed key?' he asked, holding out one hand.

Knowing there was no point arguing, I told him where he'd find it, tucked away on the shed roof. I watched him walk up the path, open the shed and disappear inside. In my head, I was counting, ten, nine. At six he came out again, staring straight at me, his hands raised. The word was hardly necessary, but he said it anyway.

'What?'

'Keeps me fit,' I replied. 'Davina McCall swears by it.'

I didn't give him time to point out that Davina McCall probably didn't dress her punchbag as a man. I turned and walked back through the flat. He'd seen everything. From the living room, I heard him lock the conservatory door. Then he reappeared. He stopped in the archway between living room and bedroom.

'First of all, I have never seen a woman's flat like this in my life before,' he said. 'Christ, Flint, don't you even have a teddy?'

He was a senior officer, we were now officially part of the same team and, in his eyes at least, he was doing me a favour. I was going to stay calm. 'Goodnight, DI Joesbury,' I replied. 'Thank you for your help.' I was standing in front of the hearth. I wasn't moving till he was out of there.

He wasn't moving either. 'Second, you can't stay here by yourself,' he said. 'Tully will have my innards for breakfast.'

Stay calm. 'I've lived here quite safely for five years, the doors will be locked and, in the circumstances, I'd rather you didn't talk about innards,' I said.

Joesbury's lips twitched again. He held up his left hand and with his right started counting off splayed fingers. 'One, there is a gate leading directly into the alley outside,' he said. 'I managed to get over it with a buggered shoulder. Two, the conservatory door has half rotted away and a good push would send it flying. Three, your front door has a Yale lock that I could open with my credit card in ten seconds. You don't even have a chain on it.' He stopped, dropped his hands and shook his head at me. 'This is south London,' he went on. 'Even without a maniac on the loose, do you have a death wish?

Probably, was the nearest I could get to an honest answer, but not one I was about to articulate. 'I'll put a chair against the door and I'll sleep with my phone,' I said. 'Now, will you please excuse —'

'I'm going to need that phone,' he said. 'I'll sort you out with a new one tomorrow. Right, have you got a blanket?'

'What?'

'I'm sleeping on the sofa.'

'Over my dead . . . no, absolutely not, get out of here.'

He crossed to the sofa and began pushing his fists into the cushions to plump them up. 'Tully can probably have you transferred to a safe house tomorrow,' he said, picking up two loose cushions and arranging them to act as pillows at one end of the sofa. 'At least until we can get some decent locks installed here,' he went on. 'We can get an alarm rigged up to the station.'

'Do you not understand the English language?'

'Any chance of a spare toothbrush?' he said, pulling off his jacket and sitting down. He was wearing a sleeveless black T-shirt and had the faintest vaccination scar just below his right shoulder. Heavily muscled arms.

'You're not staying here.'

'Flint, I'm tired.' The bastard was actually taking off his shoes. 'Stop wittering and go to bed.'

'I can't sleep if you're in the next room,' I snapped back, before I had a second to think about the consequences of admitting something so . . . oh my God.

Stalemate. Joesbury looked up at me. Then he stood. I took a step back and almost fell over the hearth stones. *Oh no. Of all the men in the world, not this one.*

'Any point suggesting I don't have to be in the next room?' he asked me in a voice that was barely audible. I wasn't even going to think about it. I shook my head.

Joesbury continued to stare at me for a moment. Then he looked at his watch and pulled out his mobile phone. 'Didn't think so,' he said.

Fifteen minutes later, a woman police constable was ensconced on my sofa, watching television with the volume turned low and drinking coffee. I was in bed, still wet from the shower and wondering when I'd stop trembling.

33

Sunday 9 September

Classical piano music was playing softly in the mortuary of St Thomas's Hospital. The room was modern, but there was something about the arrangement of so much gleaming steel, the careful placement on the counters of jars and dishes, that looked timeless. For all its grim purpose, it felt like a calm room. And given what we were about to see, calm felt good.

The pathologist, a Dr Mike Kaytes, looked at us across the central worktop. 'Not too much I can tell you,' he said. 'They normally send me a bit more to work with.'

As well as Kaytes and his technician, a boy who couldn't be much more than twenty, there were four police officers in the room: Dana Tulloch, Neil Anderson, Pete Stenning and me. This was my first post-mortem, Stenning's too, he'd confided on the way over. Anderson and Tulloch must have attended others but they didn't seem any more at ease. Didn't have to guess why. The small piece of flesh lying in the centre of the polished steel worktop looked obscene.

I closed my eyes and concentrated on the music for a second. I'm not a great music fan, I'd never think of listening to classical, but there was something about the delicate precision of the notes, the clarity of the sound, that helped.

Kaytes was a tall, barrel-chested man in his late forties. He had thick grey hair and bright-blue eyes. On the third finger of his left hand, beneath the surgical glove, a sticking plaster had been wrapped around where his wedding ring would be. He leaned forward and poked at the upper corner of the specimen. 'It's definitely human,' he said. 'Look here. See what we've got on the fallopian tubes.' He was pointing to gunmetal-grey, pea-sized objects. 'These are filshie clips,' he went on. 'Not even chimpanzees are that advanced yet; this woman's been sterilized. And it's a fresh specimen,' he finished.

The pianist played a series of notes, pure and clear, interspersed by long silences.

'Fresh as in . . . ?' prompted Anderson.

'Recently harvested,' said the pathologist.

'We're running tests to see if we can pick up any of the more common preserving solutions, such as formaldehyde, but, frankly, you can invariably smell the stuff. And this has barely begun to deteriorate. I'd say it's less than twenty-four hours old, fresh as they come.'

As the music started to build in volume and tempo, I imagined the pianist's fingers running up and down the keys. And I really hoped Kaytes wasn't going to use the word 'fresh' again.

'Can you tell us anything about the woman it was taken from?' asked Tulloch.

Kaytes nodded. 'Adult,' he said. 'From the size of it, I'd say she'd had at least one pregnancy of twenty-four weeks or over.' He stepped away from the worktop and arched his back. 'The uterus enlarges in pregnancy as the fetus develops,' he went on, 'but then very rarely shrinks back completely to its pre-pregnancy size until some time past the menopause. So this woman wasn't elderly. She'd also given birth.'

He beckoned us closer and re-angled one of the lights so that it shone directly on the organ.

'What you're looking at now is the cervix,' he said, extending a gloved index finger.

'And this little hole here is the external os of the cervix, basically the escape route for the emerging infant. Can you see that it's slit-shaped and a bit distorted?'

I told myself I was back in biology class. I'd never been squeamish then.

'How is that significant?' asked Tulloch.

'Prior to a vaginal birth the os is neat and circular,' said Kaytes. 'This isn't. She'd had at least one vaginal delivery.'

There were pronounced veins on Tulloch's neck I hadn't noticed before. The muscles of her jaw seemed tighter than usual. 'So she was a mother,' she said. 'Any idea how old?'

'Let's open it up, shall we?' said Kaytes, taking up a scalpel just as there was a surprisingly cheerful burst of music. Two fingers, tapping down repeatedly on the same keys. I glanced over at Tulloch while the incision was being made. She didn't flinch.

'Well, there are some fibroids, but none of them really large enough to distort the uterus,' said Kaytes. 'Two or three of them are calcified, which tends only to happen in later life.'

I caught Stenning's eye. He gave me a tight-lipped smile.

'I cut a few sections of the vessels before

you got here,' said Kaytes. He stepped away from the table and switched on a microscope on the bench behind him. 'Bear with me a sec.'

We waited while he adjusted the focus. The microscope was connected to a computer screen and as the screen flickered into life we saw an incomprehensible collage of pink, black and yellow. 'Here we go,' Kaytes said, tapping the screen. 'What you're seeing now is a segment of uterine artery, with some early signs of atherosclerosis, basically a thickening of the arterial wall. That's age-driven, although smoking and diet can exacerbate it. The sterilization points to a slightly older subject as well. My educated guess would be that this lady was somewhere from thirty-five to fifty-five.'

'Is it possible . . .?' began Tulloch. 'Do we . . . do we have to assume she's dead?'

At my side, Anderson sucked in a breath. It had never occurred to me that the owner of the uterus might still be . . . Jesus.

'Not necessarily,' replied the pathologist. 'Hysterectomy is still one of the most common elective operations in this country. But without medical support, there'd be a huge amount of bleeding, the pain would be close to unmanageable and there would be a massive risk of infection.'

It was getting harder, by the second, to persuade myself that this was nothing more than a biology class.

'Is it possible this was the by-product of a hysterectomy?' asked Tulloch, who seemed the only one of us with her brain fully engaged. 'Removed in the last twenty-four hours and then smuggled out of the operating theatre as a joke.'

Kaytes looked bemused. 'Not even medical students would try that nowadays,' he said.

'Are you sure?' said Tulloch. 'Because the alternative is a whole lot worse.'

Kaytes made a resigned face and bent down to the worktop again. After a few seconds he shook his head. 'There are no clamp marks across the residual uterine and ovarian vessels,' he said. 'Also a surgeon would use diathermy to control the small vessels, particularly around the cervix. There are no coagulation burns to suggest that. The incision around the cervix is by no means neat, in fact I'd say there's some evidence of pretty amateurish hacking. And you've got this piece of tissue here, which is a small segment of the ureter, indicating this was done in a hurry.' He stood upright again and let the scalpel dangle in his fingers. 'This wasn't the result of a legitimate operation,' he said.

'But he would still have to know what he was doing, right?' asked Stenning. 'I mean, there's no way I could cut a woman open and take out her uterus.' He looked round at the rest of us almost defensively. 'I wouldn't know where to begin. I wouldn't even know what it looked like.'

Anderson nodded. Tulloch gave Stenning a small half-smile.

'Well, that's true,' replied Kaytes. 'Whoever did this would need some basic knowledge of anatomy. Maybe someone who's worked in medicine without actually being a surgeon. Possibly even a butcher, someone used to cutting up large animals.'

Tulloch's eyes closed and I had a pretty good idea what she was thinking. Exactly the same conjectures had been made about the original Ripper. Someone with rough anatomical knowledge. For a while suspicion had fallen on the numerous slaughterhouse workers who lived around Whitechapel and Spitalfields.

'To be honest, though,' continued Kaytes, 'you can research just about anything on the internet these days. I wouldn't want to send you off on a wild goose chase, looking for a psychotic doctor when it's just someone who's read a couple of textbooks.'

No one answered him.

'Any truth in what I've been hearing?' asked Kaytes. 'Have we got a wannabe Ripper?'

Tulloch was about to answer when her mobile beeped. Excusing herself, she stepped to the corner of the room and took the call.

'What's the music?' I asked, after a second.

Kaytes looked at me properly for the first time. 'Beethoven,' he said. 'One of the piano sonatas. Les Adieux, in fact, played by Alfred Brendel.'

'He saves the symphonies for when the detective superintendent comes down,' said the technician in a voice that was pure estuary. 'When we get a bad one, he puts on the Fifth.'

'Gets him every time,' agreed Kaytes.

Over in the corner, we heard Tulloch take a deep breath. Then she ended the call, turned back and nodded to the pathologist.

'Mike, thank you,' she said. 'That was very helpful.' Then she looked at the rest of us and her eyes were gleaming. 'We have to get back,' she said. 'That print they found on Emma's phone. They've managed to trace it.'

I rode back with Stenning. For a while,

neither he nor I spoke.

'It seems clumsy,' I said at last. 'Leaving a print behind.'

'Only a partial print,' Stenning reminded me.

I nodded. 'How are the Jones family doing?' I asked, because I didn't want to spend the entire trip back obsessing about possible evidence and who it might point to.

Stenning shrugged. 'Not great,' he said. 'The youngest son is home now. He should have gone back to university but he's put it off a couple of weeks. The au pair thinks they're still in shock. They want answers, of course. They're starting to blame us.'

'We haven't given up on the family angle though, have we?' I said, as the lights changed and we pulled away. 'We're still talking to them, trying to find any connection she may have had with Kennington.'

'Yeah, but there isn't anything there, Flint. No financial motive that we can find, no dodgy goings-on, everyone close to her had a good alibi, husband isn't having an affair that we know of.'

'There was nothing on the bag we found the uterus in,' I said. 'If he was careful enough to keep that clear, why leave something on the phone?'

'They get careless,' said Stenning. 'That's how we catch them. If they'd had finger-printing and forensics back in 1888, they'd have caught the Ripper.'

I didn't argue, but I wasn't so sure. Nineteenth-century Whitechapel had been densely populated. Watching eyes were everywhere and at the time of the Ripper murders there was a heavy police presence on the streets. The Ripper had managed to act and escape each time undetected. I was inclined to think that whatever tools the police had had at their disposal, he'd still have stayed one step ahead.

34

'The print on Emma Boston's mobile phone has been matched, with an 85 per cent degree of accuracy, to a man called Samuel Cooper.'

Twenty people in the incident room seemed to be holding their breath. Everyone was looking at the senior crime-scene officer, a slim, bearded, grey-haired man called Peters. He pressed a key on a small laptop and we were looking at the face of the man who could be our killer. Clean-shaven, fair-haired, long face, large nose, bad complexion. And something not quite right about his eyes.

'He's twenty-seven,' said Peters. 'Last known address was a squat just off the Tottenham Court Road.'

I leaned closer. Cooper's pupils were elliptic, like those of some snakes.

'Eighty-five per cent accuracy?' questioned Tulloch.

'Best we can do, I'm afraid,' replied Peters. 'It was only a partial print. Look, let me show you.' Peters pressed another key on the laptop and two fingerprints came up on screen. One whole and perfect, the other about 60 per cent present. He pressed another key and we saw the inner segment of both prints, considerably magnified. 'What you're looking at here is a loop,' said Peters, 'as opposed to a whirl or an arch, the other two main fingerprint patterns.

'There's a short, independent ridge here, in the centre of the loop,' he went on, pointing with a pencil. 'You can see it quite clearly on the print we know is Cooper's and on the print taken from the phone. You can also see what we call a lake, a tiny, free-standing line, just above and to the right of the ridge. The lake, like the short independent ridge, is present on both images. We've also got a delta, a sort of convergence of lines, a little way down and to the left. Appears on both images and the ridge count between them is the same.'

'Looks pretty conclusive to me,' said Anderson.

'If we had more to go on than this one partial, I'd be agreeing with you,' said Peters, pushing reading glasses on to the top of his head and nodding at the sergeant.

'But nothing on either the shoe or the sunglasses, remember. Of course, 85 per cent won't be enough by itself to convict him, but it makes him someone you want to take seriously.'

'What's his history?' asked Anderson.

At the back of the room a door opened. I glanced round to find myself staring into turquoise eyes. From the look of them, Joesbury had had even less sleep than me.

'Cooper served two years of a five-year sentence in the late nineties for knife crime,' replied Peters. As I turned back to the front I could sense a notable increase in excitement in the room. 'It was gang-related, but the victim wasn't seriously injured. Hence the relatively short sentence. He was arrested several months after his release on a burglary charge, but it never went to court. Not enough evidence.'

Soft footsteps approached. The desk immediately behind me moved a fraction as someone sat on it.

'It's a big step,' said Tulloch, who had nodded to Joesbury briefly. 'From gang crime and burglary to carving up women.'

'Possibly,' agreed Peters. 'But the arrest records report him as being a disturbed individual. Violent tendencies. He injured a female sergeant while he was in custody.

Apparently he got her by the throat.'

'Looking promising,' muttered a voice from the far side of the room. I could see excited glances being exchanged. Tulloch was still looking troubled, but she got to her feet and thanked Peters. Then she updated everyone on the results of the post-mortem.

'Our corpse, when we find it,' she said, after summarizing the gist of what Kaytes had told us, 'will be that of a woman in reasonably good health, who has borne at least one child. She'll be in the age range thirty-five to fifty-five.'

'Geraldine Jones fell into that age bracket,' said one of the detectives.

'So did most of the original Ripper's victims,' remarked another.

'Yes, and so do half the women in London,' said Tulloch. 'Right, we need to find Samuel Cooper as soon as possible. George, Tom, can you get round to the Tottenham Court Road address? Take his mugshot and ask around. In fact, get some uniform round there now. They can hold him till you get there.'

The two detectives left the room.

'Pete, can you take his picture up to the Jones's house?' said Tulloch. 'See if anyone there recognizes him.'

'Anybody in here know him?' said Joesbury. He was still behind me but I knew, from the direction of his voice and its tone, that he was looking straight at me. 'Just picking people at random now, how about you, Flint?'

I shook my head as the remaining faces in the room turned my way.

'Are you sure? Name ring any bells?'

'No,' I said, looking again at the photograph of Samuel Cooper.

'He's not far off your age,' Joesbury went on. 'Pal from the old days, perhaps?'

'I'm sure,' I said calmly, because I knew I couldn't overreact in front of so many people. 'I don't know him. I have no idea how, or indeed if, he knows me.'

Tulloch had been watching the two of us.

'Did you two —' she began.

'Kiss and make up?' interrupted Joesbury. 'Absolutely. Her flat needs some serious attention, though. A three-year-old could break in at the moment.'

Tulloch shook her head, as though despairing of me and all women too stupid to take proper care of themselves.

'I've organized a home-security firm to go round today, but you need to sign the requisition order,' Joesbury was saying. 'It'll be expensive on a Sunday. If it can't be finished today, she's going to need somewhere else to sleep tonight.'

'Come on everyone, get moving,' called Tulloch. Everyone started to gather things together. I got up too.

'Hang on a sec, Flint,' Joesbury called out to me as I moved away. Without looking at him, I sat back down again and waited, until only Tulloch, Anderson, Joesbury and I were left. Joesbury got up, made his way across the room and took another seat directly facing me.

'I've got something for you,' he said, reaching into one of his inside pockets and holding out his hand to me. On it was a mobile phone that looked like a new and very advanced model. 'Your new phone,' he said.

'I was happy with the old one,' I replied.

'I've transferred all your recorded info,' he said, without withdrawing his hand. I took the phone. His hands were warm.

'We issue these to all our officers out on jobs,' he went on. 'It's got an internal tracker device built in. It links up with the GPS system. As long as it's switched on and there's juice in the battery, it will let us know where you are 24/7. OK with that?'

'Yes,' I lied.

'I can also give you a four-digit number that sends an emergency call direct to our control.'

'Is this all necessary?' I asked.

'Someone broke into Emma Boston's flat and stole her phone so that he could call you directly,' replied Joesbury. 'He spent the day sending you text messages. That does not give me a warm and fuzzy feeling about your future well-being.'

'I'll be careful,' I said.

'And I've arranged to take her over to the Yard this afternoon,' he went on, talking to Tulloch now. 'We'll get her kitted out with some basic tracking and recording stuff.'

'I can't carry a tape recorder in my pocket for the next six months,' I protested.

'We don't use them any more,' said Joesbury, before giving me a smile that didn't quite reach his eyes. 'It's all a lot more intimate.'

Any retort I could have made was drowned out by the desk phone ringing. Anderson took it, speaking quietly for several minutes before putting it down and facing us.

'That was George,' he said. 'Local uniform have arrived at Tottenham Court Road. No sign of Cooper at the address we were given. People they spoke to there seem to think he's been living on the streets for a while.'

'OK,' said Tulloch. 'Ask George and Tom

to start making their way round the places where the street people are known to congregate. They'll need more help, see who's free to join them. I want them to start straight away.'

Anderson picked up the phone again. 'You're wasting your time,' I called to him.

All three of them looked at me in surprise, Anderson with one hand over the receiver.

'Street people won't talk to those two,' I said. 'They're both built like brick shithouses, and they're about as subtle as juggernauts through shop windows.'

'I'm not sending them in to do therapy, Flint,' said Tulloch. 'They just have to show the photograph and ask a few questions.'

'The first person they collar will tell them he's never seen Cooper in his life before,' I said. 'He'll look at the ground, he'll do everything he can to get away. Anything he does say you absolutely cannot rely on, because he'll tell them anything to get rid of them. In the meantime, everyone else in the vicinity will have quietly slipped away. These people are terrified of the police.'

'How do you know so much about vagrants?' asked Joesbury.

'Street people,' I said, without looking at him.

'So what do you suggest?' asked Tulloch.

'Let me go and talk to them.'

'I really don't think —' began Anderson.

'I'll be able to track down more of them than anyone else and there's a better chance they'll talk to me.'

'Why?' asked Tulloch, although from the look on her face, I think she already knew.

'I know the streets,' I said. 'I lived on them for eight months.'

35

Official estimates say that between 1,000 and 1,500 people sleep rough on the streets of London on any given night. Many of them are young runaways, fleeing abuse of various kinds at home. Some are elderly, people at the end of their lives who have lost everything. Quite a few have mental-health problems, made worse by the impossibility of getting their required medication. All are vulnerable; always cold, always hungry, slowly getting more weak and more scared. Even that isn't the hardest part. The hardest part is making it through the day.

I started looking for Cooper in the tunnels around Tottenham Court Road where street people gather during the day to beg from Tube travellers. London Underground has a policy of moving them on, so none stay in one place for any length of time. I'd wanted to come alone and had been informed, in triplicate, that that really wasn't going to happen. Neither had I been allowed to come with women detectives.

In the end I'd agreed to take two of the youngest and smallest male detectives in the division. Both were now trying to balance two directly opposed instructions: from Tulloch and the others, not to let me out of their sight; and from me, to stay well out of the way.

I went to the women whenever I could, which wasn't always easy because around 70 per cent of street people are male. I gave them hot drinks and spoke to them for just a few minutes. By St Martin-in-the-Fields, I spotted a girl who didn't look much more than fifteen.

'Hello,' I said, crouching down and holding out a carton of tomato soup. 'I brought you this. Can I speak to you for a second?'

The girl looked distrustfully at the soup. 'What about?' she muttered.

'St John's church hall in Bayswater are giving out food from four o'clock this afternoon,' I said. 'And the Lamplight shelter in Soho has some free beds tonight.' I'd checked out various websites before coming out. There are organizations around London who offer a lot of support to homeless people. Sadly, most street people don't have access to the internet.

'OK,' she said and stretched out her hand to take the soup. I pulled Cooper's photograph out of my pocket.

'I'm looking for someone,' I said. 'Could you look at this for a second, see if you recognize him?'

She glanced at the photograph and shook her head.

'He could be dangerous,' I said. 'He may have hurt people.' Immediately her eyes went back to the photograph. Street people respond to danger. They understand violence only too well.

'Who did he hurt?' she asked.

'Some women,' I said. 'I really need to find him.'

She looked up from the photograph and saw my two minders, leaning against the wall of the tunnel only twenty metres away. If they'd had CID tattooed on their foreheads they couldn't have been more obvious.

'Are you police?' she asked, and now it was me she was frightened of.

'Have you seen him?' I asked again. 'It's really important.'

She wasn't looking any more. She shook her head and started to push herself to her feet. A few seconds later she was gone.

■ ■ ■ ■

I stayed out for the rest of the afternoon, handing out the telephone number of Joesbury's glitzy new phone and buying endless cups of soup. Most people who talked to me had glanced at Cooper's picture and shaken their heads. Just before four o'clock, I spoke to a man in his late sixties who looked properly at the photograph for several seconds and I started to hope. The street community isn't a huge one. Live rough for any length of time and you get to know most of the faces. Then the man shook his head.

'Not seen that one for a while,' he said. 'What did he do?'

I couldn't let myself sound too interested. 'But you do know him?' I asked.

'Nasty piece of work,' replied the bloke. 'Takes money from those young Eastern European girls — you know, the ones who take their children begging.'

'Where might I find him?' I asked, when I realized he wasn't going to say any more.

He shook his head. 'Took up with a young woman, I heard,' he said. 'Got a place over in Acton.'

■ ■ ■ ■

By the end of the day I was tired and more than a bit depressed. It gets to you, life on the streets, even when you know that for the moment at least you have somewhere else to go. It's like you know it's waiting, always there, for the time when the reins slip between your fingers.

Still, we knew that Samuel Cooper might be living with a woman somewhere around Acton. It was something. We could put his mugshot on posters around the area, run it in the local papers. Someone would know him.

On the way back to the station, I called in at my flat to find four men working there. I wandered around for two minutes, finding out about the various improvements Joesbury had ordered — alarms, CCTV cameras, panic buttons and hi-tech locks — but seeing that many people in a space that had previously been for me alone was unsettling and I left.

I got back to Lewisham to find no one on the team had had much luck. Neither the Jones family nor anyone on the Brendon Estate could remember seeing Cooper before. Someone placing him in Acton was the best we could do.

An hour later, I got word that the work on my flat had been finished. I wanted to go home and curl up, safe behind the barriers Joesbury had ordered be put up around me. It wasn't going to happen; I still had to go across to Scotland Yard to have SO10 fit me out with intimate tracking devices. The phone rang as I was closing down the computer.

'DC Flint,' I said.

'Yeah, right, hi,' said the voice of a young man. 'I'm worried about a shed in the park. I think there's something gone bad in there.' His accent sounded north London. His voice was slightly thick, as though he'd been drinking.

I sighed. This was a matter for uniform. Sometimes when the switchboard was busy, calls could end up anywhere. 'OK,' I said, reaching over to grab a pen, and taking down his details and where he was calling from. 'Sorry. Did you say a shed?'

'Yeah, the boat shed. In the park.' The door opened and Joesbury came in. Suddenly I found myself in a very helpful mood.

'What appears to be the trouble?' I asked as Joesbury sauntered over and leaned against the window ledge just a few feet from my desk. He was wearing a deep-blue rugby shirt. An inch or two of chest hair was just visible against the buttons of the neck.

'It stinks,' was the reply. Joesbury had a small mole just below one ear. 'And there are flies everywhere,' the caller was saying. 'I think something's died in there.'

'Probably just a rabbit or something, but we can check it out,' I said. What I'd probably do was pass the call on to the appropriate environmental-health department. 'Which park is it?'

'Victoria.'

Great. Victoria Park was north of the river. Not even our borough.

'Thank you for calling, sir. We'll get right on to it,' I said, as Joesbury gave a heavy sigh, clearly not thinking much of my policewoman-of-the-year act. I put the phone down.

'Ready?' he said.

'Just got a call to make,' I said. 'Something died up in Tower Hamlets.' I pulled out the directory we use for transferring calls around the Met.

'What did you say?' Joesbury had stepped away from the window.

I shook my head. 'A shed stinks and there are flies . . . probably just rubbish or something. Maybe a dead rat. Give me two minutes.'

I picked up the phone again. Joesbury leaned across the desk and cut the line off.

'Something died up in Tower Hamlets and you're getting the call?' he said.

'Well, of course we'd love to think the general public understands the various intricacies of the Met's internal structure, but, sadly, some of them still don't get it,' I said. 'Do I have to use another phone or are you planning to release this one?'

'Where in Tower Hamlets?'

'Victoria Park.'

He blinked, then reached out and took the receiver from me.

'Oh, be my guest,' I sulked, as he stepped away.

'Hi, this is DI Joesbury.' He'd turned his back on me now. 'The caller you just put through, did they ask to speak to anyone in particular? . . . OK, for her personally? Are you sure? . . . Are you recording calls at the moment? . . . Pity. Thanks anyway.'

Joesbury put the receiver down. I could see a pulse beating in his neck just above the mole. Then he turned and looked at me for several seconds without speaking.

'Got plans this evening, Flint?' he said finally.

'Why, are you asking me out?'

Joesbury gave a tiny half-laugh and shook his head. 'Let's hope I get the chance,' he said. He crossed the room, held the door open and looked back. 'In the meantime,' he went on, 'there is a body out there to be found and someone has just phoned here, asking for you personally, to tell you about a bad smell and flies in a park that isn't even in this borough.'

'I should let DI Tulloch know,' I said, feeling like an idiot.

'Let's just you and me quietly check it out first,' he said. 'If it's a rodent, we can stick it in the nearest skip and scoot off to the Yard. And it's just possible I'll be so relieved I will ask you out. Come on.'

36

Forty minutes later, we crossed Tower Bridge. Joesbury hadn't even bothered putting music on. Each time we stopped, he drummed his fingertips against the steering wheel until we moved on again. By the time we reached Aldgate and turned east along the Whitechapel Road it was driving me crazy.

At one point we stopped in traffic and I heard him muttering something under his breath. When I turned, he was looking out of his side window. The traffic started to move. I looked back as we drove away. Nothing I could see. Just a pub, the Victoria. Nothing else.

We crossed the canal and entered the park through the easternmost of the Crown Gates. Almost immediately we were waved down by a park keeper. Joesbury showed his warrant card and asked directions to the boat shed. The park keeper agreed to have someone meet us there and we drove on.

Victoria Park was the city's first public park, opened in the mid nineteenth century after a local member of parliament presented a petition to Queen Victoria. Regent's Canal lies to the west, while the Hertford Union Canal runs along its southern edge. The Grove Road cuts through the middle. The larger, eastern section that we were driving through has the sports facilities.

'Do you know this park?' asked Joesbury, as we spotted buildings ahead of us and slowed down.

I didn't want to talk. If I opened my mouth, there was no guarantee of what was going to come out. 'A bit,' I said, and then, for no reason I could think of, 'There are bluebells in April.'

'We'll bring a picnic. Familiar with the sheds?'

'Why would I be?'

Joesbury shrugged with one shoulder. 'You seem to have a thing about sheds,' he said.

We circled round the back of the children's play area and drove past a wild enclosure. Two deer, startled by the car, sped away from us. Then we stopped and Joesbury jumped out. I followed.

Joesbury was scanning the distance, as

though someone might be watching us. The boat shed was just a few metres away. It was a small, yellow-brick building, with a red and grey tiled roof and blue paintwork. No windows, just shutters. Another park keeper appeared and we waited for him to approach.

'Remind me where Geraldine Jones died,' Joesbury said.

'The Brendon Estate.'

'Name of the block?'

'Victoria House, why . . . oh God.'

'Penny dropped, has it?'

'Forest Hill pool,' I said. 'It's a Victorian building.'

'Victorian venues for a Victorian-style killer,' said Joesbury. 'It's quite cute in its way.'

As the park keeper drew close, I noticed that the boating lake was a concrete-lined, perfectly symmetrical oval. The water was low and dirty, probably being drained for the winter.

'When was the shed last opened?' Joesbury asked when we'd both shown our warrant cards and explained why we were here.

The park keeper glanced towards the blue wooden door. 'Week ago,' he said. 'Maybe ten days. We store the boats in there over the winter.'

'Can you open it, please?' asked Joesbury.

The park keeper looked worried but didn't argue. He produced a set of keys from his jacket pocket and walked over to the door. I stepped up to the shutter that covered one window and pressed my face up close. The man who'd called me at Lewisham had mentioned a smell and flies. I couldn't smell anything and there wasn't an insect in sight.

Close by, the park keeper wasn't having much luck. I watched him try one more key, then give up and shake his head. Joesbury sucked in his bottom lip, caught my eye and walked back to his car.

He opened the boot and a second later I heard the clanging of metal. He emerged with a large pair of pliers in his hand. Back at the door, he pushed them into the curved handle on the padlock and pulled them open. The lock sprang apart.

Plenty of airborne insects now.

As the doors opened, the park keeper and I both stepped back to avoid them. Joesbury didn't flinch.

'Wait here, please, sir,' he told the park keeper, before beckoning me forward. I drew level with Joesbury and knew that if I stayed still I might not be able to start walking again. So I stepped inside first.

I was vaguely aware of Joesbury leaning to

switch on the lights before I swayed backwards. Joesbury stepped up and caught me by the shoulders. I could feel his breath against my neck.

'Jesus wept,' he said.

37

When the body of Annie Chapman was found, on 8 September 1888, the sun hadn't come up. What few streetlights there were in the Victorian district of Spitalfields couldn't have reached the small, narrow yard behind 29 Hanbury Street. The walls surrounding the yard and the nearby buildings would have been tall. As John Davis, an elderly porter, stepped out of his lodgings that morning on his way to work, the darkness would have been close to impenetrable.

Joesbury and I weren't so lucky. Fluorescent strip lighting running along the ceiling of the boat shed saw to that.

I think John Davis must have known, that morning, that something wasn't right. I think the human race has enough left of its animal instincts to sense the presence of great evil. He reported later that he hadn't slept well the previous night. When I picture him, he is coming out of the house slowly, something inside him whispering to take great care.

I think he would have known what he was about to find, even as he stood on the back steps. Maybe he smelled something, although I doubt it. The East End was rank with the stench of slaughterhouses and poor sewerage. Perhaps he heard Annie's last cry. Maybe he even heard the sound of the Ripper's footsteps, hurrying away down the passage.

Joesbury and I had known, before we entered this shed, that what we were about to find would change us.

Back in 1888, the Ripper took Annie by the neck and half strangled her, before forcing her to the ground. Kneeling behind her head, he cut her throat so deeply he almost severed her head. Then he leaned forward, pulled up her skirts to expose her abdomen and hacked at it. He cut away pieces of skin, pulled out organs and connective tissue, leaving them strung across her body. The uterus he removed completely. He pulled up her legs, expecting to do more, no doubt, but had been disturbed, quite possibly by our friend John Davis opening the back door of the house.

I think Annie would have been conscious

for most of the attack. The strangulation disabled but didn't kill her. I think she would have felt the knife in her throat, have known the panic of being unable to scream. I think she would have lain on the cold, hard flags or wet mud of Hanbury Yard, experiencing the sort of pain the rest of us can only pray we never know, waiting for the darkness in her head to grow and knowing that when her eyes closed, it would be for ever.

Standing in the boat shed, with Joesbury's hands on my shoulders, wondering how I could go on living as I did before, I realized Annie had had it easy. Because even when it comes to murder, all things are relative.

Annie's death would have been quick. It probably hadn't been much more than fifteen or twenty minutes from the first attack to her last breath. She wouldn't have seen it coming.

This woman's death hadn't been quick. This woman had been stripped naked and bound to a work bench in the middle of the shed, the one on which boat repairs would normally be carried out. Her arms had been pulled down beneath the bench and bound at the wrists. Duct tape held her to the table at her neck, beneath her breasts and across her pelvic bone. This woman's killer had incapacitated his victim to give himself time.

Annie hadn't had time to scream. If she had, someone in the house would have heard her. No one did.

This woman had been gagged. A blood-stained cloth had been stuffed into her mouth and more duct tape held it in place. This woman had been expected to scream.

'Lacey, are you OK?' someone was asking me. I let my head fall and brought it up again. I hadn't screamed, fainted or thrown up. That must mean I was OK. My shoulders became cooler and I watched Joesbury move up towards the woman's head and look down at her face.

Her eyes were open, turning milky. I saw movement in the corner of one and realized maggots had hatched already. Flies were buzzing around her nose too and her ears, they always go for the orifices first. And the wounds. They love the smell and taste of blood.

Annie Chapman's chest had been untouched. Her clothes had protected her, her killer had had so little time.

This woman's killer had had plenty of time. Her breasts had been cut a dozen or more times. Shallow, narrow incisions, made with a sharp knife. She'd bled a lot. Her chest and the shed floor beneath her were blood-soaked. She'd bled, so she'd been alive. Her right nipple had been sliced in two.

I'd crossed my own arms in front of me, hugging myself, protecting my own chest. Joesbury glanced at me and moved down the body. The damage to her chest wasn't the worst thing we were looking at.

Almost the worst was her abdomen, where the flesh had been so hacked about and pulled apart I couldn't be sure what I was looking at. Pools of black gore were glistening on the shed floor, but nothing seemed to bear any relation to what normally lives inside a woman. And the colours were so bright. The clotted blood so very red, the fat globules a soft creamy yellow and the flies, sparkling blue and black like gems. Even that wasn't the worst.

Back in 1888, Annie Chapman's legs were drawn up until her feet were together and then her knees splayed apart, revealing her genitalia. It could have been a pose, meant to shock those who found her. It could have been in preparation for what the Ripper had planned next before running out of time.

Our Ripper had had plenty of time.

Most women, once they reach their mid twenties, will have had at least one cervical examination. We lie on an examination table, our legs drawn back so that our knees are broadly level with our chest. Sometimes our feet are held in stirrups; other times, we're asked to splay our knees. This woman looked almost like a patient waiting for an internal examination. Except that no doctor I've ever come across would use duct tape, wrapping above and below the knee, to bend the leg double and hold it in place. This woman would have been unable to move, unable even to scream, when the two-foot-long piece of wood was rammed inside her.

Joesbury was looking down at the piece of wood now. I looked too. Three inches from the point at which it emerged from her body five letters had been carved into it.

ANNIE.

'Oh, I think we get the point, mate,' muttered Joesbury. He ran a hand over his face and swallowed hard.

38

On 8 September 1888, John Davis ran immediately for help, stopping two passers-by and sending for a constable. A little over a hundred years later, Mark Joesbury steered me out of the shed and spoke to DI Tulloch on his mobile phone. Then he used the car radio to summon local uniform.

Someone, I think it might even have been our friend John, pulled Annie's skirts down to give her some element of privacy. Joesbury sent the park keeper to find another padlock. When it arrived, he locked and bolted the boat-shed door.

Already, news of what was happening had spread. Other park workers were approaching, and several members of the public. So far I'd done nothing. I'd leaned against Joesbury's car and watched events unfold. I had to get a grip.

When I asked him what he wanted me to do, Joesbury told me to stand guard at the shed door and make sure no one approached. I watched as first one and then a second patrol car arrived. Joesbury positioned officers at four points of the compass, protecting the site, and even roped some of the park keepers in to help. Gradually, more and more uniformed officers arrived and I was relieved of my post. Unsure what to do, I went to sit in Joesbury's car. I watched the inner cordon being set up around the shed and the first of the local CID detectives go inside. This murder, like the previous one, would be investigated by the Lewisham MIT, but we would need to keep Tower Hamlets CID informed.

A silver Mercedes parked on the grass and Tulloch stepped out. Joesbury met her before she'd gone more than a few paces. He put one hand on her shoulder, made her stop walking; she looked up at him and nodded her head, telling him she was OK. They talked for a few seconds longer, then the two of them looked over at me and seemed to be arguing. If they were, I had the impression he'd won. Tulloch said a few more words to him before she strode towards the shed. Then Joesbury grabbed Stenning and came my way.

'How you doing?' he asked, when he was close enough.

'I'm fine,' I replied.

'Up to taking a walk?'

I got out of the car, expecting to be sent on an errand. 'Where?' I asked.

'Just round about,' he said, not taking his eyes off me. 'Keep looking at me. I want you to go a bit beyond the outer cordon, as though you're getting some air.'

The outer cordon was being set up beyond the boating lake, keeping people at a distance.

'There's a good chance our friend will still be here. Don't look round. He'll be watching events unfold. He'll be very keen to see you. You have a walk around and Stenning and I will keep a very close eye on anyone who seems a bit too interested in you.'

It took a second to sink in. 'I'm bait?'

'Lacey, we'll be seconds away,' said Stenning. 'If anyone gets within shouting distance, we'll have 'em.'

'Goes without saying,' said Joesbury. 'I should also point out that this is not a directive, only if you feel up to it, and that DI Tulloch has informed me that if anything happens to you she will personally cut off my balls and feed them to the pigeons outside Southwark Cathedral.'

I almost smiled at that. 'Well, that sounds like something I should see,' I said.

Stenning patted me on the shoulder and then he and Joesbury walked away. A few seconds later I couldn't see either of them. I dropped my head forward and rubbed the back of my neck. With a bit of luck, anyone watching would think I was stiff from sitting too long in the car. Then I walked across the asphalt, round the lake and towards the onlookers who had gathered at the outer cordon.

'Excuse me,' I muttered and stepped through. Without looking back, I walked past the children's playground, following the line of blue-painted metal railings. I left the asphalt and took a mud track over a small, grassed hill. To my left I could see sports pitches and, beyond the park, a massive pink tower block. There were trees planted over the hill I was climbing, but not too many for me to worry about anyone lurking.

A large black crow hopped in front of me and it didn't feel like a good omen.

Daylight was fading fast now and the sky had turned that lovely deep turquoise so typical of autumn evenings. It's an odd time of day, I always think, no longer day, not yet night, a strange half-time when the world you know can — shift.

I realized my world had just shifted big time.

Back at the lake, the boat shed was lit up like a circus. The police surgeon was just arriving. I saw other people I knew milling about and knew that because of the lights they wouldn't be able to see me. To all intents and purposes, I'd become invisible.

Unfortunately for my peace of mind, so had Joesbury and Stenning, and I just had to hope they knew what they were doing. Because, otherwise, I was on my own, a couple of hundred metres from anyone, in a rapidly darkening park and at the mercy of someone who might like to take his time over slaughtering women, but who could act pretty quickly when he needed to.

I carried on walking, to the crest of the hill and down the other side, before crossing the path and drawing close to a small lake. I could no longer see anything of the activity on the other side of the children's play area. I still couldn't see my two minders either. If they left me on my own out here then when it came to cutting off balls, DI Tulloch could get in line.

Above my head a three-quarter moon was shining and the first stars were beginning to appear. Shrubs had been planted around the lake's perimeter and I decided to make my way round to the other side. It wouldn't be as safe as staying in the open, but it probably had to be done. While I was safe, he wouldn't come near.

The lake was reflecting the last of the sunset and the ripples around the reeds were a soft, deep pink. Bronze-coloured beech leaves drifted across the surface like tiny boats. The noise of the city never quite disappears in London, but in the midst of a large park it fades until it becomes little more than a background hum, like insects on a summer's day. Parks in London offer the closest thing to peace and quiet in a big city. I watched a leaf skimming the surface of the water and thought I'd rarely felt less peaceful in my life.

The darkness was coming fast now and shadows were slinking across the grass towards me. The sounds of the investigation seemed to be a very long way away. I'd reached the edge of the lake. A sudden scrabbling, then a high-pitched call of alarm made me jump, but it was only a duck startled from its hiding place among the reeds. I watched her race towards the opposite bank and the ripples she'd left behind drifted towards me like whispers.

Damn Joesbury. Wasn't it enough that I'd seen what this monster did to other women?

Did I really have to walk round carrying a neon 'pick me next' sign?

The gentle thwack of a tennis ball being bounced. And I suddenly became aware of the hairs on the back of my neck. We'd reached the time of night when the park would normally close. My colleagues back at the crime scene would be persuading people to leave. No one could be playing tennis. And the courts were too far away.

Something struck me square between the shoulder blades.

What left my mouth was more of a terrified yelp than a scream. I doubt it would have carried. I jumped round. No one there. I was spinning on the spot. Nothing. No one anywhere near me. But five feet away, nestling in some dandelion leaves, was a yellow tennis ball. I turned in the direction from which it must have come. And saw him.

A man, slender enough to be a boy. We stared at each other. He was about a hundred metres away, too far for me to make out his face, so I couldn't be sure it was Samuel Cooper, but everything I could see seemed to fit. He was white and in his mid to late twenties, fair — of complexion and hair colour — rather than dark. He was also tall and I remembered reading that Cooper was close to six foot. He wore skateboarding clothes: baggy jeans trailing to the ground, a loose dark jacket with coloured symbols and a tight-fitting beanie hat. The tennis racket was still in his right hand.

Then he was off, racing like a fox across the grass, darting behind bushes, heading for one of the side gates, and Joesbury was on his tail.

Joesbury was older than Cooper, but he was stronger and clearly fitter. The gap between them was narrowing. I heard more running footsteps and turned to see Pete Stenning speeding towards me, shouting into his radio as he went.

'You OK?' he gasped as he got close.

I'd been watching the two dark figures, could barely see them any more.

'I'm fine,' I said. 'Get after them.'

Stenning was panting, bending over to catch his breath. 'Guv'nor said I had to stay with you,' he said.

He and I looked at each other for a second and then we were both running across the grass. We couldn't see Joesbury or the man he was chasing, but we knew where they'd gone. Stenning was taller than me and no doubt faster, but he'd already sprinted across the grass to get to me. Besides, he'd been told to stick close, so we ran together, across the football pitches, to the edge of the park.

There was no gate at this point, just a blue-painted barrier to stop children running too quickly towards the nearby roads. We dodged round it and found ourselves on a small side road. Cars were parked along one edge. No sign of Joesbury or his prey.

'We should split up,' I said.

'No fucking way.'

With no clue which way to go, we jogged forward to a street of red-brick Victorian houses. Queen's Gate Villas. There were several pedestrians, a cyclist went past us faster than the traffic. No one we recognized. We waited as footsteps behind told us that colleagues, alerted by Stenning's radio call, had come to join us. On his radio, we could hear that others had left the park at different gates and were heading our way, hoping to cut our suspect off. We heard Joesbury's voice giving instructions. It didn't sound hopeful. After a few minutes, we saw Joesbury himself appear on a large, grassed area at the other side of the road. He shook his head at us and then dodged his way through the cars until he reached us.

'Lost the bastard,' he said. Then he bent over and spat in the gutter.

39

Monday 10 September

'Ketchup, anyone?' asked Kristos.

Across the table DI Tulloch looked startled. At her side, Joesbury's jaw was tight. Next to me, Stenning was staring at the blood-red bottle being offered to us. Then Joesbury and I made eye contact. As I bit back a giggle, he reached out for the bottle.

'You eating that bacon, Tully?' he asked.

Tulloch peeled back the white bread from her sandwich, lifted out three rashers of bacon and dropped them on Joesbury's plate. She licked her fingers, before replacing the bread and cutting the now empty sandwich into quarters.

'I'm a veggie,' she said, seeing Stenning and I staring at her. 'I just can't resist the flavour of bacon fat.'

It was after two in the morning and the four of us were in an all-night café not far from the station on Lewisham High Street. It was the first time I'd been here, but the proprietor, a young Greek Cypriot called Kristos, obviously knew the others well. He'd made us large mugs of coffee and put bacon on the grill without being asked.

'Wife-swapping,' announced Stenning, taking the ketchup bottle from Joesbury.

'Excuse me?' said Tulloch.

'It's a wife-swapping ring gone wrong,' Stenning went on as Joesbury leaned back in his chair and raised one eyebrow. 'Middle-class women in their forties. They're all at it. Read the *Mail on Sunday.* So, one of the husbands has had second thoughts. Decided all the women are whores and that he's going to butcher them.'

Almost to the second, Joesbury and I bit into our sandwiches. Tulloch nibbled the corner of hers.

Stenning was leaning across the table, as though physical proximity to the two senior detectives might help persuade them. 'We've seen weirder things,' he said.

'If that bloke I chased had been middle-class and in his forties, I'd have caught him,' replied Joesbury.

I looked up and caught Tulloch's eye. Difficult to say which of us smiled first.

'Both victims were the same type.' Stenning wasn't one to give up easily. 'Ladies who lunch.'

There had been no clue, either on the body or in the shed, that would tell us who our latest victim was. All we knew was that she was probably early to mid forties, slim and healthy looking, with manicured fingernails and professionally cut and coloured hair.

Arriving back in the incident room, I'd been asked to check the missing-persons list. There had been several possibilities, although none of the photographs I looked at bore much resemblance to the woman I'd seen. Nevertheless, first thing in the morning, we'd start the grim task of contacting relatives.

The name and details I'd been given by the man who'd phoned in the original call about the boat shed had turned out to be bogus.

All the time we'd been back at the station, we'd had regular reports from our colleagues out on the streets. The man we'd chased from the park — we were calling him Samuel Cooper until we knew otherwise — had disappeared. Joesbury's guess was that he'd leaped into a garden and doubled back to the main road. A helicopter had been called out, but by the time it arrived we knew it was hopeless; he'd had plenty of time to get away. Cooper's details had been wired around London, though, and every patrol car on the streets would be looking for him.

CCTV footage from late Saturday afternoon showed someone dressed exactly as our suspect had been earlier, walking into the park in the company of a dark-haired woman. The woman had been wearing a brown coat with polka dots on it and could easily be the victim. The two had been walking close together and the woman appeared to be going willingly enough.

After we'd watched it, Tulloch had sent for the footage from the Brendon Estate on the night of Geraldine Jones's murder. After thirty minutes, we'd been rewarded. A figure, again dressed exactly like our suspect, had walked into Kennington Tube station just over five minutes after Geraldine had collapsed in my arms. I'd sat watching the two clips of footage for some time, flicking from one to the other.

'Same clothes on three separate occasions,' I'd said, almost to myself.

'Different trousers on the night Geraldine Jones was killed,' Tulloch had replied from directly behind me. I flicked back to the right piece of footage. 'Those look like cargo pants to me,' she went on. 'And maybe he only has the one jacket.'

'Maybe,' I agreed. There was something bothering me, I just couldn't put my finger on it. Eventually, Tulloch called me away.

Although we couldn't be sure he was the killer, Samuel Cooper's photograph had been released to the papers. More than one national was reprinting its front page to carry the image of the man suspected of being the new Ripper.

'So you think he's choosing Victorian locations?' Tulloch said now, glancing sideways at Joesbury.

He nodded. He'd just put the last of the sandwich into his mouth and couldn't talk.

'Or with a Victorian connection,' I said. 'The pool building and the park were built during Victoria's reign, but obviously not the Brendon Estate. It was the block name that was important there.'

'Makes sense,' said Stenning. 'He can't replicate the original locations, most of them don't exist any more. They've been knocked down and built on and look nothing like what they did a hundred years ago.'

'And look how many rubberneckers were out in Whitechapel two nights ago,' agreed Joesbury. 'He'd have been playing to a packed house.'

'So we identify Victorian buildings and stake them out on 30 September,' said Stenning.

'How many of those do you think there are around London?' asked Joesbury. 'The Victorians practically built this city. There are over forty streets in the *A–Z* with Victoria in their name. I checked before we came out.'

'So we do the prominent ones, the well-known ones.' Stenning wasn't giving up easily.

Tulloch was chewing her bottom lip. 'That piece of wood,' she said, and her eyes fell to the tabletop. 'That didn't happen to Annie Chapman.'

I gave the two men a moment to chip in. Neither of them did.

'It did to Emma Smith,' I said.

'That's a new one on me,' said Stenning, looking my way.

'Emma Smith was the first Whitechapel murder victim,' I said. 'She was killed some time in April that year. A thick piece of wood was pushed up inside her, causing extensive internal injuries. She survived the attack but died the day after in hospital.'

Stenning was looking confused. 'So, hang on . . .'

'No one really believes she was a victim of

the Ripper,' I said. 'She herself said she was attacked by three men. It was probably some sort of revenge thing or punishment.'

'So what is Cooper playing at?' said Joesbury. 'He's not an out-and-out copycat, that's for sure. It's like he's sorting through and picking the bits he likes best.'

Tulloch glanced at her watch and I wondered if she were looking at the date. It was 10 September. Just twenty days before a Ripper copycat would strike again.

'We'll catch him,' I said, wondering who I was trying to convince. 'I saw him. He's real. We know who he is. We'll catch him.'

I could see her trying to smile.

'We need a plan,' said Joesbury.

'Tell me about it,' she muttered.

Joesbury was looking at me. 'I mean a plan for young Ripper-bait here,' he said.

I sat a little more upright in my seat. 'If that becomes my nickname around the station, I will personally —' I began.

'Not the testicles to the pigeons again,' he said, as his face relaxed and those great teeth appeared. 'That one's getting tired.'

'I will wear them as earrings,' I said. 'And when they start to rot, I will skewer them, alternating with your eyeballs, and give them to Kristos to serve as shish kebabs.'

Joesbury was actually smiling at me. There

was a tiny fleck of ketchup just above the left side of his mouth and I had an almost irresistible urge to reach out . . .

'Wow, she's nastier than you,' he said, turning his grin to Tulloch. She smiled back, reached up her left ring finger to wipe away the ketchup.

'I really need to get home,' I said, before realizing I had no way of getting there. 'If that's OK, Boss?'

'We should all go,' she said, before turning back to Joesbury. 'By a plan, you mean . . . ?'

'We should get her to a safe house,' he said. 'Tomorrow if we can. I'll sit outside her flat tonight.'

'No,' said Tulloch, her eyes flitting between the two of us. 'You need some sleep. I'll get uniform to do it. We can move her tomorrow.'

'Are you sure?' I asked.

Three pairs of eyes looked at me.

'We've got twenty days,' I said. 'That's not a lot of time to waste.'

Silence.

'If he's a traditionalist, he'll kill twice next time,' I went on. 'Thirtieth of September.'

'He's not a traditionalist,' said Joesbury. 'We've just established that. He's a pick-and-mixer.'

'I'll bet he finds it hard to resist the double event,' I said.

Tulloch was looking at Joesbury, who was still looking at me. 'No,' he said.

'Elizabeth Stride and Catharine Eddowes,' I said. 'Butchered within an hour of each other.'

He was shaking his head. 'Not gonna happen, Flint.'

'You were happy enough to dangle me in the snake pit earlier,' I pointed out.

'Completely different,' he said. 'It was a containable situation. We can't keep you safe twenty-four hours a day.'

'If I stay at home, he'll make contact,' I said. 'You had CCTV cameras put in the garden, didn't you? And over the front door.'

He dropped his eyes to the tabletop.

'They're linked to the station,' I went on. 'And there's a panic button by my bed?'

'Lacey,' began Tulloch, 'it's not —'

'There are intruder alarms across every door and window?' I ignored Tulloch. I was talking only to Joesbury, as though he was in charge now. He was looking at me again but his eyes weren't smiling any more. 'He can't get me inside,' I said. 'But he might try and get into the garden or put something through the front door. He might call me. He might try and contact me when I'm out and about. I'll spend a lot of time out of the station for the next few days. I'll go out on the streets again.'

Silence around the table. Over at the counter, Kristos had gone very still. He was listening too.

'We have twenty days,' I said. 'If we haven't got him by the thirtieth I'll go to a safe house.'

Still no response, but I knew they were going to agree. If we hadn't got him by the thirtieth, two more women were going to die. Tulloch dropped her head into her hands and Stenning's hand settled on my right shoulder. Joesbury was still glaring at me, but he wasn't arguing any more.

It was official. I was Ripper-bait.

40

I was woken by a shrill noise too close to my head. I groped around and found my new phone.

'Morning, gorgeous.'

'What?' I managed. 'Who?'

'It's me — Pete. Expecting someone else?'

'Whadayawant?'

'Got something that'll make your day.'

'Go on.'

'Semen.'

I struggled to sit up. 'Stenning, don't think I'm not flattered, but —'

'Not mine, you dozy mare. On the corpse.'

Wide awake now. 'Come again.'

'Apt choice of words, Flint. DI Tulloch's just got back from the post-mortem. The pathologist found semen on the corpse.'

I needed a second to take that in. It hadn't been enough then, to slice her open . . . 'He raped her?'

I heard Stenning take a breath. 'Yeah,

pretty heavy,' he said. 'But great for us. We —'

'Hang on, they've already had the post-mortem?' What the hell time was it?

'First thing this morning. Another musical one, apparently. Tulloch and Anderson went. They've just filled us in.'

I leaned across until I could see my alarm clock. Nearly half past ten.

'Tulloch said we weren't to wake you up,' said Stenning. 'But I thought you'd want to hear the good news. We'll get him, Flint. We've got a name and DNA. He's going down. Oh, and the papers have cottoned on to the Victorian connection. Your friend Emma Boston, of all people, worked it out.'

I was out of bed, wondering what I had to wear that was clean.

'Now get your ass in here. The boss wants you bringing us up to speed on the double event. Just in case.'

41

23 December, eleven years earlier

The doctor is surrounded by photographs of children. On her desk, on the shelves behind her, even on the window ledge. Some of them, the doctor's own children, the girl assumes, were taken decades ago — she can tell by the clothes worn and the graininess of the print. Others, more recent, must be grandchildren.

It's disgustingly tactless, the girl thinks, this excessive display of the doctor's own fertility, given that she's just told Cathy she will never be able to carry and bear a child.

'The infection attacked the lining of your uterus,' the doctor is explaining. 'If we'd caught it earlier, we might have got it under control. As it is, even without the damage to the fallopian tubes and the ovaries, I'm afraid the uterus simply won't be capable of sustaining a full-term pregnancy. I'm sorry.'

She isn't sorry, the girl holding Cathy's hand

can tell. She's saying all the right things, the words that are expected of her, but her eyes are too steady, her stare too intense. At best, she doesn't care one way or the other. At worst, because she's mean and she takes pleasure in other people's misery, she's secretly rather gratified this has happened to them.

'I can't have children,' says Cathy, for the third time. 'I'll never be a mother.'

Cathy, who has been a mother since she was three years old, caring for her dolls as if they were alive, cannot take in the news that she, of all females, won't make the natural progression from looking after dolls to loving real live babies.

'Well, you know, my dear,' says the doctor, 'there are more ways than one to be a mother.'

'What the fuck is that supposed to mean?' says the girl.

The doctor narrows her eyes and pulls back her shoulders. 'There's no call for language of that description, young lady,' she says. 'Perhaps I'd better speak to your sister alone.'

The girl stands up. 'Is there anything else you need to ask, Cathy?' she says.

Cathy's eyes seem to have lost the ability to focus. She shakes her head and her sister takes her arm and pulls her gently to her feet. They move away from the chairs, towards the door. Then the girl stops, turns and steps back to the desk.

'Put that down,' says the doctor. 'Put that down now, or I'll call Security.'

'There is no Security in this building, you old fool,' says the girl, as she walks over to the open window. In her right hand, she has a gold-framed photograph of the much younger doctor holding a toddler in her arms. The girl reaches the window, glances out and drops the picture. She hears the clang it makes on the roof of a red car as she steers Cathy out of the room.

■ ■ ■ ■

Part Three: Elizabeth

■ ■ ■ ■

'For this time two victims have been required in a single night to slake what appears to be an absolutely demoniacal thirst for blood.'

Evening Standard, 1 October 1888

42

Monday 10 September

'Two women were killed in the early morning of 30 September 1888,' I said. I pressed a button on the laptop and the photograph of a woman appeared on the large screen at the front of the room. Taken in the mortuary, it showed an oval face and clean, regular features. Her hair was dark, with a slight curl, and had been pinned up on the crown of her head. Her mouth was wide and generous, she might at one time have had a nice smile.

'The first victim was Elizabeth Stride, a Swedish-born woman who moved to London about twenty years before her death,' I said. 'She was forty-five, separated from her husband and homeless. The murder took place in Dutfield's Yard, a sort of courtyard that led off Berner Street in Whitechapel.'

The incident room was full, but more than one pair of eyes was drifting towards the open windows. I had a sense of people listening out of politeness. We knew who we were after now. And when we found Samuel Cooper, we could prove he was the killer. The case was all but over.

'At twelve forty-five in the morning, she was seen arguing with a man in the gateway to Dutfield's Yard,' I went on. 'That's the last we see of her alive.'

I carried on talking but my mind was wandering. I had leave due and it was too long since I'd taken a holiday. Tiredness, and shock, had been playing some very strange tricks with my head the last couple of weeks. Then the door opened and Mark Joesbury walked in. He was in a business suit, dark grey with the faintest of pinstripes. His shirt was white and his tie was dark-red silk and I'd lost my thread.

It took me a moment to find it again. 'Dutfield's Yard was overlooked by a Jewish Socialist Club,' I said, after a few seconds glancing through my notes. 'It was full on the night in question. Would have been noisy. At one a.m., fifteen minutes after Elizabeth was last seen, the steward of the social club arrived home and saw a woman lying on the ground with her throat cut. He later described the wound as a great gash, over two inches wide.'

Joesbury took a seat next to Tulloch. He'd shaved.

'He went inside to get help and the police were called,' I said, as Joesbury whispered something in Tulloch's ear.

'In the Elizabeth Stride case, three aspects are of interest. The first is the mystery of how the killer managed to incapacitate her in the way he did.'

'He strangled his victims first, didn't he?' chipped in a man at the back.

'It's believed so,' I agreed, glad of someone else to concentrate on. 'But there were no signs that Elizabeth was strangled. No bruising around the throat or face. Yet the surgeon was convinced her throat had been cut from left to right, while she was prostrate on the ground.'

'She thought she was about to have sex,' said Anderson. 'Women do that on their backs, in my experience.'

Titters from various men in the room.

'It had been raining heavily,' I replied. 'The yard was covered in mud, and maybe you need to be a bit more adventurous, Sarge,'

More titters, rather more feminine in tone this time.

'She wouldn't have lain down voluntarily,' I said. 'There were lots of people nearby, but no one heard any sound of a struggle. And she kept hold of a small packet of sweets while she was forced to the ground. He got her down quickly and without a fuss.'

'These women all drank, didn't they?' said Joesbury. 'Was she intoxicated?'

'The pathologist said not,' I replied, keeping my eyes on my notes. 'He checked her stomach contents and found no evidence of alcohol abuse or narcotics. The police at the time were completely mystified as to how he got her on the ground.'

A car horn sounded outside. Several heads turned to the window.

'Another reason Elizabeth Stride stands out is that she wasn't mutilated in any way,' I went on, anxious to get to the end now. 'The wound on her throat was the only mark on her body. No other part of her was touched.'

'He was interrupted,' said Stenning.

'In the drama I watched,' said Gayle Mizon, popping a cashew nut into her mouth, 'only one murder took place on 30 September. Elizabeth Stride was discounted as being one of the Ripper victims.'

'That's the third thing I was going to mention,' I said, giving Mizon a quick smile. 'Not every expert believes the Ripper killed Stride. Some people argue that because there was no sign of strangulation and because she wasn't mutilated, her killer was a different man.'

'The opposing argument being that because he was interrupted, the Ripper had to abort plan A and then took out his frustration on his next victim,' said Tulloch.

'Yes, that's another possibility,' I said. 'The fourth canonical victim of the Ripper was Catharine Eddowes.' I pressed the keyboard again and the post-mortem photograph appeared on the screen. It was taken of Catharine's naked body and showed a massive scar running down the length of her torso. Her facial injuries were appalling.

'At one forty-five in the morning,' I said, 'PC Watkins of the City Police found Catharine's body in Mitre Square.'

'Hang on, we're talking less than an hour after Stride was murdered in Whitechapel,' said Barrett.

'That's right,' I said. 'Catharine's throat had been cut, almost back to the spine. The police doctor referred to death being due to blood loss from the left common carotid artery. Her abdomen was ripped open from her breast down to her pubic bone. Several of her internal organs were damaged. Others, including the uterus and the left kidney, were removed. Some of her organs were left strewn around her body, almost as though he was looking for something.'

The mood in the room had changed. People were listening again.

'For the first time with Eddowes, the Ripper attacked his victim's face,' I said. 'He used his knife to make incisions on her cheeks and eyelids. The lobe of one ear was cut off and also the tip of her nose.'

My colleagues seemed transfixed by the picture of Eddowes's face. Horrible scars showed where her facial wounds had been stitched during the post-mortem examination. Beneath the damage, though, it was still possible to see that at one time she would have been a pretty woman. She'd had a heart-shaped face, high cheekbones and a smooth, clear brow, and I couldn't help but wonder if it had just been coincidence that the loveliest of the Ripper's victims had inspired his greatest violence.

43

For the next few days I was the poster girl for the caring face of the Met, or as Stenning and one or two of the others insisted on calling me, Ripper-bait. I spent less than an hour a day in the station. The rest of the time I was out, visiting schools, youth clubs and community centres around south London. I linked up with the Sapphire Units and helped them give talks to groups of girls about keeping themselves safe and the importance of reporting incidents. I met Rona and her sister, Tia, over a burger lunch and was hugely relieved to find that nothing had happened yet, and that both girls were being very careful.

Other times, I was out on the streets, buying endless cartons of soup, directing people to hostels, advice centres, sometimes just talking. The days can get very dull when you have nothing to do and nowhere to go.

At lunchtime I went swimming. In the

evenings, I sat in pubs and cafés, pretending to read a newspaper. I stayed out as late as I could bear, just waiting for the phone call, for the tall, thin figure of Samuel Cooper to appear in the distance. I even went to Camden on the second night, mainly to wind up Joesbury, and discovered there was a limit to how much I wanted to rile him. I went home alone.

Actually, I was never truly alone. Joesbury had got clearance for two of his colleagues from SO10 to take turns shadowing me. 'Your guys stand out like sore knobs,' he'd told Tulloch when she said she'd prefer her own people to do it. 'Any villain worth his salt will clock 'em a mile off.'

Whoever Joesbury's people were, they were good. Even I hadn't spotted them yet. Occasionally, at a distance, I'd see someone I knew from Lewisham. Tulloch was taking no chances.

Tulloch phoned me often, Stenning almost as much. I heard that the latest press conference had been painful and that it had been plain that Tulloch's superiors were distancing themselves. If the killer wasn't caught soon, she'd carry the can.

There had been no talk around the station about her leaving the inquiry.

Thanks to Stenning, I got a full report of

the post-mortem carried out on the woman we found in Victoria Park. Death had been the result of massive blood loss following extensive damage to the victim's abdominal cavity and organs. She'd been tortured prior to death by the infliction of fourteen shallow cuts around her breasts. The broken-off piece of wooden fencing had been rammed into her vagina while she was still alive. The internal damage had been extensive, but the presence of semen caught in her pubic hair suggested she'd been raped.

The semen, I learned, showed traces of a common spermicide. He'd used a condom. Frustratingly, Samuel Cooper's prior arrests had been before the taking of DNA samples from suspects had become routine, so we would need to catch him before we could prove categorically that it was him. But we would catch him. His photograph was everywhere. I saw it several times a day, on television and in the national papers.

Then, at the end of the fourth day, we identified our victim.

44

Friday 14 September

Daryl Weston of Stockbridge in Hampshire arrived home from a ten-day business trip to the Philippines to find his house strangely deserted. His wife, Amanda, was nowhere to be seen, his cat was half starved and his answer-machine completely full. Some of the calls were from his two children, the son who lived in Bristol, the thirteen-year-old daughter at a boarding school in Gloucestershire. Most of the rest were from Amanda's friends, who'd seen sketches of a murder victim on the news that bore a remarkable resemblance to her and who had just wanted to check she was still with us. Ha ha.

After he'd listened to the fourth such message, Daryl Weston was struggling to see the joke. He phoned his wife's parents in Sussex and her closest friends. Then he phoned us.

Forty-six-year-old Amanda Weston had been married for four years. Daryl was her second husband, her two children were from her first marriage. She had no enemies, according to her husband. She worked part-time as a nurse in a local hospice for terminally ill cancer patients.

Daryl Weston had loved his wife. He wept like a child when he saw her body. He was still crying when he arrived at Lewisham to give a statement. Tulloch and Anderson took him into the interview room, a room we keep for talking to people who aren't suspects in any sort of crime. They may be victims, family of victims or important and vulnerable witnesses. The room is furnished comfortably and there's a discreet video camera in one corner. As Tulloch and Anderson talked to Weston, the rest of us gathered round a screen in the incident room to watch the conversation.

'Mr Weston, I know you want to be getting back to your children,' said Dana, when she'd taken him through the basics, 'but I do need to ask you a few more questions. Is that OK?'

Weston nodded, without raising his eyes from the hands clasped on his lap.

'Can you think of any reason why your wife might have been in London last

Saturday?'

'Weston shook his head. 'She never comes to London,' he said. 'She hates it.'

'When did you last speak to her?'

He thought for a second. 'Tuesday night,' he said. 'I asked her what time it was in England and she said just after eight.'

'How did she sound?'

He shook his head. 'Normal. Tired. She'd been at work but she didn't have to go in again until Saturday. She was looking forward to the rest.'

'Did she have any plans?' asked Tulloch.

'Sort the garden out for the winter. Help Daniel pack his things up. He's supposed to move into a new flat next week. Jesus . . .' He put his head in his hands.

'Daniel is twenty-five, is that right?'

There were too many people crowded round the screen. It was starting to feel uncomfortably hot. I edged back a little and looked at my watch. I'd arranged to meet the local Sapphire Unit at a nearby school in twenty minutes.

'Mr Weston, we have reason to believe that whoever killed your wife may have killed another woman, just over a week ago. Did you hear about that case?'

Weston looked up and shook his head. 'I've been out of the country.'

'Of course, you did say. The other woman was a similar age to your wife. Her name was Geraldine Jones. Does that name mean anything?'

He shook his head again.

I really had to go now. I took another step back and came up against Joesbury. I hadn't even known he was in the room. Keeping my eyes on the screen, I edged my way around him and left.

For several days I carried on going through the motions, trying to lure Samuel Cooper out into the open. People like Stenning and Mizon filled me in on anything important.

Like the fact that Geraldine Jones and Amanda Weston could have known each other. So far no member of either family remembered the two women being friends, but when she'd been married to her previous husband, Amanda and her children had lived in London. They and Geraldine's kids had attended the same private school in Chiswick. Shortly after that, we learned that Cooper's mother, Stacey, had worked at the school as a cook and that Cooper himself had been known to visit it. It was looking as though the killings weren't random. There was a purpose behind them.

In the meantime, Cooper continued to

elude us. And the cranks had really come out of the woodwork. Every day we were deluged with telephone calls and Ripper letters; every day, we took a hammering in the press. POLICE CLUELESS. MET'S INCOMPETENCE. COUNTDOWN TO NEXT KILLING. The headlines got more and more judgemental. We started hiding them from Tulloch.

Then, on the eighth day after the discovery of Amanda Weston's body, we found him.

45

Monday 17 September

'The Flower Market. Ten minutes. Come alone.'

A soft click and the line went dead. I pressed the button that would end the call. My bedroom was in darkness. The luminous digits of the alarm clock showed ten minutes after four in the morning. I crossed to the wardrobe and dressed quickly. Jogging pants, trainers, sweatshirt and the jacket SO10 had issued to me just a few days ago. It had four large plastic buttons. Two of them really were buttons. The third was a tracking device that I swivelled to activate. The last contained a tiny recorder.

The second I left the flat, the cameras outside would spot me. Even if I didn't activate the jacket button, my new mobile phone sent a constant signal back to a control room in Scotland Yard. If I left my flat at this hour, someone monitoring would spot that it wasn't normal behaviour and both my team and SO10 would be alerted. They'd make contact with the unmarked car parked somewhere in my street, who would be told to follow me discreetly.

Once outside, I carried my bike up to street level and headed for the Wandsworth Road. On the other side, the streets were busier. Traffic starts building up early around here.

The New Covent Garden Flower Market is the place where florists throughout London and the South-East go for their stock. Hundreds of thousands of blooms arrive here every day from overseas and all corners of Britain. Close to the Thames and nestled between Nine Elms Lane and the Wandsworth Road, it's housed in a massive warehouse and opens most days at three a.m.

Although primarily aimed at tradesmen, the Flower Market is open to the public. Friday and Saturday mornings in particular will see a fair scattering of the bargain-hunters and the curious. Tourists who can be bothered getting up early enough; wealthy women from north of the river planning fancy parties; brides with dreams of filling their churches with blooms. And, sometimes, me.

Often, when I can't sleep, I cycle or walk down here and just wander among the stalls. Flowers have always been one of my favourite things.

I left my bike against some railings then went into the warehouse through the main cargo doors. The sticky, cloying scent of lilies was all around me. The stall to my right had hundreds of them: white, pink, yellow and the fabulous orangey-gold of the tiger lily. I moved on, heading deeper into the market, past towers of roses, cascades of daisies and boxes of blooms I could never have named. The scent of the flowers fought with that of fast food. It's an odd combination — roses and grease — but one I rather like. The place was busy. The market does most of its business between five and six a.m. and we were approaching the busiest time.

There he was.

Forty feet away from me, on the other side of a small ornamental forest of potted bay trees. He was dressed just as he had been in the park. Loose trailing jeans, black jacket with orange and lime symbols, black beanie. In the harsh electric light of the flower market, it was easy to recognize the pinched features and large nose of Samuel Cooper. A week ago, in the park, he'd been much further away and I hadn't been sure. Now I was.

He seemed to sway, then to lean closer towards me. Forty feet away and yet the way he moved seemed menacing and I had to tell myself to stand my ground. As we stared at each other, I tried to remember how many exits to the market there were. My colleagues, thanks to Joesbury's tracking devices, would know exactly where I was. Once they got here, they would surround the building. Only when confident all exits were secure would they venture inside. If I kept him in here long enough, just staring at each other across the ornamental trees, we'd get him.

Seconds ticked by and I could sense an uncertainty in him. Those odd eyes began to flicker from side to side.

It was still too soon. There might be a few officers outside, but not nearly enough. I needed my radio. So far, I hadn't turned it on, but now I needed to hear where the others were. As slowly as I dared, I moved my hand towards my jacket pocket. Cooper took a step back. I froze.

Stale-mate. If I moved, he'd run.

'Help you, love?'

The holder of the stall I was standing by had approached. I shook my head without taking my eyes off Cooper.

'Suit yourself,' muttered the man I could only see out of the corner of my eye. 'You'll have to move, though, I'm putting some stuff down there.'

'I'm with the police,' I said, knowing the chances of his believing me were slim. I was in casual clothes and still wearing my bicycle helmet. 'Give me a minute, please.'

The stall-holder was silent for a moment. 'Why don't you show me some ID?' he asked.

I ignored him.

A hand grabbed my arm. 'I'm talking to you. If you're the —'

I had no option but to turn. I saw an overweight man in his early forties. He'd made me look away from Cooper and got the full brunt of my frustration. 'Back off, now!' I hissed at him.

'I'm calling Security,' he announced.

Cooper was gone. I shook the hand off my arm and set off after him. Dodging a trolley, I pulled out and switched on my radio.

'DC Flint chasing suspect,' I called into it, using the verbal signal guaranteed to get me attention on the airwaves. 'Urgent assistance needed.' I wove my way in and out of the crowds, trying not to send anyone flying. I caught sight of the doors. 'Exit 10,' I called. 'Suspect heading for Exit 10.'

Cooper shot out into the car park and a few seconds later so did I. He was throwing himself over a railing, heading for Nine Elms Lane. I took a second to look round then I was running too, across the car park. He ran through the traffic, across the Wandsworth Road and on to the intersection.

'He's heading for the bridge,' I shouted into the radio.

As fast as I dared, I made my way across the traffic. A bus rattled past and early commuters stared out at me. For a second I couldn't see Cooper. Then I spotted the lime squiggles on his jacket.

'Suspect on the Vauxhall Bridge,' I gasped into the radio, feeling a surge of hope. On the bridge I'd have a clear run. There was a chance I could catch him. There was even the possibility someone could cut him off at the other side. Vauxhall Bridge led almost directly into Westminster, an area never without heavy police presence.

'Suspect a third of the way along Vauxhall Bridge, heading northwest.' I was fast running out of breath. 'Suspect wearing loose black jacket, jeans and black hat. Believed to be Samuel Cooper.'

The suspect believed to be Samuel Cooper suddenly stopped dead in the middle of the pedestrian walkway. I stopped too. The traffic on our side of the bridge was flowing normally. The other lane was empty and over Cooper's shoulder I could see why. Two patrol cars had stopped at the junction of the bridge and the road that skirts the north bank of the Thames. Cooper had seen that he couldn't escape that way. He'd turned and was coming back.

Ignoring the instinct that told me to step into the traffic and get out of his way, I made myself stand firm. He might make it past me but I'd slow him down. There would be back-up behind me. I didn't dare risk looking round but I knew they'd be in position by now. More officers would be arriving any second.

'Flint!' screamed a voice I knew only too well. 'Get out of the fucking way!'

Footsteps were coming in both directions and it felt like I was the one being hunted down. I had an almost irresistible urge to flee.

Cooper was yards away now, had slowed to a trot. Then he pulled a short, black handgun out of his pocket.

The footsteps slowed.

Cooper was feet away. I could see men

behind him, some of them in uniform, one of them wearing a grey jacket that had been draped across my sofa not so many nights ago. Joesbury lived just over the river from me, hardly five minutes' drive away.

Cooper was spinning on the spot, pointing his weapon alternately at me, then at Joesbury and his team. The bridge was empty of traffic now. Joesbury was mouthing something at me. I realized what it was a split second after it was too late. Get back, he'd been trying to tell me.

Cooper had grabbed me. We fell against the red steel of the bridge's safety rail and I wondered if any of my ribs were still intact.

'I'll do it!' he screamed. 'I'll blow her fucking head off!'

The gun was actually pressed into my left shoulder but I was far from arguing. Managing to get my breath, I raised my eyes from the gun. Cooper's strange eyes weren't focused. His breathing, even allowing for the distance he'd run, was too fast, and drool was collecting in the corner of his mouth. He was seriously under the influence of something.

Getting his balance, he straightened up, pulling me in front of him. He was a good six inches taller than me and a whole lot stronger. His left arm went around my waist as he raised the gun to my right temple. On balance, I wouldn't have called the situation improved. Except, while the gun had been pressed against my shoulder, I'd had a pretty good look at it and had seen the make and model number on the barrel.

'Let her go, Sam,' called Joesbury. 'Just let her go and we can sort this out.'

'Get off the fucking bridge!' Cooper's voice in my left ear was close to deafening. 'Get off the bridge or you scrape her brains off it.'

Joesbury had both hands in the air. He took a step backwards. 'Take it easy,' he said. 'We're going.'

He and the officers with him were moving back. If I was going to act, it had to be now. I wrapped my hands around the fabric of Cooper's jacket. When I had a firm hold and knew he couldn't go anywhere, I took a deep breath.

'The gun isn't real,' I called out, praying I was right. 'It's an air pistol. Come and get the bastard.'

Joesbury and the officer at his side exchanged glances. The gun that might or might not be real — I honestly wasn't that certain — was pushed harder against my temple and I felt something in my neck about to snap. Then I was being pulled backwards at the waist and my feet left the ground.

Panic shot through me like red-hot needles.

The heat of Cooper's body was gone but he still had me in a tight grip. I was being pulled backwards against the thick steel girder of the barrier. Shit, Cooper was on the other side of it, leaning out over the river, with nothing other than a tight grip on me to prevent himself falling.

'Not a good idea, Sam.' Joesbury was getting close again. 'It's low tide. The water can't be more than a metre deep. The fall will kill you.'

On the far bank of the river, there was no sign of the grimy, rubbish-strewn beaches that appear at low tide. The water would be deeper than Joesbury was telling us. Small comfort, because the only contact I had with the ground by this time was the tips of my trainers and any second now my spine was going to snap.

'It's twenty metres down, Sam,' called Joesbury. 'That's higher than an Olympic diving board. You won't survive.'

The arches of Vauxhall Bridge are twelve metres to water level at the lowest tide. Add on another couple of metres to reach road level and the fall would be fourteen metres at most. Still not one I relished. People don't often fall from bridges into the Thames and survive.

'You're right above one of the concrete piers,' said Joesbury, who was almost close enough to touch us. 'You won't even reach the water.' I couldn't look down but I was praying Joesbury was bullshitting about that, too. If we hit the water, we'd have a chance. Land on concrete — forget it.

'I've done nothing. This is a fucking fix.'

Joesbury's eyes didn't even flicker. 'Come on, buddy, back on to this side. We'll sort this out.'

'Screw you.'

Joesbury leaped for us just as Cooper pulled me up and over the railing. For a split second I felt a hand around my foot. I met Joesbury's eyes and saw them creased up with pain. His dislocated shoulder. The pressure of his hand held a second longer, then I felt a sliding sensation as my foot slipped from my trainer and I was falling.

I could see horrified blue eyes, the river gleaming like black ink and coloured lights from the north bank reaching across it like ribbons. I had a moment of surprise. I'd imagined my own death often, but it had never been like this. This strange sensation of feeling perfectly fine and completely fucked at the same time. Then instinct kicked in and I threw my arms above my head. Just in time. The water hit me so hard I thought I had landed on concrete and then the world turned into a plunging, dark hole.

46

I'm sinking, so fast it feels like I'm still falling, into a blackness that is dense enough to be solid, and I know that, against every instinct, I cannot panic. I have minutes. Fall into the Thames around Westminster in the middle of winter and it takes roughly 120 seconds before the cold paralyses your limbs and you sink to the bottom. In late September I might have a few minutes longer.

Still moving fast. Make those minutes count. Limbs outstretched now to slow me down. Looking around. Eyes stinging. Nothing to see but shifting dark shapes. Lights. The lights from the bank above me. I'm not sinking any more but moving fast all the same. The tide has got me.

Swim. Get up to those lights. Don't breathe. Don't think about the river, about the darkness below, about weed tangling in my face. Make those minutes count. Savage pain as something hits me hard. I'm being dragged against a hard surface I can't see. For a second I stop moving and know I'm caught on something. The river rips past me like a waterfall and I know this is the end. Then I'm free again, spinning off into darkness. Lights still above me. Don't breathe. Minutes have gone by. Clock ticking. I need air.

I'm breathing. I've broken the surface. Then I'm down again, but air in my lungs has given me hope. I kick. Keep moving. Don't give in to the cold. A body is recovered from the Thames every week of the year. Most of them are found in London. Don't be one of them.

I surface again. The huge wheel of the London Eye is already small in the distance. I've travelled so far already. The tide is hurrying away with me. Then I'm dragged under again. I am in the river in the dark in a heavy tide. I'll be found, days from now, probably in the U-bend around the Isle of Dogs because that's where most bodies get trapped. I'll be bloated and mutilated and the seagulls will have got to me. I'll be laid in a shallow, large bath at Wapping while the Marine Unit take fingerprints — if I have fingers left — and try to establish my identity.

But I'm still alive, still breathing and moving. Get the jacket off, the fabric is heavy and it's dragging me down. I risk reaching for the button and remember just in time.

The jacket might be my only hope. That and Joesbury's mobile phone in my pocket. He and the others will know where I am. They'll be following me downriver. Just stay alive. I catch a glimpse of something huge on the bank. Cleopatra's Needle. I'm heading for Waterloo Bridge. There's the *Queen Mary.* The river bends sharply here. This is where I run the greatest risk of being crushed to death against a bridge pier, or a tethered barge. It might also be my best chance.

I turn to face the direction I'm travelling in. I'm almost in the centre of the river and I have absolutely no chance in this tide of swimming to the side. But the north bank is busy here, it's almost a parking lot for pleasure boats and historic ships. Shit, that hurts. Something hits me in the face and for a few seconds I can't even breathe, but the boats of the Embankment are getting closer. There is a small one, some sort of water taxi, it has lines running to the shore. Several of them just above water level.

I hit them full on. The river howls and increases its grip. It's pulling me round, trying to get me free, it's not giving up on me just yet. I catch hold of a line and find myself almost horizontal in the water, so hard is the river dragging me downstream. I make the last effort I'm capable of and manage to hook my elbow around the line. I lock my hands together. It's all I can do.

Now I really do have minutes. Minutes before my strength gives up. Minutes before the cold, even in September, gets to me. Joesbury and the others will be looking for me. The control room in Scotland Yard will know where I am, will be sending back information. Someone will come for me.

I just have to hope Joesbury's swanky tracking devices don't mind the wet.

47

I woke up in a hospital room. The window blinds were drawn but there seemed to be soft light behind them. I'd lived to see another day. I lay still for long minutes. I was very hot. Then I risked moving my arms and legs. Everything hurt. Everything did what it was supposed to. I sat up and had a whole new experience of pain. My head, face, torso, everything screaming.

I sat still on the bed, just concentrating on breathing in and out, waiting for the pain to fade. After a while, when it had drifted back to a dull ache, I thought about lying down again. Only sensible thing really. Except I desperately needed to pee.

I lowered myself to the floor and experimented with standing upright. A toddler would have sneered, but at least I hadn't fallen. At the far end of the room, about eight feet away, was a door that I was praying led into a private bathroom. No way was

I negotiating a corridor.

I set off. Oh shit, it hurt. Couldn't I have peed in the river? My head was spinning by the time I got to the door. Thank God, a loo, with disabled bars. There was a chance I could sit down without falling.

Sitting down was achievable. Getting up again was a whole different story, so for a while I just didn't bother. Where was I? One of the south London hospitals, probably. I remembered bright lights shining on me. A man's hand reaching down. I hadn't been able to take my hand off the rope to grasp his, so he'd lassoed me like a runaway steer and dragged me to the back of the RIB. A pretty red-haired girl, part of the Met's Marine Policing Unit, had fastened me on a stretcher and wrapped silver heat-retentive blankets around me. Then the RIB's engines had fired up and we'd flown across the river to where an ambulance was waiting.

Realizing I couldn't spend the night on the loo, I pulled myself up. The pain might have been easier but it was marginal. And for some reason it was feeling horribly difficult to breathe. Like I had a heavy cold. After flushing the loo, I left the bathroom. The door to my room had a window that looked out into a corridor and, directly opposite my door, a man was sitting in a plastic chair. His eyes were closed, his left arm in a sling. The door to my room and his eyes opened at the same time. Joesbury stared at me for a second, then got to his feet.

'How are you feeling?' he asked, when we were both inside my room and the door had closed gently behind us.

'Like I fell in the Thames.'

Joesbury looked exhausted and I wondered how long he'd been sitting outside my door.

'You really shouldn't be up,' he said. 'They pumped you full of painkillers and sedatives two hours ago.'

Sedatives might explain why my head felt like a swarm of bees was trapped inside it. 'What happened to me?' I asked.

'Mainly cracked ribs. A few strains. And a lot of bruising.'

That didn't seem too bad. I nodded at his sling. 'Was that my doing?' I asked.

He shrugged with the uninjured shoulder. 'Well, they don't have to amputate just yet.' Then he half smiled. 'I've got your trainer in my car,' he added.

I looked down at my foot. 'I think I lost the other one,' I said.

The smile became a little wider. 'Maybe I'll keep it as a souvenir.'

'What about Cooper?' I asked. All the time I'd been in the river, I hadn't given the man who'd pulled me in a second thought. Survival had been all that mattered. Now though . . .

Joesbury shook his head. 'Nothing yet,' he said. 'But we wouldn't expect it. We wouldn't have found you if . . .'

'I know,' I said, and when that didn't seem enough, 'Thank you.'

'He's dead, Flint. The chances of both of you getting out were zero.'

'I know,' I said again. It was better, probably, that Cooper didn't survive. And yet . . . 'That thing he said just before we went in. About it being a fix.'

'They all say that.' Joesbury indicated the bed. 'Now, you really need to get some sleep,' he went on. 'Tully'll be here first thing in the morning, clucking like a mother hen and wanting chapter and verse on everything.'

'I'll just wash my hands,' I said. In the corner of the room was a washbasin.

He stepped after me. 'Lacey, that's not —'

I was at the basin. Automatically, I raised my head to the mirror. Staring back at me was a face I'd never seen before. I stepped quickly back, as though not looking at it might make it go away. It hadn't though, I could see in Joesbury's face it hadn't. I put my hands up to cover the hideous thing I'd turned into. Then one arm was wrapped around me and I was weeping against a black and grey sweatshirt.

'It's 90 per cent superficial,' he was saying into my ear. 'I spoke to one of the doctors. Most of it is swelling and bruising. In a couple of weeks it'll be gone.'

I couldn't stop crying.

'I think something must have hit you in the face,' Joesbury went on. 'Thank God you still had your bike helmet on.'

'What's the bandage for?' I managed. I hadn't seen my nose; where it should have been was a large square, surgical strip.

'There's a fracture in your nose just above the bridge . . .'

I wasn't crying any more. I was howling.

'Stop it, shush now. It's going to be fine. The Met will pay for it to be made as good as new.'

I was trying to stop. I really was. For one thing, it was getting hard to breathe.

'What else?' I muttered.

Joesbury sighed. 'There's a small cut on your right temple. If it leaves a scar it'll be a tiny one. The inside of your lip needed stitches, but any scarring will be inside your mouth.'

Deep breath. Joesbury's sweatshirt had blood on it. Mine.

'That's all. I promise you. You'll be as gorgeous as ever in a few weeks.'

I ran my hands over my face — God, it was sore — then looked up. I raised my finger to touch a scar — his. For several long seconds we just looked at each other. Then he said, 'I'm sorry.'

'For grabbing my shoe instead of my ankle?' I mumbled, knowing this wasn't about what had happened on Vauxhall Bridge.

'For giving you such a hard time the last couple of weeks,' he said.

I couldn't look at him any more. 'You've been a complete bastard,' I said.

'You've been a complete bastard, sir,' he corrected, pulling me closer still. 'And I know.'

'Why?' I asked, not quite daring to lift my eyes from the tearstains on his sweatshirt.

His left arm twitched inside the sling, as though he wanted to wrap that one round me too, and he gave a little sigh. 'Dana thinks I fancy you rotten and I'm taking the time-honoured male path of venting sexual frustration through unreasonable aggression,' he said.

So he and Dana weren't . . . ? Oh, grinning hurt like hell.

'Is she right?' I muttered to the tear-stain.

'Probably,' he said, as I was wondering how much kissing would hurt. 'Although I told myself I was just taking the time-honoured path of reasonable suspicion when faced with a still-warm corpse and a witness covered in blood.'

Smirk gone. I tilted my head back to look him in the eyes. 'You thought I killed Geraldine Jones?'

'Well, look at it from my point of view, Flint,' he said, as I realized I was doing exactly that. 'The Jones woman went to that estate to meet someone and it's been your regular Friday-night hang-out for a while now. You weren't on duty when Amanda Weston went missing, or when she was killed. You were late into work the morning Emma Boston's flat was broken into. Circumstantially, you could have done it. You have a drugs history — yeah, I know, all minor stuff and a long time ago — and you also have a mysterious habit of running round Camden in the small hours.'

Joesbury thought I'd killed Geraldine Jones? All the time I'd thought he was suspicious of my past, of my minor record with the police, he'd been investigating a potential killer? Who else had thought that about me? And what the hell had they found out?

'Did you tell DI Tulloch?' I asked, knowing my body had stiffened, my voice had become brittle and that I really couldn't let him see how much what he'd just said had scared me.

'Yep,' said Joesbury, who wasn't too keen to let me edge away. 'She told me I was nuts, but if I could find any evidence that you'd had any past dealings with the Jones or the Weston families, or Samuel Cooper after he became our most wanted, she'd take me seriously.'

'Did you?' I asked, wondering when I'd stopped breathing.

'Zilch,' said Joesbury, his hand firm on my waist, not letting me go anywhere. 'No evidence at all that Lacey Flint ever came across either family until the mothers were found dead. Or that she ever met Sam Cooper before this evening.'

His one good hand left my waist and gently touched the underside of my chin. He was tilting my face up towards his. 'And just so we're clear,' he said, when we made eye contact once more, 'your Camden-based social life will be a problem for me.'

The door to the room opened. Joesbury raised his head but otherwise didn't move. I turned. A plump black nurse in green scrubs stood in the doorway. Behind her, a young, uniformed police constable.

'You shouldn't be up,' she announced, stepping inside. 'Come on now.'

Joesbury let me go and the nurse crossed to the bed, peeling back the covers. She patted the mattress and her expression made it clear she was having no nonsense.

'Say goodnight, big fella,' she told Joesbury.

Joesbury looked at his watch. 'Good morning, beautiful,' he said. And then he followed the nurse's pointing finger and left the room.

48

Wednesday 19 September

Two days after I'd been admitted to Guy's, Samuel Cooper was pulled out of the river by the Marine Policing Unit. His body had become trapped beneath a pier just beyond the Blackwall Tunnel. I didn't go anywhere near the mortuary at Horseferry Road where he was taken, but I saw a photograph some days later.

The river is rarely kind to those who fall into its clutches and it hadn't been easy on Cooper. His body had been torn and broken and shredded until it barely resembled a human form. I wouldn't have known the scared, drug-crazed young man I'd fought with on Vauxhall Bridge just seconds before he nearly killed us both.

His mother, Stacey, identified him from a small arrowhead tattoo in between his shoulder blades. Fingerprints confirmed that he was Samuel Cooper and the results of a DNA test told us, beyond any doubt, that it had been his semen in Amanda Weston's pubic hair.

I learned all this from a succession of visitors. Tulloch came a couple of times, so did Stenning, and a few of the girls from the unit. Emma Boston came the first day and, after clearing it with Tulloch, I gave her a short off-the-record interview.

An admin officer from Scotland Yard brought me yet another mobile phone. The previous one had been ruined by the Thames but all my old details had been transferred. Gayle Mizon brought me grapes and managed to hold off eating more than half of them. Even DS Anderson came once.

They told me that, thanks to a tip-off, they'd managed to track down where Cooper had been living, a tiny room three floors above a DVD rental shop in Acton. Amidst the squalor, the remnants of drug use and medication, they found Amanda Weston's handbag.

As soon as I heard that, I asked about the woman we'd heard he was living with. No sign of anyone else, I'd been told. Cooper had lived alone.

They also found two more replica guns. The one Cooper had produced on the night we fell had disappeared, probably for ever, but it seemed a fairly safe bet I'd been right. It hadn't been real.

'How did you know?' asked Tulloch, when she came to see me. 'Those things are very realistic.'

'There was a robbery at a dealers in Southwark about six months ago,' I said. 'I did all the processing work. It was a Jericho 941, one of the more popular air pistols.'

'It does help explain how he got Amanda Weston to the park,' said Tulloch. She was perched on the edge of my bed. 'You remember we saw footage of them walking together along the Grove Road.'

I nodded, remembering that something about the footage had bothered me.

'It looked as though she was going quite willingly, but if she thought he had a gun, well . . .'

Tulloch was right. Most women, threatened with a gun, would do what they were told. Most women would not anticipate the horror that had lain in wait for Amanda in that park shed. Get a glimpse of that, and I think most might take their chances with a bullet.

'Possibly even with Geraldine Jones, too,' said Tulloch. 'If he'd said, "Turn around, face that car," she'd have expected a mugging and done it. I know I would.'

I was silent for a moment. Tulloch had brought me a white orchid in a pot and I wondered if Joesbury had told her about my plant collection. He hadn't been back to visit since that first morning, but the next day an anonymous parcel had arrived from a German company called Steiff. Inside I found a brown cuddly toy with a bright-red bow and an impossibly cute face. I had a teddy. I took my eyes away from where it was perched at the foot of my bed to look at Tulloch again.

'He claimed he'd been set up,' I said. 'On the bridge, he said it was a fix.'

'They all do, Lacey,' she replied.

I guessed she was right about that too. 'Why did he do it?' I asked her.

'We may never know,' she said, shaking her head. 'He'd been a serious drug user for a long time. The teachers we spoke to from his school report all sorts of behavioural difficulties. He was obviously someone who needed help and didn't get it.'

'But why those two women, why the Ripper stuff?'

'We found a lot of Ripper books and memorabilia in his flat,' said Tulloch. 'Including a ticket for one of the Ripper tours. As to those two women, well, he could have known them. He hung around the school a lot. Maybe he had a big problem with people more privileged than him.'

I nodded. It made some sense.

Tulloch pulled a clear evidence bag out of her jacket pocket. There was something inside.

'Lacey, we also found a photograph of you at his flat,' she said, holding it out for me to see. 'It's a snapshot. Do you have any idea where or when it was taken?'

I looked. I was on a London street, unlocking my car. Something had attracted my attention and I'd looked up. I was wearing a jacket I'd bought two years ago and jeans. I had no recollection of being photographed. I shook my head.

'We've got people working on it,' Tulloch said. 'Once we pinpoint the location, we can use light and shadows apparently to estimate the time of year. There may even be CCTV footage available. We do need to know when he became fixated on you.'

I sighed and leaned back against the pillows. 'It's really over then,' I said. 'We caught Jack the Ripper.'

Tulloch stood up and smiled. 'Oh, I think he decided for himself who was going to catch him.'

Dana Tulloch became something of a celebrity in the days that followed. Against her own inclination but faced with clear instructions from her superiors, she agreed to most interview requests. She was young, female and not entirely white. She ticked all the boxes. It was even suggested that I be put up for interview. From my hospital bed I refused on the grounds that notoriety so early in my career would be bad for it in the long term. I was commended with unusual wisdom for one so young.

I was officially convalescing, but when I went into the office to collect some things, the investigation team gave me a standing ovation. I started to cry again and got hugged so much I think the buggers cracked another rib.

I still looked like the back end of a bus, but most of the time I didn't mind. Taking medication for the pain, I found myself sleeping better than I had for years. And when I woke up, a brown bear with a red bow was never far away on the pillow.

On the first Saturday morning after my release from hospital, I made a slow and rather painful bus journey up to the South Bank. In one of the less trendy cafés, not too far from the river, I saw a thin, pale girl with dyed black hair, wearing sunglasses, even though the interior was quite dark. She didn't look up as I approached her table, but I noticed a group of teenagers nearby had spotted her. They were whispering to each other and I wondered how often she had to put up with that sort of crude and insensitive attention. The last couple of days, I'd learned a lot about how it felt to be stared at for the wrong reasons.

'Hi,' I said, when I was close enough. Emma Boston looked up and pushed her sunglasses on to the top of her head.

'Fuck, you look rough,' she said. Then she suddenly grinned at me, showing surprisingly white teeth for a heavy smoker.

'Sit down,' she said. 'Join the freak show.'

I sat. I'd never seen her smile before.

'You OK?' she asked me.

I nodded. 'Getting there.'

The waitress came over and I ordered coffee and cheese on toast. Emma asked for a refill.

'I liked that article you wrote,' I said, when we were alone again. I wasn't bullshitting or flattering her. The piece based on the interview she'd done with me in hospital, and a subsequent one with Tulloch, had appeared in the features section of one of the broadsheets two days after my night in the Thames. It had gone beyond simple reporting to ask some fairly basic questions about what drives men to kill violently.

'I'm a good journalist,' she said, almost defiantly.

'I know,' I said. 'Thanks for keeping my name out of it.'

She gave a little nod. 'So what's new?' she asked me. 'I take it you didn't invite me here to become your new best mate. Any progress on finding that woman Cooper was supposedly living with? His mum told me she never met her. Mind you, she hadn't seen Sam himself for a while.'

'Actually, it's nothing to do with the Ripper case,' I said, checking my watch. 'I may have another story for you. If you're up for a bit of controversy, that is.'

She gave a slow, sly smile. At that moment I heard the door again and turned round. Three young black girls were looking across at our table. I got up and went to meet them.

'What happened to you?' asked Rona.

'Fight with a river barge,' I said. 'Thanks for coming. Hello, Tia.'

Rona's twelve-year-old sister, a smaller, slimmer, even prettier version of Rona herself, smiled shyly at me.

'This is Rebecca,' said Rona, indicating the other girl. 'She's a friend of mine. She's been through it too.'

'It was good of you all to come,' I said. 'Come on, there's someone I want you to meet.'

The piece Emma wrote about Rona and her friends and the problem of gang rape in south London appeared eight days later. The front page of the *Sunday Times* review section showed a picture of a young black girl staring sadly out across the Thames. It was a library shot — all the girls who'd contributed to Emma's story remained anonymous — but it spoke volumes about being young, black, female and afraid in London.

The accompanying story pulled no punches and certainly didn't make for comfortable Sunday-morning reading. The Met weren't criticized as such, Emma had spoken to the head of the Sapphire Units and had included her comments, but the article did ask significant questions about whether the authorities were letting down vulnerable sectors of society, simply by refusing to confront uncomfortable truths.

Shortly after it appeared, Emma phoned to tell me that the *Sunday Times* had commissioned a follow-up story, this time talking to community leaders and schools. There was even talk of the article being submitted for an award.

I started to get something of a social life during the last few days of September. The day after the inquest into Amanda Weston's death, the team insisted I join them bowling and to my amazement I didn't argue. My ribs weren't up to active participation but I sat at the side and tried not to laugh too much.

A few days later, we went for a curry in a little café off Brick Lane where you have to take your own beer. That time Joesbury joined us, his arm still in a sling. He didn't speak to me all evening, but more than once, when I looked up, I caught his eye. And I couldn't help wonder whether the brown bear and I might find ourselves with company one of these nights.

And then, on 1 October, over a hundred years after Elizabeth Stride died in the yard behind Berner Street, my happy new existence came to an abrupt end.

49

Monday 1 October

Charlotte Benn is lying on the king-size bed of the master bedroom. The wrong way round. Her feet, still in the shoes she was wearing when she answered the door, are on the pillow. Her husband's pillow. He won't like coming home and finding it dented. Charlotte had made the bed already, pulling the bottom sheet tight at the corners, smoothing out creases, plumping up the quilt and pillows, folding the throw, arranging the silk cushions carefully. She's going to have to do it all again when this is over.

'Can I sit up?' she asks.

'No,' replies the voice.

'I think I'm going to be sick,' she says.

No answer.

'This throw won't wash,' Charlotte says. 'I'll have to dry-clean it.'

'Nice room,' says the voice. 'Did you do it yourself?'

'Yes,' says Charlotte, although she hadn't. She'd used a very expensive interior designer that one of her friends had recommended. 'I chose everything,' she continues. 'I spent weeks on it.'

'Nice use of neutrals,' says the voice in her ear. 'Are they your favourites? Neutral colours, I mean?'

'There's money in the house,' says Charlotte. 'In the safe downstairs. A couple of hundred pounds, I think. I can tell you the combination. It's six, seven, three . . .' She can hear a rustling noise directly behind her. 'What are you doing?' she asks.

'I wanted to ask you about morality,' the voice says. 'Is it absolute, do you think? Or can it shift? Don't move, or I'll blow your head off.'

Charlotte forces herself to remain still. 'I don't know what you mean,' she says. 'I think you're confusing me with someone else.' She's starting to cry and wonders if mascara will stain the throw.

'If someone you loved committed a terrible crime,' says the voice, 'what would you do? Would you stand by them, no matter what the consequences to anyone else?'

'I don't know what you want with me.' Tears are trickling down the side of her face, the first has reached her ear. She wants to brush it away but daren't move.

'This really is a nice room,' says the voice. 'Although I'm not fond of neutrals myself.'

As fingers wrap themselves around Charlotte's hair, music starts to play, an old-fashioned tune that Charlotte thinks she knows but can't quite place. In spite of the threat, she starts to pull herself up and then stops. Something is touching her throat. She glances to one side, sees the white-clad arm bent at the elbow.

'I have to be somewhere in an hour,' whimpers Charlotte, and the knife at her throat trembles against her skin.

'Yes, so do I,' says the voice. 'And they say time flies when you're having fun.'

The knife tip presses deeper. Charlotte is panting. Suddenly her body can't suck in air fast enough.

'Red's always been my favourite colour,' says the voice, as Julie Andrews starts to sing about raindrops. 'I think what this room needs is a few accents of red.'

50

I was at work when we got the call. Shortly after lunch, I'd gone into the incident room to check something with Mizon. As I approached her desk, the phone rang and she put down her sandwich to take the call. She and I were alone in the room, at least half the other team members had been assigned to new tasks. When she put the phone down, there was a crease line in the centre of her forehead.

'That was Westminster CID,' she said. 'They've been called out to Victoria Library on Buckingham Palace Road. Someone's left a clear plastic bag with what looks like a body part in it.'

I heard all the words clearly enough. I'm just not sure I processed them.

'Is DI Tulloch in, do you know?' she asked. Without waiting for an answer, she picked up the phone again. I didn't hear what she said.

Behind me, the door opened and DS Anderson came in.

'What's up?' he said, looking from Mizon to me. Mizon put the phone down and quickly filled him in. He picked up his own phone. Within minutes the room began filling up. Several people looked at me for an explanation. I shook my head.

Tulloch came in and walked straight to the front of the room.

'Everyone shut up,' she called. Normally, when spoken to like that, coppers will react. It was a measure of how tense everyone was feeling that they met Tulloch's order with silence.

'It may be nothing to do with us,' she said. 'Cooper was our killer and he is dead.'

She was right, she had to be.

'We'll go calmly and quietly,' she went on. 'Three cars — mine, Anderson's and Stenning's. The rest of you wait here and be ready to come over if we need you.'

Victoria Library. Oh no. No.

'Lacey.'

I made myself look at her.

'You'd better come with me.'

She left the room first. The men waited for me to follow and then came along behind us. Getting into Tulloch's low-sprung sports car wasn't easy but it didn't seem the moment to complain. We drove out of the station and along Lewisham High Street in silence.

'Body part,' I said, when we turned on to the A2. 'What body part exactly?'

'It's a heart,' she replied, without taking her eyes off the road. 'Among other things. I spoke to Westminster CID before I came downstairs.'

'Mary Kelly's heart was taken,' I said.

'Mary Kelly didn't die until November,' she snapped. 'And mammalian hearts are very similar in structure. I have that on extremely good authority. It could be a pig's heart, a sheep's, anything.'

I didn't reply.

'I've been expecting something like this,' she said. 'I sent emails round the rest of the force. The anniversary of the double event. I knew it would be too much for someone to resist. There are some very sick people out there.'

Once she started talking it seemed Tulloch couldn't stop. Pigs' hearts are readily available from any butcher. It was someone's idea of a joke. Maybe the press wanted to keep the story alive. She kept it up until we got to the library. I didn't say a word. I was too busy praying she was right.

The Victoria Library is beautiful from the

outside: built of cinnamon-coloured bricks, with tall rectangular windows edged with pale stone. Tulloch pulled over at a bus stop, had a quick word with the attending uniform about keeping an eye on her car, then went into the library through the very non-Victorian automatic doors. I followed more slowly. The fast drive over had done my rib-cage no good and besides, something had gone wrong with my legs. They weren't working the way they were supposed to.

Tulloch's opposite number in Westminster CID, a tall, fair-haired man who introduced himself as DI Allan Simmons, was waiting for us inside. He looked at me in surprise (I still bore a strong resemblance to the rear of public transport) and then spoke to Tulloch.

'Left on one of the desks just before one o'clock,' he said. 'Hasn't been touched. There were only three adults in the room when it was spotted. I've got them all detained and we're taking statements. No one's left the library.'

'What about footage?' Tulloch asked as we moved through the entrance hall, strode over police tape and through a doorway marked Lending Library. This was a large, rectangular room with an upper gallery running along three sides of it. A massive, arched skylight let in lots of natural daylight. Simmons was steering us towards the far side of the room, to where an arch was labelled Children's Library. We walked under it.

'Cameras picked up everything,' Simmons said. 'Someone came in here, picked up a book from one of the shelves and then carried it next door. Back we go.'

We followed him back through the Lending Library and into another set of rooms on our left. We passed a space where several people had been working on PCs, then through double doors into another large room. Black railings with a rose motif circled the raised gallery and there was a cast-iron, spiral staircase in one corner. A huge potted palm in a steel bin sat in the centre of the room, and beyond that a police photographer was blocking our line of sight. Then he moved and the three of us stepped closer to the low table.

We were looking at a clear plastic bag, fastened tight at the top end. Its contents were part solid, part gloop, mainly crimson in colour and shining in the strong overhead lights. Tulloch didn't hesitate. She walked straight up and knelt on the carpet so her eyes were on a level with the bag.

It was on top of a book, presumably the

one that had been taken from the children's section. I moved closer, saw the elaborate Celtic typeface and the image of a tall man in silvery white robes on the front cover. I got closer still and could see the title. A classic children's fantasy story I'd read many times. *The Weirdstone of Brisingamen.*

I pulled off my jacket, the room was far too hot, although no one else seemed to have noticed. A swimming pool. A park. A flower market. Now a public library. And Jack the Ripper. Dear God, who was doing this?

DI Simmons walked up behind Tulloch. He handed over a yellow Biro. 'Use this,' he said. Tulloch took the pen and pushed the bag gently. Most of what we could see looked like red mush, but there were stringy bits of tissue and something decidedly more dense. Then she stood up and turned round. Her eyes went above my head.

'Was that camera turned on?' she asked Simmons.

He nodded. 'We need to go down to the admin office to view it. Are you happy for me to get this thing taken away?'

'It needs to go to St Thomas's,' Tulloch replied. 'Dr Mike Kaytes is expecting it.'

Stenning and Anderson arrived as we got back to the main entrance. Tulloch put

Stenning in charge of taking witness statements and then Anderson joined the two of us in the lift. We went down to the basement. Simmons had already seen the footage in question. He stepped back to allow us the best view.

'Shit a brick,' muttered Anderson, as the tape started playing.

Tulloch and I didn't say a word as we watched, from above, the automatic double doors to the library open and Samuel Cooper walk in. Wearing loose jeans, a large black jacket with coloured symbols on it and a tight black cap, he walked into the Lending Library and through to the children's section. He disappeared from view and then reappeared after a few seconds with a book in his hand. Without lifting his eyes from the floor, he walked out of shot.

Simmons fiddled with the tape for a second and then we saw Cooper cross the reading room. He pulled a plastic bag from an inside jacket pocket and put both book and bag on the table. He turned and kept his head down as he left the room. Not once had he let the cameras catch a glimpse of his face.

'We didn't release any details of what Cooper was wearing,' said Tulloch. 'If someone on our team has leaked that, I will . . .' She didn't finish.

'Cooper's our killer, Boss,' said Anderson. 'He had Weston's bag in his room. We found his spunk on her . . .'

What had Cooper said on the bridge, just before he and I fell? *This is a fucking fix.*

'How did you find his room?' I asked. I'd been in hospital when this had all taken place. 'He was pulled naked from the river. How did you know where he lived?'

'Tip-off,' said Anderson. 'Anonymous. Boss, it's a wind-up, it has to be. For one thing, there was no attempt to involve Flint here.'

Oh, you think?

'Mark my words, Boss, there'll be a pig's liver at the Royal Albert Hall and an ox tongue at Madame Tussauds before the day's out.'

I think I could almost have grown fond of DS Anderson.

'Is Madame Tussauds Victorian?' asked Tulloch, in a soft voice.

'In this country, yes. Trust me, I took Abigail there just the other week.'

Tulloch's phone was ringing again. She excused herself and stepped out into the corridor.

'Why is he always wearing the same clothes?' I asked. 'He keeps his head down, so we can't see his face, but wears identifiable clothes. It's like he doesn't want us to be in any doubt we're looking at Sam Cooper.'

'No disrespect, Flint,' snapped Anderson, 'but Cooper's in the fucking morgue at Horseferry Road. Six feet of dead flesh in a fridge.'

'Say that again.'

'Why? What part of fucking morgue at —'

'No. The bit about him being six feet tall,' I said. 'That's what's been bothering me. Cooper was five foot eleven. The man we saw on camera taking Amanda Weston into Victoria Park didn't look as tall as that to me. The bloke DI Joesbury chased out of the park the next day did, but not the one on camera.' I turned from the screen to Anderson. 'I just assumed it was a funny camera angle or that Amanda Weston was wearing very high heels, but it might not have been Cooper who took Amanda Weston into the park that night.'

As Anderson's eyes narrowed, the door opened again and Tulloch stood there.

It might not have been Samuel Cooper who'd killed her.

'I have to get back to Lewisham,' Tulloch said to Anderson. 'Can you go to St Thomas's? Take Flint with you. Let me know as soon as —'

This is a fucking fix.

'No problem, Boss. And don't take any crap. It's a wind-up, I'm telling you.'

Tulloch gave him one of her tiny half-smiles and nodded at me. Then she was gone.

51

'Will they take DI Tulloch off the case?' I asked Anderson, as we pulled into the car park at St Thomas's Hospital and he stopped in a bay reserved for ambulances.

'She should be so fucking lucky,' he replied, opening his door and climbing out. 'They'll keep her on the case till the bitter end. She's the one they'll hang out to dry when it all goes pear-shaped.'

Anderson was walking too quickly as we went into the hospital through the main reception and took the lift one floor down to the mortuary. I kept up as best I could. Last time I'd been here, it had been to view a human uterus; I wondered if Kaytes would complain that we never sent him anything complete to work on.

His young assistant met us and helped us gown up. When we went into the examination room, Kaytes was leaning over a desk completing a form. He put the pen down and turned to face us.

'Never-ending paperwork,' he said. 'Your package arrived ten minutes ago. See to the sound system, will you, Troy?'

Troy crossed to Kaytes's iPod and, smiling to himself, switched it on.

A grey bag lay in the middle of the central worktop. Kaytes pulled on some gloves and unzipped it, just as the music started.

'No DI Tulloch today?' he said, as he extracted the clear plastic bag we'd seen at the library from out of the grey one. 'Right, let's see what we've got.'

Kaytes opened the bag and let its contents pour out on to a large, shallow stainless-steel tray. The soft glooping was one of the most disgusting sounds I'd ever heard and I had to force myself to concentrate on the music for a few seconds. It was an orchestral piece this time, sweeter, more harmonious than the piano sonata I remembered. Kaytes turned round and took up tongs. He began spreading the various pieces of viscera around the tray to get a better look. 'Well, it's fresh, whatever else it is,' he said.

'How can you tell?' asked Anderson.

'Smell it,' invited Kaytes. Anderson and I looked at each other. Neither of us moved any closer to the worktop. 'Yep,' continued the pathologist, 'that's a heart.'

The orchestral music gained in volume as the heart in question was gently moved to one side of the tray. It was a pale-pink piece of muscle, about the size of my fist. Two large, roughly truncated vessels full of clotted blood emerged from the wider, upper part.

'Is it human?' asked Anderson. Without the boss around to be impressed, his bullishness seemed to have diminished.

'Could be,' replied Kaytes. 'It's certainly about the right size, but we'll have to run the tests.'

Kaytes lifted something with the tongs. I took a step back. 'This is, though.' He held it closer to the light. It was almost circular, about the size of half a grapefruit.

'Please tell me that's not what I think it is,' said Anderson.

Kaytes was still looking at the object in the tongs. 'As far as I know,' he said, 'humans are the only animals with recognizable breasts, as opposed to teats, that don't have heavy hair growth around the nipple.'

Anderson turned to me. 'Did he do that? The Ripper? Did he cut off . . .?'

'He did,' I said, feeling something sticky in the back of my throat. 'Mary Kelly's breasts were both cut off. He didn't take them, though. They were left at the scene.'

'Jesus,' repeated Anderson.

'There's something else here,' said Kaytes, pushing more bloodstained tissue out of the way. He lifted it away from the tray. 'This isn't organic,' he said.

Anderson and I both waited while Kaytes crossed to a sink at the side of the room. A piano started to play, its notes light and clear, and yet sounding so incredibly sad. Kaytes had turned on the tap. A second later he came back and put something down on a clean part of the worktop. Anderson and I had no choice but to step closer.

Rinsed of gore, the tiny piece of jewellery was gleaming under the lights. It was silver, a simple, inexpensive necklace. Most of it was chain, and the part intended to sit on a woman's collarbone was made up of nine interlocking letters that formed a girl's name.

Elizabeth.

'We never released the fact that he was naming his victims,' said Anderson, running a hand over his face. 'We kept quiet about his clothes and about that. Fuck a duck, he's still out there, isn't he?'

52

'Our latest victim was found by her husband two hours ago,' Tulloch was saying as I opened the door to the incident room. 'He'd come home from work early to get changed for an evening function. Which I suppose we should be grateful for, because otherwise one of her kids would have found her.'

DS Anderson had been right. He was still out there. We'd arrived back at the station to learn that a fourth body had been reported. Anderson had gone straight to the scene. I'd stayed behind waiting for news.

Now, it was just after seven o'clock and most of the team were back from the house in Hammersmith where the murder had taken place. I spotted a vacant seat and headed for it.

'The police doctor who attended the crime scene believes she was killed some time early this morning,' Tulloch said. 'There were no signs of a forced entry or of a struggle. Apart from the master bedroom, the like of which I hope I never see again in my life, the house was untouched.'

Tulloch pressed a button on a nearby computer and we were looking at a photograph of the crime scene. A woman with short, dark hair was lying on a large bed. Her feet were on the pillow, her head at the foot of the bed. As far as the rest of her was concerned, I couldn't have said anything for certain.

The door opened and Joesbury came in. He'd taken off the sling since I'd last seen him.

'We think the killer made her lie, faceup, on the bed,' said Tulloch. 'Possibly, like our friend Cooper, he uses a gun, real or replica. He approached from behind, took hold of her by the hair and pulled her head back. He cut her throat from left to right, indicating he's probably right-handed. We'll have to wait for the post-mortem to be sure, but it looks as though he made several cuts.'

The room in the photograph looked like someone had taken a spray can to it.

'Most of the blood appears to have come from her severed throat,' continued Tulloch. 'Which suggests he waited for her to die before beginning the mutilation. No obvious sign of rape or torture this time.'

'Different killer,' Stenning suggested, sounding more hopeful than certain.

'Possibly,' agreed Tulloch. 'She had an easier death than Amanda Weston. On the other hand, the extent of the post-mortem mutilation is the worst we've seen so far. Large areas of skin were removed from the abdomen and legs, most of her internal organs were cut out and left lying around the bed. Her ribcage was smashed with something like a hammer and then forced open. Her heart was taken out and both breasts were severed. One was found at the scene. The other made its way to the children's room at Victoria Library.'

Low murmurs around the room.

'Sorry, Dana, I didn't catch her name,' said Joesbury, who was rubbing his left arm as though it was still bothering him.

I hadn't heard it either. I'd spent the afternoon in a different room to most of the team.

'Benn,' said Tulloch, glancing down at her notes. 'Charlotte Benn. Married to Nick, a criminal barrister.'

Tulloch's voice started to fade. 'Two sons,' I thought I heard her say next. 'Felix, aged twenty-six, and Harry, aged twenty-two. Madeleine, her daughter, is seventeen and still at . . . Lacey, what the . . . ? Christ, someone catch her.'

There was a sudden rush of movement around me. Someone — Stenning, I think — was holding me upright. I heard the sound of a chair being dragged and felt myself being lowered into it. The black cloud in my head started to thin out.

I was on the other side of the room from where I'd been sitting, close to the door, without any recollection of getting up and crossing the office. Mizon was in front of me, holding out a plastic cup of water. Automatically, I took it. Tulloch had crouched down beside Mizon. I kept my eyes firmly on the floor.

'I'll get someone to take you home,' Tulloch said. 'You are back on sick leave until I say otherwise.'

'No,' I said, louder than I'd intended. I took a deep breath and lowered my voice. 'I'm fine. Just give me a minute, please. I'll find a quiet room.'

Tulloch opened her mouth to argue, then looked at her watch. She didn't have time to nursemaid me. 'Go and sit next door,' she said. 'Pete, go with her.'

I found I could stand up. I fixed my eyes on the door and made it that far. Stenning was at my side.

'Now, it shouldn't surprise anyone too

much to hear that Charlotte Benn's children went to St Joseph's School in Chiswick.' Most heads had turned to face Tulloch again. Not Joesbury though. He was still watching me.

'There is a connection between these families,' Tulloch went on. 'Something that goes beyond children at the same school. We have to find out what that is. I've asked Gayle to take the lead on that.'

The door closed behind us and Stenning and I walked the few metres along the corridor to the next office.

'What can I get you?' he asked me, once I was sitting at my own desk.

I shook my head and gestured to the door. 'Nothing, I'm fine. You need to get back in there.'

Stenning didn't argue. 'Sure?' he said, but he was already turning to leave.

'Pete.' I stopped him just before the door closed. 'The second victim, Amanda Weston — she used to live in London, didn't she?'

Stenning gave a quick, impatient nod. 'When she was married to her first husband,' he replied. 'Sure you're OK?'

I forced a smile. 'Fine,' I said. 'Go on, you can fill me in later.'

I gave Stenning a few seconds to get back to the incident room before running my hands over my face, telling myself firmly I had to focus, and then switching on my desktop computer.

HOLMES — or Home Office Large Major Enquiry System — records and tracks the progress of all serious inquiries carried out by the UK police. Whilst I was still in uniform, my knack of finding and processing information had been spotted and I'd been sent on a four-week inputter course. I knew the system very well, but after coming back on light duties, I'd been inputting the endless detail that tying up a major investigation demanded. There was a lot on here I just hadn't got round to reading.

The first file I opened up was that of the Jones family. Geraldine Jones, the first victim, had been married to David, a fund manager in Leadenhall Street. He was believed to earn in the region of half a million a year, including bonuses, and they'd lived in a very nice house on the river in Chiswick. They had two sons, Jacob, who was twenty-six and a junior doctor, and Joshua, who was at university.

Jones. Such a common name.

With unusual efficiency, someone had started a file for the latest victim and her family. Charlotte Benn had been forty-nine and hadn't worked since her eldest child was born. She and Nick had two sons, Felix, aged twenty-six, and Harry, aged twenty-two. Their daughter, Madeleine, was seventeen and still at St Joseph's.

Knowing I couldn't avoid it, I opened up the file on the Westons. As Stenning had just told me, Amanda Weston, whom Joesbury and I had found in the Victoria Park boat shed, had been married before. Daryl was her second husband and she'd moved out to Hampshire when they married. Previously, she and her children had lived in London, not too far from the Jones family. Her children, Daniel, now aged twenty-five, and her daughter, Abigail, aged sixteen, had gone to St Joseph's School in Chiswick. Their name, in those days, had been Briggs.

Geraldine Jones. Amanda Briggs. Charlotte Benn.

Next door, in the incident room, the focus of the investigation would have switched to the connection between the three families. Tulloch would be ordering a trace on the money situation in each family on the off-chance the husbands had got involved in some dodgy investment and tried to pull out, resulting in the wives being killed as a warning or punishment. That would be a complete waste of effort.

Any time now, almost certainly within the

next twenty-four hours, the families themselves would realize what was going on. They would tell Tulloch and her team exactly why the three women had been killed. They would tell her who was next on the list, who victims four and five were intended to be. It would become blindingly obvious who had killed Geraldine Jones, Amanda Weston and Charlotte Benn. My colleagues would know that Joesbury had been right all along.

They would know that the killer was me.

53

I left the station twenty minutes later. No one saw me go. Before slipping out, I'd done everything I could think of, which hadn't been much. I'd also left a note saying I wasn't feeling great and would take the following day off. It would buy me a bit of time.

On top of my wardrobe at home is a bag I keep packed with things I'll need if I have to leave in a hurry. The few important papers I have are in there, and so is some money. I keep a safety deposit box at a private-security company. I change companies every year but the contents stay the same. Cash. Enough to be able to disappear very quickly.

I changed into jeans, a warm sweatshirt and trainers before grabbing a jacket. I hadn't eaten for a while but didn't want to spare the time. I would get something on the way.

I switched off the lights and left the flat. It was starting to rain and, judging from the cloud cover, it was going to continue for some time. I considered taking my bike, but only for a second. It would make me a lot harder to trace, but I just wouldn't be able to move fast enough. I planned to be in Portsmouth in a couple of hours, ditch the car and become a foot passenger on the next available ferry to France. Once on the continent, I'd take a fast train south. In a couple of days, there'd be no trace of me left. Lacey Flint would cease to exist.

As I locked the door, I could feel tears stinging behind my eyes. I'd always known that one day it would come to this; that I would take off, leaving everything behind. I just hadn't considered how much it would hurt.

I climbed the steps on legs that felt too heavy and beeped open my car.

'Going somewhere, Flint?'

I should have known it couldn't be that easy.

I turned round slowly. My nemesis had parked illegally on double yellows. He was pulling a jacket round his shoulders as his eyes went from my face to the rucksack slung over my left shoulder.

Hold it together, girl.

'Local leisure centre,' I said, stretching the corners of my mouth into what, under the dim light of a streetlamp, might pass for a smile. 'Every part of me aches and I plan to spend the next hour in the steam room. Want to come?'

Joesbury didn't look convinced. 'Tempting,' he said. 'But I already made plans.'

'Have fun,' I replied, turning back to my car, flicking my eyes across the road and back again. No one else in sight. He and I seemed to be alone in the street. 'And by the way,' I went on, 'if keeping an eye on me like this is supposed to be a covert operation, you suck at it.'

I reached for the door of my car, hardly knowing what I was going to do once I got inside. Joesbury was no fool. If he was allowing himself to be seen, he wasn't alone. There would be someone else, just out of sight. I was trapped. I looked up the street again. Still just the two of us. There was a Swiss army knife in my bag. It might not kill him, but it would slow him down, give me chance to get away.

Then I felt a hand on my shoulder and almost screamed out loud I was so pent up.

'Actually, my plans include you,' he said. 'I'm under orders to make sure you're OK.'

Tiny drops of rainwater had collected on his eyebrows. I watched one fall on to his lashes and shimmer there for a moment before he blinked it away. 'I'm OK,' I said. 'Thank you. But space would be good right now. And I really do feel like shit.'

'I'll give you a neck rub,' he said, taking the keys from my hand and locking the car again. 'Come on.' He was guiding me towards his own car, holding the passenger door open. I climbed in, telling myself I could not panic. If Joesbury got suspicious and wanted to see what was inside my bag, it was all over.

So I'd go later. I'd take the bike, after all, ride through the night. Or catch a bus or a train to Portsmouth in the morning. I could still do it. I just had to stay calm.

The inside of the car smelled of damp hair and clothes. At the junction with the Wandsworth Road, Joesbury switched on the car stereo and I braced myself for the usual rush of rhythmic club sound. Instead, a soft male voice started singing about flying.

'This is Westlife,' I said, after a few seconds.

Joesbury didn't look at me, but the crease at the corner of his mouth deepened. 'Borrowed it from Dana,' he said.

In spite of everything, I almost laughed.

'What did I miss back at HQ?' I asked, as we headed east, close to the South Bank.

'The headmaster of St Joseph's was at the station when I left,' Joesbury told me. 'Chap called Edward Seaton. Cooperative enough. He and Gayle have been using the school's telephone tree. That's a sort of list —'

'I know what a telephone tree is,' I said. 'You ring the name at the top of the list, she rings the next one and so on.'

'Right,' said Joesbury. 'They're going back ten years, contacting every family who sent kids to the school, first checking the mothers are still OK and then warning them to be extra careful in the next few days.'

'Isn't that going to cause a panic?' I asked, realizing Joesbury was driving faster than was strictly legal and had twice looked at his watch.

'Yeah, I suggested that myself,' Joesbury said as we approached some lights. He picked up speed and then braked hard when they changed. I lurched forward against the seat belt and my bruised ribs didn't enjoy the experience.

'And?' I said.

'And Tully drew herself up to her full five feet four inches, pressed her screech button and demanded to know if she was the only person in the room who understood the meaning of the phrase "double event". At which point I decided I was taking the night off.'

You had to admire the man's nerve. 'She was OK with that?'

Joesbury turned quickly and grinned at me. 'She knows I'm crap at admin, which is basically all they can do for now,' he said. 'And they're calling a meeting. Tomorrow morning at the school, for all past and present mothers.'

'What do you imagine the press will make of that?' I asked after a second.

'She's inviting them as well,' said Joesbury. 'It's looking like the school is the key to whatever's going on. She wants every woman connected with it on full alert.'

I thought about it for a moment. It was a good idea. It would also mean that some time tomorrow morning, the game would definitely be up. I had no choice but to leave tonight. Just one big problem in my way. The one in the driver's seat.

My rucksack was on my lap. Relying on the music to drown any sound, I unzipped the front pocket and found my knife. Then I slipped my hand into my coat pocket. As I was doing that, my big problem turned into a short, no-through road and pulled over. He switched off the engine and, with an exaggerated look of relief, the stereo system. 'I want double brownie points for that,' he said. 'I brought you a coat.'

He was out of the car before I had time to ask where we were, and why I would need another coat. Knowing I didn't have much choice but to play along, I tucked my bag under the seat and climbed out too.

We were in Southwark, not far from where I'd worked up until a few weeks ago, and practically on the riverbank. Directly across from us were the lights and buildings of the city. Joesbury handed over a large oilskin coat, pulled a baseball cap on to his own head and set off towards the water. I raised the coat hood and followed, very slowly.

The river was metres away, the safety barrier nothing but two iron bars held by vertical struts, and Joesbury was waiting for me at the top of some narrow stone steps that I had a bad feeling led to the beach below. As I drew close, he pulled a torch out of his coat pocket and set off down them. On the fourth step, his left foot slipped sideways.

'You need to watch it,' he called over his shoulder. 'They're skanky. Hold on to the rope.'

A weed-encrusted rope had been nailed into the embankment wall. It looked just like the one I'd clung to on the night Sam

Cooper had drowned. The night I almost had. I didn't want to touch it. And I certainly wasn't going down to that beach.

I still hadn't looked at the river, but I could hear it, had heard it the moment I got out of the car, even above the rain. The soft play of water against wooden pier struts, the insistent, rushing hum that always seems to hover around moving water.

'I'll wait in the car,' I called, but the wind had picked up and I wasn't sure he'd heard.

'That would defeat the object.' He'd turned on the last step and was looking back up at me.

'I'm not comfortable near the river,' I said. I still hadn't looked at it but I had a sense of it creeping closer. The tide was about to turn. If you spend enough time near a tidal watercourse like the Thames, you learn to hear the particular dip in sound it makes at low water. The whisper that says, *I'm coming back.* Jesus, I was getting in the car now.

'I know that,' said Joesbury, who'd taken a step back up. 'Who would be? But you can't work for the Met and be potamophobic. Come on.'

He climbed another couple of steps and grabbed my hand. Then he was pulling me down. This was the moment. The knife was in my pocket. Straight into his stomach and pull hard upwards. He'd fall to the beach and within a couple of hours the river would take him.

'Potoma-what?' I said, as I stepped on to the crunching, litter-strewn surface of the beach. I could feel my trainers sinking into what I hoped was damp sand but had a feeling probably wasn't.

'Fear of rivers,' said Joesbury, who was dragging me towards some dark shapes a few metres away. Directly ahead and soaring above us were the protruding, futuristic spikes of the Millennium Bridge. It glowed like beaten silver in the darkness. Down on the beach we'd moved out of the reach of the streetlamp and had just the thin, moonbeam trail of Joesbury's torch to light the way. 'Looked it up an hour ago,' he went on.

The dark shapes ahead had taken the form of a low pier. It looked wet, half-rotten and far from stable, and there was no way on this earth I was stepping on to it. Joesbury leaped up and I tugged my hand free. He turned back to face me.

'My grandfather worked for the Marine Unit,' he said. 'Back in the early fifties when health and safety wasn't anything like what it is now. Officers got dunked on a regular basis.'

I folded my arms. Wherever this was going, I wasn't interested.

'They had to be pretty good swimmers,' Joesbury went on, 'but even so, when they were pulled out, nearly all of them got a serious case of the potamowhatsits. So they took 'em out again, in a small, low-slung boat, just as soon as they could. Sort of like putting someone back on a horse after they've fallen off.'

So this was about doing me a favour? 'I appreciate the thought,' I said. 'But I'd rather do it some other time.'

'That's what they all say,' said Joesbury, with what I was beginning to think of as his nasty smile.

'Please can we go back to the car?' I tried one last time.

Joesbury inclined his head at me. 'Do I strike you as someone who gives up easily?'

Just get it over with. I kept close to him as we set off along the pier. Across the water, the ghostly dome of St Paul's soared above the surrounding buildings.

'This pier disappears completely when the tide's up,' said Joesbury, as I realized we were walking over water. 'The Marine Unit use it for accessing the South Bank at low tide.'

I didn't reply. I couldn't decide whether it

was better to focus on the lights of the opposite bank and have the glimmer of the river at the edge of my vision, or keep them firmly on my feet and see the swirl of the scum through the slats of the pier. Frankly, eyes tight shut and clinging to Joesbury felt like the best idea, but I rather doubted I'd get away with it.

We'd got to within two metres of the pier's end when Joesbury stopped. The tide was coming in fast by this stage and the wind blowing up the length of the river was helping it along. Every tiny wave seemed to creep a little closer to our feet. Joesbury put his hands on my shoulders and moved me to his left side, effectively screening me from most of the wind. A gallant enough gesture, I suppose, but I really didn't like the way the pier rocked.

'I've suggested to Dana that you interview the children tomorrow,' he said.

As clouds crossed the sky the river shimmered from black to purple, and bright circles of ruby-red light danced across it. I glanced up. The ruby lights were being reflected from a crane just by St Paul's.

'What?' I said, as his last words sunk in.

He was looking downstream towards Southwark Bridge. 'You're the youngest on the team,' he said. 'You'll be the least threatening.'

'Actually I wasn't planning to go in tomorrow,' I said. 'I left DI Tulloch a note.'

Joesbury glanced back at me, then down at his feet. 'Yeah, it's in my pocket,' he said. 'She hasn't seen it yet.'

I stared at him until he made eye contact again. Only for a second though. Then his eyes were back on Southwark Bridge.

'This is no time to get an attack of the vapours, Flint,' he said. 'You're needed on the team.'

He was lying. Knowing that our killer was still at large, all his old suspicions about me had come back. He'd found my note, guessed I was planning to run and was deliberately getting in the way. All this talk of getting me back in the saddle had been so much crap. He'd be watching me non-stop from now on.

I turned from him to the beach. It was covered with rocks of various sizes. All I had to do was distract him, pick one up, hold it high and then bring it down very fast. In his car, I could be in Portsmouth before midnight.

'Here comes our lift,' he said.

54

A police motor launch was heading towards us, the waves from its bow already sweeping over the low pier. It drew up alongside us and a middle-aged, uniformed sergeant threw a rope.

'Tide's fast,' he muttered to Joesbury, who'd wrapped the rope around a rusty iron cleat. The sergeant held out a large, wrinkled hand to me. 'Up you come, love.'

I'd run out of arguments. I gave the officer my hand, looked into eyes that seemed familiar and got pulled aboard. As well as the sergeant, there were two other officers on the boat, both in a sort of raised cockpit. The boat went into reverse and, at the last moment, Joesbury slipped the line off the cleat, reached for the boat rail and swung himself on board as though he'd been doing it all his life.

We were off, heading for the centre of the river, the engine loud and the rain battling spray to see which could wet us the most. A stray wave came bouncing over the bow and its tail end caught me full in the face. I could taste salt and something bitter and oily.

'DC Flint, I'd like you to meet Sergeant Wilson of the Marine Policing Unit,' said Joesbury. 'Uncle Fred, this is Lacey.'

The officer who'd helped us on board nodded to me, threw a lifejacket to Joesbury and helped me pass one over my head and adjust the waist strap. Then he gestured for us to go inside the small, windowed cabin at the front of the boat.

'Mark tells me you need to get your river legs back,' he said to me, when he'd closed the door and the noise of the engine had faded a little.

'Not sure I had any in the first place,' I replied. The cabin was surprisingly plush, with padded seats, an instrument panel and a small kitchen area. It had a faint smell of plastic and diesel fuel.

The two men exchanged a glance, then Sergeant Wilson took a long look at my face. 'From what I hear, you were about as lucky as they get,' he said. 'Well, should be a nice quiet trip,' he went on. 'We're due to go down as far as the barrier, one or two stops on the way, should have you both back by ten. Are you OK if I get back to the flybridge?'

Wilson left the cabin and we heard him walk along the deck and climb the steps to join the other two above us in the cockpit.

'Come on,' said Joesbury, steering me forwards and using the sleeve of his jacket to wipe the condensation from the window, 'you can't beat the river at night.' He glanced down, saw the look on my face. 'Course, it does help to be on it rather than in it,' he admitted.

We were almost at Southwark Bridge. I hadn't seen it from the river before and had to admit — but only to myself — that Joesbury had a point. Hidden lights had turned the stone arches of the bridge turquoise, whilst the surrounding buildings, both old and new, glowed in warm shades of gold and honey. Behind the bridge, its lights gleaming like diamonds, rose the City of London.

'Unce Fred?' I queried.

'Mum's younger brother,' said Joesbury. 'Followed his father into the Marine Unit shortly after he joined the Met. Where do you stand on the Lloyd's building, love it or hate it?'

Across the rooftops, an elongated, futuristic construction of steel and glass was radiating violet light into the sky. I'd seen few buildings more compelling. 'Hate it,' I lied.

'My grandfather was still in the force when I was a kid,' said Joesbury. 'He used to take me and my brother out on patrol with him at weekends.'

The lights of the river were both reflected in the rainfall and distorted by the cabin's windows. Deep azure blue shimmered around the top of the Nat West Tower and droplets of the same colour seemed to fall all around us. Along the embankment, lantern lights glowed like a chain of fire. I had a sense, for a moment, of being in an enchanted craft.

'He liked to tell us stories about the river,' Joesbury was saying. 'Knew it better than anyone. When he retired he got a job as a guide on one of the pleasure boats.'

As Tower Bridge loomed ahead of us like a cold, grey fortress, I had a sudden picture in my mind of two little boys playing policemen on a river launch, and it occurred to me that twenty-four hours ago, it might have been quite nice to be spending time alone with Joesbury, hearing him talk about his family. A lot can change in twenty-four hours.

'Look to your left,' said Joesbury.

'Wapping,' I said, 'Where Uncle Fred and his colleagues are based.' Wapping police station was also where Samuel Cooper's body had been taken after it had been lifted from the river. Where mine would have been.

'Yeah,' said Joesbury. 'Also, the site of Execution Dock, where they used to hang murderers and pirates and other assorted villains. Pirates were hanged on short ropes so they suffocated slowly and then three tides had to wash over them before they pulled the bodies down. I tell you, police work's not what it used to be.'

The river had changed. Beyond Tower Bridge it becomes commercial, the buildings, black as soot against the skyline, are functional rather than beautiful. As we travelled on, all the colour in the world seemed to be seeping away.

'That's a very sweet story,' I said.

Joesbury gave a short laugh. 'They had something called dirty money back in Grandad's day.'

The embankment lights we were passing now were stronger and colder than the touristy ones we'd left behind. They cut through the dark water like needles. 'You're going to tell me what that is, whether I want to hear it or not, aren't you?' I said.

'It was the bit of extra pay the river men would get for retrieving a body from the water,' said Joesbury. 'Made quite a difference to pay packets back then, so finding a floater was always a bit of an event.'

Not much more than a week ago, I'd come very close to being a floater. Was this about punishing me, as well as keeping me from running?

'As you can imagine, it all got a bit competitive,' Joesbury went on. 'And there was the added complication that if they found a body towards the end of the shift, they might not have time to get it all the way downriver to Wapping.'

'I'm not going to ask,' I said.

I didn't need to. Joesbury was on a roll. 'So rather than let the next shift get the extra cash, they'd hide it somewhere. Tie it up out of sight and then collect it next day.'

By this time, it felt like the boat was travelling through a black and white film. On the south bank, the lights were a cold white, their reach hardly penetrating the gloom around them, their reflections just teardrops on the black river.

'I have heard few stories more gross than that,' I said.

'I think it just goes to prove that, given time, you'll get used to anything. How are you feeling?'

'Fine,' I said automatically and, a second later, realized I was. I was absolutely fine. I still had a pressing need to get off the boat and head for the English Channel, but otherwise, being on the river hadn't been nearly as bad as I'd expected.

Joesbury stepped away and faced me. 'You look fine to me,' he said, with a half-smile. 'It takes a lot to throw you off kilter, doesn't it?'

'Yep,' I said, turning back to the river, thinking the events of the past few hours might just qualify. 'You could say that.'

Without warning, the engine fired up and the boat surged forward. Joesbury and I both staggered backwards before getting our balance. We looked at each other and he told me to stay put. Before he could reach the door, Uncle Fred poked his head inside.

'We've just had a call about a small craft heading for the Royal Docks,' he said. 'Bloody suicide in these conditions. We're picking up speed to try and find them. Now do I need to tell you two to stay in here and keep out of the way?'

'No, sir,' said Joesbury. I shook my head.

We were skimming along the water now, the searchlights on the front of the boat turned up to maximum, and I caught sight of Greenwich on the south bank. Joesbury moved behind me and opened one of the cupboards that ran along the back of the cabin. He took two coiled yellow straps from inside. Both had metal clips at either end. Lifelines.

'I was a real pain in the arse as a kid,' he said, unwrapping one and clipping the end of it to my lifejacket. 'Never did what I was told.' He passed the line over my head and then fastened the second clip to the first at my waist. He did the same on his own jacket and then reached for a pair of binoculars from the cabin wall.

'Feel free to stay in here,' he said, opening the door that led to the port deck. 'In fact, I'm giving you a direct order to do exactly that.'

'I was a pain in the arse as a kid too,' I said, following him to the door.

'Why am I not surprised,' he replied. 'As soon as we're outside, find something solid and clip yourself to it.'

Leaving the warm, if diesel-rich air of the cabin was like getting out of a hot bath. Once on deck, the wind hit us full on. The rain had picked up in the short time we'd been on the river and was bouncing off the water like bullets. We were speeding against the tide and the double effect of tide and wind was creating angry waves all around us.

'Who'd take a small boat out on a night like this?' I shouted into Joesbury's ear.

He had binoculars clamped to his eyes and was looking downstream. 'Nobody up to any good,' he said. 'Smugglers of some sort, possibly. Although my guess would be illegal immigrants. Are you clipped on?'

'To the rail,' I said, glancing down to make sure. 'Immigrants? Coming up the Thames?'

'It's not uncommon,' he told me. 'Container ships bring them across the North Sea. They get off a mile or so downriver, usually at Tilbury, and then head up in smaller crafts. Fred's right though, it is bloody suicidal.'

'We'll be lucky to even see them in this weather,' I said.

'There they are,' said Joesbury, reaching out and taking hold of my shoulder. 'Ten o'clock. About two hundred metres away.'

He passed over the binoculars and guided them in the right direction. After a second or so, I could just about make out a medium-sized inflatable dinghy with a small outboard engine and no lights. Three people on board.

'This is the Marine Policing Unit, switch off your engine and remain exactly where you are!' Sergeant Wilson called out over the loudspeaker, making me jump. I handed the binoculars back to Joesbury. I didn't have a good feeling about this and I really didn't want to watch someone else go in the water. When Cooper and I had fallen in, the weather had been fine and the surface of the river smooth. In these conditions, it would be close to hopeless.

'Shit,' muttered Joesbury.

'What's happening?' I asked.

'They're making a run for it,' he replied.

The launch veered round in the direction of the north bank. We were flying across the water now. The small craft couldn't hope to match the speed we were travelling at. Above my head I could hear someone on the radio. They'd be requesting back-up on the bank. Even if the dinghy made it the fifty metres or so to the side, there'd be police waiting for them. They were stupid to try to escape. But desperate people do stupid things, desperate people panic. I knew that better than anyone.

The launch veered round again and I half fell against Joesbury. 'If I tell you to go back inside and get your head down, I expect you to do it,' he said. 'These twats could be armed.'

We were getting much closer now and our

boat cut its speed. Joesbury lowered his binoculars and replaced them in the cabin just as our searchlight picked out the dinghy. Its occupants stared at us like startled wildlife.

We were less than forty metres away. Joesbury had positioned himself directly in front of me and I had to look round his shoulder. Two of the dinghy's occupants were men. The other looked smaller and I could see hair blowing around a pale face.

The dinghy swerved to the left and I thought I heard someone crying out. Thirty metres away. When our searchlight found it again, I could see white hands clutching the rope that ran around the rim of the boat.

The dinghy swung round again as Fred repeated his warning. This time the small boat went head-on into a large wave. It seemed to hover on top of it for a second then went racing down the other side, just as a second line of wash hit it. When I saw it again, it looked lower in the water.

The sound of a second large engine told me another boat was heading towards us. Taking my eyes off the dinghy for a second, I spotted the flashing lights of another police launch just a short distance away. It cut its engines about thirty metres downstream of the dinghy. We were just upstream.

Surely now they'd give up?

The people in the dinghy weren't wearing lifejackets, I could see all three of them quite clearly now. They all looked soaked to the skin. The men had dark hair and heavy brows. The girl didn't look much more than eighteen.

Then one of the men in the dinghy stood and raised his hands above his head, just as wash from both motor launches hit the small boat head on. It rocked one way, then the other, before tipping completely. Immediately, our boat went into reverse, backing away, positioning itself to be able to spot people in the water.

'See anything?' Joesbury yelled to me as the searchlights and powerful handheld torches from both police boats swept across the water.

I couldn't. It was too dark, the water too choppy. Then the dinghy appeared, upside-down in the water, two large hands clinging to the rope that ran around its rim. The other police launch surged forward.

'There's another one,' said Joesbury, just as our searchlight picked out the second of the two men in the water, swimming towards the bank. For a few seconds he made progress and then the tide took hold of him and he began to drift upstream and back towards the centre of the river. We gave chase.

It took just a few seconds to catch up with him, but by the time we did, he was visibly tiring. I glanced back to see that the other police boat had reached the upturned dinghy. The other man was probably safe.

On our boat, Fred and one of his constables were on the starboard deck trying to reach the swimmer. Joesbury unclipped his line and moved round the front of the boat to join them, leaving me alone on the port side. I could hear Fred and his colleague calling to the man in the water, telling him to catch hold of their hands. I turned back and began scanning the river again. There was no sign of the girl and it really wasn't looking good for her.

Then I saw a white hand, not fifteen metres from the boat, moving quickly towards us. The tide had got her, would be taking her upstream, in just a second she'd be past us.

'She's here!' I yelled. Her head surfaced and went down again. 'I can see her!'

On the other side of the boat, I could hear cursing. Joesbury's voice. Then more shouted instructions. The boat went into reverse and then moved sideways, further from the girl.

'Sir! Sergeant Wilson! I can see her!'

Up in the cockpit, the driver seemed to glance at me, but keeping close enough to the man in the water needed his full attention.

The girl appeared again. She was trying to swim but she'd be tiring already. She'd have been cold and wet even before she went in. By now, her core organs would be drawing blood away from her arms and legs, making it harder for her to keep moving; she'd be dangerously close to giving up.

There was nothing I could do but keep her in sight. And hope she stayed on the surface for a minute or two longer. She went under again. Her small hand seemed to clutch at the air before it disappeared.

She was small and thin. She probably hadn't eaten for a while. She'd be weak. And panic would make her too quick to suck in air. Even when her head was below the surface. One big gulp of river water and she'd go down.

There was nothing I could do. Even if I could bring myself to go into the river again, I'd never reach her and get her back to the boat.

Right next to where I'd been standing was a coiled metal wire, probably used for towing other craft or hauling heavy objects out of the water. On the loose end was a large steel clip. Without any real idea of what I was planning, I unclipped my lifeline from the boat rail and fastened it to the wire. Then I tugged the wire quickly so that around three metres of it was free. The rest should unravel.

Still with no plan whatsoever, I swung first one leg, then the other over the rail. A thin wooden ledge ran around the hull of the boat. Just wide enough for me to stand on.

The girl was level with me. I looked into eyes that seemed black as the water. I'd like to say I dived. To be honest, I think the boat swerved and I fell.

Got you, whispered the water rushing past my ears. For a split second I felt panic reaching up for me, like a huge, barnacle-encrusted hand from the river-bed. Then I was on the surface again.

Don't think about the river, think about the girl. Where is she?

I'd fallen in ahead of her, she should have hit me full on by now. No sign. A small cry behind me. I kicked myself round. There she was, being carried by the tide, already in front of the boat. I probably had seconds before the wire anchoring me to the boat would reach its full length. I took a deep breath and started swimming.

Cracked ribs and swimming? Before I'd taken four strokes I knew I'd never keep it up for long, but I'm a good, strong swimmer and, when I want to be, I'm fast. Four more strokes, she was almost close enough to touch. Two more. Her hand grasped my arm and slipped away. One last, huge effort and she was clinging to me and, tiny though she was, her weight was pulling me down. Both hands were on my head, as though she was trying to push me under. My lifejacket had inflated seconds after I'd hit the water but I wasn't sure it was enough to keep us both afloat. Not with the almost demonical strength that people have when they're fighting for their lives.

I was going to have to do the same thing myself.

For long seconds the girl and I struggled in the river. Several times I went under. Each time I managed to kick up to the surface again, but I could feel myself getting weaker and colder. She, though, still had the strength to yell. She was making terrified, animal-like cries that rang in my ears every time my head broke the surface.

'Lacey!'

A different sound, directly above me. I blinked away river water and realized I was a metre away from a dull, white hull striped with blue. We were at the boat. They'd tugged us back in using the wire. The girl had seen the boat too and her panic had shifted its focus to the men above her. I felt her foot kick hard against me and then she was lifted up and pulled over the side. She disappeared.

'Give me your hand, Lacey.' I looked up to see Sergeant Wilson reaching down towards me and somehow managed to lift first one hand, then the other. A second later, I was dangling above the water and, no time after that, was back in the cabin wrapped in a silver, heat-retentive blanket. I was shaking like a jelly on a washing machine — and the inside of my mouth felt like I'd swallowed neat engine oil.

The two immigrants were across the cabin on another bench. Neither gave any reaction to being handcuffed and cautioned. When it was over, the three of us resembled nothing more than oven-ready turkeys and I felt a ludicrous urge to laugh. The door to the cabin opened and Joesbury came in. He ignored the others, looked only at me. I discovered I could smile.

'Now can we go to the steam room?' I said.

55

'What's the worst thing that could happen to you, Karen?'

This, thinks Karen Curtis, her eyes tightly closed. This is the worst thing that could happen to me.

'Most people answer that question the same way, had you noticed,' says the voice that's tickling her neck. 'Most people say the worst thing would be to lose someone they love. Would you agree?'

Karen doesn't reply. As a child, terrified of the dark, she'd keep her head beneath the bedclothes and her eyes tightly closed, as though what she couldn't see couldn't hurt her. She's doing the same thing now. Keeping her eyes closed.

'Would you agree?' The voice has hardened now, grown a little impatient.

'Yes,' Karen manages, although what she really thinks is that the worst thing that could happen to her right now is for the sharp object at her throat to be pressed closer.

'You know, it's only polite to look at someone when they're talking to you,' says the voice. 'I'd feel a lot better if I knew I had your full attention.'

Karen forces her eyes open. She sees the face above hers, the glossy black hair and pale skin and almost closes them again. Instead, she fixes her gaze on a spot of damp on the ceiling. She needs to get that looked at. If she focuses on the damp, on what she's going to have to do to get it sorted out, nothing can happen to her. Nothing bad can happen to a woman who's planning home repairs.

'Who do you love most, Karen?' she is being asked. The damp might be coming in through the loft. Probably a loose tile on the roof. She'll have to organize someone to go up there.

'I asked you a question, Karen.'

'My son,' Karen says, and in speaking feels her throat rise up a little closer to the knife. The ceiling may have to be re-plastered. It will be expensive.

'Oh yes, Thomas. And does he love you? Would it be the worst thing to happen to him, if he lost you?'

Probably not, is the honest response. Karen barely sees Thomas any more. She doubts he gives his mother much thought from one day to the next. The tip of the knife is pressed into her and she can feel her skin break around it.

'I suppose so,' she says, as hair brushes against her face. Her captor is leaning closer, getting ready to whisper in her ear again.

'I lost someone I loved,' says the voice. 'Did you know that?'

'How could I know?' Karen whimpers. 'I have no idea who you are.'

Karen hears a deep breath being sucked in and then slowly trickling out again. 'I loved only one person my whole life and I lost her,' says the voice. 'Do you like the zoo, Karen?'

This is insane. She is at the mercy of someone who is completely insane.

'I like the zoo,' the voice says, as music begins to play softly, a tune so incongruous that Karen thinks, for a moment, it must be coming from outside. 'I'm going very soon,' the voice continues. 'And I think I might just be taking someone — or should I say, something — with me.'

Karen Curtis had never thought she would die to the sound of Julie Andrews.

56

We didn't make it to the steam room. We took the three immigrants back to Wapping police station, from where, over the next couple of days, they'd get a crash course in the English legal system. I showered, changed into yet another orange boiler suit, drank several mugs of scalding hot tea and gave a statement. I also got a thorough ticking-off from Uncle Fred on the subject of stupid and irresponsible behaviour that put the lives of his officers at risk and was completely unacceptable on any boat he was master of. I told him he was absolutely right, I hadn't been thinking and I was terribly sorry. By the time he finished, I'd decided I rather liked Uncle Fred.

While all this was happening, Joesbury retrieved his car from Southwark and, when the Marine Unit were done with me, he was waiting to take me home. He still hadn't spoken to me and I had no idea what was going through his head. We drove in silence and it was after midnight when we arrived.

'Can I tell Dana to expect you tomorrow?' he asked, when he pulled over outside my flat. He hadn't switched off the engine.

'Of course,' I said, looking him directly in the eyes. I picked up my bag, realizing then that Joesbury had been alone with it for a couple of hours while I'd been in Wapping station. He might know exactly what was inside. As I turned away from him I caught sight of the clock on the dashboard. The early trains to Portsmouth would start in just over three hours.

I said goodnight and heard him drive away as I was going down the steps. Inside the flat I turned the electric heater up to maximum and thought about running a bath. I decided against it. My body was perfectly warm. The cold was in my head. Besides, a bath would make me sluggish, even sleepy, and I needed to stay awake.

I'd already planned my escape route. I knew I couldn't leave by the front door, there would be somebody in the street watching me. From the conservatory, though, I could sidle along the back of the house, turn the corner and creep very close to the alley wall. Joesbury's cameras wouldn't spot me. I could climb the wall, cross the park and make my way to the main road. The Tubes had long since stopped but Waterloo Station wasn't too far away. I could walk. The trick would be in the timing. Go too soon, and I'd run a greater risk of being spotted by a camera. Leave it too late and I'd be missed before I had chance to board a ferry.

I changed into warmer clothes, found what food I could and walked out into the garden. The night air would keep me awake. Anyone watching would just assume I was having trouble sleeping after the events of the evening. I looked at my watch. Fifty minutes before I had to leave. Stay awake, keep your nerve.

Then, as I closed the door of the conservatory behind me, music started playing. It was coming from somewhere very close, possibly even the garden itself. I stood there, listening to the clear notes of the violins, waiting for the moment when Julie Andrews would sing the first line.

She didn't. I heard the click of a button being pressed and then the music stopped. In its place was the heavy silence of someone listening. Then, loud enough for me alone to hear, that same someone said my name.

57

Was this it then? Was it all going to end here and now? So many years since I'd heard that voice. It hadn't changed.

On the other side of the alley wall, something scraped against the stone. It was a sound so soft it could almost have been a cat, even a rodent. I knew it was neither. I opened my mouth, tried to form the name on my tongue, but nothing came out.

From the main road came the sound of a police siren. On the other side of the wall, that of footsteps moving away.

'No, wait. It wasn't me. I didn't call anyone.'

I had no idea whether I'd been heard. The footsteps had gone. It took me seconds to pull back the heavy-duty bolts on the gate and get into the alley. It was empty. Instinct told me not to run towards the street so I went the other way. Thirty metres and I'd arrived at a pathway that circled the park.

Still no one in sight.

We were taught in training that it's human instinct to turn left rather than right and that, with no other motivation, people will head to their left. That's the way I went. The gateway to the park was open and I stopped to get my breath back. I could hear the music again. The tinkling tune, light as air bubbles, was trilling away from somewhere inside the park.

Careful now. The shrubs around the perimeter were tall and dense. Plenty of hiding places. On the other side of the park were recreation fields, several football pitches that became cricket pitches in summer. Every step now took me further away from people. I'd brought no radio with me, no phone, no weapon of any kind. I'd acted without thinking, running out here. I'd have been spotted leaving the garden but it would take time for back-up to arrive. In the meantime, my police-officer status would be no protection. I was just a woman, alone at night.

The park was long and narrow. Clumps of shrubs and ornamental trees prevented me from seeing the full length, but I knew it well enough. To my right was the young children's play area. There were swings, a roundabout, a large treehouse complex with slides and stepping stones. Lots more hiding places. The eastern side of the park was aimed at older children and teenagers. There was a skateboard ramp and a BMX track.

Ahead of me was a circular structure of sheltered seating. In the darkest corner, I thought I could see movement among the shadows.

After the rain of earlier, the night was now dull, damp and mild, with no stars or moon that I could see. Just a thick covering of cloud. Not much wind either, and yet all around me the leaves that hadn't yet been claimed by the autumn were shivering. I was shivering too. So much it was starting to hurt.

Then everything fell silent. Even the distant noise of traffic seemed to retreat and I had a sense of a defining moment approaching. I realized I'd stopped breathing and I began to wonder how long it had been exactly since I'd checked behind me.

I didn't move.

'I'm waiting,' I said and could almost feel the hand reach out to touch my shoulder.

Then the silence broke, as though someone had waved a wand and brought the city back to life. I could hear traffic on the Wandsworth Road, leaves rustling like crisp packets, a car door being slammed.

And another police siren, one that — instinctively I knew — was heading this way. We were out of time.

I walked out of the park and back to my flat. As I left the alley I could hear footsteps running down the front steps and then someone banging on the door. I crossed my bedroom, picked up my rucksack and put it back on the wardrobe. I wouldn't be going anywhere tonight.

I had things to do.

58

Tuesday 2 October

Next morning, I dressed carefully. I don't often wear a skirt but I have a couple of more formal outfits for when the job demands it. The smarter of the two, a dark-blue suit from one of the high-street chains, is plain but respectable. I wore it with a loose cream blouse and twisted my hair into a knot at the back of my head. It could almost have been a trainee barrister staring back at me from the bedroom mirror. From the neck down, of course.

My face was still a mess. My nose was swollen and discoloured and the bruising around both eyes, whilst fading, was still very much in evidence. The stitches were visible at my left temple and my lips were twice their normal size. Joesbury hadn't been lying that night in hospital; my injuries were 90 per cent superficial and already improving. I was still barely recognizable though.

Every cloud, as they say.

I spent less than an hour in the office, drinking strong coffee, trying to summon up enough nerve for what I had to do. When the police left my flat the night before, it had been nearly two o'clock in the morning. They'd carried out a thorough search of the park and the alley leading up to it, but had found nothing. By the time they finished, the words 'wild goose chase' were practically hovering in the air above their heads. It wasn't even as though I had anything concrete to tell them. Scuffling sounds and footsteps. It could have been anything. Anyone. I didn't mention the music. To do so would have been to face too many unanswerable questions. I drank a third cup of coffee, collected Mizon from the next room and left the station.

First on the list were the Benn children, whose mother had been found dead the previous evening in a room sprayed liberally with her own blood. Out of respect for the immediacy of their grief, we'd arranged to see them at the home of friends, where they'd stayed overnight.

Felix Benn was twenty-six years old. I'd put his height at six two and his weight at around 180 pounds. He was a sportsman, it was clear from his walk, the way he held his shoulders, from the muscle visible through the pale-blue polo shirt. He was fair-haired, freckled, thin-faced. His younger brother, Harry, was similar but darker, maybe not so tall. Madeleine, at seventeen, was slender as a willow with long blonde hair. She was the only one who'd been visibly crying. I introduced myself and Mizon and said how sorry I was for their loss. They nodded and thanked me, three polite, well-brought-up kids.

'Can you think of any reason why anyone might want to kill your mother?' I asked, once I'd gone through the basics. 'Why someone might want to kill Mrs Jones and also Mrs Weston — Mrs Briggs, as she was when you knew her?'

Felix shook his head. 'My mother never did anyone any harm,' he said.

I turned to Harry and Madeleine. 'You both still live at home, I know,' I said. 'How did she seem yesterday morning?'

They looked at each other, then back at me. 'Mornings are always a bit hectic,' said Harry. 'But she seemed OK.'

'She was pissed off about that journalist,' said Madeleine quietly. 'The one that kept calling her.'

‘Someone was calling her?’ I asked.

Madeleine nodded. ‘A reporter. Calling about Geraldine and Amanda. She said she was talking to several of the mothers from the school, wanted to get a feel for what everyone thought, whether they were scared.’

‘When was this?’ asked Mizon.

‘It started a few days ago,’ Madeleine said. ‘In the end, Mum told me that if she rang again, to say she wasn’t in.’

‘Did your mother mention a name at all?’

Madeleine nodded. ‘I wrote it down. It’s in my bag in the hall.’

Mizon and I and the two boys waited while Madeleine fetched her bag. She handed a small notebook over and the two of us looked down at the name Charlotte Benn had warned her daughter about.

Emma Boston.

As Mizon drove us back to the station, I phoned in the news about Emma Boston being in contact with Charlotte Benn and was told that someone would be sent out to find her. We arrived to find that Tulloch, Anderson and several of the team were still at the public meeting over at St Joseph’s and that it had already featured on several morning news programmes and London-based radio stations. We learned that Emma had yet to be located and people in her building thought she might have gone away for a few days.

The Jones children, sons of the blonde woman who'd died in my arms the night all of this started, were waiting for us.

Jacob, aged twenty-six, had prematurely greying hair and startling blue eyes. His mother's eyes. He was tall, with long arms and legs, good-looking and aware of it. He was a junior doctor in Sheffield. Joshua, at nineteen, was taller than his brother but very slight. We spoke to the boys for twenty minutes and got the same old story. Their mother had had no enemies. They had no idea why she had been on the Brendon Estate that night. They couldn't imagine why anyone would want to hurt her. They weren't aware of her having been in contact with Charlotte Benn in years. Amanda Weston, formerly Briggs, they barely remembered.

The Weston/Briggs children, just like the two Jones boys, were sad, scared and angry. Like the Jones boys, they could tell us nothing. By the time Mizon and I had finished with them, Tulloch and the others were back. The public meeting had been an ordeal, by all accounts. Nearly seventy confused and frightened families wanting answers we didn't have. The mothers in particular had been told to take extra care in the coming weeks, to report anything suspicious, to let people know where they were at all times, to pass on the warning to others connected with the school.

The post-mortem examination on Charlotte Benn's body had now taken place and we'd had early results emailed through. Death had been caused by massive loss of blood when both carotid arteries were cut. She'd probably died some time between eight and ten o'clock on the morning of Monday 1 October. A little late to mark the exact anniversary of the Ripper killing, but I guess our killer had to wait for her to be home alone.

At the end of the day, I drove home, but instead of going inside, I walked to the South Bank, bought a burger and sat on a bench to eat it, watching the river that I knew couldn't scare me any more. I sat there for as long as I could bear it, waiting for the shadow drawing closer, for the voice whispering in my ear. When I needed a change of scene I crossed Vauxhall Bridge and headed for Westminster. I kept in the open, in well-lit spaces, easy enough to spot, not too vulnerable to being jumped on. Just by the Houses of Parliament, I turned quickly on the spot and saw a dark shape disappearing into a side road. I was being watched. Impossible to tell who was watching.

Nothing happened. No one came anywhere near me. By ten o'clock, I was cold and exhausted. I made my way home and went to bed. For a few hours, I actually slept.

When I arrived at work the next morning, Mizon was finishing a cigarette at the front door. She stubbed it out as I approached.

'Everyone's upstairs,' she said. 'A woman arrived five minutes ago, asking to talk to the DI. She's claiming she's the next victim.'

59

Wednesday 3 October

Jacqui Groves was thin and pale with chestnut hair in a chin-length bob. She wore nice clothes, good jewellery and a little more make-up than the average woman in her late forties. I watched the internal TV screen as first Tulloch and then Anderson joined her in the interview room. Around me, the team crowded close.

'Two kids,' said someone directly behind me. 'Twins. Boy and a girl. Toby and Joanna. Both went to St Joseph's. Twenty-six years old now.'

On the screen we watched Groves reach into her bag and pull out a narrow white envelope. She handed it across the desk to Tulloch. 'This arrived this morning,' she said. 'In the post.'

Tulloch made no move to take it. 'Can you tell me what it is?' she asked.

'Cuttings from a newspaper,' Groves

replied. 'Two of them. One about the murder of Geraldine, the other about Mandy.'

'Do you know who sent them to you?' asked Tulloch.

Groves shook her head. 'There's also a note,' she said.

Tulloch inclined her head. 'Please go on,' she said.

'It says, "TIME FOR NUMBER FOUR",' said Groves. 'Meaning me, I suppose. I'm number four.'

Tulloch nodded at Anderson, who got up and found gloves from a drawer in a nearby desk. He put them on and then pulled the contents out of the envelope. The camera was too far away for us to see them clearly, but they appeared to be exactly what Groves had described. Almost. The press reports weren't cuttings, they'd been lifted off the internet and printed out on standard office A4 paper.

'Postmarked late Monday night,' said Tulloch. 'In central London. Do you have any idea why someone might want to send you this?'

Groves shook her head.

'She's lying,' muttered someone behind me.

'Not sure,' said Joesbury, who'd moved closer to my chair. 'She looks scared to me.'

Then the door of the interview room opened and someone we couldn't see stuck their head inside. Tulloch suspended the interview and then she and Anderson left the room.

We waited for Tulloch and Anderson to go back into the room, for something else to happen. Nothing did. People began to drift away from the TV screen. Someone offered to get coffee. No one seemed able to get on with any work. Just when we were ready to give up, the door opened.

Tulloch had no need to call for silence. I could hear people around me breathing.

'Jacqui Groves's husband, Philip, is downstairs volunteering to make a statement,' she said. 'So are Geraldine Jones's husband, David; Jonathan Briggs, Amanda Weston's first husband; and Nick Benn, who found his wife's body on Monday. And three heavy-duty solicitors.'

Silence around the room. I wondered if anyone could hear my heart beating.

'The detective superintendent wants to be present,' Tulloch went on. 'We're starting in five minutes. I guess this is it, everyone.'

'Talk to them individually,' said Joesbury. 'It's too easy for them to stick to their story if they're together.'

Tulloch and he held eye contact for a

second. 'I know that,' she said. 'But they're here voluntarily in the presence of some very aggressive legal help. For now, I think we just have to listen to what they've got to say.'

As soon as she left, the rest of us turned back to the TV and flicked it to the main interview room on the top floor. As the screen flickered into life, we saw Anderson checking the recording equipment. Then the door opened and the room started to fill with tall men in expensive suits. I saw a resemblance to Felix Benn in one man. Another looked a little like Joshua Jones. The two lawyers were easy to spot. They didn't look scared. The superintendent came in with the third lawyer and they all took seats around the large glass table. Through the windows behind them we could see the rooftops of Lewisham and a cloudless autumn sky.

Anderson took a seat. They were all waiting for Tulloch. Minutes passed and still she didn't appear.

'She's making them wait,' muttered Mizon, who was just behind me. I wasn't so sure. I rather thought she'd gone via the ladies' room. At my side, Joesbury looked at his watch and his frown got more pronounced.

Another minute and one of the solicitors turned round to look at the clock on the wall. The detective superintendent breathed out heavily just as the door opened.

'Good morning,' said Tulloch as she closed the door softly behind her. The men got to their feet, including, after a second or two, Anderson and the DS. All of them towered over Tulloch. She moved to the nearest vacant seat and pulled it away from the table.

As the men sat, the youngest of the three solicitors started scribbling notes. Out of the corner of my eye I saw Joesbury biting his thumbnail. We all waited for Tulloch to begin. She was sitting with her back to the camera and we couldn't see her face. We could see her hands though, on the table in front of her, pale and very still.

'I understand you have a statement —' she began.

'One moment, please,' interrupted one of the lawyers, a tall man with ginger hair. 'Can we establish some ground rules, first of all?'

Tulloch inclined her head.

'These gentlemen are here voluntarily, in the spirit of being as helpful as possible. What they have to say is almost certainly not relevant to the investigation, but in the interests of full and frank disclosure. As such —'

'I understand that perfectly,' interrupted Tulloch. 'But my team has a great deal to do today. Who's going to start?'

'Miss Tulloch,' began the ginger-haired solicitor.

'Detective Inspector Tulloch, and no disrespect, sir, but I think we've heard quite enough from you for the time being.'

A short flurry of appreciative noises from people around me.

Without giving the solicitor a chance to speak further, Tulloch turned to the husband of the latest victim. 'Mr Benn, why don't you begin?'

Benn looked down at the glass table. 'It's probably nothing,' he said. 'It was a long time ago and no reason why —' He stopped and ran a hand over his face. 'Somebody else is going to have to do it,' he said.

Three husbands and one ex were exchanging glances around the table. The young solicitor was still scribbling away.

'There was an incident,' said David Jones, Geraldine's husband, after a moment. 'Years ago. We don't see how it can be relevant, but —'

'Whenever your people have talked to us, Miss Tulloch,' said another man — 'Jonathan Briggs,' I heard someone mutter at my side, 'Amanda Weston's first husband' — 'they've been trying to establish a connection of some sort between the families. At first, with Geraldine and Amanda, we just thought it was the school. Then when Charlotte was killed too, I started thinking. I phoned Dave and then we got in touch with Nick. We agreed we should come and talk to you.'

'With three lawyers,' murmured Joesbury. 'Sounds like more than a cosy chat to me.'

'You mentioned an incident,' said Tulloch. 'Can you tell me what that was?'

Silence again.

'It was in Cardiff,' said Jones after a moment. 'Eleven years ago this summer just gone. It involved the boys.'

'Your sons?' asked Tulloch.

Jones nodded. 'They were in a rowing team — coxed fours. They'd gone to take part in a regatta in —'

'I'm sorry, can you explain that term for me? Coxed fours?'

'Four oarsmen in the boat, one oar each,' said Jones. 'When they have two oars it's called sculling, not rowing. Our boys rowed. And there was a fifth team member, little lad, he was the cox.'

'I understand,' said Tulloch. 'Please, carry on.'

'The boys had gone to compete in the South Wales regatta. Starts up at Llandaff and finishes in Cardiff, in Bute Park. They did well, they won one of their races, were placed in another.'

'Get on with it,' someone near me muttered. Someone else shushed him.

'They were allowed to go out on Saturday night,' said Philip Groves. 'Bloody stupid idea, if you ask me, kids that young, but they were allowed to go to the centre of Cardiff. I got a phone call at one a.m. to say they'd all five of them been arrested.'

'We were phoned at home,' said David Jones. 'I drove up. Got to Cardiff about six. Nick was there already, then Jon arrived. And the other lad's dad.'

'Who was he?' asked Tulloch.

'Chap called Robert Curtis,' said Groves. 'Lives abroad now. We couldn't get hold of him.'

'What had they been arrested for?' asked Tulloch.

'There'd been an accusation,' said Jones. 'Completely fabricated, of course, but the police claimed they had no choice but to investigate.'

'What sort of —'

'They'd been drinking in one of the town-centre bars,' said Benn. 'Makes me bloody livid even now. None of them were older than fifteen. They should never have been served.'

'They were big lads,' said Groves. 'Oarsmen have to be.'

'They were arrested for underage drinking?' asked Tulloch, as puzzled glances were being exchanged around me.

'No,' said Jones. 'If only. They met up with two girls, you see, local girls. Both well known to the police in Cardiff. The eldest in particular a known trouble-maker.'

Over Tulloch's shoulder I could see her fingertips were starting to tap gently on the glass table. 'Go on,' she said.

'They left the bar shortly after eleven,' said Jones. 'The girls went with them. They went into the park. The big one in the middle of Cardiff.'

'Bute Park,' said Benn.

'They were young, they'd been drinking, they had two pretty girls with them,' said Briggs. 'You can imagine the rest.'

'Actually I can't,' said Tulloch, her voice like ice. 'Please fill me in.'

'They had a good time,' said Jones. 'They gave the girls some money to get a taxi home and they said goodnight. That should have been the end of it.'

'And it wasn't?' Tulloch's hands were so still now they could have been made of glass like the tabletop.

'Next thing they know, the girls are at Cardiff Central police station, claiming they've been raped. The police have no choice but to go through the motions, get the girls examined, go down to the scene, bring the boys in. Because they were all underage, the parents were contacted.'

'Let me get this straight,' said Tulloch. 'Your sons, and one other boy, were arrested and charged with the gang rape of two girls.'

Jones slapped his hand down on the table. 'No, Miss Tulloch. They were never charged.'

Joesbury moved away from my side and walked to a desk at the far side of the room. He started moving the computer mouse around.

'There was no evidence against them,' Jones was saying. 'Neither of the girls had a mark on them. There wasn't even evidence that sex had taken place. All the boys used condoms, thank God. And the girls supplied them.'

Joesbury had picked up the phone. He turned his back on the room.

'None of the boys tried to deny that they'd

had sex,' said Benn. 'But they were all very clear that it had been the girls' idea, that they'd suggested going to the park in the first place. God knows we're all vulnerable to hysterical females crying rape.'

'How old were these girls?' asked Tulloch.

'The eldest was nearly seventeen,' said Briggs. 'Well known to the local force. She was in with a joy-riding gang. Used to steal cars and drive them around the docks and then torch them.'

Joesbury was talking to someone. I forced myself to concentrate on the screen. At the other side of the room, another phone began ringing. Barrett picked it up.

'And the youngest?' asked Tulloch.

No one answered her.

'How old was the younger girl?' repeated Tulloch.

Still no response.

'All the boys were under the legal age of consent,' said the ginger-haired lawyer. 'These were kids. A situation got out of hand. The police at the time did everything by the book, but no charges were brought.'

Barrett finished talking, put the phone down and looked at me.

'It came down to the word of two working-class girls with reputations against those of five public schoolboys with influential fathers,' said Tulloch.

'Not exactly,' said Ginger Hair. 'The police found the condom packets. The girls' fingerprints were on them. Why would they be if they hadn't bought them in the first place? Those girls went into Bute Park expecting to have sex and then, possibly because the boys didn't give them as much money as they were hoping for, they got nasty. Now, I think my clients have been as cooperative as you could expect, given the very considerable distress they've been subjected to and —'

Tulloch was on her feet. 'What were their names? The girls?' she asked.

Glances exchanged around the room. More than one man shrugged. Either the names of the victims hadn't been important enough to be remembered, or they'd been as helpful as they were prepared to be.

'Thank you for your time, gentlemen,' said Tulloch. She left the room, followed by Anderson. The detective superintendent got up and switched off the recording equipment. In the incident room, someone reached up and turned off the screen.

'Hey, Flint,' called Barrett, from across the room. 'Your mate Emma Boston's turned up. Want to talk to her?'

I did. Anything to get out of that room.

60

'What's going on?' Emma demanded as I walked through the door. 'I've got a bloody story to write, I can't spend all day waiting for you lot to talk to me.'

The call Tom Barrett had taken upstairs had been to inform us that Emma Boston had returned home to get the message that we needed to see her urgently. Not wanting to miss out on anything interesting, she'd come straight down to the station. Her sunglasses were on the table in front of her and I was struck again by how lovely her eyes were. And how I might never now have the chance to ask her why she kept such beautiful eyes covered up.

'Tell me where you were between eight o'clock and twelve noon on Monday morning, Emma,' I said. The light on the monitor wasn't switched on. I didn't think anyone was watching us but I still couldn't afford to be chummy. Certainly not with

Joesbury back on my case.

She shrugged. 'At home.'

'Can anyone confirm that?'

'I might have popped out for a coffee. Why, what's happened?'

'Let's take turns to ask questions, Emma,' I said. 'Me first. Now, where did you go for coffee, what time was it, who served you and who did you see in the coffee bar?'

I made notes while she talked. Emma was a good journalist, she noticed things; she gave me plenty of detail of her morning and the trip to Nero's. She shouldn't have too much trouble proving she'd been nowhere near the Benn house when Charlotte was killed.

'Why have you been trying to phone Charlotte Benn the last couple of days?' I asked.

Her eyes narrowed. 'You mean the woman who was murdered? I haven't.'

'Her daughter told us,' I said. 'Her mother had several phone calls from you, asking to interview her about the Jones and Weston murders. Apparently, you were talking to several of the mothers from the school, trying to find out how they felt about the killings.'

Emma's creased face screwed up even further. 'That's bullshit,' she said. 'Someone was phoning Charlotte Benn? Pretending to be me?'

I knew Emma was telling the truth. Still had to go through the motions, though.

'Are you telling me you haven't tried to speak to Charlotte Benn?' I asked.

She shook her head. 'No way. I might have done, if I'd thought of it, but I didn't. Tell me what happened.'

For a moment it was difficult to talk. 'Still my turn,' I said, when I'd pulled myself together. 'I'm going to need your phone. And any you've got at home. I need to confirm they weren't used to call the Benn house.'

Emma sat back in her chair. 'Oh, you are kidding me. Again? How am I supposed to get anything done?'

'If I were you,' I said, 'I'd concentrate on staying out of harm's way. Can I have the phone, please?'

I put Emma's phone into an evidence bag and got up. 'Emma,' I said, turning in the doorway. She looked up. 'Please be careful,' I added, as I left the room.

61

When I got back upstairs, the incident room was quieter. Several people had left; there was no sign of Tulloch, Anderson or Stenning. Joesbury was still on the phone.

'The boss has ordered the five boys to be brought in,' Mizon told me. 'They don't all live in London, so it will take a while. And we've traced Karen Curtis, you know, mother of Thomas, the fifth member of the rowing team. She lives in Ealing. Stenning's on his way over there with one of the new recruits.'

'Where's the boss?' I asked.

'She and the sarge are still with DS Weaver.'

'Still can't see it,' said one of the older sergeants, whose voice was never pitched low and who now seemed determined that the whole room hear him. 'Two young Taffy girls get it a bit rougher than they bargained for and ten years later someone starts slicing up mothers? Gotta be coincidence.'

No one answered him. Three dead women seemed to be stretching coincidence for most people. Joesbury was talking into the phone again, but he was too far away for me to hear what he was saying.

'Those guys were ashamed of themselves,' said Mizon to me. 'None of them wanted to talk about it. They were defensive from the word go. I'll bet they pulled some serious muscle with the Cardiff force.'

We heard footsteps and saw Tulloch and Anderson making their way along the corridor. The door opened and they came in.

'I need somebody to get on to Cardiff,' Tulloch said. 'Find out their version of events. We need to know who the girls were.'

'Their name was Llewellyn,' said Joesbury, as we all turned to the corner of the room. He'd put the phone down. 'They were sisters,' he went on. 'The eldest had just turned sixteen, the younger one was fourteen. I spoke to the records clerk at Cardiff Central. She couldn't give me much, just that an accusation had been made and investigated. Two days later the girls withdrew their complaint.'

'Which you might expect them to do if the accusation was spurious in the first place,' said Anderson.

'Or if enough pressure was applied by people they were scared of,' said Mizon.

'Our killer can't be a woman,' insisted Anderson. 'Women don't rape and they don't slice up other women. It's men who get up close and personal with a knife in their hands.'

Across the room, turquoise eyes fixed on me.

'Couple of other things you should all know,' said Joesbury, when he finally let himself blink. 'The alleged rape we've just heard about took place on Saturday 31 August. The date of Jack the Ripper's first murder. And the date someone got up close and personal with Geraldine Jones.'

'What else?' Tulloch asked.

'The younger girl was called Cathy. The older one was Victoria.'

He waited for us all to think about it.

Tulloch pursed her lips and blew out a long, slow breath. 'Victorian locations,' she said. 'Victoria Park, Victoria House, the Victorian swimming pool.'

'Gov, it still makes a bollocks of the whole Ripper business.' Anderson raised his voice and spoke directly to Joesbury over several heads. 'Unless you're telling us that was just a giant smokescreen right from the start.'

Joesbury was watching me again. 'Oh, it

was a bit more than that,' he said. 'What do you think, Flint?'

'What are you talking about?' asked Tulloch as, around the room, eyes went from Joesbury to me and back again.

'Let's go back to the original murders,' he said, and it could almost have been just the two of us in the room. 'In a place as densely populated as Whitechapel, how come nobody spotted a man covered in blood? Not once?'

'It was dark,' someone offered.

Joesbury didn't even turn his head. 'More to the point,' he said, 'how come five streetwise prostitutes, more than accustomed to dealing with aggressive punters, allowed a bloke with a knife to get close enough to slice them open?'

'They had to take risks,' said Mizon. 'If they didn't, they didn't eat.'

'Not long before Polly Nichols was killed, there were two violent murders in Whitechapel,' said Joesbury. 'Nothing to do with Jack, but I'll bet every working girl in the city was on her guard. After Polly, definitely after Annie, they'd all have been jumpy as crickets. Yet he managed to kill three more times. Silently and invisibly. You're our undisputed Ripper expert, Flint. How did he do that?'

'What has this got to do with Lacey?' asked Tulloch, stepping a bit closer to me and frowning at Joesbury.

'Good question,' he replied.

Tulloch turned to me again, saw the look on my face and took a small step back.

Joesbury, quite deliberately, had dropped me completely in it. Everyone was waiting for me to speak and now I had no choice but to tell them what I'd kept back so far. My own pet theory about who Jack the Ripper had been, exactly as I'd told my classmates all those years ago. My favourite character from history? Jack the Ripper, of course, because Jack kept his secret, right to the very end.

'What DI Joesbury is driving at,' I began, surprised at how calm my voice sounded, 'is that Jack the Ripper was a woman.'

62

4 September, ten years earlier

Tye Hammond is coming down from a high and, when that happens, he likes to sit on deck and watch the lights bounce across the river. Somehow, they always manage to soothe him, to make the transition from bliss to the pressing crush of real life a bit more bearable.

As he climbs the steps of the houseboat, he thinks perhaps he hears someone calling out his name. When he reaches the cockpit the boat rocks against its mooring. He isn't alone on deck.

'What's up?' he asks the fair-haired girl at the port stern. Her back is to him, she's clutching the guardrail. Her head twitches round, then back again, too fast to make eye contact.

'The bow rope's been cut,' she calls. 'This one's loose too. I can't catch hold of it.'

It takes a second for the words to sink in. Then Tye sees that the bow of the boat has swung away from its mooring. The current has caught hold of it and is pointing it directly downstream. Only the rope at the stern is keeping them against the bank now. Unsteady on his feet, he stumbles over to where Cathy is still reaching out for the cleat the boat had been tied up to.

Tye is taller than Cathy. He throws himself against the rail and leans over. His fingers brush the cold steel for a split second before the boat drifts too far away. The rope is still wrapped around the cleat but not tied. It's slipping, only the friction of wet rope against steel is preventing the boat from spinning away at speed. He has to leap to the bank. Cathy can throw him the rope and he can catch the boat before the momentum gets too strong. He straddles the rail just as Cathy grasps hold of his leg.

'It's too far,' she says. 'You'll go in.'

She's right. Already they're two metres away, three. But they have to go in. There's no engine on the boat, no way of steering or stopping it. They cannot be loose in the river, at night, without any means of controlling the boat.

'We have to jump,' he says, taking hold of her arm. 'We're still close enough to swim.'

Cathy's eyes are wide and pale with fear. 'The others,' she says, looking down towards the cabin. 'Jen and Al are asleep. There's four people down below.'

'I'll get them,' he says. 'You jump.'

Tye turns his back on Cathy and heads for the hatch. Four people. He'd thought five. Jen and Al, Rob and Kit, and that new girl who pitched up a day or so ago. That made five, seven with him and Cathy. But Cathy thinks four and she's never wrong. He hears Cathy cry out behind him and spins round for a second to see her striding towards the bow. 'We're on fire,' she calls. 'The boat's on fire.'

The explosion throws him high into the air, burning into his skin, sucking all the air from his body. When he hits the river, it feels like a relief.

■ ■ ■ ■

Part Four: Catharine

■ ■ ■ ■

'The most agonizing of the East End mysteries is that of the utter paralysis of energy and intelligence on the part of the police.'

Daily News, 1 October 1888

63

Wednesday, 3 October

'This theory might seem a bit wild, but it certainly isn't new,' I said. 'It was the inspector in charge of the original investigation, a chap called Frederick Abbeline, who first suggested that the Ripper might not actually be a man after all.'

'On what grounds?' asked Tulloch.

I glanced over at Joesbury and said, 'You've just heard. When the whole of London was looking for a suspicious male, Abbeline couldn't understand how a man with bloodstained clothing could make his way around the streets without being spotted.'

Faces around me were a mixture of sceptical and interested. I decided I might as well sit down, I wasn't going anywhere in a hurry.

'Abbeline talked it over with colleagues,' I went on, as I perched on a desk. 'They came up with the mad-midwife theory. In later years it became known as the Jill-the-Ripper theory.'

Some small sounds that might have been titters.

'Keep going,' said Tulloch. All eyes were still on me. Sceptical or not, everyone wanted to hear what I had to say.

'They asked themselves who could get up and go out in the middle of the night without arousing suspicion in their own households,' I said. 'Who wouldn't attract attention if seen walking the streets in the small hours.'

Heads were starting to nod. Across the room a phone rang.

'Who could even appear heavily blood-stained without anyone thinking it out of the ordinary,' I said. 'The answer they came up with was a midwife. Or an abortionist. Quite a few women were both.'

'A midwife would have the anatomical knowledge to locate things like the uterus, the kidneys and so on,' said Mizon. 'Better than a butcher, at any rate.'

Out of the corner of my eye, I saw Joesbury leave the desk he'd been sitting at and approach the TV screen. The phone was still ringing. Tulloch signalled for someone to answer it.

'That was also part of the argument,' I said to Mizon. 'Another thing being that if prostitutes were approached by a woman, especially one they knew to be a midwife, they wouldn't be alarmed. It would explain why no one heard a scream or a struggle. The women weren't scared until it was too late.'

'And it was common practice at the time for midwives to knock their patients unconscious by using pressure points,' said Joesbury, who'd switched the TV on and was flicking through the list of stored information. 'A midwife who could do that wouldn't have much trouble subduing a tired, drunk prostitute,' he said. 'Could explain how he, or she, got Elizabeth Stride on the ground.'

I hadn't realized quite how much reading Joesbury had done on Ripper lore. He'd stopped fiddling with the TV and was watching me again. 'Seems to me women invariably get nervous if approached by a man they don't know,' he said. 'Completely different story if it's a woman. As a rule, women don't fear other women.'

'Geraldine Jones didn't scream or run the night she was killed,' said Barrett. 'If she had, Lacey would have heard her.'

'Flint, you've been banging on about a height discrepancy,' said Joesbury. 'Remember, you pointed out that the chap we saw on CCTV escorting Amanda Weston into Victoria Park didn't look as tall as the one we chased out of it?'

I nodded.

'Here we go,' said Joesbury. 'This is what the camera on Grove Road picked up on Saturday 8 September, the day before Amanda Weston was killed.'

Joesbury pressed a button and we all watched the recording of a busy London street on a Saturday afternoon. Two people walked into shot and along the pavement before turning into Victoria Park. The woman was wearing a brown coat with polka dots. We hadn't found the coat, but Daryl Weston had confirmed that his wife had owned one just like it. The woman's companion was dressed in black and was a little taller than she. Only a little.

'How tall was Amanda Weston?' asked Tulloch.

'Five five,' replied Mizon, reading from some notes.

'We need to compare this to the footage from the library,' said Tulloch. 'See if the heights are comparable.'

Joesbury was still looking at the picture of Amanda Weston and her killer that he'd frozen on the screen. 'In the meantime,' he said, 'I can't see anything to suggest that isn't a woman with her.'

'It is a woman,' I said. 'Our killer is a woman.'

Everyone turned to me. 'Go on,' said Tulloch.

'Charlotte Benn was being pestered by a woman claiming to be Emma Boston in the days leading up to her death,' I said. 'If Emma can prove it wasn't her . . .'

'I think we need her to prove it beyond any doubt,' said Tulloch. 'Emma Boston has always been a bit close to this investigation for my liking.'

'She will be able to prove it,' I said. 'I've just spoken to her. She didn't make the phone calls and she didn't go to the Benns' house that morning. The killer was using her again. I know I'm right. It's a woman.'

'That was Stenning,' called someone from across the room. 'He's stuck in traffic.'

'Hang on,' said Anderson. 'We know Amanda Weston was raped. We found semen — Cooper's — on her body.'

'Cooper was living with a woman,' said Tulloch. 'Or at least he was according to that street bloke Lacey spoke to. A woman we still haven't managed to track down. If the two of them had sex, it would be a relatively simple matter for her to save a condom. The pathologist found traces of a spermicide, remember?'

Several heads nodded. We heard another phone ringing.

'We don't know for certain Amanda Weston was raped,' said Mizon. 'At least, not in the usual sense. We just know someone pushed a piece of wood up inside her. A woman could have done that.'

'But why go for the mothers?' said Anderson. 'That makes no sense.'

Something tight inside me broke loose. 'Oh, you think?' I said, turning on him. 'Because it makes perfect sense to me. If you really pissed me off, and I was a bit of a psychopath, I wouldn't go for you, that would be too kind. I'd go for someone whose death would tear you apart. Your three-year-old daughter, maybe.'

'Steady on, Flint,' Anderson managed, as people around us started to look nervous.

'Or if you didn't have a daughter, maybe I'd go for that other relationship men always feel really protective about.'

'Mothers,' said Tulloch, looking like she'd swallowed a peach stone.

'Exactly,' I said. 'In fact, I can think of few better ways of getting your revenge on a man than by carving up his mother.'

'OK, OK.' Anderson was holding up both

hands. 'All I'm saying is, it seems a bit extreme to me.'

'Rape changes women,' I said, and waited to see if anyone wanted to hear what I had to say. Nobody turned away. 'Rape victims talk about themselves before and after the rape as though they were two different people.'

'We know people are impacted by trauma,' said Anderson. 'But it doesn't —'

'I'm not talking about a period of depression or getting a bit edgy,' I said. 'Rape victims are very specific in the language they use. They talk about the rape killing the person they were and then having to get used to the new person they've become.'

'Yes, but with all —'

Tulloch put her hand on his arm. 'Go on, Lacey,' she said.

'For most of these women, their life after the rape is governed by fear,' I said. 'They become afraid of the dark, of being alone, of strange noises in the night, of meeting strangers, of crowds.'

'Of everything,' said Mizon.

'Yes,' I said. 'Once a woman has been violently raped, the dominant force in her life, sometimes for years afterwards, becomes fear.' I stopped, suddenly having no real idea where I was going with this.

'Sorry,' I went on, 'I'm probably not making any sense.'

'You're making perfect sense,' said Joesbury. 'What you're not making is a connection.'

I looked at him and saw the connection. 'Well,' I said. 'What if, for one of these Llewellyn sisters, the dominant force in her life afterwards wasn't fear? What if it was rage?'

For a moment no one spoke.

'Boss,' called Barrett from the other side of the room. Tulloch looked up.

'Pete and Joe are at Karen Curtis's house,' said Barrett. 'Local uniform were waiting for them. They can't get any reply and it looks like there's mail behind the door. What do you want them to do?'

Tulloch glanced over at Joesbury. He nodded.

'Tell them to go in,' she said.

64

Barrett passed on the instruction and I sensed the room holding its breath. We waited the several minutes it would take for strong young coppers to break down a door.

'They're inside,' said Barrett.

'If anybody here's religious, this would be a good time to put it to use,' said Tulloch in a quiet voice.

'Nothing on the ground floor,' said Barrett. 'They're making their way upstairs.'

I am not remotely religious, but I was still repeating an old prayer from my childhood, over and over in my head.

Seconds ticked by. Barrett was talking quietly on the phone again. He looked up.

'Nothing,' he said. 'Not a trace of anything out of the ordinary.'

There was a sound of exhalation and I wondered if everyone in the room had been holding their breath. Tulloch sank on to a chair. 'Thank God,' she said, dropping her head into her hands.

'Hang on a minute, Boss, they have found something.'

Every head in the room turned in one direction.

'It's an envelope behind the door,' said Barrett. 'It's not been opened but it looks a bit like the one Jacqui Groves had. What do you want them to do?'

'Open it,' said Tulloch.

We waited.

'Another warning note, Boss,' said Barrett after a second. 'Press coverage of the Jones and Weston murders and a typed note saying "TIME FOR NUMBER FOUR".'

Tulloch was on her feet. 'We need to find Karen Curtis as a matter of urgency,' she said. 'She hasn't seen the note, so may not be on her guard. Tom, can you sort that out?'

Barrett nodded.

'And get a team talking to her neighbours,' Tulloch went on. 'Find out where she works, who her friends are, when she was last seen.'

'Who's sending these notes?' asked Joesbury. 'The Jones, Weston and Benn mothers weren't warned.'

'That we know of,' said Tulloch. 'They could have had a note of some sort, just not kept them. Or the killer could have taken them.'

'Doesn't make sense to me,' said Joesbury. 'If you want to take someone by surprise, you don't put them on their guard. And why two number fours? Surely the killer knows who he or she's going for next.'

'Gayle, get back to the three families,' said Tulloch. 'Find out if the mothers received any unusual mail in the days before they were killed. Then find out where these letters were posted. And get them down to Forensics, see what they make of them.'

'On my way.'

'OK,' said Tulloch, as Mizon left the room. 'After finding Karen Curtis, top of the list is tracking down the Llewellyn sisters. Mark, do you have contacts in Cardiff?'

He nodded. 'Helped bring down a paedo ring couple of years ago,' he said.

'Find out as much as you can about the girls, please,' said Tulloch.

'Yes, ma'am.' Joesbury sat down and picked up the phone.

'And I want someone to get on to Social Services in Wales,' said Tulloch. 'See if they have any record of them. We need to know about family background, school, that sort of thing.'

Across the room, someone volunteered.

'Neil and Lacey, can you make your way through the other agencies. Start with the DSS.'

DS Anderson and I nodded. It was standard procedure when trying to track someone down. Start with the Department of Social Security. If the two girls had ever claimed benefits, they'd be on the system. Failing that, we'd work our way through the others. If they paid tax, the Inland Revenue would hold records; if they drove a car, the DVLC would have them on file. We'd try the utility companies in Wales and then London. If they'd ever paid a gas, electricity or phone bill, they'd appear on a database somewhere.

'We'll meet back in an hour,' called Tulloch as she left the room.

Fifty minutes later she was back. 'Jacqui Groves is going to stay with her sister's family for a few days,' she said. 'With a police escort. Anything on the letters, Gayle?'

'None of the other families can remember their mothers getting any sort of warning letter,' said Mizon. 'We've got uniform going through the Benns' dustbin just to be on the safe side. Both the notes and the press coverage were printed out on the usual

A4 office paper on a completely bog-standard printer. We've got umpteen similar ones here, apparently. No prints yet.'

'Thanks, Gayle,' said Tulloch. She turned to the corner desk. 'Mark?'

Joesbury glanced down at his notes. 'I ran them both through the box,' he said. 'Nothing on Catherine, the younger sister.'

By 'the box', Joesbury was referring to the Police National Computer. Anyone who has ever been charged with an offence or accepted a caution will be on it.

'The older one, though, Victoria, she was a different story,' continued Joesbury. 'Two reprimands on her record, both for being in the company of joy-riders. Shortly before the incident, she accepted a final warning for knowingly being a passenger in a stolen vehicle and for exhibiting abusive and anti-social behaviour.'

'So we'll have her fingerprints?' said Tulloch.

Joesbury shook his head. 'It all happened on the street,' he said. 'No prints taken.'

'They must have been printed,' said Tulloch. 'We've just been told the girls' prints were on the condom packet.'

'Yep, both girls had their prints taken that night,' said Joesbury. 'But they went back a couple of weeks later with their social worker and witnessed them being destroyed.'

Tulloch muttered something under her breath.

'The night Victoria disappeared, she was caught on camera breaking into a car in the city centre,' Joesbury was saying. 'They put out an APB on her, but never found her or the car. Technically, she's still on Cardiff's wanted list.'

'They can join the queue,' said Tulloch.

'I spoke to everyone I know at Cardiff Central,' Joesbury went on, 'but none of them were around eleven years ago. They suggested I speak to a Sergeant Ron Williams. He's not on duty till tomorrow.'

'I talked to Social Services in Cardiff,' said Barrett. 'The girls' mother, Tina Llewellyn, was a drug addict and an alcoholic. She served time when the girls were small.'

'What for?' asked Tulloch.

'Dealing,' said Barrett. 'All minor stuff. She wasn't a big player, but it wasn't her first offence. The girls were sent to a children's home in the city and then, when they were eight and six, they were fostered.'

'Go on,' said Tulloch.

'The foster placement broke down when the older girl went to secondary school,' said Barrett. 'She had a history of truancy, abusive behaviour towards the teachers and suspected shoplifting, although that was never proved. They went back into the children's home.'

'Both of them?'

'Yeah. The foster family were happy to keep the younger girl, but she wouldn't be separated from her sister. There were several other foster placements over the years — apparently the younger girl was very pretty and could be quite engaging in a quiet sort of way.'

'Did any of them last?'

Barrett shook his head. 'They followed a pattern, Boss. It worked for a while, then Victoria would get into trouble, the foster parents would give up and poor little Cathy got dragged back into care. In spite of that, she still managed to do pretty well at school. She was considered university material. Until the alleged rape, of course.'

'Then what?'

Barrett took a moment to look at his notes. 'Well, ironically, Victoria seemed to pull herself together for a while. She stopped hanging round with the gangs, made an effort to sort herself out, even started trying at school. But the headteacher says she had a sense of real anger bubbling away inside. Several of the teachers became genuinely afraid of her. And it all started to go wrong for Cathy. She started missing school, she was suspected of taking drugs. There'd be very public rows between the two sisters. One day, Cathy just upped and left.'

'To go where?'

Barrett shrugged. 'No one knows for sure. She'd said nothing to any of her friends, not that she had many left by this time. The view at the time was that she'd come here, to London, and was living rough. A few weeks later, Victoria left too. In the stolen car we've already heard about.'

'Are they on the missing-persons list?' asked Tulloch.

'Haven't checked yet,' replied Barrett. 'There's just one snapshot on file. It was taken two years before the rape and isn't that clear. I've blown it up as much as I can without losing too much clarity.'

He passed round a sheet of A4 paper. Joesbury looked at it for a long time. Eventually it came to me. It had been taken in a photo booth, two young girls messing around. The older girl, whom we could only see in profile, was a Goth. Dyed black hair sticking away from her head at angles and falling down over her forehead to meet eyebrows that had been plucked to a pen-stroke. Her mouth had been painted in very dark lipstick and was pursed up as she pouted at the camera. She was wearing a torn black T-shirt that didn't hide very generous breasts for a fourteen-year-old, and a black leather jacket with lots of metal.

Twelve-year-old Cathy was quite plump, with a wide-mouthed grin and even teeth. Her fair hair was shiny as toffee. She was model-girl pretty and the glint in her eyes said she knew it.

'And that's that?' asked Tulloch. 'Nothing else?'

DS Anderson held up both hands and shrugged. I shook my head. We'd found nothing. Whatever had happened to Victoria and Cathy over the last eleven years, they hadn't claimed benefits, paid tax or utility bills or legally driven a car. They'd fallen off the grid, as so many do.

'Tina Llewellyn, the girls' mother, died of cancer seven years ago,' said Barrett. 'She was a lifelong smoker apparently, got a tumour in her lungs that spread very quickly. She died in a hospice in Mid Glamorgan. No father that we know of. The girls might not even have had the same father.'

'Actually, Victoria did re-emerge briefly, after about twelve months,' said Anderson. 'The girl's grandfather, their mother's father, lived up in the Rhonda Valley. They hadn't had much contact with him even when they were kids, but when he died he didn't leave a will and the girls inherited his house. Went for about a hundred thousand quid. Victoria claimed it.'

'All of it?' asked Joesbury.

'As far as I've been told,' said Anderson. 'If she's a psycho, she's a psycho with money.'

'Is that it?' said Tulloch.

Nobody spoke. That was it.

'OK, we keep looking. Lacey, we might need you to go out on the streets again, take a team with you, show that picture around.'

'I can start now, if you want,' I offered.

'Actually, I have another job for you and Gayle first,' said Tulloch. 'Karen Curtis hasn't been seen at work for two days, but according to one of her neighbours, she had an elderly mother living close to the river in Fulham. She used to visit her several times a week. It could well be where she's gone to ground.'

'You want us to go and check?' asked Mizon.

'The mother is frail, by all accounts,' said Tulloch. 'No point scaring her with the heavy brigade. Go and see if she can help.'

65

Mrs Evadne Richardson, Karen Curtis's mother, lived on a street of houses that probably sold for over a million pounds each. It ran north, perpendicular to the river, and the kerbs were crowded with expensive-looking cars. Number 35 was shabbier, more old-fashioned than the rest.

'Bet she bought this for a couple of grand fifty years ago,' said Mizon as we stood on the tiny, tiled path that led to the front door. 'Do you think this bell's working?'

I lifted the door-knocker and rapped. We waited. Mizon stepped back and looked up to the first floor. 'Got a bad feeling about this,' she said.

'Don't,' I replied, because whatever bad vibes Mizon was picking up, I could sense them too. I leaned forward. 'Someone's coming,' I said.

I could hear footsteps approaching the door. Then the sound of a bolt being drawn.

A key was turned and the door opened just four inches. A brass chain held it in place. I had to look down to make eye contact. A tiny, wrinkled faced stared up at me. Soft brown eyes behind thick, gold-rimmed glasses. Invisible lips.

'Mrs Richardson?' I asked.

'Yes.' She nodded her head once, looking scared. I realized that with my bruises I probably wasn't what a frail old lady would want to see on her doorstep. I took a step back. Mizon held up her warrant card so Mrs Richardson could see it through the gap in the door. The old lady took a step closer and her eyes narrowed.

'Mrs Richardson, we're trying to find your daughter, Karen,' she said. 'We were hoping to ask you a few questions.'

A bluebottle flew out of the gap between the door and the frame and hit me on the forehead.

'She's not here,' said the old lady.

'Can we talk to you for a few minutes?' asked Mizon.

'Mondays, Wednesdays and Fridays at five o'clock. That's when she comes.'

I forced a smile. 'Mrs Richardson, we need to ask you some questions,' I tried. 'Is it possible to come in?'

The woman disappeared and after a second the door was opened.

'Close it behind you,' she told us, as she made her way back along the corridor. 'Make sure it's locked.'

The hall floor was covered with black and white tiles that looked as old as the house. The walls were covered in pictures, decorative plates and mirrors. A wooden staircase led up to the next floor.

The house didn't smell too good. It wasn't strong but it was nasty. Like damp. Like rubbish that had been left too long in the bin. Like something gone off. Mizon wrinkled her nose at me as we followed Mrs Richardson along the corridor. As she pushed open a door we could hear the soft buzzing of houseflies.

We were in a sitting room, large but so full of furniture it seemed cramped. There were lots of family photographs over the fireplace and on the lid of an upright piano in the corner. I could see a dead housefly in Mrs Richardson's silver hair and several more buzzing around the large bay window.

'Would you like a cup of tea?' asked the old lady, once we were all settled in easy chairs.

At my side, Mizon shook her head. 'No, thank you,' I said. 'We won't keep you long. Can I ask when you last saw Karen?'

'Monday night,' she replied. 'She comes at five, cooks me some dinner and helps me have a bath. She goes about half past seven. Just as *Coronation Street* starts.'

'So you're expecting to see her tonight?' I asked. Today was Wednesday.

Mrs Richardson was nodding at me. 'She'll be here at five,' she said. 'She comes straight from work.'

I glanced at my watch. It wasn't far off five, but Karen Curtis hadn't shown up at work for the last two days.

'Mrs Richardson, how did she seem on Monday?' asked Mizon. 'Was she her usual self?'

Evadne Richardson nodded. 'Just the same,' she said. 'She'd had a phone call from Thomas. Said he had a new girlfriend.'

She pushed herself to her feet and crossed to the fireplace. Her hand went up and she seemed to be counting off the frames that were lined up along it. When she got to the fifth, she stopped. 'This is my grandson,' she said, taking down a photograph of a boy in graduation robes. 'Thomas.' She held the photograph out. I took it and passed it quickly to Mizon, just getting a glimpse of a dark-haired boy. He was smaller and slimmer than the other boys we'd met. The cox of the rowing team.

'Did she say anything about planning to go away?' I asked.

Evadne looked puzzled and shook her head. 'She doesn't go away,' she said. 'Not without arranging for a home help to come in and see me. I have health visitors calling every day,' she said. 'Just for ten minutes. They make sure I take the right pills. But they don't do any cooking or cleaning up.'

'Did she seem worried about anything?' asked Mizon.

'No. What would she be worried about?'

'Hopefully nothing,' said Mizon. 'I don't want you to get worried, but she didn't go to work today. Can you think of anywhere she might be?'

The old lady was on her feet again. 'I'd better just phone her,' she said.

Mizon and I watched Evadne cross the room to the phone, dial a number and wait to be connected to her daughter's answer-machine. I saw Mizon bat a fly away. Evadne put the phone down.

'Mrs Richardson, is there anything you can tell us, anything unusual about her vis—'

'She went upstairs,' Evadne said.

'Upstairs?' repeated Mizon.

The old lady nodded. 'I heard her,' she said. 'The music on *Coronation Street* had just finished and I heard her going upstairs.'

'And that was unusual?' I asked.

'We don't use the upstairs rooms,' she said. 'I can't manage the steps any more. My bedroom's downstairs in the room we used to call the back parlour. A few years ago, we had the pantry turned into a bathroom. I haven't been upstairs in years.'

'But your daughter went up?' I asked.

'Did she come back down again?' said Mizon.

The woman looked startled. We were scaring her. 'Yes,' she said. 'After about fifteen minutes. I remember because the ads were on. I heard her come back down and go out the front door.'

'Did she speak to you again?' I asked. 'Call out goodbye or anything?'

The lady shook her head. 'No,' she said. 'She'd already said goodbye.'

I had no need to look at Mizon.

'Mrs Richardson, have you let any strangers into your house over the last few days?' I asked. 'Anyone you hadn't seen before?'

'No, dear, I'd never do that. Wouldn't dream of it.'

I was starting to breathe again.

'Only the nurse,' said the old woman.

I waited for a second. 'Which nurse was that?' I asked.

'The new one,' said Evadne. 'The one that came on Monday. About mid afternoon. She had a card and a uniform and everything. Should I not have let her in?'

'I'm sure it was fine,' I said. 'Did she come to give you your pills?'

Evadne shook her head at me. 'No, dear, I'd already had those,' she said. 'She came to give me a health check. I'm not sure she checked much, though. Just talked to me for a few minutes, asked when Karen was due. Then she left.'

'Did you show her out?'

'She said not to get up, that she'd show herself out. I heard the door, though.'

I looked up at Mizon. She was pale, her hands clasped tight in front of her. I stood up.

'Mrs Richardson,' I said. 'Do you think we might look round the house?'

66

There was nothing out of the ordinary on the ground floor, but we hadn't expected there would be. I wasn't even surprised to find a nearly empty rubbish bin in the kitchen and a fridge in which everything seemed fresh. There was nothing to explain the bad smell. Two minutes after starting our search, Mizon and I stood at the bottom of the stairs.

'We could call it in,' she said.

'What if we're wrong?' I replied.

'We didn't bring gloves.'

'We're only going to look.'

Still we didn't move.

'We have to,' I said, and before I could change my mind, took the first step up. That seemed to bring its own momentum and I was soon at the top. Mizon, to do her justice, was right behind me. There were five closed doors on the first floor.

'Start at this end,' suggested Mizon,

indicating the door nearest to us.

'Not sure that's necessary,' I said. Mizon followed my sight line and gave a quiet moan when she saw the cluster of flies hovering around the furthest door.

'I'm calling this in,' she said. She got her radio out of her bag.

'Wait just a sec.'

The corridor wasn't wide enough for two of us so I led the way towards the front of the house. When we reached the door, I pulled my sleeve down over my hand and pushed it open.

Behind me, Mizon made an odd gulping sound and stepped back into the corridor. I could hear her on the radio, contacting Control, requesting immediate presence. I took a step further into the room. Quite close enough. The flies sensed an intruder and their steady drone took on an angry sound.

The body of Karen Curtis lay on the large double bed. The bedspread was the old-fashioned type that I think is called a candlewick. Long narrow grooves ran across the fabric. The grooves had acted as channels for Karen's blood, taking it away from her terrible wound, across the bed and down on to the flower-patterned carpet. Karen had been overweight, dressed in blue trousers and a brightly patterned smock. Her shoes on the pillow looked expensive and she'd been killed wearing a chunky amber necklace. It lay at the foot of the bed.

I heard Mizon come back into the room.

Karen hadn't been tortured that I could see. She'd probably been killed quickly. All this was assuming, of course, that it really was Karen I was looking at. Because it was impossible to be sure. Mizon and I had seen Karen's photograph downstairs, we knew exactly what she looked like. It wasn't going to help us much. This woman's head was nowhere to be seen.

67

'I don't think so, dear,' said the poor old lady. 'Same colour hair as this one, but . . .'

Evadne Richardson was in the interview room at Lewisham. Shortly after calling in news of Karen Curtis's death, we'd taken her mother out of the house and I'd driven her back across London. She knew we hadn't been able to identify formally the woman found upstairs in her house, but the description she'd given us of Karen's clothes left little doubt. She'd asked several times to see her daughter and couldn't understand why we kept telling her it wasn't possible.

She was braver than I think I would be, in her situation.

'Take your time,' I told her. 'It's important that you're sure.'

She looked again at the snapshots of Victoria and Cathy Llewellyn, before taking off her glasses and bringing the photograph closer to her face. I gave her time, conscious that upstairs in the incident room, people would be watching us. She shook her head again and I thought I saw a tear shining in the corner of one eye.

'These photographs were taken a long time ago,' I said. 'The girls would be older now, in their twenties. What about this one?' I was pointing to the older of the two girls.

'She looks, I don't know, I may have seen her,' Evadne said, looking up at me and then back down at the photograph. 'She was pretty, dear, like you. Nice little thing.'

My face was still swollen and discoloured. I wasn't remotely pretty. I began to suspect that Evadne Richardson would be little use in court as an eye witness.

'Did you get a good look at her face?' I asked, knowing I had to go through the motions. 'Did you, for example, notice a scar at all?' Tulloch had told me to check whether our nurse bore any resemblance to Emma Boston. So far, Emma's alibis checked out but Tulloch wasn't letting her go easily.

Mrs Richardson thought for a moment, then shook her head. 'No,' she said. 'I didn't notice a scar. Do you think she could have hurt my Karen? A nurse?'

'I don't think she was really a nurse,' I said.

■ ■ ■ ■

I got back upstairs to find Tulloch had returned from Evadne Richardson's house. Karen Curtis's severed head — we had to assume the murdered woman was Curtis until we knew otherwise — had been nowhere in the house. Nobody had asked the obvious question out loud.

'The woman at Mrs Richardson's house was killed between thirty-six and forty-eight hours ago,' said Tulloch. 'That's according to the attending surgeon. We know Karen Curtis was alive at seven thirty on Monday evening because that's when her mother last saw her. The chances are she was killed shortly after that.'

'By this nurse,' said Anderson

'Probably,' said Tulloch. 'Our killer, knowing Mrs Curtis's habit of visiting her mother on Monday evening, arrived at the house that afternoon wearing the uniform of a district nurse. Mrs Richardson is used to being visited by nurses, the woman appeared unthreatening and had ID. She had no real reason not to let her in.'

I found a vacant chair and sat on it.

'Mrs Richardson didn't see the nurse leave,' continued Tulloch. 'She just heard the front door close. What seems likely is that the killer remained inside and quietly made her way upstairs.'

'Waiting for Karen Curtis to arrive,' said Anderson.

Tulloch nodded. 'A few hours later, Mrs Richardson said goodbye to her daughter but heard her going upstairs, which was unusual. A short time after that, she heard someone coming back down again and assumed it was Karen leaving the house. It seems safe to say it probably wasn't.'

'Whoever it is, she knows these families well,' said Anderson. 'She persuaded Geraldine Jones to go to the Brendon Estate late on a Friday night. She found out where Amanda Weston was living and that she was on her own in the house. She may even have known Amanda wasn't due back at work for a few days. Then she called on Charlotte Benn when she was on her own. Now we find out she knows where Karen Curtis's mother lives and when Karen visits.'

'She does her homework,' said Tulloch. 'But so would I in her position.'

The door opened and Joesbury came in. Tulloch gave him a half-smile as he settled himself down at the desk opposite mine.

'What we don't do is panic,' Tulloch went on. 'We know who her next victim is and we have her safe. We can keep Jacqui under armed guard if necessary. And we have time. The Ripper didn't strike again until 10 November. That's nearly six weeks away.'

'She won't wait that long,' I said. 'This isn't about the Ripper any more.'

Everyone turned to face me. 'What do you mean?' asked Tulloch.

'If it hadn't been for all the Ripper business,' I went on, 'the coincidence of the dates, the letters, the body parts turning up all over London — if it hadn't been for all that, we might have realized earlier what was going on. Someone might have spotted the connection when Amanda Weston was killed. But the whole of London was on alert for a copycat serial killer and that was exactly what she wanted. It gave her time to get to Charlotte and Karen. It was all just smoke and mirrors.'

Nobody answered me. I couldn't see anyone about to disagree.

'She'll know we'll have figured it out by now,' I said. 'And she'll have planned for it. She'll have a way of getting to Jacqui Groves that we haven't anticipated.'

'Who's she, Flint?' asked Joesbury. 'Who are you talking about?'

No choice but to look up at him. 'One of the Llewellyn sisters,' I said. 'It's got to be.'

Joesbury stood up, a tiny smile on his face. 'Say that again,' he said.

'Say what?'

'The girls' name.'

'Llewellyn,' I repeated, sensing people around us looking puzzled.

'Now that's interesting,' he said. 'Everybody else in the room is pronouncing the name phonetically, Loo-ell-in.'

'And?' I said, my heartbeat picking up.

'You're making that odd guttural sound in your throat,' he said, 'more like a "cl" than a "l". You're saying the name the way the Welsh do.'

I stared at him for a second, conscious of everyone watching us. 'I'm from Shropshire,' I said. 'Last time I checked, it was on the Welsh border.'

'Yeah, whatever, you two. We need to find them both,' said Tulloch. 'Lacey, I'm putting you in charge of interviewing the homeless. If they came to London penniless, they would have lived on the streets for a while. Flint, are you even listening?'

Joesbury and I were still glaring at each other. I turned away and fixed my attention on Tulloch.

'You can have a team working with you,' Tulloch went on. You can have some WPCs out of uniform. We also need to get people to Cardiff.'

'They inherited money,' said Stenning. 'They could have got off the streets. And they could be working together. We could be looking for two women.'

'We can't rule anything out,' said Tulloch. 'We need them both.'

'I found Cathy this afternoon,' said Joesbury in a quiet voice.

Silence.

'Excuse me?' said Tulloch.

'An hour ago,' he repeated. 'Just after lunch.'

Tulloch looked like he'd slapped her. 'Why in God's name didn't you say anything? I want her brought in. Now.'

'Hardly possible, I'm afraid.'

'Why?'

Joesbury was looking at me again now. 'She's been dead for nearly a decade.'

68

Tulloch stood, strode across to the window, put her hands on the ledge and took a deep breath.

'Go on,' she said.

'I got suspicious when I heard Neil say that Victoria had claimed her grandfather's inheritance,' said Joesbury. 'If he died intestate then his money would be divided equally between his nearest surviving relatives. Victoria would have been given half of it, the rest saved for Cathy when she eventually showed up.'

'For Victoria to be given it all meant she was the only one left alive,' said Tulloch. 'Shit, I should have thought of that.'

'Cathy Llewellyn died in an accident ten years ago,' said Joesbury. 'She left home about six months after the alleged rape. I assume she made her way to London, because the following summer she was living in a semi-derelict houseboat near Deptford Creek. Squatting along with a group of other kids.'

'Go on,' said Tulloch.

'It broke away from its moorings one night and caught fire at the same time. Nobody is entirely sure how many kids were on board, but five bodies were found in the river. One boy survived, a lad called Tye Hammond, and he could only remember another five people.'

'How do you know all this?' asked Tulloch.

'I checked the death register,' said Joesbury. 'I found the date of Cathy's death and checked the coroner's report and then press archives.'

'There's no doubt it was Cathy?' asked Tulloch. 'Did they check dental records?'

'Not that was recorded,' said Joesbury. 'But they didn't need to. The body was identified. It wasn't badly burned, apparently. She drowned.'

'Who identified her?'

'Big sister Victoria. Once the coroner's inquest was over, she claimed the body and arranged cremation.'

Tulloch closed her eyes. For a few moments we watched her breathing. Then she opened them again.

'What about Victoria?' she said.

'Still nothing,' said Joesbury. 'Nothing's been heard of her since she claimed her grandfather's money.'

Tulloch raised her head. Her face was drawn and pinched. 'Well, it makes things simpler,' she said. 'Victoria's the one we want.'

69

Thursday 4 October

The afternoon of Geraldine Jones's funeral was a perfect autumn day. Bright and clear, with just a smattering of leaves in the gutters to remind us that summer was beating its retreat. Most of the MIT went along. Afterwards, Tulloch and Anderson went to a press conference at New Scotland Yard. The rest of us returned to Lewisham.

I spent the afternoon at my desk, pretending to be working. We were notified that Joesbury was following up a lead on the Llewellyns, but we heard nothing from him directly.

Time had picked up speed, it seemed to me. Every clock, every watch in the room was running fast. Options were disappearing like ice on a griddle and I had no idea what to do next.

It was still only twenty-four hours since the body — albeit incomplete — of Karen

Curtis had been discovered and the world's press were having a thoroughly good time with the story. The new Ripper had claimed his fourth victim, he'd managed to stage a double event, and the country was revelling in gleeful outrage.

He was still being referred to as a *he*.

So far, the public had been told nothing about the alleged rape in a Cardiff park that might just have been the catalyst for everything. The photograph and descriptions of the Llewellyn girls had been sent to every police station in the country and Victoria had temporarily become the most wanted person in the UK. We just hadn't said why.

Neither had we publicly released the information that Karen Curtis's head was still missing, but it was only a matter of time. We'd had to warn our colleagues around London that a severed human head was likely to turn up any day now, probably at a prominent Victorian location. It was the sort of news that was going to leak pretty quickly.

At six the day shift ended and people started to drift away. Soon just Mizon, Stenning and I were left in the incident room. Anderson arrived back at six thirty, just as we were about to give up on him and Tulloch.

'How'd it go, Sarge?' Stenning asked him.

'Blood bath,' said Anderson. 'Everyone else gone?'

'Anything you need, Sarge?' asked Mizon. 'Or shall we get off?'

'The boss has asked us all round for dinner,' said Anderson, looking uncomfortable. 'Only if you're free, she says, nothing formal.'

Stenning and I raised eyebrows at each other. 'Dinner?' said Stenning. 'As in, at her place?'

Anderson shrugged. 'Must be a gender thing,' he said. 'You get a bloke DI, he invites you down the pub. A woman asks you to dinner.'

'Are we supposed to bring flowers?' asked Stenning.

Dana Tulloch lived in a modest-sized terraced house in Clapham, but when she opened the door to us there was nothing modest about its interior. The walls were a soft smoky cream and the wooden floors walnut. The pictures on the walls were limited-edition prints and even one or two that looked like originals.

Her living room had three matching sofas in pale green and a large, square rug patterned in squares of green, rust and oatmeal. A real fire was burning in the hearth. As Dana took our coats, we could hear someone moving around in the kitchen and my heartbeat stepped up a pace. A few seconds later, I was disappointed. It seemed safe to say, though, that Anderson and Stenning probably weren't.

The blonde woman smiling at us was tall and athletic, with a perfect oval face, a clean jawline and brown, puppy-dog eyes. She was older than Dana, possibly around forty, but you only had to look at her to know she would probably look much the same at fifty.

'I'm Helen,' she said. 'Dana's partner.'

Dana's partner? Where had I been?

The six of us ate around the table in Dana's dining room and I found myself shy as a child. I was sitting next to Helen, who, it turned out, was Detective Chief Inspector Helen Rowley from Tayside police in Scotland. Fortunately, none of the others were quiet and no one seemed to notice I wasn't saying much. When all the plates but Dana's were almost empty, Helen put down her glass just a little more heavily than she needed to. We all looked her way.

'Right,' she said. 'Everybody ready to talk?'

Tulloch sighed and shrugged.

Helen's smile didn't falter. 'Or are we just

here for the pleasure of our company?' she asked.

'Always,' Tulloch replied.

Helen gave a short laugh. 'Yeah, well no offence, you lot, but I didn't fly down from Dundee for the fun of meeting my girlfriend's new team.' She turned to me. 'Dana says you've got a good feel for what's going on. You think it's Victoria Llewellyn?'

A little surprised to be singled out, I nodded. 'I think it has to be,' I said. 'What's happening now has to be linked to the rape. Her sister and her mother are both dead. No other family that we know of. She's the only one left.'

'And she's going for the mothers because she thinks that's the best way of getting back at the boys,' said Helen.

'Well, the mothers will be a softer target,' I said. 'Those boys are big blokes now; they all look like they can handle themselves. The mothers will be a different story entirely.'

Around the table, Anderson and Stenning were nodding to themselves. Mizon was watching me carefully. Dana's eyes were going from me to Helen.

'And, yes, I think if maximum revenge is what she's going for, she's got it right,' I went on. 'When those boys know for certain that what they did eleven years ago caused their mothers' deaths, and that they died so horribly, I think it will eat them up.'

'And the Ripper business was only ever just a smokescreen?' asked Helen, who seemed happy to ignore the others.

This was where I had to be careful. 'I think so,' I said. 'I think she wanted us thinking Ripper from the word go. A real copycat, on the other hand, would have stuck more rigidly to the historical trail, letting us cotton on gradually.'

Helen's eyes didn't leave mine.

'By sending the *Dear Boss* letter to a journalist, she made sure London got Ripper fever,' I said. 'Everyone was counting down to the next murder.'

'I'll say. Whitechapel was like the first day of the Harrods sale on 8 September.' That was Anderson.

'She was playing with us,' I said. 'She let the whole day of the 8 September go by with nothing happening until the evening, when she staged a fake call to get the team out to Southwark and, using Emma Boston's phone, she tricked me into going to the swimming pool.'

'To find the uterus,' said Helen. 'Nice touch. And a day later, she sends you out to Victoria Park to find the rest of Amanda Weston. She does have a bit of a thing about you, doesn't she?'

'She chose her second victim quite carefully,' said Tulloch. 'By going for the one mother who'd moved out of London, who didn't have any contacts with the capital, she slowed down the process of someone making the connection between the first two victims. It was days before we realized the school was the key to it.'

'She sounds like someone who knows how the police operate,' said Helen.

The others fell silent for a moment, as they all thought about that one. I kept my eyes down.

'How do you think she got Amanda Weston to London?' Helen was still talking to me.

'I'm not sure we'll ever know,' I said, glancing up. 'But her accomplice, Sam Cooper, used a replica gun. Those things can be quite convincing, especially if you're not used to weapons.'

'And after the second body was discovered, it became open season for Ripper hunters,' said Helen.

'She made sure of that,' I said. 'A hundred years ago, the press seriously got in the way of the police investigation. Reporters got to witnesses first, they bribed them, they ran stories that were just pure invention. Almost as much time was spent dealing with the effects of press speculation as it was hunting the Ripper. I think our killer wanted that happening with this investigation too.'

'But all the publicity worked against her as well,' said Mizon. 'She had every mother connected with that school on full alert.'

'Yes, but she had a plan for that too,' I said. 'Before we really cottoned on about the school, she gave us Cooper. We'd seen him at Victoria Park, we had a DNA link to the semen on Amanda Weston's body. He was a slam-dunk suspect and we caught him. Because she let us.'

'Do you think he was involved in the actual killings?' asked Helen.

I shook my head. 'The last thing he said, before he pulled me off that bridge, was "This is a fucking fix." He realized he'd been set up.'

'And we all thought it was over,' said Anderson, leaning back in his seat.

'She'd killed two more women before we even knew there was still a threat,' I said. 'But she knew we'd figure it out then. She knew that one of the husbands, if not all of them, would talk.'

'So why is she still ripping?' said Mizon. 'That's what I don't get. Why all the dramatics with the entrails and the heart and Karen Curtis's missing head? If she knows we know, why bother?'

Outside, I thought I heard a car pull up.

'She's keeping the pressure on,' said Tulloch. 'She wants us focusing our attention on where the head's going to turn up, so we take our eye off the ball.' She turned to Stenning. 'And don't think I don't know you bozos have a sweepstake running.'

Stenning blushed bright pink. 'Just a bit of fun, Boss,' he muttered to the table. 'To relieve the tension.'

'What's this?' asked Helen.

'My caring young DCs are taking bets on where the head is going to turn up,' said Tulloch. 'They've narrowed it down to twenty well-known Victorian sites around London.'

Helen smiled. 'What odds will you give me for the Albert Memorial?' she asked Stenning.

'It's not funny,' said Tulloch. 'All she has to do is get to Jacqui Groves and she's beaten us.'

A knock sounded at the door. Helen got up and left the room.

'She can't get to her,' said Anderson. 'Jacqui Groves has got round-the-clock bodyguards and no one knows where she is.'

'Hey, gorgeous,' came the familiar voice

from the hall.

I straightened up in my seat before I realized what I was doing. Out of the corner of my eye, I could see Tulloch watching me. And smiling to herself.

'You're late,' we heard Helen say, as the front door closed.

'Save me any grub?' Joesbury appeared in the doorway and glanced round the table. 'Evenin' all.'

He took Helen's seat, next to me, as Helen left the room. He reached across the table, brushing his left shoulder against me as he helped himself to the water jug.

'Do you want a beer?' offered Tulloch.

He shook his head. 'I'm off in a minute,' he said. 'Anybody here still sober?'

'Why?' asked Tulloch. 'What have you found?'

'Tell you in a sec,' he said, as Helen reappeared with a plate piled high with risotto. She put it down in front of Joesbury and then walked round the table to perch on the side of Dana's chair. Joesbury shovelled several forkfuls into his mouth while we all sat and waited. My shoulder was still tingling.

'Be great with a bit of chicken,' he said eventually, putting down his fork and refilling his glass.

'If you've nothing sensible to say, eat up and go,' said Helen. 'We're about to convene the poetry club.'

'I may have found Tye Hammond,' said Joesbury.

Helen, Mizon and Anderson looked puzzled. 'The survivor of the river-boat fire,' Stenning said as Joesbury carried on eating. 'The one in which Cathy Llewellyn died.'

'Where is he?' asked Tulloch.

'Living in a warehouse just east of Woolwich,' said Joesbury. 'It was sold off to developers who went bust. It's sitting empty while the lawyers fight over it, and a couple of dozen low-lifes — sorry, Flint, street people — have moved in. Word has it that if we pop along in the next hour, we might just find him at home and coming down from one of his highs. He might be able to tell us more about Cathy. He might even remember Victoria.'

'And how do you know this?'

'Contact,' said Joesbury mysteriously, continuing to eat.

Tulloch glanced up at Helen. The older woman shrugged. 'We can have pudding later,' she said.

'Should we call out uniform?' asked Anderson.

Tulloch was looking at Joesbury.

'Your call,' he said. 'But personally, I'd keep it nice and low key for now. If you send the numpties in you could have every morning paper running with the story that we suspect one of London's homeless is the Ripper. That's not going to make for good community relations.'

Tulloch stood up. 'Just you and me then,' she said to Joesbury. 'Helen can stay with the others.'

'No,' said Anderson, getting to his feet. 'No disrespect, Boss, but you're not going down some semi-derelict doss house at this time of night with a one-armed man. Pete and me are coming too.'

Joesbury was looking down at his injured arm, wriggling his fingers as if to make sure it was indeed still working. He looked up at Mizon and winked. She smiled back and then let her eyes drift to me.

'You'll be less threatening with more women in the party,' I said to Tulloch. 'These people that DI Joesbury calls low-lifes are easily scared.'

'I want to come too,' said Mizon, pushing back her chair.

A moment's silence. Helen and Joesbury were the only ones still sitting.

'Well, you're sure as hell not leaving me with the washing-up,' said Helen.

70

We took Tye Hammond to an all-night diner and ordered food he didn't seem too interested in. We'd found him, as Joesbury had predicted, in the warehouse, another Victorian building on the riverbank at Woolwich, and had persuaded him to come with us for a short chat. I sat with him at a Formica table, together with Tulloch and Mizon. Not wanting to intimidate him with numbers, Helen and the three blokes sat a few tables away.

'Am I under arrest?' he said, grabbing the sugar bowl and spooning grimy white powder into his mug. Tulloch nodded at me to reply.

'No,' I said. 'We just want to ask you about something that happened a few years ago. There was a fire on a houseboat, at Deptford Creek, do you remember?'

He began stirring his tea. 'What if I do?' he asked his spoon.

'People died,' I said. 'Either in the smoke or drowned in the river. You were the only one who survived.'

He shrugged. 'Got lucky, didn't I?'

'How?' I asked him. 'How did you get lucky?'

He didn't reply, just wrapped his hands around the mug and looked over at the sugar bowl. He'd half emptied it. He still hadn't looked me in the eyes.

'Tye,' I said, 'nobody here wants to take you down the station to talk to you formally. But we will if we have to. Why don't you —'

He looked up then. 'You think I'm scared of that?' he said. 'They'll have to feed me in the nick. It'll be warm. There'll be a proper bog I can use.'

'We don't have to give you smack, though,' I said. 'Is that what you're on? In fact, we'll have to wait till you come down off whatever it is and get the DTs out of your system. Could be twelve hours or more. Won't be much fun.'

Tye's eyes went back down to his tea. He picked up his fork and began pushing beans around on his plate.

'OK, let's go,' said Tulloch, pushing back her chair.

'Wait.' Tye was holding up one hand. 'There was a — what do you call it? — an inquiry?'

'An inquest?' I suggested.

He nodded. 'In court,' he went on. 'I told them everything I knew. I can't tell you anything else.'

'Tell us how it happened,' I said. 'How did the boat get away from its moorings?'

'The rope was cut,' he said. 'That's why I was on deck. This girl, Cathy, she called me up. Someone had cut the rope and we were drifting.'

I could sense Tulloch and Mizon sharing a look. I kept my eyes on Tye.

'Cathy?' I said. 'Cathy who?'

He shook his head. 'Just Cathy. We didn't use second names. Not even real first ones, most of us.'

'Go on,' I said.

'We were well away from the bank by this stage. It's serious shit, you know, being loose in the river, especially at night. We knew we were in trouble. Then Cathy said there was a fire.'

'On the boat?'

He nodded. 'I didn't see it, but she ran up the front. Then there was a huge flash and a couple of seconds later, I'm under the water. I must have fallen in.'

'Were you rescued?' I asked, remembering the light shining down on me from the RIB, the moment I'd known I would live.

He shook his head. 'No, I managed to swim to a pier. I caught hold of one of those wooden columns and made my way to the shore.'

Out of the corner of my eye I saw Tulloch gesturing to the other table.

'You were very lucky,' I said. 'Tye, how many people were on the boat with you that night?'

For a second, Tye looked uncertain. His brows contracted, his lips pressed tighter together, as though he was trying to remember something. Then he shook his head. 'There was six of us,' he said. 'Five people died and I survived.'

I nodded. 'Yes, that's what the inquest report said,' I replied. 'Three men, including you, and three women, including Catherine Llewellyn. Is that right?'

He shrugged. He supposed that was right. Over my shoulder, someone handed a photograph to Tulloch. She put it down on the table in front of Tye. It was the snapshot of the Llewellyn sisters.

'Do you recognize either of these girls?' she asked him.

He pointed to the younger of the two. 'That's her,' he said. 'That's Cathy.'

I watched Tye's eyes start to glint as he

looked down at the photograph. 'Was she your girlfriend?' I asked him, sensing someone from the other table closing in.

He shook his head.

'But you'd have liked her to be?' I asked. Joesbury had approached our table. He crouched down, so that his head was on a level with ours.

'Do you recognize the other girl in the photograph?' he asked. 'Did you ever see her with Cathy?'

Tye looked at the photograph again. He glanced up at me, then back down again. He shook his head.

'When you knew Cathy,' Joesbury said, 'did you ever have the feeling that she thought someone might be looking for her?'

'We've all got someone looking for us,' Tye answered. 'Filth, Social Services, families who can't take no for an answer,' he went on. 'Toe rags who think we owe them money. No one gives us any peace.'

'But Cathy specifically. Was someone looking for her?'

Tye looked at his plate for a second, then nodded.

'Did she say who?' Tulloch asked.

He shook his head.

Joesbury reached into his pocket and pulled out two twenty-pound notes. He put them on the table and laid his hand on top of them. 'I don't hand over money for bullshit, Tye,' he said, 'so don't waste your time. Tell me something useful and I'll leave this behind when I go.'

Tye's eyes were on the money, working out what it would buy him and, somehow, I didn't think he was planning a trip to the nearest Tesco Metro to stock up on salad and live yogurt.

'Was she afraid?' asked Joesbury.

Tye shrugged, gave a weak, half-hearted nod, shrugged again. 'I know she didn't want to be found,' he said. 'She would never move north of the river. I think that's where this bloke — she never said it was a bloke, I just sort of assumed — I think that's where he was. I think she knew he was north of the river and that's why she wanted to stay this side.'

My three colleagues were exchanging glances. I kept my eyes on the young man directly opposite.

'Did she ever mention a sister, Tye?' I asked him. He looked at me vacantly for a second, then shook his head. 'Do you think he found her?' he asked me. 'Do you think he cut the rope that night? Set the boat on fire?' Tye took his eyes away from me to look at the others. 'Do you think whoever did that to us was the one Cathy was scared of?' he asked them.

Joesbury was looking at me. 'Anything's possible,' he said and pushed himself to his feet.

71

Friday 5 October

'I'm sending a team to Cardiff,' Tulloch was saying to the assembled throng as I pushed open the door of the incident room the next morning. 'I'm not sure who yet. But we need to find any other photographs of Victoria, talk to people who knew her, try and find out where she might be staying.'

The door opened again and I turned to see Joesbury holding it for Gayle Mizon. She walked through holding two paper mugs from Starbucks. She held one out to him and he grinned at her as he took it. The smell of coffee came drifting over towards me. Joesbury's hair was still wet from the shower. A phone started ringing. From the corner of my eye, I thought I saw Barrett answer it.

'We need to go over Cooper's place again,' Tulloch said. 'We may have missed something. A partial print, anything.'

'Boss.' Barrett's voice.

'That outfit she wears, the black-hooded coat with squiggles on it, it may —'

'Boss.' Louder that time. We all turned to Barrett, whose normally glossy black skin had taken on a duller shade. 'You need to take this,' he went on. 'The head's turned up.'

Tulloch seemed to freeze. 'Where?' she asked.

'The zoo,' he answered. 'It's at London Zoo.'

'This is one sick bitch,' muttered Anderson, as we bypassed the zoo's queuing system and went in through the main gates. A couple of uniformed constables were already in place. We'd passed another one on the street outside, patiently explaining to the growing queue why they couldn't go into the zoo just yet. I hoped he wasn't telling them the whole truth.

Ahead of us we saw two men in suits and a woman in black trousers and a green sweatshirt approach Tulloch.

'The tall bloke's local CID,' muttered Anderson. 'I knew him when I worked in Islington.' He pointed over to a group of primary-school children gathered by the gift shop. 'Look,' he said. 'The place is crawling with school parties midweek. Is it even Victorian?'

'Strictly, it pre-dates Her late Majesty by a few years,' I said. I'd done a quick Google search before we'd left the station. 'Although she was on the throne by the time it opened to the public.'

'My bloody daughter comes here,' said Anderson.

'Take it easy, mate,' said Joesbury.

The tall detective introduced himself and the zoo's general manager, a man called Sheep, comically enough. The woman was one of the head keepers. She was shaking.

'How long ago was it found?' asked Tulloch.

Sheep looked at his watch. 'About quarter to ten,' he said. 'We'd only just opened. Luckily the place was quiet. Just a few dozen early birds and that school party you can see over there.'

'Is there anywhere they can be taken until we can talk to them?' asked Tulloch.

'The Oasis might work,' said Sheep. 'The main site restaurant. It's not far from here and there's plenty of space.'

'Thank you,' said Tulloch. 'Gayle, can you organize that? Coordinate with the keepers to get everyone over there, including all non-essential staff.'

'It's our busiest time,' said the woman in green. 'All the enclosures need to be made ready for the day, the animals all need feeding.'

'I understand,' said Tulloch. 'We'll keep the disruption to a minimum. Now, where can we see CCTV footage?'

'My office is probably the best place,' said Sheep. 'I can take you there now.'

'Can you take DC Stenning, please?' said Tulloch. 'Pete, get hold of everything for the last twenty-four hours for starters. We'll take it from there.'

Stenning and Sheep set off towards the zoo's main admin buildings.

'OK, let's walk and talk,' said Tulloch. 'How far do we have to go?'

With the CID detective, a man called John Hallister, in the lead, we set off down the hill and along the zoo's main avenue. To our right were the original brick buildings of the aquarium and the reptile house. Tiny cafeterias on either side of the path had just started business for the day. The serving staff watched us with undisguised curiosity as we made our way past.

'Our local office got the call at ten minutes to ten,' said Hallister. 'We followed down about fifteen minutes later. When we got here, uniform had already closed the zoo to new punters and roped off the enclosure. The zoo staff had to get the animals back into their sleeping accommodation. Wasn't easy. They were very upset.'

'And which animals . . .' began Tulloch. We'd stopped at the police tape. 'The Gorilla Kingdom,' she said, with something like dismay in her voice.

'Gorillas are extremely sensitive,' said the keeper in a shaky voice. She was wearing a name badge that told us she was called Anna. 'They don't react well to the smell of blood,' she went on.

'Neither do I,' said Tulloch in a low voice.

'This is one of the newest enclosures,' I said. 'And probably the most popular. If anyone were going for maximum shock value, this is the one they'd choose.'

'Are you telling me the gorillas found the head?' Tulloch asked Anna.

'We knew something was up,' she replied. 'They started screaming the minute we let them out. They wouldn't go near it, of course.'

'They didn't touch it then?' asked Tulloch. 'It's still where it was found?'

'I couldn't say for certain about the Colobus monkeys. We had quite a job getting them rounded up. And they are very inquisitive. The gorillas are a different story. Very distressed. Our alpha female is pregnant.'

There wasn't much we could say to that — it certainly didn't seem like the moment to offer congratulations. We stepped through a long fringe of plastic sheeting and found ourselves in a semitropical environment. Lush foliage, running water, decorative bamboo structures and jewel-coloured tropical birds. We carried on through more plastic fringing and came into the enclosure itself.

It was a large space. A dead tree looked sculptural against the pale October sky. I looked up. No roof of any description.

The gorillas were still upset. Even some distance from their indoor accommodation, their calling and chattering was uncomfortably loud.

'There it is,' said Hallister. 'Over by that rock.'

With Tulloch in the lead we approached a viewing point. Between us and the gorillas' enclosure was a metre-high fence and a water-filled moat. The head was face-down about five metres away on the other side of the moat. The chin-length brown hair was damp from dew. What looked like congealed blood surrounded the stump.

'She could have thrown it from here,' said Joesbury. 'One big swing would do it.'

'Has anyone been near it?' asked Tulloch.

The CID detective shook his head. 'Nope. Once we got the animals back inside and knew what we were dealing with, we waited for you.'

Tulloch nodded and turned to Anderson. 'Any idea when SOCs will get here?' she asked.

Anderson stepped to one side and made a call to find out.

'Are the animals kept inside overnight?' asked Joesbury.

'Yes,' said Anna. 'It's safer. And at this time of year, much warmer.'

'So it could have been left some time in the night and no one would have spotted it till this morning?' he asked.

'Well, the zoo's locked at night,' said the keeper. 'No one's supposed to come in. There are nightwatchmen.'

Joesbury was looking round. 'Mind if I take a walk, Tully?' he asked.

She shook her head and he left the enclosure. He had to step to one side to let some new arrivals through. SOCs hadn't taken long to show up.

Ten minutes later, covered head to toe in Tyvek, Tulloch, Anderson, the senior crime-scene investigator, Anna the keeper and I stepped out from the gorillas' house and into the enclosure. We were halfway across the outdoor area and the head was in view when we spotted Mike Kaytes, the duty pathologist that morning, making his way towards us. He was already suited up. We stopped to wait for him.

'No flies,' I said.

'Sorry?' said Tulloch.

'Look,' I pointed out. 'Over there, it looks like dung, am I right?'

'Well, we haven't had chance to clean yet,' said the keeper.

'There are flies on it,' I said. 'I can see them from here.'

'OK,' said Tulloch.

'But none on the head,' I went on.

Tulloch stared at it for a second. 'You're right,' she said. 'Maybe she used something to preserve it that's keeping them away.'

Kaytes had arrived. He nodded at us all and then we let him approach the head by himself. He took his time, walked close and stopped. Then he made a circle around it, looking down all the time. When he'd completed the 360 degrees he crouched low, blocking our view. We could see him reach out but not what he touched. He got down on to his knees and peered forward. Then he pushed himself back and stood up.

As he walked towards us there was an

expression on his face I couldn't read. He almost seemed on the verge of a smile.

'You haven't heard from Madame Tussauds this morning, have you?' he asked the CID detective.

'Not our patch,' Hallister replied. 'Why?'

'I think you might be about to,' said Kaytes. 'Go and take a look.'

He followed close behind as we moved over to the head. We formed a circle and looked down. I breathed in hard through my nose. The smell stayed the same. Earth, coffee from the nearby cafés, the detritus of warm-blooded animals. Nothing else.

Tulloch dropped to her knees. After a second so did the rest of us. We must have looked like some sort of bizarre prayer meeting.

'It's not human,' said Kaytes, unnecessarily. This close, it was unmistakable. 'What you've got there is a waxwork.'

72

'A hoax then,' said Hallister.

'Not necessarily,' said Kaytes. 'That red stuff around the stump wasn't paint. That was blood.'

Tulloch, the pathologist, Hallister and I were sitting at one of the zoo's smaller outdoor cafés, a fish and chip bar near the bug house. The day was getting colder but no one seemed to want to go indoors. Anderson had been left in charge of the crime scene. Mizon was interviewing visitors and Stenning was still looking at CCTV footage. I had no idea what had happened to Joesbury.

'Human blood?' asked Tulloch.

'Impossible to tell till I have a good look at it, run a couple of tests,' he replied. 'I'll probably know later today.'

'It wasn't a hoax.' We looked up to see Stenning and Joesbury had arrived. 'I've seen the CCTV footage,' Stenning went on.

'She got into the zoo last night wearing her trademark clothes. You know — baggy black jacket with coloured symbols, black beanie. One of the cameras picked her up by the Komodo dragons at three twenty-four a.m. She was carrying a small holdall.'

'How did she get in?' said Tulloch, looking round.

'Over the fence,' said Joesbury. 'Budge up, Flint.' He pulled a chair up and squeezed in between me and Tulloch. Leaning forward, he put a map of the zoo on the table. 'There you go,' he said. 'Other side of the camels. There's an iron fence between the zoo and the park. It's barely five feet high. I think I even found the exact spot.'

'How?' said Tulloch.

'There are four indentations in the grass,' said Joesbury, 'forming the four corners of a rectangle about two feet by fifteen inches. Someone's gone over to photograph them. They were just there.' He pointed to a spot on the map and we all leaned in closer.

The perimeter of the zoo formed a right-angled triangle, with two roughly equal sides that ran along the Prince Albert Road and the main avenue through Regent's Park. The hypotenuse ran diagonally south to north-west through the park. About halfway along it, between the enclosures for camels, pygmy hippos and bearded pigs and the new Komodo dragon exhibit, was the tip of Joesbury's index finger.

'I could see similar marks on the other side of the fence,' he said. 'This spot isn't directly overlooked by any cameras. I think she had a light aluminium stepladder that she used to give herself a bit of height on the park side of the fence. She jumped over and reached through the railings to lift the ladder up and across. Then she left it on the zoo side ready for a quick getaway.'

'It's that easy to break in?' said Tulloch.

'Well, sooner or later, anyone wandering around at night will be picked up on camera, trip an alarm or bump into one of the security staff,' said Stenning. 'But if the guv'nor's right, she had hardly any distance to go before she got to the gorillas. I'll bet she was in and out in ten minutes.'

'Why, though?' asked Tulloch. 'What is she playing at?'

'That's exactly what she's doing,' I said. 'She's playing.'

Joesbury leaned back in his chair and gave me the full benefit of his 'nasty' smile. 'And she's really starting to enjoy herself,' he said.

By the end of the day we knew that the wax head had been liberally smeared in human blood, which is why the gorillas had reacted to it. Whether it was Karen's blood we'd find out in time, but none of us had any doubts. Tulloch had assigned two detective constables to try and track down where the head had come from. They'd started with Madame Tussauds, who couldn't report any missing exhibits, either from the main collection or the warehouses. Staff there had been happy to hand over a list of other possible suppliers. Searches through eBay and other internet sites were proving surprisingly fruitful. Likenesses of severed human heads really weren't that hard to find.

'The world's gone fucking nuts,' was Anderson's reaction to that, when he got back from the zoo. Stepping into the incident room, he had a moment of unprecedented popularity. In response to numerous questions, he said that the gorillas were fine, none the worse for their upset of the morning, that the keepers were watching the pregnant female closely but weren't unduly concerned, and, just so he knew where he stood, was anybody in the room still interested in the ongoing murder investigation?

When he'd got over his huff, he told us that the zoo had been opened again, with only the Gorilla Kingdom still out of bounds. None of the morning's visitors that Mizon had talked to had seen anything out of the ordinary, but we hadn't expected them to.

The figure in the black skateboarding clothes had come and gone by moonlight. I sat and watched the few seconds of film showing her cross the main avenue over and over again.

'She's five eight, possibly five nine,' said Stenning, who had come up behind me without my hearing him. 'And those clothes look loose to me. I'd say she was quite thin.'

'Karen Curtis's mother described the nurse as a little thing,' I said. 'Five nine isn't little.'

'Perhaps she just meant skinny,' said Mizon. I hadn't realized she was there either. 'And she said black hair. In the photograph we have, Victoria had black hair. Impossible to see under that cap though.'

'Some women change their hair colour more than I change my socks,' said Joesbury. I must have been really engrossed not to see him coming. 'And clothes make a huge difference to body shape. What do you think, Flint?'

'About what?' I said, without taking my eyes off the screen. 'Your chances of pursuing a second career as a personal stylist?'

He leaned against the back of my chair. I could feel his knuckles against my shoulders. 'Do you think she's wearing heels?' he said. 'Wind it back a bit.'

Mizon leaned over and clicked the recording back to the beginning.

'Look at that,' said Joesbury. 'Look at the way she's walking.'

We watched the black figure keep her head down as she crossed the main avenue and disappeared into the gorilla enclosure.

'Gayle, are you wearing heels?' asked Joesbury. Mizon raised her right foot to give us the benefit of her two-inch court shoes. It was a modest heel by most women's standards but about the maximum a serving police officer could get away with.

'Can you walk over to the far wall?' asked Joesbury. 'If anyone wolf whistles, I'll clobber 'em.'

Mizon made a face that was somewhere between a simper and a silent giggle and set off.

'Flint, are you in your usual Doc Martens?' said Joesbury. 'Why don't you do the same?'

Reminding myself that telling a senior officer to eff off wasn't the way to keep a low profile, I got up and walked to the wall. I didn't even own a pair of Doc Martens.

When I reached Mizon I turned round. Joesbury was an asshole.

'OK, both of you, come back. Slowly.'

We did what we were told. Only one of us was smiling.

'I hope there's a point to this,' said Tulloch from the doorway.

'I'd say what we can see on screen is a woman trying to make out she's bigger than she is,' said Joesbury. 'She wears baggy clothing and heels.' He pointed to the screen. 'Look,' he said. 'She's walking like Gayle. Heels throw a woman's hips forward. And I'd say she's being careful, like she's worried about stumbling. Flint, on the other hand, is stomping around like a man.'

A couple of people in the room sniggered. I wasn't one of them.

'I'd say Mrs Richardson got it right,' said Joesbury. 'She is quite small. How tall are you, Flint?'

'Five six,' I said, through gritted teeth.

'Really?' He walked over and lifted my jacket from the back of my chair. 'This is a size twelve,' he said. 'And it drowns you. So you're an eight? Ten on a fat day?'

'Thank you, Mark, we get the point,' said Tulloch. 'She's a small to average-sized woman who tries to disguise it when she knows she's likely to be filmed. Now, before

I forget, are you free to go to Cardiff over the weekend? You can take Gayle to keep you in order.'

I excused myself and left the room. I needed to find something to break.

73

Saturday 6 October

I was waltzing. So I knew immediately it was a dream. I've never waltzed in my life. But in my dream I was whirling, Viennese style, spinning like a top, round and round as the music grew louder, and everywhere I turned there were red balloons and streamers and bright-scarlet confetti falling like petals from the ceiling.

I spun faster, and the music in my head started to hurt. Then suddenly the balloons and the streamers and the petals were changing, taking on odd shapes, gleaming wet. The streamers weren't paper any more, they were entrails. The petals were blood spatters and the balloons — oh Christ — the balloons were severed human heads, staring at me with milky eyes everywhere I turned.

With something between a gasp and a scream I was awake. I was out of bed, standing at its foot, shaking. The room was dark and for a second I could see nothing but the lights of Joesbury's alarm system. Tiny red lights.

I'd had no idea how disorientating it would be to wake suddenly in the middle of the night and not be in bed. How vulnerable it would make me feel. I stumbled across the room and switched on the light.

As soon as I could see, the first thing I did was to check my body, my arms, legs, torso. The dream had been so vivid that even now I was convinced I was covered in blood. There was nothing, of course. The sticky dampness I'd felt on waking was just sweat. Harder to explain away, though — in fact, impossible — was the music.

The music hadn't been part of the dream. The music was still playing. At first I thought it was in the room with me, but I knew I'd checked all the locks and alarms before going to sleep. It was coming from outside. I was wearing a running vest and loose shorts. I don't own nightclothes. I found a sweatshirt on the chair and pulled it on.

Outside, the music was louder. I was surprised other people in the house hadn't woken and heard it. It was an instrumental version, but of course I knew the lyrics off by heart. *Raindrops, roses, copper kettles and wild geese.* All the best things in the world. Favourite things.

Through the shed window I could see a light flickering, like a candle flame. And the door didn't seem properly closed. I was halfway down the garden now, my bare feet cold on the stone path. The shed door was unlocked and just an inch ajar.

Door bells, sleigh bells, girls in white dresses. My own list of favourite things hadn't been quite the same as Maria's, although I couldn't argue with most of her choices. My list, though, had included being the first to dive into a swimming pool and break the lovely clear stillness of the water. Also the steam that comes off ponies' bodies on winter mornings. And the velvet soft feel of their noses. I'd adored ponies.

I'd been in the shed earlier. When I got home from work I'd changed and unlocked it. I'd stared at the dummy's head on top of my punchbag and imagined it with turquoise blue eyes, tanned skin and even, white teeth. An hour later I'd returned to the flat exhausted.

Books were my other great passion as a child. I'd practically taught myself to read and it rarely took me more than a term to get through everything on the classroom reading shelves. With never enough spare cash to buy books, the lending library had been a godsend. Every Saturday morning I was there. And my favourite book ever? *The Weirdstone of Brisingamen,* of course.

The music was coming from the shed.

I'd liked city parks, too. The way the grass and the trees seem to form a bubble around you, shielding you from the noise and smells of the city. And the zoo, I shouldn't forget that. I'd always, from being a toddler, loved visits to the zoo. Pools and ponies, parks and the zoo; and public libraries full of books. My favourite things.

I was at the shed. All I'd done was walk the length of the garden path, but it seemed to have taken a very long time to do so. Even longer to stretch out my hand and push the shed door gently.

From the very beginning, this case had been about me. At some level, I'd always known that.

There was no need to go into the shed. From the doorway I could see the punch-bag swaying to and fro, as though remembering the hammering I'd given it earlier. Or as though someone had not long left it. It had the look of a clock's pendulum, marking time. Tick tock. I could also see that the inanimate head I'd pictured earlier as Mark

Joesbury's face was no longer on top of the punchbag. Something else had taken its place.

There was no need to switch on the lights. Five candles in a circle around the punchbag made extra lighting unnecessary. They flickered and danced in the breeze that the open door had allowed in. Their light was soft, golden, warm as the morning. They made Karen Curtis's severed head look almost alive.

74

'You'd better come and stay with us tonight,' said Helen, looking down at me. 'Dana keeps the spare room made up in case the two of us have a row.' I looked up and tried to smile. Helen's long blonde hair was plaited behind her head. It made her look younger.

'I'll stay with her,' said Joesbury from the doorway. He'd spoken to Helen, but then dropped his eyes to me. 'If you'd prefer to stay here, Lacey.'

I could sense Helen's eyebrows rising towards her hair. I nodded. 'Thank you,' I said, to no one in particular.

'How're they doing out there?' asked Helen.

'They're done for now,' said Joesbury. 'They're going to seal off the shed and the garden. Just in case there's anything left to find in daylight. Let's hope the rain holds off.'

'Have they taken it away?' I asked.

'Yep,' said Joesbury.

'You've been very brave,' said Helen, her hand on my shoulder.

The three of us were in my sitting room. The clock on the cooker told me it was nearly four in the morning. I was on the sofa, Helen perched on one arm. Dana and the rest of the team were processing the crime scene my garden and shed had become. I hadn't moved since Helen had sat me down and wrapped the duvet around my shoulders shortly after she'd arrived. She'd made me tea, but my hand had been shaking too much to drink it. She'd suggested I might be in shock and that perhaps I should be taken to A&E. I'd refused and begged her not to mention it to Dana. So far she hadn't.

'Did the cameras pick anything up?' I asked Joesbury.

'Not a sausage. We had them all angled towards the house, not the ruddy garden shed.'

'How did she even get in there?' asked Helen.

'The key wasn't hard to find,' said Joesbury. 'Tully has just torn me off a strip for not securing the shed as well as the flat.'

'Is she leaving uniform outside for the rest

of the night?' asked Helen.

Joesbury nodded.

'Good. Not that I don't have complete faith in you, of course.' She gave my shoulder a squeeze. 'Lacey, you need to be very careful. Just because she hasn't hurt you yet doesn't mean she won't. She could just be saving you for last.'

'Way to cheer the girl up,' said Joesbury, shrugging off his jacket and draping it over the back of a chair.

'Yeah, well I don't know about you, but I prefer my girls scared and alive,' said Helen.

Ten minutes later, Dana and Helen said goodnight. I still hadn't moved. The clock on my cooker is silent and yet I swear that night I could hear it ticking. Steady, relentless. I heard Joesbury turning the key in the conservatory door, pulling the bolts. The alarm beeped as he turned it back on. Then the door between the bedroom and the conservatory was locked and bolted. He came into the living room and crossed it without looking at me. The front door got the Joesbury treatment. We were shut off from the world.

'Can I get you anything?' he said from the door.

I shook my head and felt, rather than

heard, him come closer.

'Come on,' he said. He was standing in front of me, holding out his hand. I took it and stood up, holding the duvet around me.

Time was running out. I didn't know how much longer I had. I didn't know what or when it was all going to come to an end. All I knew was that I wanted Mark Joesbury — impossible to pretend otherwise any longer — and this might be my last chance.

Together, we walked into the bedroom.

I think he flicked off the lights. I know I put the duvet down on the bed and pulled it straight. I climbed beneath it without removing my clothes. I wanted to feel his hands pulling them off. He sat on the edge of the bed with his back to me and took off his shoes.

The rooms at the back of the house are so dark. He was little more than a shadow now but I caught the glint in his eyes and heard the rustle of the mattress and knew he'd turned to face me. I pulled the duvet back, inviting him in, holding my breath, waiting to feel his weight pushing me down.

Instead he wrapped the duvet round me, before leaning away as if about to stand up.

Well, I wasn't giving in that easily. I sat upright and caught hold of his arm. The tip of my nose brushed against his face and I found his mouth. Taking his bottom lip between both of mine I pulled gently. Then I did the same with his top lip. I ran my tongue lightly around the outline of his mouth and blew gently across it. He didn't move.

I raised my hand and reached for his face, meaning to hold him still while I kissed him long and deep. Moving faster than me, he caught my hand in his.

'No,' he whispered. Then he stood up.

I could have persisted. Gently stroking fingers, soft kisses in the right places. He was only a man, when all was said and done. But I learned something that night. When everything else is slipping away, pride is one thing you cling on to. I didn't push it. Instead, I lay back down on the bed and waited for the morning.

I didn't expect to sleep, but I must have done because some time later I woke to hear breathing. I turned, soundlessly. Joesbury was in the chair at the foot of the bed, his head turned my way, his eyes open. I stared at him, at his face that was just starting to emerge from the darkness, and he didn't move.

That's when what I'd suspected for a while became certainty. Mark Joesbury wasn't here for my protection. He was here to protect other people. From me.

He thought I was Victoria Llewellyn.

75

13 September, ten years earlier

Victoria Llewellyn is struggling to breathe. Air is going in, and out again, faster than feels normal, but it's just not having the right effect. There isn't enough oxygen getting to her brain and that light-headed, drifting-away-from-reality feeling is coming over her again. It's a common enough reaction to grief, she knows, sudden breathlessness, but what she can't deal with is this sense of the world slipping away, leaving her behind, alone, in the void.

She's sitting, bent forward almost double, her head just above her knees. She can't remember finding a bench on the towpath, the last thing she can remember is seeing a houseboat like the one Cathy had been living on, and then stumbling away, but the wooden slats are hard and damp beneath her and she's grateful. Because while she's sitting down, she won't fall.

They are getting increasingly common,

these periods when she can't remember anything. When her life has just been wiped away like an old lesson from a school white-board.

A cardboard drink cup floats past her down-river and she tries not to think of Cathy and those other kids being swept away, sinking down into the depths. She tries not to think about the washed ivory skin and the matted fair hair of the drowned girl she identified only a few days before.

Cathy is gone.

She has a sense of someone hurrying past. She glances up in time to see the suspicious look, the hurrying footsteps, and she realizes that the knife is in her hand again. Her knuck-les are white, her fingers starting to hurt. Without noticing it, she's been slicing into the wooden seat beneath her. A dozen or more score marks show where she's dug the blade repeatedly into the wood. She almost drops the knife, then, with a huge effort, manages to close it and slip it back into her pocket.

Cathy is gone. Nothing will bring her back now. Might as well get used to it.

She gets up and makes her way home.

■ ■ ■ ■

Part Five: Mary

■ ■ ■ ■

'. . . he watches to strike his blow with unfailing and remorseless cunning . . .'

Star, 10 November 1888

76

Saturday 6 October

When I woke again, Joesbury was still in the chair. As I sat up, he took a long, deep breath and let it out slowly. For a second he seemed to stop breathing. Then his chest rose and fell. His eyelashes flickered and settled again. Some time in the very early morning, my guard had fallen asleep.

I got up and found clothes. When the shower had washed away some of the weariness I dried myself, cleaned my teeth and dressed. As I left the bathroom, I could hear someone moving around in the kitchen.

'Morning,' said Joesbury, glancing up from the previous day's copy of the *Evening Standard.* The kettle was coming to the boil.

'Sleep well?' I asked him and got a grin in return that I think could have broken my heart, had it not been far too late for any nonsense of that sort. I'll say one thing for Joesbury, he kept his sense of humour till the end.

'Ready for a road trip?' he asked me, handing over black coffee.

'Where?' I said.

'Cardiff.'

He squeezed past and I heard the bathroom door being closed and locked. It wasn't quite six in the morning and the two of us couldn't have had more than four hours' sleep; in his case, half of it had been in a chair. And now he thought we were going to Cardiff?

'No offence, but three's a crowd in my book,' I said, when he emerged damp around the edges ten minutes later. 'Gayle Mizon will be packing her best underwear as we speak.'

'Well, you've got fifteen minutes to pack yours. We can get breakfast on the way.'

'I'm not coming to Cardiff. And I don't have any best underwear.'

He yawned and scratched behind one ear. 'Flint,' he said, 'we're leaving in fifteen minutes, in my car, and you can come with underwear or without it. Your call.'

'I want to talk to DI Tulloch,' I said.

Joesbury leaned against the worktop, effectively blocking my way out of the kitchen. 'First, she gets very grouchy in the morning, so sooner you than me,' he said. 'Second, Helen's flying back to Dundee today, so she'll be in an extra-bad mood, and third, she'll only tell you what she and I agreed a few hours ago. We need you out of London for a while. Last night was a bit close to home.'

I couldn't leave London right now. And I certainly couldn't go to Cardiff.

'Here is where I need to be,' I said. 'Llewellyn's done with number four now. She'll be ready for number five. She'll do it soon and I'm still the best chance of catching her. You and Mizon don't need me tagging along.'

'Gayle isn't coming,' said Joesbury. 'It's just us two.'

'And that's supposed to make a difference?'

Joesbury finished his coffee and rinsed the mug out in the sink. 'If sulking keeps you quiet, that's fine by me,' he said. 'Ten minutes.'

Eight minutes later, with a soundtrack of the house/jazz/funk rhythms that Joesbury didn't seem able to operate a car without, we were heading for the river. On Vauxhall Bridge I closed my eyes and pretended I'd fallen asleep. We stopped for five minutes outside the big white Georgian house in

Pimlico where Joesbury had a flat. As we reached Chiswick I risked peeping and saw a rosy glow in the passenger wing mirror. The sun was coming up.

When we hit the M4 Joesbury turned up the volume and picked up speed. A lot of speed. Given the events of the previous night, there seemed a significant risk of his falling asleep at the wheel and killing us both.

All things considered, there were worse ways this could end.

So I closed my eyes again and tried to ignore the nagging voice telling me that every mile took me further from where I needed to be. I managed to stay calm enough for the sleep act to be reasonably convincing. Somewhere along the way, exhaustion got the better of adrenalin and the charade became reality. When I woke, Joesbury had pulled into a service station.

'Where are we?' I asked, as he parked the car and switched off the engine. The music died.

'Membury,' he answered. 'Hungry?'

Surprisingly, I was. We both ordered the full English breakfast and took a table beside the window. I managed about half my plate before my stomach started knotting itself up again. If I walked out on Joesbury now, what were the chances of hitching a lift back to London?

'So, are you going to ask why we're off to Cardiff?' asked Joesbury, as I concentrated on the industrial-strength tea.

I knew exactly why we were going to Cardiff. Joesbury was going to parade me in front of people who'd known Victoria Llewellyn in the hope that one of them would recognize me.

'Why are we going to Cardiff?' I asked.

'First up, we're going to talk to Sergeant Ron Williams,' he answered. 'He was the custody sergeant the night of the rape. He may be able to give us some background on the Llewellyn girls. Or at least, a more accurate idea of what really happened than we'll ever get from the boys or their dads. Are you eating that?'

'Help yourself.' I pushed my plate across the table.

'Then we're going to see a woman called Muffin Thomas,' Joesbury went on, in between mouthfuls. 'She lived next door to the girls for a while, a couple of years before the rape. Lives somewhere called Splatt or Splott or some such.'

'Muffin being a very common Welsh name,' I said.

Joesbury reached into his pocket and

pulled out a notebook. He opened it and turned it to face me.

'Myfanwy,' I said, deciphering his scrawl.

'Say again?'

'Muff-an-wee,' I repeated.

'Do you actually speak Welsh?'

'No. Why would I?'

'Just wondered. Fancy driving from here? I'm wrecked.'

Joesbury's car was effortlessly fast, so much smoother and easier to handle than my Golf. In a little pocket by the gear stick I found a Black Eyed Peas album and put it on. In very different circumstances, I might actually have enjoyed the journey.

As we drove into South Wales, an autumn mist started to creep closer to the edges of the motorway. Sleeping Beauty woke up just before Newport and spent the next twenty minutes on the phone to Tulloch.

'Definitely Karen Curtis's head, no forensic evidence in your shed or garden that will help us, and Jacqui Groves is still very much alive and under close guard,' he said, after ending the call. 'Tully wishes us a good trip and told me to behave myself.'

'She'd be proud of you so far,' I muttered, without taking my eyes off the road.

Out of the corner of my eye, I thought I

saw Joesbury smiling to himself.

The traffic was heavy going into Cardiff centre and it wasn't far off noon when I pulled up in the Sophia Gardens car park. Joesbury jumped out and went to the ticket machine. There was drizzle in the air and a thick mist was coming off the River Taff.

'Police station?' I asked when Joesbury got back.

He shook his head and pulled the collar of his jacket up. 'Nope,' he said, nodding towards the footbridge. 'We're going for a stroll.'

Bute Park is long and narrow, stretching several miles out from the city centre towards the surrounding countryside. Once over the footbridge, we started walking directly across it. After a few minutes the outline of modern buildings on a nearby main road began to take shape. A water-course, that could have been a backwater of the Taff, or even a drainage ditch, marked the furthest boundary of the park. When we reached it, Joesbury turned right and we headed back towards the city. He hadn't explained why we were here and I wasn't going to ask. It wasn't like I couldn't guess.

'What do you reckon, Flint? Look like a copper to you?'

I raised my eyes from the path to see a tallish, plumpish man in his early sixties standing on a narrow, red-brick bridge that crossed the backwater. As we drew closer, the shortness of his hair, the stubbornness of his jaw and just something in his bearing marked him out as one of us.

Sergeant Ron Williams greeted Joesbury first and I waited quietly for my turn. I was wearing my best suit, with a stiff white blouse and tights. My hair was scraped back into my neatest librarian bun and I was wearing glasses. No make-up, of course.

When they'd exchanged a few pleasantries, Sergeant Williams turned to me. Conscious of Joesbury watching the two of us, I gave them both a few seconds.

'You should see the other guy,' I said, when I figured they'd had long enough. Forcing a smile, I held out my hand for Williams to shake. 'I'm DC Lacey Flint.'

'Nice to meet you, DC Flint,' replied Williams, his accent marking him immediately as a man from the Valleys. 'Now, you're stretching the old grey matter a bit. It was all a long time ago. Shall we start with where it happened?'

Joesbury agreed and Williams led us further along the path in the direction of the city. We were close enough now to see the tall Norman keep and, beyond it, the Gothic-fairytale elegance of Cardiff castle. As we drew level with the castle wall, Williams left the path and set off across the grass. Joesbury followed and, a little way behind, so did I.

'This is the magnolia lawn we're crossing now,' said Williams. 'It's quite something in spring.'

The twisted branches of the old trees looked like tendrils reaching out for us. A little way ahead, tall stones began to emerge through the mist.

'So, you think what's been going on in London is something to do with the Llewellyn girls?' asked Williams, taking out a large white handkerchief and pressing it to his face as we drew nearer to the stones. I'd already noticed his eyes were bloodshot and his nose reddened. Williams was fighting a losing battle with a heavy cold.

'Just covering all angles,' said Joesbury.

'I can't see it myself,' said Williams. 'They were nice girls.'

Joesbury's walk slowed a fraction. 'That's not the way the boys' families tell it,' he said.

Williams stopped when we were metres away from the stone circle. 'Aye well, I'm not saying they were angels,' he replied. 'Cardiff lasses rarely are and the older one did run a bit wild. The younger one, though, good as gold she was. Didn't deserve what happened. She died, I heard.'

In front of us, eleven rough-cut stones made a circle of about thirty metres in diameter. The two largest seemed to form a natural entrance. Williams and Joesbury walked through. I trailed along behind.

'You were on duty the night of the alleged rape?' asked Joesbury.

'I was. And then I came down here with the older girl as soon as it was light,' answered Williams. When we were almost in the centre of the circle he stopped.

Joesbury turned on the spot, taking in the upright stones, and the huge flat central one like a sacrificial altar. 'Is this an ancient monument?' he asked.

Williams blew his nose and shook his head. 'No,' he said. 'It was put up in the late seventies. Although the central stone was supposedly part of something Neolithic found in the park. So, do you want me to talk you through it?'

'Please,' said Joesbury.

'Victoria and Cathy met up with the boys in the Owain Glyndwr on St John Street,' said Williams. 'The girls left about twenty past eleven and headed towards the bus stop. When they got to the main road just outside the park, they heard the boys running up after them.'

'The boys followed them from the pub?' asked Joesbury.

'Probably, but what they told the girls was a gang of local lads had started some trouble back in the pub and were hot on their heels. They asked how they could get away quickly.'

'They came in here?' said Joesbury.

Williams nodded. 'Victoria said she wasn't worried about the boys at that point. In the pub they'd been polite, well behaved. She knew that once they were in the park, they could make for the pedestrian bridge across the river and get into the Sophia Gardens car park. They climbed that gate over there, the one in the wall, the boys helping the girls over.'

Joesbury and I both turned to where Williams was pointing. We could just about see a darker line in the mist where we knew the huge stone perimeter wall of the park would be.

'And then it all went wrong,' said Joesbury.

'Victoria said she and Cathy set off through the park and the boys followed behind. Before long, though, she knew something wasn't right. The boys fell back, out of sight, but they could hear them, cat-calling, whispering to each other. Victoria told me she realized she'd made a big mistake so she grabbed hold of Cathy and scarpered.'

'She tried to outrun them?' asked Joesbury, his eyes flicking from the park entrance to where he judged the bridge would be.

'They hadn't got a hope,' said Williams. 'Girls in high heels, half-cut on cheap booze. Cathy fell over, they got separated and that was that.'

'Is this where it happened?' asked Joesbury, looking back towards the flat central stone.

'They pulled them over the stone,' said Williams. 'One on either side. They could see each other's faces while it was going on.'

He stepped closer to the stone. It was raised on a mound of earth. On each side, two smaller flat stones had been laid to form steps.

'They pulled Vicky over this side, held a knife to her throat and raped her,' said Williams. 'Over a dozen times, she told me. She stopped counting at twelve. And all the time she had to watch her fourteen-year-old sister going through exactly the same thing.'

I turned away from the two men and fixed

my eyes on the treetops.

'She said the worst of it, though, was that the city seemed so close,' continued Williams. 'She could see lights, hear traffic, even people, and none of them could help her. She told me she'd never felt so helpless.'

'You're very quiet, Lacey,' said Joesbury.

'I'm not particularly enjoying the story,' I replied, forcing myself to look at him.

'No, love. I'm not sure anyone would,' said Williams, dabbing his nose.

'How did they get away?' said Joesbury, turning back to Williams. 'Did the boys just get tired of it and go?'

'No, they threw them in the river,' said Williams.

Joesbury almost did a double take. 'They did what?'

'Undressed them, carried them naked over to the bank and threw them in,' said Williams, nodding in the direction of the Taff. 'Getting rid of evidence, if you ask me. They were being extra cautious, because they all used condoms. And they made Vicky touch a packet before they threw her in. Tried to make out she'd bought them.'

'So the girls got out of the river. Then what?' asked Joesbury.

'They found their clothes, got dressed and made their way to Cardiff Central. That's where they found me. Tell you what, I'm fair freezing out here. Anyone fancy a cup of tea?'

77

The cafeteria at Cardiff Central was lunch-time busy but Williams managed to find us a table.

'So what happened after they came in?' asked Joesbury.

'I played it by the book,' said Williams. 'I had a feeling it was one that could get very nasty. I separated the girls and got a WPC to sit with each until I could get the doc over. We have a dedicated rape unit now, with officers trained to deal with sexual violence, but in those days we just had to do our best.'

'What about the boys?'

'The girls knew where they were staying, so I sent a couple of cars out to fetch them in. They arrived thirty minutes later and I arrested all five of them. That's when it all started to go pear-shaped.'

'How so?' asked Joesbury, leaning back in his chair.

'The games teacher came with them,' replied Williams. 'Started throwing his weight around. He was an old public-school type himself. He insisted none of the boys talk to anyone until they each had a solicitor. It was nearly two in the morning by this time. You can imagine the picnic trying to find five solicitors. And these were minors we were dealing with, remember?'

'Oh, I can just see it,' said Joesbury.

'The girls' foster mother arrived and started getting hysterical,' said Williams. 'Then we had Social Services pitch in.'

'How were the girls coping?' I asked.

Williams looked at me. 'Victoria was holding up well,' he said. 'Quite self-possessed, that one. Cathy was a mess. Sobbing and crying, begging to go home.'

My hands were shaking. I wrapped them around my mug to keep them still.

'Then the doctor who attended refused to examine Cathy. He said that because she was underage, she needed to be seen by a paediatrician.'

Joesbury gave a small, sympathetic smile.

'Well, there was no finding one of them in the middle of the night.' Williams had a pinched look on his face and I didn't think it was just the effects of the cold any more.

'So you let them go home without Cathy

being examined?' I asked.

Williams held up one hand. 'Love, I knew it wasn't right,' he said. 'But I had two social workers, the foster mother and the lass herself telling me to let her go. And by that time, the boys' parents were starting to arrive. It was bloody mayhem, if you'll excuse my Welsh. And I didn't let them go. Someone else took that decision.'

'OK, but Victoria was examined properly?' prompted Joesbury.

'She was,' replied Williams. 'But the examination wasn't conclusive. No traces of semen at all.'

'The boys used condoms,' I said. 'There wouldn't be.'

Williams nodded. 'They did,' he said. 'And the dunking in the Taff would have got rid of any accidental spills, if you get my drift. The examination did find some minor lacerations and bruises, but nothing that couldn't be consistent with consensual sex.'

'It was starting to look like their word against the boys',' said Joesbury.

'As soon as it was light, we did a search of the park,' said Williams. 'We found the condom packet with Victoria's prints on it. And the batch number showed that it had been bought from the girls' lavatory in the pub where they'd been drinking.'

'When did you let the boys go?' asked Joesbury.

Williams ran his hands across his eyes. 'We were getting towards the end of the twenty-four-hour period,' he said. 'The parents had brought in some heavy-hitting legal help by this stage. It was either charge them or let them go.'

'What did the girls want to do?' I asked.

'Cathy was falling apart big time,' Williams answered. 'She had a counsellor advising her not to talk to us if she didn't want to. Victoria wanted to press charges and I didn't blame her. Them lads were nasty pieces of work. We see it a lot. Kids with rich parents think they can get away with murder.'

'But Victoria changed her mind?' I asked.

'She did, love,' said Williams. 'And this is the bit I'm really not proud of. The lawyers requested a meeting with her and eventually she agreed to it. I went too, with our own legal help. We weren't going to be walked all over.'

'And?' said Joesbury.

'It was very short and to the point. They pointed out that she was the only one in the park that night over the legal age of consent and that sex with a minor, of either sex, is considered statutory rape. They would agree not to press charges, if she did too.'

'They threatened to charge her with rape?' Joesbury, to give him his due, looked incredulous.

Williams inclined his head.

'Would they have got away with it?'

Williams shrugged. 'Possibly. They had the fingerprints on the condom packet and technically they had the law on their side. If the sex had been consensual, Victoria would have broken the law. They also pointed out that her sexual history would be brought up in court. As I said, she was no angel, even at sixteen she had a past.'

'You allowed a juvenile rape victim to be intimidated out of pressing charges?' said Joesbury.

'We broke the meeting up at that point,' said Williams. 'But the damage was done. Victoria knew she was on a hiding to nothing. And she didn't want to put her sister through a court case.'

Williams showed us out. We stood on the front steps of Cardiff Central police station and thanked him for his time.

'When did you last see Victoria?' asked Joesbury.

'That day,' said Williams. 'I came across Cathy a few times after that, she turned into a bit of a tearaway, but Victoria I never saw again. We had a bit of a hunt for her when she disappeared, you know. She took a stolen car with her.'

I'd been looking at the graceful white buildings around me. 'What do you think, Sergeant Williams?' I asked, turning back to him. 'Were the girls telling the truth?'

His eyes held mind steadily. 'I never doubted it for a moment, love.'

78

'Alice fostered thirty-two children in twenty years. She never got tired of telling people.'

Myfanwy Thomas, who at one time had been next-door neighbour to the Llewellyn girls and their foster parents, was in her early fifties, but still vain enough to wear clothes that were too tight and use shop-bought hair dye to cover up the grey. She'd given me a quick once-over when we'd arrived. 'My goodness, love, you have been in the wars,' she'd announced, before turning her attention to Joesbury.

'Do you remember the Llewellyn sisters?' I asked.

She frowned at me, before concentrating on Joesbury again. 'Biscuit, love?'

Joesbury helped himself to a HobNob and smiled at her. I swear the woman practically simpered at him.

'In trouble, are they?' she asked him. 'I'm not surprised, not with Vicky anyway. The problems Alice had with that girl.'

'So Vicky was a bit of a handful?' asked Joesbury.

'You wouldn't know the half of it, love. If she went to school one day in three it was going well. Pleased herself when she came back for meals. Stayed out till all hours.'

'Sounds a fairly typical teenager to me,' I said, raising my eyes above Myfanwy's head to the small, walled backyard.

'There was something not right about that one,' said Myfanwy, giving me the briefest of glares. 'Her bedroom was full of nasty books, used to give Alice the creeps. Stephen King, James Herbert, you know the sort.'

'So she read a lot?' I asked.

The woman shook her head. 'Nothing nice,' she said. 'She'd get true-crime books out of the library. Serial killers and mass murderers and the like. She wasn't normal.'

I could sense DI Joesbury taking just a little bit more notice.

'And that dye she used on her hair.' Myfanwy was on a roll now. 'Black as soot, it was. The mess she made on Alice's bathroom carpet.'

'Sounds a real delinquent,' I muttered, sitting back in my chair and looking round the not-very-clean kitchen.

'She took up with a boyfriend shortly after they came to live here,' said Myfanwy. 'Proper waster, he was. Used to steal cars and race round the docks in them.'

'We're struggling to find photographs of Victoria,' said Joesbury. 'Can I ask you to describe her for me? We're trying to get an artist's impression produced. As you lived next door to her for two years, you'd be a big help.'

'She wasn't pretty, not like her sister,' said Myfanwy. 'She used to cake her face in that horrible white make-up. Like a ghoul. How she got away with it at school, I don't know.'

'Actually, we know about her hair and make-up,' said Joesbury. 'I'm more concerned with bone structure. You know, I sometimes think it helps to have a reference point. Why don't you look at my colleague here and tell me how Victoria was different?'

Oh, nice one, DI Joesbury. Very slick.

'Sit still, Flint,' instructed Joesbury, although I already was. 'How do the eyes compare?' he asked Myfanwy.

'Victoria was all eyes,' she replied after a moment. 'This lady's are much smaller. And Victoria didn't need glasses.'

'Neither does DC Flint,' said Joesbury, with something like impatience creeping into his voice. 'Hand them over.'

Without taking my eyes off Myfanwy Thomas, I removed my glasses and put them on the table in front of me.

'What about my mouth?' I said.

She shook her head. 'Thicker lips. More pouty somehow. And she wasn't as thin as you.'

'Nose?' I said.

'No offence, love, but yours is so swollen I can't tell what it's like normally. And I never saw Victoria with two black eyes or a split lip. I won't lie to you, she did get into fights, but she knew how to handle herself. The other girls always used to come off worst.'

'I think they still do,' said Joesbury under his breath.

79

'Sorry to keep you,' the woman from social services said to us from the doorway. 'Normally, we can't give out details without a court order.' Mrs Rita Jenkins reclaimed her seat in the small interview room in one of Cardiff's municipal buildings. She'd come into work on a Saturday specially to meet us. Joesbury stepped away from the window and sat down beside me.

'But confidentiality expires if the person in question is dead?' he asked.

'Well, yes, it does,' Mrs Jenkins agreed. 'There's a note on file about Catherine's death,' she went on. 'Ten years ago, does that sound right?'

I nodded.

Mrs Jenkins frowned. 'As far as Victoria's concerned, the director's happy for me to tell you what I can,' she said.

'We're hoping to find someone who knew the girls,' said Joesbury.

Jenkins pursed her lips. 'Eleven years is a long time,' she said. 'Social work has a high staff turnover. And back then, adoption and fostering came under South Glamorgan County Council. That was abolished a few years ago and the department transferred to Cardiff. People got moved around in the restructuring. I can try and track some down for you. It'll take a while though.'

'I appreciate that,' said Joesbury, who was starting to run out of steam.

Jenkins was flicking through one of the files. 'It doesn't often go that badly wrong,' she said. 'A young girl dead. And pregnant at fourteen. Bloody mess, I must say.'

The man at my side was paying attention again.

'Excuse me?' he said. 'Cathy was pregnant?'

Jenkins nodded her head sadly. 'Yes, it was confirmed a few weeks after the incident in Bute Park.'

Joesbury looked at me. 'Hang on a minute,' he said. 'The boys used condoms.'

'Condoms aren't bulletproof,' I said. 'Isn't there something like a 3 per cent failure rate?'

Joesbury raised both hands in a surrender gesture. 'Flint, I bow to your greater —'

'Don't even go there,' I snapped.

Joesbury turned back to Jenkins. 'So what happened to her?' he asked. 'Did she have the baby?'

Jenkins shook her head. 'No,' she said. 'The pregnancy was terminated at eleven weeks. The trouble was, that wasn't the end of the matter.'

'How so?' asked Joesbury.

'She got a form of postnatal depression that we see a lot in young girls who've had terminations,' Jenkins said. 'She was prescribed antidepressants and was allowed to get addicted. She was suspected of taking other things as well. Then she contracted an infection as a direct result of the operation. There was irreparable damage done to her insides. Things just went from bad to worse after that. Her school-work plummeted, there were all sorts of behavioural issues, but she wouldn't see any of the counsellors we suggested. She became a very sick girl.'

'And then she ran away?' said Joesbury.

'Yes,' agreed Jenkins. 'Then we lost her.'

80

By six o'clock, Joesbury and I were both shattered. We'd visited the children's home where Victoria and Catherine had lived, on and off, for most of their teenage years. Neither care workers nor files had little to offer that was new. Cathy was the quiet, pleasant-natured one, Victoria the problem child, in and out of trouble, suspected of being up to worse than she was ever caught at.

Joesbury got excited when we managed to track down Victoria's former English teacher. The look on his face when the tiny woman opened her front door and we realized she could barely see was the highlight of my day.

Miss Munnery's eyesight might have been failing, but her brain was razor sharp. She remembered both girls, Victoria in particular. 'I remember her leaving,' she said to us, as we were getting ready to go. 'I was sad, but not surprised. That trouble with her sister in the park — something died inside her when that happened. She became — what's the word I'm looking for? — cold. Her eyes looked, I don't know . . .'

'Unhappy?' I suggested as we stood on the doorstep.

'No, dear,' she replied. 'They looked like shark's eyes. Dark and dead.'

Police budgets don't stretch to luxury hotels, but business centres like Cardiff often have empty hotel rooms at the weekends. The Met had got us a good deal on a new and rather glitzy hotel in the bay area and we checked in shortly after six.

'Where do you want to eat?' asked Joesbury, stifling a yawn as we took the lift up.

'Actually, I don't,' I said, without taking my eyes off the lift buttons. 'I'm just going to crash. I'll see you at breakfast.'

The lift got to my floor first and I left it without looking back. My room was beautiful, quite the classiest place I'd ever been in. The bed was king-size, the décor understated but elegant in shades of soft cream and biscuit. Most of one wall was glass. I walked over and pulled back drapes that were fine as cobwebs.

Night had fallen properly by this stage and

lights were shining across the water. Not far from shore a yacht had anchored. It gleamed like a jewel on dark velvet and I could see people moving around on deck. The lights seemed to stretch away from it like coloured streamers across the water. I watched the yacht until everyone went below and the loneliness felt like something that could smother me.

Then I ran a bath and lay in the water for a long time, thinking of Joesbury a floor or two above me and of what could never be. And I thought about two young girls, who hadn't had much to start with except each other, and who had lost even that when an evening in the city had gone so very badly wrong. I lay there, thinking that finally, at last, I might have found enough courage to take my own life. And that I probably would do exactly that when this was all over; in a warm, sweet-scented bath just like this one.

When the water was starting to cool, I got up and dressed in jeans and a sweater. I pulled on trainers and my jacket and left the hotel. Outside, I fastened my coat and started walking. Within a few metres, the smooth brick path became rough stone and shingle. Most of the remaining light slipped away and rough grasses, taller than me, rose up on either side, turning the path into a tunnel.

I was walking through an area of natural wetlands, preserved as part of the bay development. Signs along the path warned of deep water, life buoys at intervals suggested the signs probably weren't kidding and soft splashing sounds told me I wasn't alone out here.

To my right, through gaps in the grass I could see a single row of brick-built terraced houses. Lights were shining in most of the windows. I saw a woman of about my own age, with a toddler in her arms, pull the curtains in an upstairs room. She stopped for a second to look at the solitary figure walking through the wetlands, before shutting herself off from view.

A normal life. It had never seemed so far away.

I kept on walking, listening to the sounds of the city on one side of me and those of the bay on the other, until I reached a wooden pier that zigzagged out across the water. As I made my way along, water gurgled gently below it and a swan flew close enough for me to feel the air under its wings. It landed close by and disappeared into the bullrushes.

I'd reached the end of the wooden structure when, a hundred metres or so behind me, someone else stepped on to the pier.

I bent forward, leaning my elbows against the wooden railing. To my right was a small marina, the yacht riggings clinking gently in the wind like tiny bells. The port buildings of the old Tiger Bay were across to my left and I could just about make out tall cranes and a few boat masts against the skyline.

The footsteps on the pier were getting closer. They were heavy, the steps of a man. I watched a water taxi skim across the bay like one of the water fowl.

'I told you I wasn't hungry,' I said a second later, to the reeds in front of me.

'What you said was, you were going to crash,' came the response. 'And what makes you think they're for you?'

'A man who stalks me with chips in his hands had better be prepared to share,' I said, turning round.

Joesbury had two wrapped packages under his arm and a carrier bag in one hand. The smell of hot chips had given him away. We set off back along the pier and, once on dry land, stopped at a large stone sculpture that looked a bit like a wave and a bit like a sail. It had a circular base and we sat down together. Joesbury handed over a package that had *Harry Ramsden* stamped on it.

'I'm feeling surprisingly warm towards you right now,' I said, unwrapping it. I honestly hadn't realized quite how hungry I'd become.

'Well, that sounds like progress,' he replied and I could tell from the tone of his voice that he was smiling. I heard the sound of a ring-pull being torn and then Joesbury handed over a cold can of lager. I drank and put it down on the stone beside me. In the tall grasses in front of us something was rustling. For a few minutes we ate in silence.

'Have you heard from DI Tulloch again?' I asked, when the more pressing hunger pangs were starting to fade.

'The image enhancers have got back to her,' Joesbury replied. 'You know, the boffins who take a picture of a three-year-old with a bad diet and age it so that you know the kid will be Lard Man with prostate cancer when he's forty.'

Wishing I hadn't asked, I nodded. A few days ago, Tulloch had sent the snapshots of the Llewellyn girls away to see if a computer programme could indicate what they might look like in their late twenties.

'Any good?' I asked, realizing my hunger had mysteriously disappeared.

Joesbury popped another chip in his mouth and shook his head. 'Not promising, from what she told me,' he said, in between chews. 'They didn't have much to work on with Victoria, given that the picture was in profile. They had a bit more with Catherine, but nothing conclusive.'

'Shame,' I said, putting my fork down.

Joesbury looked at me sideways. 'Turns out the kit works best on distinctive features,' he said. 'Big noses, pointy chins, wide foreheads. Classically pretty women like the Llewellyn girls, especially Catherine, have very bland features. How they look when they're older depends on things we can't predict — weight loss or gain, skin condition, that sort of thing.'

'Worth a try, I suppose,' I said, and pushed a few chips around the tray to give the impression I was still eating.

Joesbury finished his first can and opened another. 'Some wag in the department aged Cathy's picture twenty years, darkened the hair and skin tone, and now it's a dead ringer for Tully herself,' he said.

I managed a smile. 'Well, let's hope she has a good alibi.'

Silence fell again and I found I could eat some more, after all.

'Is Dana all right?' I asked after a few seconds.

Out of the corner of my eye, I saw Joesbury's head flick in my direction. 'She's fine,' he said. 'She's tougher than she looks.'

Joesbury was so full of shit. 'Yeah, OK,' I said.

'What?' He had his hard-man voice on. This wasn't something I should have brought up. Well, tough. I was way past worrying about upsetting senior officers.

'I know she's struggled with this case,' I said, turning to look at him properly. His eyes had narrowed, one brow was higher than the other, he was just daring me to say something disrespectful about his precious Dana. 'She told me so herself,' I finished. I wasn't scared of Joesbury any more.

'We're all struggling with this case,' said Joesbury, in a voice that told me he intended to have the last word.

'Yeah, well, we don't all have eating disorders,' I replied. 'And we certainly don't all have suicide scars.'

Joesbury took a deep breath and let it out noisily. He leaned slightly closer. 'There is absolutely nothing wrong with the way Dana has been leading this investigation,' he said in clipped tones.

I leaned closer too, until I could smell vinegar on his breath. 'I didn't say there was,' I came back. 'I asked if she was OK.

You're not the only one who likes her, you know.'

Joesbury turned away from me, finished his meal and screwed up the paper. For a moment, I thought he was sulking. Then, 'Those scars weren't self-inflicted,' he said, in a soft voice.

Now that I hadn't expected. 'Someone else did that to her?'

He gave a sharp nod. 'She doesn't like to talk about it,' he said, before standing up. 'Are you done?'

I folded the greasy paper carefully and stood up. I'd got the message. We set off back and for a minute or two Joesbury didn't speak. I had the impression, though, that he was thoughtful rather than angry.

'Have you thought what you might do when you finish training?' he asked me, when we'd deposited the chip papers and empty cans in a bin.

I was waving my fingers in the air to get the smell of fat and vinegar off them. 'To be honest, I'm finding it difficult to see much beyond this case,' I said, which was certainly the truth, if not the whole truth. For me, there was nothing beyond the case.

We set off again and before long were approaching the hotel. Leaving the shingle path, we re-joined the smooth red-brick one that would lead us to the front door. The path circled around another sculpture, this time a large brick circle decorated with massive rocks and cast-iron seagulls. Joesbury stopped walking and turned to face me.

'We should have a chat,' he said. 'When this is all over. About where you go next.'

Not far from us, people were milling around outside the hotel. A couple getting into a taxi. Two middle-aged women smoking and shivering. A man strolling up and down, talking loudly into his mobile; in Welsh.

'You're offering me career advice?' I said.

'Let's just say I have a couple of ideas,' he replied. 'As does Dana, by the way. If she survives this case, she'll be after you for the MIT.'

The wind was picking up. My hair blew across my face and I reached up to push it away. Joesbury's hand got there first, brushing against my right ear. I pulled away and turned to face the bay.

'What have I said?' he asked.

'Nothing.' On the sculpture in front of us, some of the iron seagulls had broken off. Only their feet remained, clinging to the rocks.

'How has that upset you?'

I swallowed hard. Both he and Tulloch

were assuming I had a future in the Met. Shit, I could not cry.

'Lacey Flint, you are one weird girl.' He'd moved closer.

'Tell me something I don't know.'

'I still think you're trouble,' he said. One finger was brushing the sleeve of my jacket and I could feel his breath against the side of my face.

'Can't argue with that,' I muttered.

He was holding my hair now, winding it round in his hand, gently pulling me back towards him. 'So why is it that every morning when I wake up,' he said, as I felt his cold fingers on the back of my neck, 'the first thought in my head is you?'

81

13 September, ten years earlier

By the time Victoria Llewellyn arrives back, it's dark. She climbs the fence and slips across the abandoned ground. At the metal gate, she finds her torch and makes her way inside. The tunnel is dark and damp, but cheap lanterns light the way. She climbs steps and, still in almost complete darkness, makes her way around camps and prone bodies. When she sees the hospital screen and the calor-gas stove she slows down.

A girl is lying on the mattress the two of them share. Victoria shines her torch softly on the girl's face. She doesn't want to wake her up.

The girl isn't asleep. Her eyes are wide open. A second later, Victoria is on her knees, checking for a pulse, for breath, anything. Her friend isn't dead yet, but close.

'Oh God no, not you too.' She has to get her up, get her to where they can find help. She slips an arm beneath the other girl's shoulders and tugs. 'Come on, wake up. You have to help me. Come on, Lacey, I can't lose you too.'

Lacey's eyes focus for a second on Victoria's and she struggles to her feet. Slowly, the two girls make their way back out to the night.

82

In my room, I sat in darkness for a long time, staring out at the water. One by one lights across the bay went out, and as each one disappeared, a tiny chunk of time seemed to be slipping away. Eventually, all movement ceased and the bay settled down for the night.

At one o'clock in the morning, I knew I couldn't play a waiting game any longer. I had to get back to London. More importantly, I had to get Mark Joesbury off my back.

Against all odds, coming to Cardiff had helped, I realized. I'd got through the various traps he'd set and he was starting to get some measure of trust back. Not enough, though. It was time to take a huge gamble.

I was going to have to tell him the truth.

Not giving myself the chance to chicken out, I left my room and walked barefoot to the lift. I'd changed after getting back and was dressed in loose jogging pants and a running vest. At the door of his room, I knocked gently.

When he opened the door, he was bare-chested, with brightly coloured, button-up cotton trousers slung low on his waist. The way he was squinting at the bright corridor lights told me I'd dragged him from a pretty deep sleep. When he registered that it was me, the look in his eyes became a mixture of bewildered, curious and hopeful. I didn't give him chance to open his mouth.

'There's something I need to tell you,' I said.

He rubbed both eyes and then turned and walked back into the room. I followed, letting the door swing shut behind me.

Joesbury's room was even bigger than mine, with two double beds. As he switched on a reading lamp, I saw that the bed he'd been sleeping in had a pillow laid lengthways and that it was dented. He'd fallen asleep hugging it.

On the other bed, glossy pages from a souvenir book of the Ripper mystery had been spread across the counterpane. I had a copy of the book myself. As a reference work it had been close to useless, but it did have perfect reproductions of much of the original documentation, including the mortuary photographs of the five victims. Joesbury, who I guess had fallen under the Ripper's spell like so many do, had spread them out across the bed in chronological order. Polly Nichols, Annie Chapman, Elizabeth Stride, Catharine Eddowes and Mary Kelly.

He walked the full length of the room. I picked up the photograph of the mutilated Mary Kelly and moved it further up the bed, before perching on the corner.

'Want a drink?' he offered. I shook my head.

The huge windows were open a fraction and the room was cold. The night air was goose-pimpling the skin on his shoulders and I found myself shivering. I watched him walk to the bathroom, reach inside and bring out a large, white towelling robe. He wrapped it round himself and then, from a pile of clothes over a chair, found a sweatshirt and threw it across.

'Central heating at night gives me a headache,' he said.

I pulled the sweatshirt over my head. It was the one Joesbury had been wearing all day. It was cool, like the room, but its smell made me think of a warm body, moving closer. When I could see again, he was pouring himself a drink from the minibar. More awake now, he sat in an armchair in front of the window and looked at me.

I took a deep breath. 'I know this is something I should have told you before,' I said. 'But I think you'll understand why I didn't. At least, until I was sure there was no alternative.'

A glass with about two centimetres of amber-coloured liquid was in his left hand. He brought it to his lips.

'You remember me telling you I lived on the streets for a while?' I asked him. He inclined his head and the glass went down on the table beside him with a soft clink. 'And you know I had a drug problem once?'

Another nod from him. Another deep breath from me.

'The truth is, I was a complete mess,' I said. 'Completely addicted to heroin for nearly two years. It was far, far worse than I told the Met's selection process.'

One eyebrow went up.

'What I told them was that I'd had a problem in the past,' I went on. 'That it had been the main reason why I didn't finish my degree, but that I'd been clean for several years before I applied to join the police.'

Joesbury's eyebrow relaxed. His eyes hadn't left mine.

'They did lots of tests,' I said. 'And they found out that as far as that part was concerned, I was telling the truth. I was completely clean when I applied. I'd been lucky in that I'd always managed to avoid any serious trouble with the police. If I'd had a record of any kind I wouldn't have got past first base, I know that. But when I applied, they were broadening their admissions criteria. The fact that I knew so much about what you call London's low-life was seen as an advantage. They thought people like me would bring something new to the service.'

I could see from Joesbury's expression what he thought about the Met's relatively recent relaxation of its selection procedures. 'They'll let anyone join these days,' was a refrain heard a lot around stations.

'I had to be routinely tested all the time I was going through training,' I said. 'And I had to see counsellors. The Met didn't take any stupid risks. But I kept my nose clean and I got good marks in all my exams.'

'So they let you through,' said Joesbury.

'They let me through,' I agreed. 'But if they'd known the truth, it would never have happened. When you report what I'm about to tell you — and I know you have to — I'll be finished in the force.'

I stopped, giving myself a moment.

'I have no family,' I went on, after a second. 'And as you've probably seen for yourself, not much of a social life. My career is everything and I couldn't give up on it until there was no choice. Can you understand that?'

'Consider it understood,' said Joesbury. 'But you haven't really told me anything yet.'

'My home life was abusive,' I began. 'You don't need the details. I went to live with my grandparents, but they couldn't cope. So I spent most of my childhood in and out of children's homes and foster care.'

'Sounds like someone we know,' said Joesbury.

'By the time I was sixteen I was smoking weed, using cocaine when I could get it, experimenting with all sorts of weird cocktails. Cocaine and meth was a popular one at the time. For all that, I was pretty bright and I managed to hold things together enough to get a university place. But on a campus it was all so easy to get hold of. By the end of my first year, I barely knew what day it was. I was thrown off the course, naturally. I had nowhere to go. My grandparents were both dead by this time and the State stops looking after you when you're eighteen.'

'You went to London?' Joesbury said.

I nodded. 'It seemed as good a place as any,' I said. 'I found a group of kids in north London who taught me the ropes. We used to sleep in abandoned buildings, until we were moved on. Then we'd look for the next one.'

'Where did the drugs come from?' asked Joesbury.

This was the bit I was going to struggle with. I dropped my eyes to the carpet.

'Were you on the game?' he asked me.

I kept my eyes down and nodded. 'There was a boy called Rich,' I said. 'He was Jamaican. Young, but big and nasty with it. He was . . . my pimp . . . I suppose. He had a few other girls working for him as well. He'd take us out, sometimes to clubs or bars, sometimes just street corners and derelict buildings, and send the punters to us.'

I risked looking up. Joesbury's eyes seemed to have lost all their colour.

'I never saw any money,' I said. 'None of the girls did. We did tricks and then we got the gear. There was a brief window every day when we were just about functional. Rich would collect us, take us to places where we could get cleaned up and fed, and then we'd go out. By the time the business was over, we were desperate. All we could think about was the next hit and just being able to forget.'

Joesbury's empty glass made contact with the table.

'Sometimes, Rich would just turn up wherever we were sleeping with some of his mates,' I said. 'He didn't even charge them. They just took turns until they'd had enough. That's why I want to work with the sex-crimes unit. Because of what happened to me.'

Joesbury got up and poured himself another drink.

'I think it would have gone on like that,' I said, 'until one day I took the wrong stuff or just too much of it and didn't wake up any more.'

'So what happened?' he asked me, sitting down again.

'I met a girl,' I said.

Joesbury sat a little more upright in his chair.

'I'd been on the streets for a few months when she just turned up one day,' I said. 'She was about my age, maybe a year or so younger, and completely naive about street life. But she was different somehow. She was focused.'

Joesbury put his drink down. 'Focused how?'

'She didn't take drugs,' I said. 'She had nothing to do with Rich and his friends. She wasn't — I don't know how to put it, really — she wasn't hopeless.'

'Go on,' said Joesbury.

'She was looking for someone,' I said. 'Another girl. She had a photograph. She spent her days just making her way around London, around all the places where homeless people gather, showing the photograph, asking around.'

'Did she tell you who it was?'

I shook my head. 'Never,' I said. 'She really didn't talk much about herself. I knew she'd grown up in care, like me, and that she had nowhere else to go, like me.'

'What was her name?'

'I called her Tic.'

He frowned at me. 'Tic?' he said.

'People on the street don't use their real names,' I said. 'Most of them are hiding from something or someone. They use nicknames, made-up names, several names. She told me to call her Tic and I did.'

'Do you think she was Victoria Llewellyn?' asked Joesbury.

I nodded. 'I think she must have been,' I said. 'But you have to believe me, she looked nothing like that photograph we have. Her hair was much longer, for one thing, and she was fair, not blonde exactly, but close. She wore practical, sensible clothes and no makeup. Ever. And she had, I don't know, a sort of poise about her. There was no way she was some screwed-up Welsh teenager.'

'Welsh accent?'

'Possibly.' He raised his eyebrows, gave me an incredulous look. 'Look, I was a total sleepwalker, I couldn't have told you about my own accent most of the time. I remember a lovely, soft voice. That's all.'

'OK, OK, calm down. What happened to her?'

'I think — I have problems remembering time frames, I was out of my head so much of the time — but I think she found the girl she was looking for and it wasn't good.'

He leaned forward. 'She was dead?' he said. 'Well, that would fit. We know Cathy died round about —'

I shook my head. 'I don't think so,' I said. 'I remember getting back one night and Tic was like all the fire had gone out of her, but it didn't seem like grief somehow. After that, she stopped going out, she just hung around all day, brooding. When I tried to cheer her up, to say there were other places we could look, she just said there was no point, that some people just didn't want to be found.'

'Maybe she got tired of looking.'

'Maybe,' I said. 'But I think if that had been the case, the change would have been more gradual. This happened instantly. I think she found her — Cathy — and it wasn't a happy family reunion.'

Joesbury sighed. 'You know, it would really help if you could put a timescale on this,' he said.

'Ten years ago. End of the summer,' I said. 'August, maybe September. I remember because we knew the place we were living in wouldn't be suitable when the weather got colder, we knew we'd have to find somewhere else.'

'The houseboat accident when Cathy died was 27 August,' said Joesbury. 'What happened to her, this Tic girl?'

'I don't know,' I said. 'But I do know that she saved me.'

'How so?'

'She started talking about leaving,' I said. 'Saying that there was no point staying on the streets any longer. I'd got so dependent on her by that stage. I just couldn't face the thought of being on my own again.'

'So?'

I ran a hand over my face. A decade later, this was still a memory I struggled with. 'So

I took too much stuff one night,' I said. 'Maybe it was just corrupted shit, I don't know. When I came round the next morning, I was in hospital.'

'She took you there?' asked Joesbury.

I nodded. 'She managed to get me to the main street. It was the middle of the night and there was no transport. She couldn't find a phone either. So she stole a car and drove me to hospital. I'd have died if she hadn't.'

'Then what?'

'When I was well enough, she took me to a private clinic and gave them enough money for me to stay there for a month. I'd no idea she had money, but suddenly she produced thousands.'

'Her grandfather's house,' said Joesbury.

I nodded. 'She told me this was my one chance to sort my life out and I shouldn't blow it. Then she went.'

'Did you ever see her again?'

I shook my head. 'Never. But I stayed at the clinic. It was hell, but I got through it. Social Services arranged for me to go to a hostel as long as I stayed clean. After a few months I got a job. Then my own place. I got accepted in the RAF reserves and found I quite liked the discipline, the camaraderie. A couple of years later, I started thinking about applying to the Met. I know she's a monster, but she saved me.'

'OK,' said Joesbury, leaning forward with his elbows on his knees. 'I can buy that you came across the Llewellyn girl when you were an out-and-out and that the two of you hung out together for a while. I can even just about accept that you didn't recognize the photograph. But what I'm struggling with is why she's fixating on you after all this time. Why involve you in her little revenge games? You had nothing to do with what went on in Cardiff.'

'No, but she knew what was happening to me in London,' I said. 'About all the punters I was expected to service, about Rich and the gang rapes. It made her furious. She kept begging me to put an end to it, to get myself out. I was a victim, just like she'd been.'

Joesbury leaned back in his chair, a frown line running down the middle of his brow.

'I only knew her for a few months, but she was the closest I'd ever come to someone I really cared about,' I said. 'We lived together, if you can call a few square feet of concrete floor surrounded by cardboard any sort of home. I think this thing that she's doing now, this revenge business, killing the boys' mothers — in some weird way, I think she's doing it for me too.'

Seconds ticked by. I took deep breaths, hoping my heartbeat would slow down.

'I'm sorry I didn't say anything before,' I said. 'But even now, I still can't be sure that it's her. And I had so much to lose.'

Joesbury gave a deep sigh, then stood up. He turned his back on me and pulled open the window. The room hadn't been warm, but the air coming in felt like it was straight from the Arctic. I tucked my knees up inside his huge sweatshirt and watched him walk to the balcony rail and lean over. When the Ripper photographs started to blow around the room I got up too and stepped to the open window. He was looking across the bay, directly out to sea.

'That's it,' I said to the back of his head. 'Everything. And I'm dead on my feet. Can we pick this up again in the morning?'

He nodded without turning round. I waited another second, then went back into the room. As I walked past the bed, I caught sight of the photograph of the butchered Mary Kelly. The one Ripper killing still to be replicated.

The lift was about fifteen metres away along the corridor. I'd raised my hand to press the call button when the last piece of the jigsaw fell into place.

Oh Christ.

83

I was back at Joesbury's door, rapping loudly, hardly caring who I woke up. 'Let me in,' I hissed, the second I heard him turning the lock. I pushed on the door, making him step back into the room.

'What the —' he managed.

'We have to get back to London,' I said. 'Right now. Get Dana on the phone. We've been absolute idiots.'

'Lacey, calm down. What the hell's got into you?'

I pushed past him to get to the bed. The photograph of the horribly carved-up body of Mary Kelly was on the pillow. I reached out and picked it up.

'I should have seen it,' I said. 'I knew she'd have a way, some way of getting to number five. She's got her already, I bet you anything, we have to —'

Two warm hands were on my bare shoulders.

'Right, deep breath. Stop talking.'

'Sir, there isn't —'

'Shut up. Now.' One hand was across my mouth. He was right. I had to get a grip. But Jesus, why hadn't I seen it, why?

Carefully, reminding me of someone about to let a wild animal out of a cage, he peeled his fingers away from my mouth.

'Slowly,' he told me.

'She knew we'd work it out after she killed Charlotte and Karen,' I said. 'Victims three and four. She knew we'd put a guard on number five.'

'And we have,' said Joesbury, speaking slowly. 'Three hours ago, Jacqui Groves was fine and dandy. Are you saying she —'

'Jacqui Groves wasn't the one. Llewellyn never had any intention of going after her.'

Joesbury shook his head. 'She's the last of the mothers,' he said.

'The Ripper's first four victims were women in their forties,' I said. 'Just like the mothers. Then he changed. He went for a younger woman. He upped his game.'

'I still don't see —'

'How many people are there in the Groves family?'

Joesbury shrugged. 'I don't know, the mother, father, the son — what's he called, Toby — and the — oh shit.'

He'd got it. At last. He was stepping away from me, looking for his phone.

'Toby Groves has a sister,' I said, just in case there was any doubt, although judging by the look on Joesbury's face, I didn't think there was. 'A twin sister,' I went on, as he picked up his phone and started to dial Dana Tulloch's number. 'She's twenty-six. And I think Llewellyn has her already.'

84

Sunday 7 September

Darkness isn't still, Joanna Groves has learned, it moves. It shimmers, gathers itself, wafts closer and forms strange, drifting shapes. Sometimes, darkness becomes so heavy it presses down on her scalp, on the back of her eyes, her throat. Joanna had never really thought about darkness before she was brought to this place. Now, she finds it difficult to think about anything else.

Except, maybe, the cold. It's difficult not to think about cold when the pain of it is ever present, even when she sleeps. She has no sense of time, has no real idea how long she's been here, but she knows there came a point when she stopped shivering and when moving her limbs became a struggle. Her world has become darkness and cold.

And soft, scrabbly noises. Scrapings and scratchings and tiny, mewling cries. Movement all around her. She wouldn't have believed this cold, black, empty place could sustain life, but it does. And they're getting bolder, the scratchy things. Creeping closer all the time. Maybe they've already worked out that she can't move.

She tries to swallow and can't. Even breathing isn't easy any more. The first time she was left alone, she screamed until she could taste blood. And then duct tape was wrapped round the lower part of her face. When it was taken off, great handfuls of her hair had been ripped away with it. She hadn't screamed again.

She has a sudden sense that the darkness has changed. It isn't random any more. The darkness has taken on a purpose and that purpose is drawing closer.

'You're there, aren't you?' she whispers in the direction from which she might have heard something heavier than a scratch. 'You've come back. I know you have.'

Another sound. Definitely a footstep this time.

'I know why you're doing this,' says Joanna, and every word hurts. 'I know about what you say my brother did to you and your sister.'

The movement has stopped.

'I'm sorry,' says Joanna quickly. 'I didn't mean that. I'm just scared. What he did to you, I mean. What my brother and his friends did to you.'

Another footstep, getting closer, and Joanna has a sense that she has to speak quickly. 'What they did was terrible, I know that,' she says. 'They should never have been allowed to get away with it.'

A sound of fabric rustling. Someone is crouching just in front of her.

'But it was nothing to do with me,' says Joanna. 'Why are you doing this to me?'

Something cold brushes against her face. A sloshing sound. She can smell plastic. She tilts back her head and lets the water flow into her throat. It helps a bit. She pushes the bottle away with her mouth when she's had enough. Her captor is very close. If Joanna's hands weren't strapped behind her back, she could reach out and touch the girl's face.

'Can I ask you something?' asks Joanna.

For a second there is no reply, but she knows the other girl is still there. She can hear her breathing. Then, 'Why didn't I just kill the boys?' a soft voice says. 'Is that what you want to ask me?'

'Yes,' says Joanna, and feels guilty just for saying the words. Toby is her twin. She loves him more than she does her parents. Yet Toby is the reason she's here.

'How tall is your brother?' the voice says. 'Six one, six two? And he weighs about two hundred pounds? You've seen how big I am. There's only one way I could kill a man of that size and that's a bullet through the head from a distance.'

She stops and Joanna waits. Then she feels her captor moving closer.

'Well,' the girl whispers in her ear, 'where's the fun in that?'

85

We left the hotel the next morning. I'd wanted to leave immediately; Joesbury had insisted we stay the rest of the night. There was nothing in London that Dana and her team couldn't do without us, he'd argued, and another night of no sleep would render both of us useless. As we approached the Severn Bridge his phone rang and he gestured for me to take it.

'Lacey, it's Dana.'

'We're just over two hours away,' I said. 'Depending on traffic. Is there any news?'

'None of it good,' she said. 'Joanna Groves hasn't been seen by her flatmate for two days. She assumed she'd gone away for the weekend, but she can't be found anywhere.'

I turned to Joesbury and shook my head. He swore under his breath.

'Lacey, I know what you told Mark last night,' said Tulloch. 'Now, listen to me, I don't want you to worry about anything except helping us catch her. When this is all over, whatever happens, I'll support you, I promise. So will Mark.'

'Thank you,' I managed.

'Now you are our best chance,' said Tulloch. 'You know this woman. You'll have a better idea than anyone what she'll do next. It's all up to you now. I'll see you when you get back.'

She hung up and I replaced the phone in its holder. Tulloch was right, it was all up to me now. But she was wrong about seeing me. I wasn't going back.

We reached London just before eleven. At Earls Court we dropped south towards the river. As we approached Vauxhall Bridge, my heartbeat started to race. Now or never.

'Sir,' I said, as we reached the summit, 'I'm sorry, but I'm going to be sick. I think there are public loos at the Tube station. Can you stop?'

He glanced over, saw me sitting upright, one arm around my waist, the other hand at my mouth. He indicated and pulled over just before we left the bridge. I muttered thanks, grabbed my bag and jumped out of the car. Using my Oyster card to get past the ticket barrier, I turned the corner and was out of sight.

There are no public lavatories at Vauxhall Tube station. I jogged to the platform, praying there'd be a train going south before Joesbury realized I wasn't coming back. The overhead indicator told me the next train was due in one minute.

Every second seemed to stretch, but at last I heard the rumble of the train's engines and felt the rush of wind that always precedes them into stations. I travelled one stop to Stockwell and ran the few hundred metres to my flat. Fewer than ten minutes had passed since I'd left the car.

As I opened the door, I told myself that before I counted to a hundred I'd be out again. I raced round, grabbing my bag from the top of the wardrobe, gathering what else I'd need. Behind the door, there was the usual Saturday-morning delivery of mail-order flyers and official-looking envelopes. And a long, thin box, wrapped in brown paper. I didn't have time to open it, but I tore the paper apart all the same.

Seeing what was inside cost me a few seconds. Then I left my flat for what would surely be the last time, grabbed my bike from its lock-up and set off.

86

An hour later I switched my mobile back on and called Joesbury. He answered on the first ring.

'You had better have a fucking good explanation —'

'Shut up and listen,' I said. 'Or I hang up.'

No response.

'I'm going to save you some time,' I said. 'I'm just outside Waterloo Station. In twenty seconds I'm going to switch the phone off, take a train and disappear. There is absolutely no point in your trying to trace me.'

A second's silence, then, 'Go on,' he said.

'My career is over,' I said, knowing that Joesbury would be instigating the trace as I spoke and scribbling notes to colleagues to get the nearest uniform here. 'Any talk of damage limitation is just bullshit, so let's cut to the chase.'

'Which is?'

'Joanna Groves is still alive,' I said, turning away from the traffic.

'How the fuck —'

'Listen! The minute I know for certain where she is, or where Llewellyn is, I will call you, so keep your phone close. Until then, the best thing you can do for her is let me get on with it.'

I could almost hear a whole bunch of expletives bursting to get out of Joesbury's mouth. Somehow he managed to keep it together. 'Flint, we have spent weeks searching London's underclass,' he said in controlled tones. 'She isn't living on the streets any more, you won't find her.'

'I don't expect to,' I said. 'She'll find me.'

A sharp hissing sound. Then the noise a chair makes when it's being pushed roughly over the floor. 'Lacey, you are going to get yourself killed.'

'Least of my worries,' I said. 'Now, one more thing.'

'I'm listening.'

'When you go to my flat, you'll find something that was delivered early this morning. It's a rectangular package and inside is a knife. The name Mary is scratched into the edge of the blade.'

'Jesus, fuckin —'

'Shut up. The knife is perfectly clean. It hasn't been used. Joanna is still alive.'

I gave him a second to think about it. Only a second, though. I really had to hang up. Already I was looking nervously up and down the street.

'It makes no fucking sense,' he said. 'Why send you a weapon that hasn't been used?'

I almost smiled at that. 'It's lucky you're cute, Joesbury,' I said, 'because you have shit for brains. The knife is squeaky clean because I'm the one who has to use it. I have to kill Joanna.'

87

'Those women you killed, the boys' mothers,' says Joanna. 'My mother, too. Do you blame them for what happened? Do you think it's their fault their sons did that to you?'

The girl has begun spending time with her, as though she too feels the loneliness of this place. Sometimes they talk, sometimes they just sit in silence, listening to each other breathing.

'They brought them up to believe they could have anything they wanted,' answers the girl. 'Anything that took their fancy and to hell with the consequences.'

'Is that why you did it?' asks Joanna, after a moment.

'The next day, when they met us at the police station,' says the girl, 'their dads were embarrassed, they couldn't look at us. They were ashamed of their sons. They didn't want them facing charges, I'm not saying that, but they weren't trying to make out it was all our fault, that we'd asked for it.'

'And the mothers did?' asks Joanna.

She hears the hiss of a sharp breath. 'Those women weren't prepared to consider, even for a second, that their precious baby boys could do anything wrong,' the voice says. 'So we had to be the evil ones, my sister and me.'

Joanna thinks for a moment. There is something she wants to say. It feels like a horrible betrayal, but it's her life at stake. 'I understand that,' she says. 'But the people who really hurt you and your sister, they're getting away with it.'

She hears a soft laugh, then the girl leans in closer again. 'No, Joanna,' trickles a voice into her ear. 'Killing them quickly — which is what I would have to do — would be letting them get away with it. They wouldn't even see it coming. This way, they'll suffer for the rest of their lives. Just like me.'

88

I'd told Joesbury the truth when I'd said I was close to Waterloo station. I'd lied about getting on a train. The London Underground network is riddled with CCTV and finding me would be too easy. Instead I jumped back on the bike and headed east, following the course of the A202 but avoiding the main road. I kept my hood up and my head down and pedalled steadily.

Seventy minutes later, I was high above the city, watching southeast London idle its way through a Sunday. At the entrance to Greenwich Park I'd bought coffee and sandwiches. I ate and drank now, watching the weak sun trying to cast reflections on the river, keeping an eye on anyone who got too close. The sky was getting cloudier all the time and the park wasn't overly busy. A few dog-walkers, kite-flyers and some families over at the children's playground. Overnight, the temperature had dropped.

It must have been the proximity of the Greenwich Meridian Line, the centre of the world's time, that made my sense of time running out so very strong now.

The team I'd walked out on would have two priorities. First, they'd want to find Joanna Groves and Victoria Llewellyn, who it seemed reasonable to assume were in the same place. Their second objective would be me. Already my photograph would have been sent around every police station in London. Every CCTV control room, every copper in uniform, every patrol car, every police community support officer, would have been told to look out for me. I could expect to see myself playing a leading role on the lunchtime news. Then everyone in London who cared would be looking for me too.

And so would Llewellyn. She had my phone number. She would tell me where I was expected to go. All I had to do was avoid being picked up for long enough to give her the chance.

So I sat, and tried not to get too cold, as the hour went past. At twelve fifty-five, the great red time-ball rose halfway up the mast on the top of Flamsteed House. Three minutes later it floated to the top, and at one p.m. it sailed back down again. I waited half an hour more and then pulled out my mobile. No messages.

Switching off the phone, I got back on the bike. I had to assume Joesbury and the MIT now knew I was in Greenwich. Time to move on.

I cycled out of the park and found a market stall that sold cheap clothes. I bought a waterproof blue jacket and a baseball cap and put both on. Then I made my way to the glazed dome entrance of the Greenwich foot tunnel. I pushed the bike through, keeping my head down in case there were cameras inside. On the north bank, I found another bench close to the river and sat, staring at the ornate Wren-designed buildings of the old Greenwich Hospital until another hour had gone by. By this time rain was starting to fall. I switched on my phone again. Nothing.

By mid afternoon I was freezing. I cycled up the Isle of Dogs and found a small internet café that was open on a Sunday. Keeping my head down to avoid CCTV cameras, I went in and found a vacant computer. Then I started making my way through the various news websites.

Joanna Groves's abduction was on every site I pulled up. She was a fair-haired, blue-eyed, slim girl, not quite pretty but far from plain. She lived in a flat on the ground floor of a house in Wimbledon and worked at the local primary school. She'd left the school at three thirty on Friday afternoon and disappeared. As I flicked through site after site, my insides started to twist themselves into knots.

There was nothing about me. Even on the Met's own website. Nothing.

My hour wasn't up, but I couldn't stay here any longer. Tulloch's computer skills were legendary and it was perfectly possible that she'd know I'd been on the Met's website and be able to trace the computer I was using. I got up and left the café in a hurry. The MIT were doing the exact opposite of what they were supposed to. I needed them to be looking for me, damn it, and I needed it to be public knowledge. How else would Llewellyn know I'd gone AWOL?

OK, think, think, think. I cycled for fifteen minutes and found another café with internet access. When a machine became available I typed 'Ripper' into the search engine and pressed go.

Run a Jack the Ripper search and you can expect to see several million results. Search for his twenty-first-century copycat and it's not quite so many. Just under forty-three thousand. Still a pretty impressive performance for someone who's only been around a matter of weeks. I started making my way through the sites, looking for blogs. On each one I left a message.

Cardiff Girl: Call me. L.

It was risky. Officers in the team had been monitoring the various websites since the case had started. When they spotted my posts, they'd start tracing them. I left and found a small, half-empty branch of Starbucks. After forty minutes, I switched my phone on. Nothing. And I was getting paranoid. A woman had entered the coffee bar shortly after me. Three-quarters of an hour later, she was still there. It almost certainly meant nothing, she was probably just another Londoner with too much time to kill, but I didn't like her being close.

I found another café, this time with a TV, and asked permission to change to the twenty-four-hour news channel. I watched for twenty minutes and saw several references to Joanna. None to me. I switched my phone back on. Still nothing. Move on.

Shit, this was not what I'd planned. Panic was rising inside me like milk coming to the boil. Llewellyn didn't know I was out here. She wouldn't contact me.

And my sense of paranoia was growing

too, because everywhere I went I had a sense of people looking at me. It was impossible; I'd kept my phone switched off, I'd stayed on the move, I'd avoided cameras, the attention I was getting had to be down to my still-bruised face. But as every minute went by, the sense of being watched increased.

I could just run.

But if I did that, Joanna Groves would die. There had to be another way. I knew this woman. I knew how she thought. Where would she take Joanna?

She'd killed Geraldine Jones in a south London housing estate. She'd cut Amanda Weston to pieces in a park. Charlotte Benn had been murdered in her own home, Karen Curtis at her mother's house. There was no pattern.

I left the café, unchained my bike and just pushed it along the street, forgetting even to watch out for cameras. For the first time that day I had no plan, no idea where to go next.

Llewellyn had sent me a knife. She wanted me to kill Joanna Groves. That meant she had to believe I'd find her. I passed a newsagent's, a children's clothes shop, a second-hand record shop. I'd stopped walking, was staring at my reflection in the record-shop window. On the pavement, people were having to make their way around me, but I couldn't move, couldn't take my eyes off the stack of vinyl recordings of old musicals. *The Sound of Music* wasn't there, but it didn't have to be. I'd got it.

Of course there was a pattern, there had been all along. It was me. It was all about me and my favourite things. Because a couple of times, I'd played that game with someone else. We'd had long lists, that other girl and I, but one day, we'd narrowed our choices down to just five each. We'd laughed because I'd tried so hard to make my five all begin with P, but it didn't matter how much time we spent, we couldn't think of another word for zoo that began with P.

So my list was the (P) zoo, Parks, Pools, Public libraries and Ponies.

Geraldine Jones had been killed where I would be bound to find her, to make sure I became involved from the outset. Amanda Weston had been murdered in a park I visited, part of her body left for me in one of my favourite swimming pools. Charlotte Benn's heart had been found in the children's section of a Victorian public library, on top of one of my favourite books. We'd been sent on a wild goose chase to London Zoo to find Karen Curtis's head. Parks, libraries, pools and the zoo. Four out of five boxes had been ticked. One left.

Ponies.

Finally, I knew where they were. Poor terrified Joanna Groves and the Llewellyn woman who was holding her hostage, waiting for me to arrive and draw a knife across her latest victim's throat.

When I'd told Joesbury the story of two young women sharing cardboard walls and body warmth in a derelict London building, I hadn't been specific. The exact location of that half-forgotten, freezing-cold place hadn't seemed significant. And, of course, it didn't take a genius to spot that when I mentioned a particular London district to Joesbury his eyes had a habit of narrowing and his jawline of becoming that bit tighter. When it came to me — and Camden — Mark Joesbury had a bit of a blind spot.

I'd wanted him listening and sympathizing, not getting mad. So I hadn't mentioned that the place where I'd met and lived with the other young runaway had been less than half a mile from where I now regularly — to use his words — go shagging.

But it made perfect sense that Llewellyn would choose Camden. I'd lived there for months, knew it well, and although much of it had changed beyond recognition in recent years, the entire development had been themed around that other favourite of mine. Ponies. Llewellyn was holding Joanna somewhere around Camden Stables Market. Almost certainly in the Camden Catacombs.

89

'You can see me, can't you?' says Joanna. 'I don't know how you do it, but you can see in the dark.' She's had her suspicions for some time now. The girl moves softly and silently around the dark space, never stumbling. Joanna has never seen her use a torch.

'Yes, I can see you,' the girl replies. 'I have night-vision equipment. Gives me a headache after a while, but it's useful down here.'

'Please,' says Joanna, 'can we have some light? Just a torch. I already know what you look like, it can't make any difference.'

'We can't, I'm afraid,' says the girl. 'We're waiting for someone, you see. And I need to know exactly when she's coming.'

90

It was almost six o'clock by this time. In a hardware shop I bought a torch and a large pair of pliers and then it took me nearly two hours along the back streets to reach Camden. Once there I found somewhere to chain my bike and jogged down to the towpath that runs alongside Regent's Canal.

Mention the Camden Catacombs and few people in London, even those who know Camden, will have any idea what you're talking about. But they exist, all the same: a buried network of underground chambers and tunnels, constructed nearly two centuries ago as part of the railway development. In recent years, lots of old tunnels have been opened up and developed as part of the Stables Market. Not all of them.

On the lock side of the railway bridge, built into the wall that edges the canal, is a solid black-metal door. I stopped in front of it. This was the time to phone Joesbury. He,

Tulloch and the team would stand a much better chance of getting Joanna out than I would alone.

On the other hand, if I was wrong, they'd arrest me. I'd never get away again, and Llewellyn wouldn't keep Joanna alive indefinitely. Having me kill her might be the icing on the cake, but when people are hungry enough, they'll usually eat their cakes without icing.

The padlock on the door looked new. After a quick glance around I pulled out the pliers. Copying Joesbury's actions in Victoria Park a few weeks earlier, I pushed them beneath the curved lock and pulled them sharply apart. The padlock fell to the ground. When I opened the door, I'd be inside an old tunnel that would take me to a vast underground structure called the Stationary Winding Engine Vaults.

In the old days, the noise made by trains travelling up the steep hill from Euston to Camden had driven wealthy residents bananas. That was before you got on to the subject of smoke. So, to avoid noise and smoke pollution, the trains at this point were pulled up by two steam-powered winding engines and a very long circular rope. The winding engines, the driving wheel and other large sheaves and pulleys were housed in a huge, vaulted underground space, nearly 200 feet long and 150 feet wide, that still sits directly beneath the main railway line. Up until the mid nineteenth century, two tall chimneys indicated the building's position. These days, practically nothing of this massive cavern can be seen from the surface; very few people even know it's there. Ten years ago I and a few dozen others had called it home. And this rickety piece of black metal had been my front door.

The best plans are the simple ones, they say. All I had to do was find Joanna without Llewellyn spotting me, guide her out of the vaults to safety and then get the hell out of London. Simple.

Except, when I tried the door it didn't budge. There was no handle as such, just the metal clasps that the padlock had held together. I tried inserting my fingers into the gap between door and frame and pulling, but nothing happened. Somehow it had been locked or jammed from the inside.

What the hell was I supposed to do now? Knock?

There were two other entrances to the Engine Vaults that anyone who knew about the catacombs would be aware of. I left the towpath and climbed back up the steps to railway level. At the top I stopped dead. I'd seen someone, something, dart out of sight not twenty yards away. I stepped into the shadows and waited.

After five minutes nothing had happened, so I took a pedestrian path that brought me past a development of terraced waterside houses. I walked the path's full length until I reached the huge wooden gates that prevent casual access to one of the more extensive tunnels, known as the western horse tunnel. The adjoining railing gave me just enough height to leap over the gates.

The door to the tunnel was padlocked shut, and breaking this padlock didn't help either. The door held as firm as the metal gate had done. Time to check out entrance number three.

This time I took the main road through a housing estate called Gilbey's Yard and then climbed the boundary wall between the estate and the railway. Graffiti all along the other side of the wall suggested I wasn't the only one to make this journey in the last ten years. It wasn't easy underfoot but there was enough light, mainly from Morrisons supermarket not too far away, for me to see where I was going. The third 'official' way in was a narrow spiral staircase in the north-eastern corner of the vaults. Whether I actually went down it was another matter; for now, I was simply going to look.

Ahead of me was the fencing that surrounded the staircase. As I drew closer, I could see that two upright struts had been broken, creating a gap that someone of my size could easily squeeze through. So I did.

On the other side, the staircase was open to the air, just as I remembered it. This was the way I was supposed to come in. Llewellyn had blocked the other two entrances so that I had no choice. This was where she was waiting.

What she didn't know, though, what I was willing to bet very few people knew, because I'd only stumbled across it myself by accident, was that there was a fourth way into the vaults. I'd told no one about it, not out of any desire for secrecy, I just didn't think anyone would be interested. I was willing to bet, though, the way in was still there. If I could bring myself to take it.

Over the boundary wall again — easier said than done, but I was running on pure adrenalin by this stage — I jogged back towards the towpath, thinking back ten years, to when once I'd tried to leave the Engine Vaults without a torch. I'd taken a wrong turning and found myself in a section of tunnel that instead of leading to the canal, as I'd expected, took me parallel to it. After a hundred metres or so it came to a dead end.

Curious, I'd gone back the next day with a torch and found that part of the wall that blocked off the tunnel had collapsed and that it was possible to climb through into another large underground chamber that had once been the basement of a large goods shed. The shed itself had long since been demolished. Housing and even part of Morrisons had been built in its place, but the vaulted brick basement remained.

Amazed at my own daring, I'd gone through it, into another section of tunnel and then a second basement, this time beneath another Victorian building called the Interchange Warehouse. I'd heard the sounds of traffic and of water, and without warning had stepped through an archway and into dim daylight. I was still in a tunnel, but one that contained a short offshoot of Regent's Canal.

I could see the Interchange Warehouse ahead of me now, a four-storey red-brick building with lots of arched, cast-iron windows. The offshoot I'd found that day was a man-made backwater that had originally functioned as a private dock, allowing boats to unload cargo into the warehouse. Today, it's still used by narrowboats needing to turn round. It even has a name, after an unofficial debris-collection function it serves. It's called Dead Dog Hole.

In theory, if I took that same route now, in reverse, I could make my way through the catacombs and enter the Engine Vaults from a direction Llewellyn wouldn't be expecting.

To do so, I'd have to jump into Regent's Canal.

By this time, I'd reached the towpath and was at the foot of the small bridge that takes pedestrians over Dead Dog Hole. A boat had been moored against the bank. Without stopping to think, I climbed down on to it and made my way along the narrow ledge that rimmed its port side. When I reached the bow, I took another look around, partly to check that no one could see me; mainly, I think, to put off a bit longer what I had to do. I was alone, rain was falling steadily and the black water seemed to shimmer beneath me. I could smell diesel fuel and rotting vegetation.

Canals aren't rivers. They have no tide and no flow. The Regent's Canal isn't much more than a metre deep. In theory, I could stand upright. I would be able to wade. It would be for a few seconds at most, just long enough to get me under the pedestrian bridge and into the hole itself.

No point thinking about it. I took off my jacket and sweatshirt and pushed both into my rucksack. The rucksack stayed on the boat as I lowered myself into the water.

There aren't words to describe properly that feeling of being squeezed on all sides by a force powerful enough to crush, or a cold that seemed to freeze my lungs and stop them functioning. The water came up to my neck. The one-metre depth had been a gross underestimate. Holding my rucksack high with one hand, gripping the bank with the other, I began wading.

Every step seemed to take an age, as I groped around the canal bed that was alternately hard as granite and soft as putty. The bed was littered with objects, some of them so big I had to make my way round them, hating each second I wasn't in contact with the bank.

Light diminished under the arch of the tunnel, but after a second or two my eyes started to adjust. A few more seconds and I could make out stone steps just ahead of me. I bumped up against them and managed to throw my rucksack on to the bank and grab hold. Then I hauled myself out.

For a minute I couldn't do anything but shudder. Then I pulled off my soaking

T-shirt and got my sweatshirt and jacket from my bag. That helped a bit. As did taking off my shoes and emptying them of filthy canal water. When I felt I could face it, I stepped through the arched doorway and towards the far wall. Then I began to make my way through a series of small arches, each only six feet high and around twelve feet wide.

The vaults smelled of stagnant water, sewage and something sharp and acrid, almost chemical. The air was still, and the further I went in, the more the sound became unnaturally distorted. The steady dripping of water, the rustling of rodents among rubbish. How rubbish got in here I had no idea, but it had. I passed supermarket carrier bags, the remains of take-away dinners, a dead cat, clothing, even a camp stool. With every step I took, noise from the street was fading away until there was nothing but my own footsteps, softly squelching across the cobbled ground.

Every few paces took me past wide archway footings, behind any one of which someone could be waiting. I shone my torch ahead of me, keeping as quiet as I could, watching out for shadows that weren't mine, for sounds that hadn't originated with me.

After a few minutes, the north-western

wall loomed ahead and I could make out the black space that was the entrance to the horse tunnel. If my memory served, I had to follow it for a short distance before it met the basement of the old goods shed.

The tunnel was easier to travel through than the huge underground chamber. For one thing, the way wasn't in doubt. For another, there was some light, coming in through ventilation grilles in the ceiling. Before more than a few seconds had gone by, I was in the basement under the old goods shed.

Halfway there.

I walked on, through pools of water that looked like slime, past gated archways and around tall, riveted iron columns. I almost cried out loud when something fluttered close to my ear, but managed to hold it together. I was practically at the far end when I heard something I couldn't steel myself against and ignore. A man's voice.

91

Instinctively, I flicked off the torch. The voice was followed by a crackling sound like paper being torn. Or the hiss of a police radio. Impossible. They could not know I was here. I'd heard something from street level, that was all, a sound that had travelled down through one of the ventilation grilles.

I wasn't anywhere near the ventilation grilles. I was crossing the basement, the grilles were in the horse tunnels.

For God's sake, I'd been ultra careful, there was no way the MIT could have found me. They hadn't even been looking. All the surveillance and tracking equipment Joesbury had given me had been wrecked the night I fell in the river; he hadn't replaced any of it.

Except the phone.

Only the growing conviction that someone was close enough to hear kept me from moaning out loud. I'd been issued with a new phone while I was in hospital, one that had come from the specialist crime directorate that sends its officers into dangerous situations and needs to keep track of them. I'd kept it switched off for most of the day, thinking a phone needed to be on to be traceable. What if Joesbury had put some sort of device inside mine that was permanently active whether the phone was on or not?

Gently, I pulled it out of my pocket. As I did so, any doubt I might be clinging to disappeared. From not too far away came the sound of someone stepping into water.

The MIT hadn't needed to look for me. They'd known exactly where I was all day, probably from the moment I'd left Joesbury's car. They'd been watching and following; waiting for me to lead them here.

I almost gave up there and then, almost switched on the torch and called out to them. But something stopped me. It wasn't over yet.

I'd been following the south wall of the goods-shed basement. If I reached out it was close enough to touch. I bent down and soundlessly put Joesbury's traitorous mobile by the wall. Then, with the fingers of one hand tracing the outside wall, I set off. After a few more minutes I reached the corner.

By a massive stroke of luck, my left hand found the hole in the wall that would take me through to the western horse tunnel. I risked the torch for less than a second, and went through, knowing I was very close now. A corner, a few more metres and I would be able to enter the Engine Vaults at the upper, gallery level. If I'd got it right, Llewellyn would be at the far end of the structure watching the stairs. If I were wrong, well, all bets were off.

I waited just before the corner, listening. Then, in almost total darkness, I turned and walked into the vaults. I was near water again. A lot of it. The floor of the Engine Vaults is permanently underwater and ten years ago we'd built our little homes on the gallery that runs around three sides of the perimeter.

I moved slowly, praying the gallery floor was still solid. A lot can happen in ten years. The structure was 170 feet long. Maybe a hundred slow steps to take me along the main gallery to the upper floor of the eastern boiler room. The boiler rooms were smaller spaces and less draughty; in the old days they'd been the most coveted spots. They were where Llewellyn would be holding Joanna.

It was far too dark to see the water beneath

me but I could hear it moving, soft little ripples and splashes, and the smell of it seemed to be coating the inside of my throat. I could almost imagine it had grown deeper, deeper even than the ten feet I remembered, stretching up towards the gallery, that if I leaned out from the edge, my hand might touch it. I had an unnerving sense of walking around the perimeter of a vast underground swimming pool.

My fingers found the corner of the gallery and I took a few sideways steps. When I touched the suspended sheet of polythene, I knew I was at the entrance to the boiler room. As I pushed it silently to one side and stepped through, I heard movement.

The darkness in the boiler room was absolute. I remembered the space all too well, had made my way around it before in almost complete darkness, but there is a difference, I was discovering, between the almost complete and the absolute. A decade ago, there had always been a candle, or a gas lamp, or an oil drum somewhere. Now, someone could be inches away from me, staring straight into my eyes, and I wouldn't know it. Torch or voice, I would have to use one of them.

'Joanna,' I whispered, knowing that, of the

two, a low sound would be the less noticeable.

Another movement, this one more urgent. And the sounds a woman makes in the back of her throat when she can't speak.

'Shush,' I risked. 'Don't talk.'

She whimpered a couple of times more, enough to give me a fix. She was about three metres away. I moved forward, one small step at a time, until my foot came up against something soft. Another whimper.

I crouched low.

Not daring to put the torch down in case I never found it again, I reached out and touched her legs. She was wearing nylon tights and was freezing. I ran my hand down her legs to her ankles and found them duct-taped together. I was just pulling my rucksack off to find the knife when she pulled her knees up towards her chin and kicked out at me.

As I went down, I couldn't stop the yelp slipping out. I pushed myself up but had no idea where she was, where the torch was, where I was. I made myself keep still and listen, it was the only thing I could do.

The darkness felt solid, as if it was pressing into me on all sides. Then two distinct sounds: the first, that of someone scuffling along the ground away from me; the second, footsteps behind. Before I could turn, a powerful beam of light shot across the room. I had a moment to see Joanna, curled up like a filthy, terrified child. Less than a moment really, before I was grabbed from behind and dragged to my feet.

'Victoria Llewellyn,' said a voice in my ear, as my right arm was twisted up behind me, 'I am arresting you for the abduction of Joanna Groves and for the murders of Geraldine Jones, Amanda West, Charlotte Benn and Karen Curtis.'

92

Joesbury was only holding me with one arm. I managed to break free, stagger away and twist round to face him. The situation I wouldn't have believed could get worse had just plummeted and what came out of my mouth was little more than a wail.

'Mark, no —'

'You do not have to say anything . . .' Joesbury was striding towards me, torch in one hand, his voice far too loud.

'Mark, get out of here now.'

'But it may harm your defence if you do not . . .'

Could I hear something else? More footsteps? 'Mark, listen to me, you have no idea —'

'. . . mention when questioned something you later rely on . . .'

I was backing away.

'. . . in court. Anything you do say may be given in evidence.'

'Stop it!'

'Get down.'

I took another step away. 'Mark, I'm begging you —'

'On the ground, now.'

I was frantically looking round. The torch he'd brought was powerful, but there were still too many shadows.

'I won't ask you again.'

I fell to my knees. 'Mark, please, just give me one —'

'I don't want to hear it, Flint,' he said, dropping down behind me and pushing me down flat. He grabbed first one hand and then the other, being far rougher than he needed. 'And I really have to stop calling you that,' he said. Then he leaned forward, pressing me harder against the concrete, grazing my face against the rough surface. 'I've been following you all day, you stupid bitch,' he half spat into my ear. 'I've known where you were since you ran off this morning. And you know what, I really wanted to give you the benefit of the doubt. I waited hours for this other girl to show up, but that was all just bullshit, wasn't it? It was always just you.'

He left me where I was, face-down on concrete. For a second I couldn't move. Then I struggled up on to my knees. The handcuffs behind my back held tight. Joesbury was on his feet, crossing the dark space to where Joanna lay whimpering behind the duct-tape mask. His torch was in one hand, his radio in the other. I watched him try to contact Control, praying he'd do it. Help was what we needed right now. It didn't matter what happened to me any more. Shit, I was probably the only one of the three of us *not* seconds from death.

Joesbury cursed into the radio and replaced it in his pocket. We were too far underground. He crouched down over Joanna and spoke softly to her.

'You're all right now, love,' he said. 'Take it easy, let me get this off.'

More whimpering from Joanna. And a harsh cry of pain as the duct tape was pulled off her mouth. Using a small knife not dissimilar to my own, Joesbury cut the tape binding her wrists and ankles. 'We need to get you out of here,' he said. 'Can you walk?'

Standing up himself, he pulled her to her feet. She leaned against him for a second, then grabbed his arm and directed the torch back at me, completely dazzling me.

'It's not her,' I heard her say. 'She's not the one who brought me here.'

The torch beam fell away. I blinked hard and could see them again. Joanna was holding on to Joesbury with both hands, her eyes shooting from him to me.

'There's someone else,' she went on. 'She'll be back any second. She never goes far.'

She couldn't bring herself to step away from Joesbury. She was like a child clinging to an adult. A child terrified of monsters. Mark looked as though he hadn't understood her. He certainly wasn't reacting fast enough.

'Get these off me,' I told him, half turning and holding up my handcuffed wrists. The torch was back on my face again.

'What the . . . ?' he said, sounding lost, miserable and not nearly as scared as he needed to be. 'Who the fuck *are* you?'

I couldn't answer him. I hardly knew myself. All I knew was that one of us had to get a grip. 'You need to get these off me and we need to get out of here,' I said. 'Please tell me you're armed.'

'She is,' said Joanna. 'The other one. She has a gun. That's how she got me here.'

Mark stepped forward and clinging Joanna came with him. When they reached me, he pushed her gently away and gave her the torch. Then he found the key for the cuffs in his pocket. 'Try anything and I will kill you,' he muttered, before the handcuffs sprang free.

'She's waiting by the main steps,' I said, spotting my own torch and grabbing it. 'If she hasn't heard anything, we can get out the way we came in.'

'Who?' he said. 'Who's she?'

I grabbed his arm, made him look at me. 'If she appears,' I said, 'you're the one she'll go for. She'll want me and Joanna alive. You, she'll have to get out of the way as quickly as she can.'

'Noted. Now get moving.'

We crossed the boiler room, I leading, Joanna following me, Mark at the rear. At the entrance to the gallery, I shone the torch around the dark space. There was something almost cathedral-like about the vast area, now that I could see it. Massive brick archways ran the length of the building, their detail reflected in the water that covered the lower part completely. I turned back to Mark.

'If we can get across here, we have a good chance,' I said. 'You should be in the middle.'

He shook his head. 'Go,' he told me.

I went. Not much more than a hundred feet to travel and we would be back in the horse tunnel. In there, we might get reception on the radio. We'd gone barely twenty feet when music started to play. 'My Favourite Things'.

First Joanna, then Mark, walked into me.

'Where's it coming from?' someone asked. I think it must have been me. Neither of the others would know the significance of that particular tune. The music was menacingly soft, but nevertheless bouncing off walls and pillars. It was impossible to tell its origin. I could almost have believed it to be in my own terrified head. Mark was directing his light around the structure, but the space was vast. 'Behind us, I think,' he muttered, just as the music stopped and a woman's voice took its place.

'Hello, Lacey,' she said. 'It's been a long time.'

The world seemed to stand still for a second. It was over then. I watched the beam of Mark's torch flashing around the cavern. Then it fixed on a point on the opposite gallery, maybe eighty feet from where we were standing.

'I thought you'd never get here,' said the voice again, cutting through the darkness, a second before Mark's torch found her. In its beam we saw a slender woman in her mid twenties, with the sweetest face I think I've ever seen. Her hair was chin length and bright blonde; the black crop we'd heard so much about had clearly been a wig. Those eyes would be blue once I got close enough to look at them properly, with tiny flecks of hazel brown. I knew that face almost as well as I knew my own.

At my side, I heard Mark make a soft hissing sound, as he sucked air in through his teeth. 'Is that her?' he asked.

'Yes,' I said, without taking my eyes off her. 'That's Llewellyn.'

'I've met her before,' he breathed. 'She's Geraldine Jones's au pair. Stenning actually took her out for a drink.'

She was looking at me now, just me. 'Raindrops and roses,' she sang. 'Do you remember, Lacey? That game we used to play?' Then that sweet face broke into a smile. She looked completely relaxed, maybe a little surprised, as though we were two old friends who'd met by chance at a party. Her arms hung loosely by her sides. In her left hand she held something I couldn't quite make out, except it seemed to have a black headband. In her right hand was a small handgun.

'Let these two go,' I called across the vaults to her. 'We don't need them any more. It's about us now.'

Her eyes went from me to the man at my

side. She seemed to be thinking about what to say next. I risked taking my eyes away from her.

'Mark, take Joanna and get out of here,' I said to him. 'She'll let you go.' I looked back at Llewellyn. 'You will, won't you?' I asked her. 'Please, just let them go.'

'I'm not going anywhere,' said Joesbury.

'I need you both to step to the front of the gallery and drop your torches down into the water,' said Llewellyn.

When neither Joesbury nor I moved, Llewellyn's face screwed up like that of a thwarted child. 'You have three seconds to lose those torches before I shoot your boyfriend,' she said to me.

'Do it,' I said, stepping forward and raising my arm.

Joesbury caught hold of my shoulder. 'Oh, I think you've played enough games with those replica weapons of yours,' he called across to her. 'And don't imagine I came here alone. There are armed police at every exit, just waiting for my signal to come in.'

Joesbury was so full of shit.

'Mark,' I said, 'I really don't think that's a —'

'Then we're running out of time,' said Llewellyn. 'Drop the torches now.'

'Mark, please just do —'

'Without light, we'll be sitting ducks,' he whispered into my ear.

'I know this place better than she does,' I replied quietly. 'I can get us out in the dark. The minute she switches on a light, we'll know where she is. Now drop your torch, take hold of me and then back up to the wall.'

He muttered something that I took as agreement, then first my torch, then his, went over the edge of the gallery. A second later we heard them splashing into water and then all light disappeared from the world. Joesbury's hand was on my shoulder. We backed away from the gallery's edge and I heard him speak softly to Joanna. A few more steps and we were up against the wall. I reached out and found Joanna's hand.

'Move slowly and stay together,' I said.

'Wait,' insisted Joanna. 'She can see in the dark. She has some sort of night-vision equipment. She can still see us.'

A hand was on the back of my neck, pushing my head down. 'Stay low and move fast.' Joesbury's mouth brushed against my ear. 'Go now.'

I didn't need telling twice. Bent almost double, one hand keeping contact with the brick wall on my left, the other holding fast to Joanna, I moved as fast as I dared. From the gallery she'd been standing on, Llewellyn couldn't access the horse tunnel. She'd have to head north along the length of the gallery, make her way across the width of the building and into the boiler room where I'd found Joanna. Only then could she follow us down this, the more easterly of the two galleries. If Joanna was right and Llewellyn could see in the dark, she'd be able to move a lot faster than we could. On the other hand, we had a head start.

It was impossible to move at that speed and stay quiet, so we didn't. Three sets of footsteps thumped along the wooden slats, making it impossible to hear if anyone was gaining on us. Somehow, I made myself keep moving when there was nothing but blackness ahead of me. At the end of the gallery I stopped to get my breath back.

'Get moving,' came Joesbury's voice out of the darkness. Upright again, I turned into the tunnel. Ten feet along it and I had a choice. Turn left and make our way into the vaults of the old goods shed, heading back the way I'd come in, or go straight on and within minutes be at the metal gate that opened on to the towpath. If we could get through it, we'd be safe immediately. If we couldn't, we'd be caught like rats in a pipe.

Too risky. I went left, just as Joesbury tried

his radio again. No luck.

The basement of the goods shed was a hundred metres long and the only way to get safely across it in pitch blackness was by following the south wall.

It seemed to take for ever. Realistically, it couldn't have been more than a few minutes. At one point Joanna slipped and fell headlong into a pool of something that smelled vile. When we pulled her out, we had a hard job persuading her to get moving again. Then there was a grunt and a squeal.

'I've got her,' said Joesbury. 'Firemen's lift. Let's go.'

I set off again, screamingly slowly, one hand on the wall, the other on Joesbury's arm. The ground was treacherous in here. Fallen bricks, holes in the concrete, debris scattered around, every step had to be taken with care.

'Lacey, hold it,' said Joesbury, when I judged we were about ten metres from the next stretch of tunnel. 'Listen.'

Silence. Then the soft plinking sound of something falling into water.

'We have to move,' I said.

Silence for another second. The sound of Joanna's breath like tiny sobs. Then, 'Go on then,' said Joesbury. 'Slow and quiet. I think we may have company.'

We made it to the next stretch of tunnel. It was less than thirty metres long. I think I actually started to hope. The vaults beneath the forecourt of the interchange warehouse weren't more than the length of my garden at home. There would be light in there. And that jump into the canal was going to feel very good this time.

As we entered the warehouse vaults, the blackness all around us was weakening, becoming greyer. I could make out pillars, the reflection of water at our feet, and an orange glow at the far end, where the light from a canal-side lamp could just about seep into the building.

'Hi.'

We stopped. Llewellyn was about five metres ahead of us, had just stepped out from behind an archway footing. The night-vision goggles had been pushed on to the top of her head. In her left hand she carried a torch that she switched on now. In her right, she still had the gun. If it was a replica, we were safe. She was no match for Joesbury. Not even for me. But if it wasn't . . .

I stepped in front of him and faced her. Behind, I heard Joanna being lowered to the ground. Then Joesbury's hands were on my shoulders.

'Out of the way, Lacey,' he said, trying to pull me behind him. I wasn't moving.

'She won't shoot me,' I said, without taking my eyes off Llewellyn. 'It's over,' I told her. 'You heard what he said. There are police at every exit.' I stopped and took a deep breath. 'I'll stay with you,' I went on. 'Just let Mark and Joanna —'

I didn't get chance to finish. At that moment, poor, terrified Joanna Groves made a run for it. Without thinking, I dived after her and gave Llewellyn a clear shot. I saw her raise her arm and then there was an explosion that sounded like the roof had fallen in. I turned back in time to see Mark jump forward as if he'd been scalded. I think I must have closed my eyes because when I looked again, he was on the ground.

A split second later I was with him. He'd fallen against a pillar and had collapsed into a sitting position. Llewellyn's torch focused on him and I could see a pool of blood spreading across the right side of his sweatshirt. His eyes were still open. There was a scuffling sound behind and then Joanna was flung on to the ground beside us.

'Handcuff her,' Llewellyn told me. 'Quick. There isn't much time.'

Mark didn't have much time. His body was trembling and each breath sounded like it was whistling through a blocked pipe.

'I'm sorry,' I mouthed, before reaching into the left pocket of his jacket and taking out the cuffs. More blood poured out of the wound on his chest. I pulled my jacket off and pushed it against the blood flow, then lifted both his hands and put them against the wound too.

All the time, Llewellyn hadn't taken her eyes off us and the gun was still raised. Pointing at Mark. Behind her, Joanna Groves was crouched, shivering and sobbing, against another pillar. I crossed to her quickly, pulled unresisting arms behind her back and slipped the handcuffs on. Then I ran back to Mark and touched the side of his face. Already it felt far too cold. I turned back to the girl with the gun.

'Please don't let him die,' I begged her.

She dropped her head on to one side as she looked at us with something like interest in her eyes. Then she crouched down and fumbled around in the shadows.

'Guess that's up to you now,' she said, as she stood and held out something that gleamed in the torchlight. 'Brought a spare,' she went on, holding the knife out towards me. It looked exactly like the one that had arrived by post at my flat the day before.

I'd been holding Mark's hand, but I let it

go now. There wasn't going to be an easy way out of this.

'Thought you might,' I replied, getting to my feet. The place couldn't possibly be surrounded by armed police, as Mark had claimed. He'd never have been allowed to come in here by himself. He'd gone AWOL, just as I had. We were on our own. Mark had taken a stupid risk because he'd wanted to believe in me and it was going to get him killed.

'I've got a car parked by the canal,' Llewellyn said to me. 'We can still make it.' She held the knife out towards me. Her grip on the gun hadn't faltered.

'Let's go now,' I said, knowing that the minute we left him, Mark would be able to summon help. We were barely any distance underground here, both his radio and his phone would work.

'Job to do first,' Llewellyn replied, glancing over towards Joanna Groves, who hadn't looked at anything but the knife since Llewellyn had produced it. As I took the weapon, she started to cry. On the other side of me, Mark's breathing sounded like an old pair of bellows. I looked into turquoise eyes that had gone dark with pain and knew I had a very simple choice.

If I killed Joanna and fled with Llewellyn,

the police might arrive in time to get Mark the help he needed. If I refused, we'd stay down here as hostages and he would die.

'Lacey, what are you doing?' he whispered.

I didn't even look at him. I'd made my choice. I just needed to get it done. I strode across, dropped to my knees, and took hold of Joanna Groves by the hair. The poor girl was too terrified even to scream.

'Lacey, don't you dare.'

I couldn't help but turn then. He was slipping away, right in front of me. Flesh seemed to have fallen from his face, his body had shrunk.

'I can't live if you don't.'

That's what I tried to say. Whether any of the words came out I don't know, I think I might have been crying too hard. Just do it. I leaned back so that I was holding Joanna's head at arm's length. Then I took a firmer grip on the knife and brought it down. At the second it made contact with flesh, I closed my eyes, clenched my teeth together and made the cut with every ounce of strength I had left.

Three screams rang out around the vaults. None of them had been mine. I'd neither the breath nor the energy. The pain beating a tattoo against my brain was too intense and all I could do those first few seconds was to live through it. I'd let go of Joanna's hair. She sprang away from me, her face covered in blood. Mine. Hearing movement behind, I passed the knife into my left hand and placed the knife edge, gleaming scarlet in the cold light, against my right wrist.

'I'll do it,' I said, stopping Llewellyn in her tracks. She'd been diving towards me but she stopped now. Her eyes dropped from mine to the blood that was pumping in waves from the gash on my left wrist. I'd slashed vertically down the artery, as determined suicides always do. It had been seconds since I'd made the cut but already I was starting to shiver.

'How long do you think it takes to bleed to death?' I asked her. 'Ten minutes? Twenty?'

She stared at me for another second.

'Tick tock,' I said.

For a moment she looked angry. Then she shuddered. Finally, she smiled and it was still the sweetest face I'd ever seen. She bent down, and when she stood again, she wasn't holding the gun but something that looked like a towel. She came towards me, crouched down and wrapped it tightly around my wrist. The pressure of it eased the pain just slightly. I still didn't trust myself to move. I just watched her, as she reached inside Joesbury's pocket for his radio and held it out to me. Mark's eyes were still open, still focused on me, and there was a gleam on his left cheek that looked like a diamond. Or a tear.

Hold on, Mark, hold on.

I expected her to run. I never, for a moment, thought she'd give up. But she just sank down on to the ground next to Joesbury.

I picked up the radio.

'I love you,' I told her, just before I made the call for help.

93

Friday 9 November

On Friday 9 November, a little over eleven decades after Mary Kelly was hacked to pieces in a small, rented room off Dorset Street, I followed a line of people along a brightly lit, yellow-painted corridor. We'd all travelled some distance, waited for what felt like hours. The people around me all appeared to be used to it. I wasn't.

It was the first time I'd visited a prison.

In the five weeks since I'd been carried out of the catacombs, the young woman who'd abducted Joanna Groves had made a full confession. Starting that night at Lewisham police station, she told Dana Tulloch and Neil Anderson the full story of how she was raped at knifepoint as a teenager by a group of boys high on drugs, alcohol and arrogance. She remembered every threat, every taunt, every insult, with the screams of her sister ringing in her ears the whole time. She told them she'd genuinely believed, at one point, that she'd died, that this was hell, and that it was never going to end. There were times, she said, when she still thought that.

I heard from colleagues that DS Anderson left the interview room unusually pale and spoke to no one for several hours.

Giving information that only the killer could have known, she freely admitted murdering Geraldine Jones, Amanda Weston, Charlotte Benn and Karen Curtis. She signed the confession Victoria Llewellyn.

At the end of the prison corridor, a door led into a large, high room. The windows were way above our heads, but they had bars across them all the same. Twenty or so small tables were evenly spaced around the floor. Already, people ahead of me in the line were settling themselves down on spare chairs.

In the hours they spent talking to her, Llewellyn told Tulloch and Anderson that she'd gone abroad after her sister's death, that she'd learned how to fight with knives and guns, and had returned several years later. She came with no papers, no passport, nothing to indicate her identity or her home country. It's quite commonly done, I learned. If people arrive in the UK with nothing to prove where they've come from, we can't send them back.

After a few tough months, she'd been granted leave to stay and apply for a work permit. She'd worked her way into the west London community around St Joseph's as a nanny, an au pair, even a house-sitter and a dog-walker. She'd been hardworking and reliable. The families had liked her. She'd come across Samuel Cooper and, spotting a future use for him, had become his lover, feeding him drugs and sex in equal measure.

I looked over at the last line of tables. Closest to the far door sat a young woman in her own clothes. Unconvicted prisoners don't have to wear prison uniform. The bright-blonde hair dye had begun to grow out and at her roots I could see a centimetre of the soft toffee brown I remembered. Exactly the same colour as my own. She wasn't wearing make-up. She didn't need to. She was still one of the prettiest girls I've ever seen.

That pretty girl had insisted, several times, that she'd had no contact with me since she'd returned to the UK and that I'd taken no part in any of the abductions or murders. She was determined that I would carry no blame for what she'd done.

She saw me and smiled, watched me make

my way towards her table and sit down. I glanced round. Those people in earshot were chattering away, intent only on themselves. No one would hear us talk.

'Hey, Tic,' she said.

I hadn't heard that nickname in a very long time. Certainly not coming from the girl who'd given it to me in the first place, when her plump toddler's mouth hadn't been able to form the four syllables of my real Christian name. My baby sister hadn't been able to manage 'Victoria', so she'd called me Tic.

'Hello, Cathy,' I replied.

94

For what seemed like a long time, Cathy and I didn't speak. Then she laid a hand across mine on the tabletop. Wrapping her fingers around my bandaged wrist, she turned it over.

'Will you be all right?' she asked.

I gave a little shrug. 'Well, you know those piano lessons I talked about having one day? Turns out I might have to give up on that idea.'

She put my hand down and smiled again. 'I'm sorry about what I did,' she said, and she might have been apologizing for scratching one of my CDs.

'For killing those women?' I whispered.

'Lord, no. I'm not sorry about that,' she said, with an odd little shudder. 'I'm sorry about trying to make you kill the Groves girl. I should have known that would never happen.'

I had nothing to say back to her.

'When you sent the warnings to the Curtis and Groves women, I should have known you wouldn't play ball,' she went on. 'I told those detectives I sent them, by the way — that I was trying to stop. I think they believed me.'

'They did,' I said. I'd been careful when I'd sent the notes to Karen Curtis and Jacqui Groves, there was no way they could be traced back to me. I might as well have not bothered. My warning hadn't saved Karen, and Jacqui had never been a target anyway.

'And I'm sorry for what I said all that time ago,' Cathy said, leaning back a little. 'You know, when you came to the boat and I went a bit mental. It wasn't your fault, what happened to us in the park, with those boys, I just had to —'

'Get me off your back,' I finished for her.

She nodded. 'You'd spent eight months looking for me,' she said. 'I knew you were never going to leave me alone. I'm sorry, Tic. I just needed space. And some time.'

I let my head nod slowly, as though I understood completely. Which I did, in a way. My sister had needed space and time. To plan the destruction of five families.

'Did you set fire to the houseboat?' I asked, and when her eyes fell to the table I knew she had. More deaths on my conscience, then. She leaned forward across the table. 'Why did you do it?' she said. 'Why did you tell them that girl in the river was me?'

'To set you free,' I replied. 'I knew that's what you wanted. A couple of days later, a friend of mine died and it seemed like I had the same chance. I didn't think the world would miss the Llewellyn girls.'

'Was that Lacey?' she asked me.

I nodded.

My whole life long, I'd allowed only one other person to call me Tic, and that was the sad, sweet, drug-crazed young woman I'd met and become close to when we'd both been homeless ten years ago. The story I'd told DI Joesbury in a Cardiff hotel room had been almost 100 per cent true. I'd just told it from the other girl's point of view. And I'd made up the happy ending. Not long after officially declaring Cathy dead, I'd come back to the Engine Vaults to find Lacey seriously ill. I'd managed to drag her to the street and, with no other options at hand, I'd stolen a car that hadn't been properly locked. I'd intended to drive her to the nearest hospital, to put her in a private clinic when she was better, but by the time I got the car back to where I'd left her, she was dead.

So I'd taken a chance on a new life. Lacey's record with the police was relatively clean; mine wasn't. I'd driven to the coast, taken what few papers she'd had and replaced them with my own. Then I'd pushed the car and my friend into the sea. At three o'clock in the morning on a clifftop in Sussex, I'd become Lacey Flint.

And it had worked. I'd taken the time to grieve for both my friend and my sister, then set about building a new life for myself. I'd walked away from the streets, kept my distance from anyone who might know either Lacey or me, and gradually gathered up the reins of another woman's life. Neither Lacey nor I had much in the way of family, which significantly reduced the number of people I needed to avoid; and I'd had money, which had helped a lot.

When I'd felt I was ready, I applied to join the Metropolitan Police. Never having taken drugs in my life, I sailed through the drugs tests and then the various entrance exams. I'd taken a law degree and been accepted on to the detective programme. It had been an OK life, while it lasted.

'We're going to have to tell them,' I said. 'Who we really are.'

Cathy had a trick I remembered from years ago, of crinkling up her eyes until they became bright, sparkling slits. She did that now. 'In the eyes of the world, Victoria Llewellyn is a sadistic, bloodthirsty killer,' she said. 'I made sure of that. Do you really want to be her again?'

Sitting there, looking into those glinting, hazel-blue eyes, I couldn't have said whether she was trying to protect me or destroy me. And yet it all made a twisted sort of sense. My neglect of Cathy all those years ago had started the process that had made her what she was. I'd turned my sister into a killer; and now she'd done it right back.

'That reminds me,' she went on. 'Did I kill that butch detective friend of yours?'

I waited, and watched her smile die.

'No,' I said, when it had. 'You punctured a lung. The doctors managed to stitch it up. He'll be OK.'

I was relying on reports from mutual friends. I hadn't seen Mark since the night we'd both almost died. Nor would I, for as long as I had any control over the matter. It was enough, surely, that never a second went by when I didn't think of him.

At the news that he would live, Cathy gave a little shrug and nodded her head. I judged she was pleased, on balance, that he wasn't dead, because she'd realized how important he was to me. Otherwise, it was of very little interest. That was the moment when I finally accepted that my sister was insane.

'Cathy,' I said.

'Shush.' She leaned forward again. 'Don't call me that. I'm Vicky now. I always liked your name better anyway.'

'Cath— do you realize you're going to prison for life?'

She sat upright in surprise. 'Get real, Tic,' she said. 'I'll be out in ten.'

We were slipping into la-la land.

'Cathy,' I began. She held up a warning finger and I realized there was nothing I could do but let her have her way. I was to blame for the dreadful things my sister had done in my name. The least I could do now was to let her keep that name if she wanted it.

'Vicky,' I began again, and just saying the word made me feel like something essential inside me had slipped away for good. 'You killed four women. They are never going —'

'Oh for God's sake.' She leaned forward, holding up the fingers of one hand and started to count them off. 'One, I'm going to plead guilty and show lots of remorse. That always reduces the sentence. Two, I'll be a model prisoner. I'll get therapy, I'll go to church, I'll study for a degree. You just watch me. Parole in ten years.'

The officer in charge of the room started making his way in between the tables, letting everyone know visiting time was almost up. She looked up at him in surprise, then at me with something like panic on her face. I caught a glimpse then of the scared little girl I remembered from her first day at primary school.

'You'll come and see me again, won't you?' she said and I could only nod. She was my responsibility, now more than ever. I'd made her what she was.

Everyone was leaving, the prisoners were standing up and walking towards the door that would take them back to their cells. I stood up too, let her kiss me and then watched her head for the door. Before she disappeared, she waved, just as she'd always done when she'd gone through the school doors as a child.

I turned and made my way out, knowing that the next time I saw her, life in prison would have knocked a little more of the spirit out of her. And the time after that, a bit more. And so it would go on, for a very long time.

She was wrong about the leniency of the system. However she chose to plead in court, however she behaved in prison, she wasn't going to be out in ten or even twenty years. My sister would spend the rest of her life paying for what she'd done.

And so would I.

AUTHOR'S NOTE

Jack the Ripper: Man or Myth? (or Miss!)

Eleven decades of fascination with the sadistic serial killer whom the police never caught have given rise to endless ideas, stories and beliefs about his crimes and his identity. As Lacey says, 'Jack was a real man, but he's become a myth.' Here are some of my favourite daft Jack theories.

1. Jack was a prince of the realm. Any mention of Jack the Ripper will invariably be met with: 'Wasn't he a member of the royal family?' The royal in question was Prince Albert Victor, grandson to Queen Victoria and in direct line to the throne, who allegedly contracted syphilis after an assignation with a prostitute. His subsequent murderous rampage was hushed up by the authorities (who possibly had Masonic connections) to protect the queen from scandal. It's a lovely idea, but the prince's where-

abouts on any given date are a matter of public record and he was, sadly, nowhere near Whitechapel when the murders took place. We all love a royal conspiracy, but this one simply doesn't stack up.

2. Jack was a surgeon who collected internal organs. Annie Chapman and Catharine Eddowes were both partially disembowelled and are believed to have been missing organs. This gave rise to the theory that the Ripper himself took the organs and must have been surgically trained in order to locate and remove them. Equally likely, though, is that the organs were taken some time after death by unsupervised and unscrupulous mortuary assistants, who knew their value on the black market. Jack may well have had nothing more than the most basic knowledge of anatomy.

3. The Ripper was a smartly dressed gentleman who carried a Gladstone bag. Countless depictions of the Ripper portray him as a Victorian 'toff', an elegant gentleman who easily lured women to their deaths. In fact, the relatively few eye-witness accounts differ so much in terms of age, appearance, dress, nationality, that it is impossible to form any reliable idea of what Jack looked like. Certainly, there are as many accounts

of his being roughly dressed as there are of his being respectable. The Gladstone bag arises from two eye-witness accounts of passers-by carrying 'shiny black bags'. Although nothing concrete connects either bag-owner with the crimes, these reports gave rise to a dozen or more black-bag stories, to the point where mere ownership of such an article became a cause for suspicion.

4. The Ripper was the subject of a massive police and Masonic cover-up. A barely literate chalk-written message near the site of Catharine Eddowes' murder, referring to 'Juwes', along with similarities between the murder and a certain Masonic legend, gave rise to the theory that the Ripper killings were part of a Masonic conspiracy. In reality, the graffiti may have been completely unconnected with the murder, whilst the link between the word 'Juwes' and three Masonic murderers, Jubela, Jubelo, Jubelum (the Juwes — are you keeping up?) is pure speculation. As far as the police are concerned, they faced massive public, press and government pressure to identify the killer, not to conceal his identity, and it is hard to believe that over a hundred years later, hard evidence of a cover-up would

not have emerged.

5. The Ripper taunted the police with letters and postcards. During the months of the murders and for several years afterwards, the police, the press and even prominent members of the public received letters supposedly from the killer. Many of them were signed 'Jack the Ripper'; one was accompanied by a human kidney. The letters have been subjected to endless investigations by police and independent experts of various kinds and are generally believed to be fake. In recent years, the crime writer Patricia Cornwell built a very convincing case that the artist Walter Sickert was the author of many of the letters. She fell short, in my view at least, of proving that Sickert was also the killer.

And finally . . .

6. Jack was a woman. Inspector Abbeline, the officer in charge of the original investigation, took seriously the theory that the killer could have been female, and so we should too. If, as was argued at the time, the Ripper was a midwife, she would have been able to leave her house and wander the streets in the small hours without attracting undue attention, her bloodstained

clothing would not have been remarked upon, she would have been able to approach women without alarming them and would have had the medical knowledge a) to subdue her victims and b) to locate and remove reproductive organs. True, there is no direct evidence to suggest a woman committed these crimes, but until the worldwide jury agrees on one prime male suspect, I think Jill the Ripper has to stay in the mix.

ACKNOWLEDGEMENTS

Writing a police procedural proved seriously challenging and I'm grateful, once again, to Adrian Summons, not just for his patience and good humour at school pick-up, but also for introducing me to some very useful mates and former colleagues. The ones I'm allowed to name and thank are Detective Inspector Brian Cleobury and Inspector Harvey Martin of the Metropolitan Police's Southwark Borough Command, and Chief Inspector Derek Caterer of the Marine Policing Unit. As for the one I'm not allowed to name, I thank him too.

I'm indebted to Mike Katesmark for checking the medical and pathological detail and for his contribution to the text and characterization. Thanks, also, to Denise Stott and Jacqui Socrates, who never seem to mind my pestering them with daft questions; to Gareth Cooper for some eagle-eyed proofreading; and to Edward Teggin, who knows stuff his parents probably wouldn't approve of.

Any remaining mistakes are mine.

The Camden scenes, both above and below ground, owe their accuracy to Peter Darley of the Camden Railway Heritage Trust, and their inaccuracies to my overheated imagination. I have to point out that any attempt to retrace Lacey's final journey through the catacombs would be illegal, highly dangerous and, thanks to several demolished basements and tunnels, quite impossible. I would like to thank Peter for being so generous with his time and his local knowledge; and also the Trust for the work they do in conserving this fascinating part of London.

Reference books I relied on include: *Telling: A Memoir of Rape and Recovery* by Patricia Weaver Francisco, *After Silence* by Nancy Venable Raine, *Recovering from Rape* by Linda Ledray, *The Complete History of Jack the Ripper* by Philip Sugden, *Jack the Ripper* by Andrew Cook, *Jack the Ripper: The Twenty-First Century Investigation* by Trevor Marriot, *Portrait of a Killer* by Patricia Cornwell and *Jack the Ripper: The Casebook* by Richard Jones.

Transworld continue to be the best publishers in the world, with St Martins Minotaur in the US coming a very close second. My especial thanks to Sarah Adams, Lynsey Dalladay, Nick Robinson, Kate Samano and Jess Thomas on this side of the Atlantic and to Kelley Ragland and Matthew Martz on the other.

Anne Marie Doulton, Peter Buckman, Rosie Buckman and Jessica Buckman remain wise, supportive and diligent. My thanks and love to them once more.

ABOUT THE AUTHOR

S. J. Bolton was born in Lancashire. She is the author of three previous critically acclaimed novels, *Sacrifice, Awakening* and *Blood Harvest,* all available in paperback.

Sacrifice was nominated for the International Thriller Writers Award for Best First Novel, and for the prestigious Prix Polar SNCF Award. *Awakening* won the Mary Higgins Clark Award for Thriller of the Year in the US.

In 2010 *Blood Harvest* was shortlisted for the CWA Gold Dagger for Crime Novel of the Year.

S. J. Bolton lives near Oxford with her husband and young son. For more information about the author and her books, or to check out her popular blog, visit www.sjbolton.com.

The employees of Thorndike Press hope you have enjoyed this Large Print book. All our Thorndike, Wheeler, and Kennebec Large Print titles are designed for easy reading, and all our books are made to last. Other Thorndike Press Large Print books are available at your library, through selected bookstores, or directly from us.

For information about titles, please call:

(800) 223-1244

or visit our Web site at:

http://gale.cengage.com/thorndike

To share your comments, please write:

Publisher
Thorndike Press
10 Water St., Suite 310
Waterville, ME 04901